ALSO BY DAVID CARL MIELKE

A DISH BEST SERVED COLD
A Novel
Winner: Reader Views
"Reviewers Choice Award" 2010
(Mill City Press, 2009)

Please visit author's website:
DAVIDCARLMIELKE.com

Sue —

Prepare to be "Lena-tized"...

Enjoy —

D) Miller

A NATION BEST SERVED HOT

A NATION BEST SERVED HOT

DAVID CARL MIELKE

COPYRIGHT © 2010 BY DAVID CARL MIELKE.

MILL CITY PRESS, INC.
212 3RD AVENUE NORTH, SUITE 290
MINNEAPOLIS, MN 55401
612.455.2294
WWW.MILLCITYPUBLISHING.COM

ALL RIGHTS RESERVED. NO PART OF THIS PUBLICATION MAY BE REPRODUCED, STORED IN A RETRIEVAL SYSTEM, OR TRANSMITTED, IN ANY FORM OR BY ANY MEANS, ELECTRONIC, MECHANICAL, PHOTOCOPYING, RECORDING, OR OTHERWISE, WITHOUT THE PRIOR WRITTEN PERMISSION OF THE AUTHOR.

ISBN - 978-1-936107-98-8
ISBN - 1-936107-98-8
LCCN - 2010929806

COVER ART AND AUTHOR PICTURE BY ETHEL ENGLAND
FRONT AND BACK COVER DESIGN BY S.C. SHISLER

PRINTED IN THE UNITED STATES OF AMERICA

The author wishes to dedicate this novel in memory of Jean Weis, who passed from cancer in her early fifties. With her husband Wally, her legacy is defined by their two outstanding sons—Keith and Dan*—both highly-successful law officers and family men.

* See acknowledgments at the end of book.

PROLOGUE
CUIDAD JUAREZ, MEXICO
WEDNESDAY, JANUARY 24, 2007

AT ONE WITH SCRUFFY UNDERBRUSH, Drug Enforcement Agent Tracy Henderson was invisible to the most observant eye. Trained in the art of camouflage, her face, skin and uniform blended perfectly with the terrain.

She studied the target at seventy yards through a magnified rifle sight. Over six feet tall with slick black hair, pockmarked face and thick mustache, the man wore a black guayabera shirt covering a bullet-proof vest. *Deadly handsome*, she thought.

And the eyes. She had never seen such deep set eyes. Bushy brows shielded barely visible whites surrounding horizontal retinas—pit viper fossae scenting prey.

Her mother Anne talked with animals and the dead. She was a medium who believed the ancient saying: "Eyes are windows to the soul."

Studying these eyes, Tracy was sure. *This man has no soul.*

"*El Gato,* The Cat" was one of Mexico's major drug lords, Felix Carón. Scanning the open field, his mouth barked orders in Spanish. Ten men were loading large crates from a remote warehouse aboard three eighteen-wheelers destined for the States. Another ten men holding automatic weapons, poised to fire on anything threatening the operation, patrolled the immediate perimeter.

Tracy's team of eight—half Mexican regulars—threatened the operation. Each camouflaged member was separated by at least twenty feet of bush. Heavily outnumbered, they held two advantages: bricks of molded c-4 implanted with electronic detonators carefully wedged under the frame of each truck the previous evening, and the element of surprise.

A NATION BEST SERVED HOT

This was her fifth search-and-destroy mission around Juarez, El Gato's turf. The previous four had been executed with precision and devastating effect. Many kilos of cocaine and other illegal substances had gone up in flames during the month following Felipe Calderon's inauguration as Mexico's new *Presidenté*. Upon assuming office, he had immediately made good on a vow to cooperate with American agents against the drug lords—something the previous corrupt Fox administration had promised in word but failed in deed.

Carón had been absent on the previous missions. His appearance and beefed-up security meant greater danger. In addition, the first four operations had taken place under cover of darkness. Daylight removed this advantage. Prudence dictated retreat and detonation from afar, but the opportunity to nail this major drug lord overrode caution. Tracy's DEA team was in a support role, guests of the Mexican government. *Sargento Primero*—First Sergeant Ernesto Nieves—was in command and held the radio-controlled detonator.

Communication was kept to a minimum. All eight operatives wore shoulder radios and used standard police 10-codes. The plan was to wait until all trucks were fully loaded before triggering the explosives. An expert marksman, Tracy was assigned El Gato and the nearest guard. The others had been assigned other targets and awaited the signal.

Tracy adjusted the rifle sight for a head shot, her finger resting lightly on the trigger. El Gato and all other targets were to go down on command prior to detonation. It would be over in less than five seconds—if all went well.

Tracy sensed trouble. *Something isn't right*, she thought to herself. *The command is late.* El Gato was staring in her direction, reaching for his holstered pistol. Her finger increased pressure on the trigger.

Huff, huff, huff. The sound approached from her rear.

A crushing load of American Staffordshire terrier landed on her back, its jaws latching onto her right arm. Her shot went astray. In less than a second, three huge explosions were followed by fire from surrounding rifles and assault weapons. Screams blended with growls as other dogs attacked team members. The guards moved in with Uzis to make short work of her comrades. It was over quickly. Releasing the rifle, Tracy had turned on her back and was wrestling with the eighty-pound pit bull. Her helmet came off, revealing a tousled mass of jet black hair. One of the guards stood over her, aiming to kill.

"*¡Alto!* Halt!" commanded a strong voice. The dog released its prey and backed away. "Thees one I wan' alive." El Gato's face was contorted in rage, his eyes flaming fire. Four sets of hands forced her into submission and dragged her off toward the warehouse.

Seven commandos lay dead.

All too soon Tracy Henderson would wish there were eight.

SLICK AND SON
CHILDESS, TEXAS
1969

THE COUNTY OF PECOS, Texas is the second largest county in state land mass, but one of the smallest in population. In 1969, one of its three towns was Childess—often confused with a more populous eastern cousin, Childress. No one knew who founded the dusty town or why it existed. No one cared. Childess had three kinds of residents: transients who stayed less than a year, transients who stayed longer but eventually left, and the very few who tired of moving and waited to die. Most of the men worked as wildcatters in the surrounding oil fields. That year, the population of Childess was exactly one hundred twenty-one scruffy souls.

In addition to a McDonald's, the town consisted of a Texaco filling station, the Shady Lady Motel, a mom-and-pop food market, and a town hall which also contained a post-office, local bank, barber shop and greasy-spoon diner. No one trusted the bank's security, so townsfolk kept most of their money under mattresses, stuffed in coffee cans or buried in back yards, guarded by Messrs. Smith and Wesson. Since the diner's chef was also the barber, few trusted the menu offerings after hair clippings and dandruff were found floating in bowls of soup. The postmaster also moonlighted as banker but could be found either playing checkers, snoring in his easy chair or fleeing his irate wife of forty years, who chased his "fat ass" with a broom around the block at least once a day. It was the only entertainment in an otherwise comatose town.

Childess boasted three saloons and one Baptist church with its Boot Hill cemetery out back. All agreed to the ratio, for the slaking of thirst was at least three times more prevalent than reciting of prayers in this forgotten way stop.

The first baby of the year arrived August thirtieth. It was also the last baby of the year. With only nine females of child-bearing age, the town might as well have been named "Child*less*". In a vain attempt at societal bonding, the unelected mayor—his designation won in game of stud poker—announced a ceremony honoring the occasion. The young couple would receive a bouquet of desert flowers and all the McDonald's hamburgers and fries they could consume in a half hour of gluttony, witnessed by His Honor and others of self-appointed prominence. Much to everyone's dismay, the proud parents declined to participate. The husband gave less than a rat's ass regarding Childess society and declared disdain of fast food restaurants, believing the ground beef contained morsels of similar rodents.

The first baby of the year was named Jerry, born of Edna and Clive Custer Calhoun. Edna was a stark, angular woman with a tremendous capacity to forgive and an equally abiding stoicism, both qualities necessary to live with a nomadic husband who made his money in confidence scams and gambling. Edna knew what he was, but she married him anyway. Tall, dark and handsome, Clive was a smooth-talking con artist who never worked an honest job in his life but could produce an inside straight when necessary. Stud poker was his game. He had earned the nickname Slick from many years practicing sleight-of-hand palming, often purloining from the bottom of a deck. Only the sharpest eyes could detect his deceit.

If discovered, his attitude would change from gregarious confidence to abject apology, groveling and lavishing praise upon his accusers. More often than not, the ploy worked and he exited with his skin and ill-gotten winnings before his victims realized they had been doubly duped. If that act failed and he faced physical harm, Slick would resort to a more basic skill—he was a very fast runner.

The Calhouns were the first type of Childess residents—transients passing through. Temporarily residing at the Shady Lady, Slick was busy plying his deceptive skills upon a few unsuspecting locals when Jerry was born. If it hadn't been for the caring assistance of the motel night manager, Edna would have deposited her baby on the linoleum room floor. Instead, when her water broke at four a.m., Edna was whisked one block down to the care and comfort of the town's only midwife, a slovenly drunk suffering from her latest bender. Trembling, the woman performed her duty in

A NATION BEST SERVED HOT

a semi-stupor, belching invectives with staggering halitosis. Fortunately, Mother Nature was alert and sober. The result was the normal birth of a healthy, vociferous bundle of indignant male child, whose first intake of air was a malodorous, maggot-gagging downdraft from the midwife.

Slick, flush with the evening's winnings, arrived at the scene just after six. With neither acknowledgment nor apology to his exhausted wife, he lifted his son from her arms. Cradling the sleeping child, for the first and last time in his life, Clive fell in love.

BORN TO RUN
DALLAS
1969 – 1988

ONE MONTH LATER, after declining the first baby awards and pissing off the town council, Slick was caught in an evening of poker turned ugly. Threatened with death, Slick ran from the bar, grabbed his family and departed in haste, leaving behind most of their clothes and stiffing the innkeeper. Driving their '65 Buick LeSabre flat out, they headed east, seeking the anonymity of a large town.

Dallas fit the bill, affording Slick a seemingly endless number of neighborhood venues in which to ply his nefarious trade. He and his family played musical motels, never staying in one for more than two weeks. Once Slick had ill-gotten money in hand, he and the family would move. When the law became involved and victims were asked to provide a physical description, Slick's other skill came in handy. He was a master of disguise.

Edna stayed married to this charming sycophant for three reasons: He was a good, though unconventional provider, so far as she knew he did not stray to other women, and he was a loving father. She accepted the nomadic existence and never asked Slick how he earned his money.

Edna was a career dependent. Being a wife and mother were her only goals. On many occasions she gave voice to her opinions and concerns, only to be cajoled by her husband's charm.

Slick had two loves in his life. Edna was not one of them. She was a good woman, but any lustful desire was soon gone after a couple of years of nagging. He loved his son and gadabout lifestyle equally.

Nothing was too good for Jerry. As he grew from a gangly colt into a rakishly handsome copy of his father, Slick passed to his son dreams of riches and tricks of his trade. It mattered little to Jerry that none of his father's dreams saw the light of day. Slick was his mentor and the young protégé strived to make his father proud. Before he was a teen, Jerry had learned most of his father's card tricks. By the age of twelve he could palm and switch cards with the best.

At this early age, Jerry also assumed an air contrary to his father's outgoing bluster. Convinced success could coexist with a different personality, he eschewed Slick's bravado for an air of confidence. With his father's encouragement reinforced by Texas bravado, Jerry developed an attitude of superiority by copying rough-and-tough "King of the Wildcatters" Glenn Herbert McCarthy. Nicknamed "Diamond Glenn", McCarthy was the prototypical Texan, making and losing many fortunes in oil and other ventures during his lifetime. Immortalized by Edna Ferber in her book and the 1956 motion picture by the same name, *Giant*, he was portrayed in the movie by James Dean, the original American rebel. Rock Hudson co-starred. To Jerry, his father was "Diamond Glenn" and James Dean rolled into one superhero.

Slick, an inveterate con artist by choice, considered legitimate employment beneath him. Jerry learned that working smart far outweighed working hard. Knowledge, wit and charm were tools of the trade, the combination often skewing luck in his favor.

Schooling for Jerry came easily in spite of the family's unconventional existence. Edna was saddled with the details. She soon learned that a fictional permanent address, in addition to a few forged documents, sufficed to soothe the bureaucratic beast. No one ever checked the documents' veracity.

Jerry assimilated smoothly into each new school. Highly intelligent, he learned just enough to pass his courses, discarding information he considered useless to his future. He was also a loner, choosing to observe human nature and its foibles rather than join in discourse.

On the day after Jerry's high school graduation, the inevitable came to pass. A homeless person discovered Slick's remains in a trash bin near a Morningside office complex. His face was mutilated and the skull and most of his bones were broken. Lacking dental and fingerprinting records, if not for a concerned wife reporting his two- week absence, the body would likely have remained unidentified. Edna recognized his clothing. A comment on the coroner's report stated, "Severe trauma to skeleton and cranium inflicted with intent to mutilate. Cause of death: murder."

After three weeks of investigation and intense questioning, neither Edna nor Jerry were implicated in this crime of passion. The deceased was indeed one "Clive Custer Calhoun, age 46, residence: Dallas, Texas. Survived by wife, Edna Walker Calhoun and one son." Through additional interviews by stiffed gambling victims, it was also determined that Calhoun was an all-around ne'er-do-well who likely deserved his fate, though the punishment was particularity egregious. The case remained open but rapidly worked its way to the back of the "unsolved" file section due to lack of interest.

Edna's period of mourning was short-lived. It was replaced by fear and outrage. Slick had left her with a son and nothing of monetary value—no life insurance, bank account, investments or home. She had no marketable skills or relatives to rescue her and saw little hope in a future doomed to minimum wage. Railing against her husband for his selfishness and lack of financial foresight, she cursed herself even more for being obliviously dependent.

Jerry thought his world had ended. Clive's murder brought forth a depth of anger matched only by his grief. Edna bore the brunt of his wrath. Instead of feeling sympathy or concern, Jerry launched into a vicious verbal tirade that cowed her into a defeated lump.

Jerry gathered his clothes and a few personal items. He left abruptly, vowing never to see his mother again. Nor would he learn her fate. Rather than face a future of loneliness and poverty, Edna chose to end her life, overdosing on stolen sedatives less than a month later.

STRIKING OUT, CASHING IN
EL PASO
1988 - 1996

AT NINETEEN, the son of Slick Calhoun was of legal age. Six feet tall, smart, handsome and street-wise with eyes that missed nothing, he was ready to face the future. Armed with a legitimate Social Security number and a Texas driver's license, Jerry was not intimidated by circumstance. Anger fueled determination. Tempered by the knowledge that his brashness, innocent good looks, ability to ingratiate and manual dexterity with cards were more than adequate assets for success, he hitchhiked west on I-20 with fifty dollars in his pocket. In three days, he landed in El Paso, broke in every way but spirit.

Jerry held a deep-seated resentment for his nomadic childhood. When asked, "Where are you from?" he always answered with a flippant, "Nowhere." Anxious to establish roots, he started his adult career by seeking something Clive would never consider—legitimate employment.

Consulting local want ads for a job compatible with his skill set, he settled on automobile sales. After a couple of rejections due to his age and inexperience, the owner of a Ford dealership took a chance on Jerry and hired him. With a minimum of training, Jerry rewarded his boss by selling more cars in his first three months than any other sales person had in the last six. Within a year he was the dealer's top salesman, breaking all previous records.

Praise from his boss did not impress Jerry. Sales commissions did. For a while, he was pleased with his new lot in life. By asking questions, he had an uncanny ability to ferret customers' hot buttons of greed, status and pleasure.

"This car has 'YOU' written all over it," he would say to a wife while her husband sat in a corner sweating bullets.

"What will the neighbors think when you drive home in this cream puff?" he would cajole a bald-headed introvert with delusions of grandeur.

"This is a Cadillac in Chevy clothing. The car rides so smooth, the only thing you'll have to worry about is falling asleep at the wheel," he would soothe the bank V.P. looking to enhance a low-grade salary with an upgraded ego.

After a half-hour dose of Jerry-atrics, most customers left with a vehicle far in excess of need, paid for or financed at full price, convinced they had just received the deal of a lifetime.

Between the ages of nineteen and twenty-seven, Jerry sated his raging hormones with a stable of beautiful, young West Texas fillies. Captivating each by good looks, youthful self-reliance and a burgeoning bank account, Jerry was the envy of his male acquaintances. Quick to bed but loath to wed, his stable had a revolving door, triggered by the first hint of commitment. During those eight years, "Callous Calhoun" humped and dumped over a hundred women.

By 1995, Jerry had accumulated over a half-million dollars after taxes, but he was bored with the routine. Convinced he deserved more than constant pats on the back and commissions, for some time and to no avail, he lobbied the owner for a portion of stock in the business. Threats to quit were met with condescension and false promises. After allowing the owner six months to make good, Jerry gave his two-week notice and quickly secured employment in something far more lucrative—commission sales of life insurance.

Texas insurance companies hired almost anyone without a criminal record or drug addiction, throwing each prospect against a wall to see who stuck. Anyone with an IQ north of zero could pass the state licensing exam. Training costs were minimal and offset by continued premium flow from each failed agent's policies after termination. Over ninety-five percent failed within the first year.

After initial training which emphasized prospecting for potential clients and basic product knowledge, new recruits were handed a rate book, some glossy advertising brochures and told to go out and shake the bushes. Agents could earn between fifty and ninety percent commission based upon collected first-year premium from the sale of cash value "whole life" insurance. The fortunate few who made the cut enjoyed a schedule of bonuses for exceptional production.

A NATION BEST SERVED HOT

To Jerry, all this seemed too good to be true. Trans-Texas Life, a company with precarious financials, hired him after the first interview. Lax compliance laws and worse enforcement allowed most Texas insurance companies to generate misleading and often false advertising with little or no consequence. Trans-Texas produced glossy sales brochures graphically touting high ratings from fictional third-party agencies and impossible growth projections as well as glowing comments from non-existent clients. Powerful magnification was needed to reveal disclaimers at the bottom of each page.

Armed with a fierce determination to succeed, Jerry Calhoun was loosed upon the population of El Paso after one week of training. Striking up conversations with total strangers, he elicited sympathy as a handsome young man trying to make a start in the business world. Quickly gaining rapport, scheduled appointments were easily obtained. Once in the door, Jerry turned on the charm.

Most prospects turned into clients who gave Jerry full access to their life stories and checkbooks for premium payments, unaware his promises and brochures were lies. After delivering each policy with profuse thanks, positive reinforcement and obtaining leads to their acquaintances, Jerry never contacted his clients again. One year later, when premium renewal notices arrived with future policy projections, each victim learned the ugly truth. But it was too late. Jerry had long since cashed his hefty commission and bonuses.

He worked tirelessly and reaped huge rewards, realizing income over two hundred-thousand dollars his first year with Trans-Texas, over five hundred-thousand the second. Jerry won every "Out-of-the-Chute" and "Yee-ha" company award, all by record-breaking production. Company executives flew from Houston to give him a good ol' Texas slap-on-the-back. He was wined, dined and paraded as the company's "Golden Boy." Women flocked to be defrocked, and he was more than happy to oblige.

Jerry had arrived! His Texas ego was massaged while his net worth grew to over one million dollars by the middle of his second year, most of which was deposited with previous car commissions in an offshore Cayman Islands account.

Like storm clouds, ominous signs began to appear. Many wealthy clients hired lawyers to go after Jerry and his company. Trans-Texas had its own cadre of lawyers, but their sole objective was to protect the company, not the agents thrown under the bus during litigation. Jerry's slack record-keeping would be little help in his defense. Attorneys lined up, circling his errors and omissions liability coverage like sharks trolling for first bite.

In addition, the Internal Revenue Service was demanding its pound of flesh with interest and penalties. Since all Trans-Texas salespersons were "statutory employees," they were responsible for reporting and payment of their own income taxes on a quarterly basis. Jerry had not only neglected to file quarterly, but also to pay the first dollar of income tax obligation since becoming a Trans-Texas agent.

Served with a pile of court summonses, Jerry remembered his father's solution to similar situations. He planned well and disappeared one night across the border into Mexico, using a pilfered passport under the name of Eric Allen Simmons, a fellow salesman bearing a reasonable resemblance who had carelessly left his desk drawer unlocked. Months went by before Simmons discovered his passport was missing.

THE GOOD LIFE
SAN JOSE, COSTA RICA
1996 - 1999

JERRY USED THE PASSPORT only once, gaining access to a new life in Central America, where the weather is great, living is cheap, questions are few, and American greenbacks buy luxurious privacy. True to Slick's legacy, he had stiffed his company, Eric Simmons, the IRS and his current stable of lovers. Jerry was reborn in Costa Rica—a new man in a new land. Using the name Jerome Calvin, he acquired new expertly-forged identification. After six months and a liberal greasing of palms, he was a naturalized citizen.

Life in Costa Rica was everything Jerry expected. Unlike El Paso's arid climate, frequent sand storms and provincial natives, San Jose and surroundings were warmly tropical and humid, with a vast array of flowering vegetation and fauna. In addition to fawning natives vying for gringo greenbacks, many ex-patriots welcomed him as one of their own. Eager to share past adventures, they usually exaggerated for effect. Jerry listened to his new acquaintances and concocted elaborate lies of his own. His well polished, charming approach won many a confidence while he deftly avoided reciprocation.

Pleasantly surprised to learn two thousand dollars US per month bought all requisite comforts, he purchased a spacious villa high on the side of a dormant volcano. With a vista overlooking a spectacular river valley, he furnished his abode with top-of-the-line products and the best food available. For an extra one thousand monthly, he acquired the live-in services, both domestic and sexual, of a beautiful young senorita with flowing black hair, a smooth almond complexion and the brown eyes of a fawn. Long, perfectly contoured legs conjoined in a torrid zone of pleasure. Miriam de la Rosa demurely served his every need and kept her mouth shut— with frequent sensual exceptions.

Costa Rica boasted one of the more stable governments and economies in Central America, and its banks welcomed a good portion of Jerry's money transferred from his Cayman account, while assuring similar secrecy. Interest alone from these local accounts was more than enough to finance his lifestyle.

Jerry had it all—health, wealth and an enviable lifestyle. But he was his father's son. After three years coasting in luxury, he was bored with a restless need to "get back into the game." It was 1999 and he was thirty years old.

WITH MODEST GROWTH, Jerry's net worth now exceeded three million US. Excepting his house and vehicles, all assets were liquid in Cayman and Costa Rican accounts. He never invested in securities, real estate, collectibles, ventures, or loans. Though this conservative investment philosophy was at odds with a restless desire to gamble, his knowledge of human behavior, skill at card counting and techniques of deception made gambling more a study in advantage than risk.

During his stay in Costa Rica, Jerry had cultivated a low profile while keeping alert to opportunities. As before, he made many acquaintances but no friends. His kindness and generosity toward Miriam was reciprocated with loyalty and love. Tripling her monthly salary, Jerry also surprised her by purchasing a small but adequate home nearby for her parents. Realizing Jerry's reluctance toward commitment, a grateful Miriam wisely accepted his emotional separation, giving freely and receiving graciously while demanding nothing. She fulfilled his every need and he repaid her handsomely.

Invited to play an occasional game of stud poker with expatriates and locals, Jerry purposely lost more than he won. Over time, he developed a reputation as someone who was honest and more interested in having a good time than winning. He made sure to accept invitations sparingly and his patience was rewarded by invitations to games with increasingly higher stakes. He could afford to lose and wait for the big score.

Jerry's acquaintances assumed he was wealthy, but in Costa Rica no one pried. Secrecy was the reason most had moved to this country. His lifestyle, comfortable without seeming excessive, was at odds with a devil-may-care gambling attitude, for he often lost thousands of dollars during an evening of poker. Jerry was known to play an honest game, so he judiciously avoided every tantalizing opportunity to utilize his talents. Winning small and losing large, Jerry demurely played coquet to his anxious suitors. Adding fuel to the fire, he regretfully turned down consecutive invitations to three very large stake games, citing previous engagements and an out-of-country excursion to the Caymans. Every time the intrigue reached a fevered pitch, he and Miriam would leave for another vacation.

Jerry had sown his seeds. He was about to reap the reward.

THE INVITATION came one month after his latest vacation. Admission was one million dollars US. Six of Central America's biggest fish were invited. One of his wealthy acquaintances was on the list but declined, citing recent market losses. A man of influence, he recommended Jerry in his place. Producing the required collateralized letter of credit from Banco Internationale in San Jose, Jerry was approved and graciously accepted.

The acquaintance could not keep a secret. The rumor of Jerry's invitation circulated among the local elite. In the close-knit community of high stakes gambling, his status rose immediately. Jerry had hit the big league. Most thought he was a fool destined to lose, but no one doubted his courage.

The game was an annual event at a location revealed only to the participants. The game of Texas Hold'em hadn't yet reached universal popularity. Seven card stud with no-limit raises was still the preferred game of chance. Only the host, a man with a reputation of impeccable honesty, knew the identity of each participant. In addition to the six players, the host, a bartender, server, and five large, armed off-duty policemen would be the only people in attendance. Weapons were to be checked at the door. The price of admission was an advance fee of ten thousand dollars US, which would remunerate the host and his staff for the facility, their service and sworn silence before and after the event. No actual money would change hands during the game, only chips. This was winner-take-all poker, the sum to be paid by the host with a bank wire transfer two business days after the event.

Jerry had reached gambling nirvana. Nothing before or after would compare to this event, the culmination of his dreams. He was no longer his father's son, playing petty games and preying on unsuspecting marks with guile and deception. He was sure the adversaries would be equal or better than he in judging character, body language and odds. They would also be aware of any attempt to cheat, so he would have to abandon any notion of palming and switching. This was a straight-up test of luck and fortitude—his chance to do or die. A million dollars was at risk—the price for the greatest adrenaline rush of his life.

THE GAME
FEBRUARY, 2000

THE EVENING ARRIVED with mild weather following a typical afternoon downpour. Armed with his passport for identification and an address with map, Jerry Calvin wound his way up a steep mountain road that terminated at a villa larger but quite like his own. Having left early, he pulled in the driveway with ten minutes to spare, only to find he was the last player to arrive. Jerry was admitted, identified and introduced to the others by number only.

He was Player Six. Only the host talked. No one smiled. Handshakes completed, the players retired to the gaming table and were each supplied with chips in various denominations, each pile representing a total of one million dollars US. All table talk except betting was forbidden. The rules were reviewed and acknowledged by nods of the head. Cards were shuffled, cut, and the game began.

To the uninitiated, stud poker is relatively simple to understand. It consists of the ante—in this game, ten thousand per person per hand—then two alternately-dealt cards (face down) followed by the first round of wagering, starting at the dealer's left and continuing clockwise. Each player may stay in the game with a match—"call"—or a raise. If at any time a player quits his hand—"folds," he loses his ante and additional bets to the eventual winner. Four rounds of face up cards are then dealt each player, each round followed by a similar series of calls, raises or folds. The final card is dealt down. After a last round of wagering, all hands remaining in the game are shown. The player with the best hand wins the pot.

Add a study in human nature, eye gestures and body language and the simple game becomes complicated. A player determines whether to hold or fold from a combination of factors. He judges the strength of his own hand as it unfolds and guesses the relative contents of all other hands by counting the "up" cards, each player's betting and mannerisms. A player may have a weak hand but try to bluff his way to a win by continual raises, hoping all others will fold. Each player tries to remain stoic, but even the best have mannerisms that become clues when repeated. An unconscious raised eyebrow, twitch, cough or slight smile may be enough to sway an opponent's decision to bet or fold. It is a game of non-verbal cat and mouse enhanced with luck.

The first hour was like a boxing match, each player sparring conservatively. Jerry won the first two hands straight up but knew his luck was temporary. Player Three, a small, balding Latin with beady eyes, went on an immediate losing streak that continued into the second hour. He was very aggressive, seldom folding, always believing that the next hand would be his salvation. It was not his night. By the third hour, he was broke and withdrew, visibly upset with his bad luck and stupidity.

Player Five was the greatest beneficiary of Three's misfortune, amassing a large pile of chips by the end of the second hour. Roughly fifty years of age and over six feet tall, he was obviously a master of the game. Winning or losing a hand did nothing to alter his surly demeanor. Sporting a pencil-thin moustache, coal black hair that matched a set of sunken eyes, the Latino wore a neutral facial expression that belied deep passion. After the first hour, Jerry felt this swarthy man would be his most dangerous adversary.

Player One, a slim, blond-haired Caucasian in his forties, kept a perpetual grimace on his face, as if he were in pain. He wagered too conservatively, more than once folding with superior hands. Jerry guessed he was the player least able to afford a loss. But for exceptional luck, he would have retired by the second hour. Instead, he survived to the end of the third with approximately half his original stake.

Player Four, the only other non-Latino in the game, tried his best to remain stoic, but after the second hour, Jerry could read him like a book by his eyebrow twitch and rapid blinking. An older man in his seventies, his betting was sound. By the third hour, he still retained a large pile of chips.

Player Two was a nervous, chubby man in his fifties. Forcing style over substance, always clearing his throat with great fanfare before each bet,

A NATION BEST SERVED HOT

he resembled a hamster on a treadmill. During the first hour, with a bad hand he would smile and with a good hand sigh. Then he changed tactics, reversing his actions into the second hour. The attempted ruse only served to confuse him into a losing series of bets. By the end of the second hour, he was gone.

Jerry tried to remain calm and analytical. Except for Player Five, these gamblers weren't any more proficient than those he encountered in lesser games of the past. This observation helped to lessen Jerry's anxiety over the amount of money at stake. But as the evening progressed, his hands seemed to get worse. By the end of the third hour, he had lost two-thirds of his stake. The end seemed near. Two and Three were gone. He and Player One were on the ropes. Four was winning with blind luck and Five was well ahead, continually staring daggers at all remaining opponents while polluting the air with acrid cigarillos.

Each hour's play ended with a five-minute break. At the end of the third hour, Jerry took stock. He could afford to lose the entire million, but could he afford the self-doubt that would follow? By now, the remaining players held no mystery. Head to head he could beat One or Four. Five was the hardest to read, but Jerry felt evenly matched in skill. Only luck stood in his way. Quitting was out of the question. Too many eyes were watching to contemplate cheating. For better or worse, he was all in to the end.

Up to this point, Jerry had played each hand straight. At the beginning of the fourth hour, he bluffed a win with a pair of jacks showing. The conservative Player One had folded after being dealt the first up card. Four and Five probably had better hands, but through a series of bold raises, Jerry forced each to fold. If all others fold, the winner need not show his winning hand. Having won the hand by default, Jerry quickly stuffed his cards into the remaining deck. Enraged, Player Five's dark eyes threw daggers as his nostrils flared and lower lip roiled. Sensing the animosity, Player Four twitched and blinked, surrounding his pile of chips with protective arms.

The host sensed trouble. Eyeing his five bouncers, he interrupted play with, "Gentlemen, all is in order. Player Six has the right to privacy upon all other hands folding. Please resume play."

Player Five won the next three hands, Jerry folding with poor down cards after the ante. Player One had come out of his shell to join in the bidding war with one of the hands. Convinced he had the winning hand, he went all in. When his three aces were trumped by Five's nine-high spade flush, he lost his grimace along with his composure. He quickly downed three shots of scotch before exiting the game in a semi-stupor. Desperate to regain his stake, Four had also bet heavily on all three hands, losing a substantial portion of his remaining chips to Five.

Jerry remained stoic on the outside but enjoyed winning the next two hands straight up from Players Four and Five. Bets and raises rose with each hand. With the end drawing closer, Jerry was now more than even on his stake. He felt the outcome was between Five and him, leaving Four a very nervous bystander.

The fifth and last hour became a study in character. Hands were subordinate to strategy. Five was still ahead of Jerry, but not by much. Four was on his last leg, twitching and blinking at a palsied pace. With fifteen minutes remaining, it was Five's deal. Jerry started with two eights down, followed by an ace, king and another eight up. Four had a good hand and kept raising. Five stayed in reluctantly.

Looking at his hand, Jerry faced a difficult decision. His ace, king and eight showed on the table. He knew the odds of another ace or king were better than landing the fourth eight with his last two cards. Player Four wasn't capable of bluffing at this level. His aggressive raising meant that three eights alone would not be enough to win.

Five had two pair—a ten and king down and the same up, with a deuce kicker. Four had three queens, two down, one up with an additional four and seven showing. He knew this hand was his last chance to win. The betting escalated.

After three sets of raises with the third up card, the pot had grown to nearly a million. Player Four had lapsed into such heavy breathing the host called a timeout, inquiring about his health. Dangerously low on chips, Four quickly waved off the concern and play continued. The last raise was called. Player Five dealt the fourth up card around.

Upon receiving a third ten, Player Five was incredulous. A full house of tens and kings was a sure winner. With steely-eyed composure, he waited his turn, determined to vanquish both adversaries with this one hand. To his left, Player Four was dealt a four which triggered more hyperventilation. Sure he held the winning hand, a full house of queens and fours, Four called another timeout, requesting a private conference with the host. Wanting the game to end quickly, Five was restless. To his dismay, Four's request was granted. Both he and the host retired to an adjacent room.

A NATION BEST SERVED HOT

Jerry was not a religious person, but a benevolent God had to be smiling upon him this night. He had been dealt another king! With eyebrows raised and an abrupt intake of breath, his body seemed jolted with electricity. His table hand was strongest of the three. Eights and kings—a full house. He cursed himself for the lapse in demeanor.

Upon seeing the last king drop, Five was livid. Anger oozed from every pore. Dark eyes aimed two blow torches of malice toward Six. That king should be his!

Across the table, Jerry felt the heat. Grateful for the five guards in the room, he also wished for a swift ending, whatever the outcome. Maybe it would be better to lose and depart with his bones intact. For an instant, the ghost of Slick Calhoun invaded his thoughts. No longer his father's son, Jerry was his own man, determined to see this game through. His lips pursed with resolve.

After three minutes, Four returned with the host who stated, "Player Four wishes to communicate an offer to both of you. He wants to remain in the game but is low on funds. I have in my hand a title to his company, of which he is the sole stockholder. This company holds a patent on a product that has an appraised value of two million dollars US, certified by a top accounting firm. He has recently received offers to sell in excess of that sum, offers that are still valid.

"He wishes to pledge his business as collateral for an additional two million US. I will allow this only if both of you agree. I have known this man for many years and vouch for his sound mind and honest character." The host added, "If Player Four says his business is worth two million, you can believe him. Gentlemen, it's your decision. Time is running out."

Player Five wanted to be rid of Four and concentrate his efforts in defeating the real enemy, Player Six. Still fuming, he believed Four had a good hand, but would it beat a full house, tens and kings? Not likely. If he were wrong, he could still come back for a last hand or two to take revenge on Six. He consented to the offer.

As did Jerry, anxious for a quick conclusion. It was his turn to bet.

With the best hand showing, Jerry threw in a half million. Two kings showing didn't sway Four or Five from raising aggressively. Jerry called. Five wasn't going to let these punks get the better of him. He raised another half million, shoving the chips to mid-table with a snarl. After a quick count, the host announced the pot now held over three million dollars. Shaking like a dead leaf about to fall from its tree, Player Four blanched, twitched and snorted. With a great sigh he called.

Jerry collected his composure and also called, praying to his newfound God.

Five dealt the last down card. His was a useless three.

Four's card was a six, also of no value to his hand. His full house was solid, but was it enough? A final round of bets would seal the pot.

Jerry's brow beaded with sweat. Convinced his was the winning hand, with an inspired gesture of macho impudence, he left the final card down on the table. Player Five studied his young adversary. Was it gall, a bluff or stupidity that drove this fool to leave his card untouched?

It was Four's turn to bet. With a nervous whimper he shoved his remaining chips to mid-table. "I'm-m-m all in," he declared.

Summoning his remaining courage, Jerry met Player Five's cold stare with his own. Slowly sliding his remaining chips to the center, he replied with a croak, "Me, too."

Five was in a quandary. Now in panic, rivulets of sweat cascaded down his face. Damn this gringo punk and stuttering geezer! "As am I," he shouted, boldly shoving his remaining pile to the center. The mountain of chips spilled over with a few falling to the floor.

Gone were the strategies, stoic reserve and enforced silence. The host, five policemen, waiter and bartender gathered around the table. It was time to read 'em and weep!

Player Four shouted in joy, throwing down his two queens and six while reaching out with both arms to encircle the pot. Like an erupting volcano, Five's cards exploded from both hands while he spewed Spanish invectives, yelping like a scalded dog. Knocking his chair backwards, he was quickly restrained by two policemen.

Amid the mayhem, Jerry calmly placed his two eights on the table to join the third eight, ace and two kings. With a somber nod, he silently acknowledged Player Four who was raking in the pot as spittle flowed down his chin.

Jerry stared at the final down card as if it were dusted with anthrax. Surely he was beaten. Player Five halted his rant. The room was suddenly silent, sucked free of oxygen. Twenty-two eyes stared at the card—and waited....

With his right hand hiding the view from everyone else, Jerry slowly lifted a corner. As if hit by an invisible fist, his body shot back in the chair, nearly tipping it over. Composure abandoned, he turned sheet white, consumed by uncontrollable shaking.

A NATION BEST SERVED HOT

The host stepped forward and turned over the card...

The fourth eight.

A chorus of gasps filled the room. Player Four fainted in a frightening heap. Two guards rushed to his aid while a third called for an ambulance. Realizing he was defeated not only by the pathetic geezer but incredibly by this rat-bastard gringo punk, Player Five went berserk, flailing fists and screaming at the remaining two policemen, who dragged the enraged Latino out of the villa, chucking him into his car.

During the last three years in Costa Rica, Jerry had become fluent in Spanish, but Five cursed with words he'd never heard. Giddy and celebrating with a scotch on the rocks, Jerry laughed at the man's tantrum. It was music to his ears.

Player Five fishtailed his car down the mountain in a shower of gravel and sparks. Four was stabilized until the ambulance arrived to cart him off. The host congratulated Jerry, patting him on the back. After deducting the one million stake and adding two million for the mystery business, Jerry's profit for one evening's work was a staggering seven million dollars! Adding back Jerry's stake, the host gave him a signed receipt for six million in cash, promising a quick wire transfer of this amount into his Banco Internationale account. In addition, he handed Jerry the business title.

It was four a.m. With the top down on his Mercedes SL500 convertible and bathed in the light of a three-quarter moon, Jerry floated down the mountain toward his villa on a cloud of euphoric ecstasy. Arriving home, he rushed to wake Miriam and make passionate love until the break of dawn. Life couldn't get any better. He was master of the universe, flush with cash and the invincibility of youth.

But Lady Luck is fickle—smiling with good fortune one minute, snarling with malice the next. It was only a matter of time before Jerry Calvin would find the sweet reward of chance dashed by the pernicious penalty of retribution.

THE EVENING'S DRAMATIC ENDING haunted Jerry. Winning at games of chance was a high wire act. One slip and he would come crashing to earth. Though gambling was part of the genetic blood coursing through his veins, unlike so many others, he was not addicted to the thrill.

Rather, he was able to analyze emotion. High stakes poker was a calm lake hiding a steep ledge. He vowed never again to test the water.

The fourth day after Jerry's dramatic windfall, a courier delivered a package of documents from a company named Rely, Inc. based in El Paso—Player Four's business. In addition to legal documents was a letter typed on a legal firm's stationery:

> *Señor Calvin:*
>
> *Enclosed you will find documents pertaining to the transfer of Rely, Inc. to you, the new owner and sole stockholder. This settles your account with one Edward L. Johnson, known to you as "Player Four." Pursuant to his request, I am acting in his stead with limited power of attorney solely for this transaction. In this capacity, since I must reveal my identity, I implore you to keep secret my name as host of the game.*

Jerry paused. Now the owner of someone else's business, he felt a tinge of sympathy for the older man—this Edward Johnson. Sure he had held the winning hand, Johnson must obviously be devastated at the sudden turn of fortune. Clearing his head, Jerry's new feeling was short-lived. He would be selling the business as soon as possible.

The letter continued:

> *To effect this transaction, please complete, sign and have notarized all the enclosed paperwork. Then register this transaction with the proper inter-governmental authorities. I suggest you retain the services of an international corporate attorney. Again, I congratulate you on your success and wish you the best with your future endeavors.*
>
> *Marco de la Vega, Attorney at Law*

Before reviewing the paperwork, Jerry read the letter three times. This situation could complicate his life. Dealing with attorneys was one thing, government authorities quite another. He was, after all, living under an assumed name and was doubtless wanted for income tax evasion and unlawful flight in the States. This Rely, Inc. was U.S.-domiciled. His first choice—crawling under a rock—was not an option.

Jerry took a week to decide the next move. Realizing de la Vega was right, advice from a legal expert was mandatory. But so was anonymity.

A NATION BEST SERVED HOT

Jerry viewed attorneys as blood-sucking leeches who twisted laws to their advantage. Until now he'd had no use for them. From local poker games, he had made the acquaintance of a retired ex-pat, formerly a lawyer in the States. Former attorneys were a slight improvement, and this one seemed to have a sense of humor—always a good sign.

Knowing he would be grilled for details of "The Game," Jerry was reluctant to contact anyone in the local poker crowd. Seeing no other choice, he called the former attorney. Anticipating the inevitable question, he had prepared an oblique comment: "I survived the evening with the shirt on my back."

Pleased to learn his acquaintance had been a corporate lawyer, Jerry asked to meet with him on a legal matter. Happy to listen, the attorney invited Jerry to his home the next day.

The attorney-client privilege is sacred, even to retired lawyers. Still, Jerry reinforced his demand for absolute confidentiality with an envelope containing ten thousand dollars US. Delighted with the cash, the attorney was happy to oblige. For the first time in his life, Jerry trusted someone with his secret past. He related the story of his former name, background in sales, income tax problems and his flight to Central America. To Jerry's amazement, the attorney was amused. "Why do you think most of us live here?" he laughed. "All of us have skeletons somewhere back in the States and many of us face arrest if we return. You're definitely not alone, friend."

Jerry then brought out the paperwork, minus the letter, transferring the company to his name and asked the attorney how to proceed. Again to his amazement, the solution was simple: submit all the paperwork through a U.S. attorney hired to act on his behalf through a limited power—the same procedure used to transfer ownership to Jerry.

"It's done all the time, bud," said the attorney. "That's what an attorney does—act as the client's representative in legal matters. Countless U.S. businesses are owned by foreign nationals, a good many of them with illegitimate purposes. Your company is legitimate. It already exists. Piece o' cake!"

The retired attorney then gave Jerry the name and address of an active stateside corporate lawyer, saying, "I trust this man. He is brilliant finding solutions where none seem to exist."

The next day, Jerry contacted the attorney and, through private courier, exchanged the documents to execute the limited power, thus transferring de-facto ownership of Rely, Inc. to himself.

Legal matters temporarily aside, Jerry called the company's telephone number and asked to speak to the general manager.

"Henry Adams, how may I help you?" asked a slightly out-of-breath voice after a thirty second Muzak interlude.

"My name is Jerry Calvin. I'm calling from San Jose, Costa Rica."

"Oh, the new owner. Mr. Johnson said you'd be in touch," Adams answered. His breathing seemed to accelerate.

"Yes, how is he? Is he there?" asked Jerry.

"You didn't know?" Adams replied. "Mr. Johnson passed away two days ago. Bad heart, they think."

Incredulous and stricken with remorse, Jerry knew he was indirectly to blame. "Oh!" he gasped. "What about his family?"

"I guess you didn't know him well, Mr. Calvin," said Adams. "He had no family, other than his employees. Mind if I ask you a question?" he continued.

"No, of course not," Jerry answered, relieved to know he wasn't responsible to any Johnson heirs.

"What do you intend to do with the company?" Henry came right out with it.

"That's what I was calling about. Will you fly down here in a couple of days so we can discuss the matter? I can make the flight arrangements for you at this end."

"Yes, sir, certainly."

Jerry thought, *This Adams seems competent.*

"By the way, what does the company do—this Rely, Inc.?" he asked.

"You mean you bought our company and don't know what we make?" It was Henry's turn to be incredulous.

"I'll fill you in on how I came to own the company when I see you." Jerry was getting impatient by the second. "Now, what is it you make?"

"Disposable adult diapers," was the curt reply.

Jerry sat back in his office chair, dumbstruck.

"You still there, Mr. Calvin?" asked Henry Adams.

"See you in two days," was the answer, followed by a click.

Jerry had slammed the receiver.

What have I stepped in now?

UP TO THE WAIST IN WASTE
SAN JOSE, COSTA RICA

CURIOSITY CAN BE a mental aphrodisiac every bit as powerful as an illicit drug. Rather than follow his original plan to contact a broker and liquidate the business, Jerry spent the next two days accumulating knowledge. He learned dozens of companies around the world were making disposable diaper products. He wondered what made this Rely, Inc. able to compete with the big companies like Johnson and Johnson, Procter & Gamble and Kimberly Clark and products like Pampers, Huggies and Luvs.

Henry Adams arrived toting a briefcase stuffed with corporate records. Stocky with a slight Irish accent, Adams was no more than five and a half feet tall with short brownish-red hair and a ruddy complexion. Jerry remembered his father's advice: "A man with a firm handshake is a confident man." Adams was confident.

After brief personal small talk, Adams explained to his new boss that Rely was a small company in relation to the competition, which captured ninety percent of the adult bladder control market. Although the business headquarters was in El Paso, its manufacturing wing had relocated two years ago for cheaper labor an hour south of Ciudad Juarez, a large Mexican town named after the former Mexican president, Benito Juarez. Less than a two-hour drive south across the Rio Grande, the venue was a logical choice. After governmental bribes, Mexican labor still produced less expensive product, allowing the company a foothold in this competitive market.

Rely's biggest advantage was Johnson's patented formula of the sponge-like absorption material. Not only could Rely products be manufactured at less expense, but they also absorbed more liquid than the competition. The company was rapidly increasing market share. Mr. Johnson, a former chemist, had created the formula, which was kept in an El Paso bank box. Johnson and Henry were the only signatories. Adams produced and Jerry signed a revised signature card for box access.

Seeing that Henry had held Johnson's total confidence and trust, Jerry explained that he had won the company in a high stakes poker game. "You must have known Mr. Johnson well," he said. "Why would he do such a risky thing?"

Henry sadly shook his head. "He was lonely. That much I know. The business was his whole life. Mr. Johnson started it five years ago. We have one hundred seventy-six employees on both sides of the Rio Grande. He operated on a shoestring. I've been curious why he was always short of money. This company is a cash cow. Maybe he ran up other debts I don't know about and hoped the game could save him. Desperation can make anyone take risks. Could be he knew he was dying and that game was his last hurrah. The patent was his alone.

"Mr. Johnson was a very generous man with all of his employees, and we were really making a go of it. It's so sad, and we're all worried about the future."

Jerry studied Adams, who was close to tears. Never before had Jerry felt pity toward someone in business, let alone an entire company. "I can see you were close to him," he interrupted with a tinge of envy.

Nodding his head and gathering himself, Henry continued. "One problem has been bad marketing. Mr. Johnson paid a local advertising firm a big fee to produce a catchy slogan. The admen were creative but their offerings were crude, offensive and self-defeating. The first slogan was, 'Rely—While You Re-load,' and their alternate was a pathetic poem: 'Lower price and high capacity, for all your wet and wasteful nassity'." Adams sighed, "Johnson fired them on the spot."

Jerry chuckled, warming to Henry even more. "Thank you for coming down and explaining everything to me," he said. "I can't promise you or the other employees anything at this time, but I will be in touch soon after some more investigation. Until then everyone's job is secure. Please pass the word along for all employees to keep the business running as efficiently as possible. I'll do my best to see the resolution works to the benefit of all."

During the visit, Henry had also been studying Jerry and his surroundings, which bespoke wealth and good taste. He was impressed with the villa and its majestic view. The interior was richly furnished, replete with Navajo Indian artwork, ancient artifacts and subtle lighting. This was a man with means. But what were his intentions? Somewhat mollified, Henry left the documents with Jerry and flew back to El Paso.

Contacting his stateside attorney, Jerry launched a full business evaluation, not only of Rely, but also the competition and odds of success. "Cash cow" was Henry's term. Jerry wasn't about to sell the business without first securing due diligence. Given the right odds, this venture could be his next life challenge. During the brief car and insurance careers, he had promoted ideas that would have manifested in greater employee motivation and business revenue—ideas that fell on deaf ears. Now he was the owner of a fledgling company, a David among Goliaths, which possessed a secret formula—a rock in a sling that made the competition uncomfortable. He had more than enough money to finance such a venture. The thought intrigued him.

In two months, the attorney flew down to meet with Jerry. Simon Morris of Canter, Morris and Blackstone, P.A. was the opposite of Henry Adams. Tall, thin and prematurely bald with coke bottle glasses that often slid down his nose, he wore a rumpled three-piece suit quite out of place in the tropics. Portraying a man in disarray, he talked so fast most of his sentences finished before him. The one similarity with Adams was a strong handshake, and Jerry knew immediately Morris had perfected a demeanor calculated to deceive. Calvin took an instant liking to this legal pit bull.

Morris arrived with a large briefcase full of documents and an equally large bill for services. He had studied the battlefield of corporate adversaries. "Assuming adequate funding and capable leadership, Rely has the opportunity to kick butt," he announced with bottom line bravado and flailing arms.

Jerry was tempted to offer Morris a Valium. Simon settled for a double scotch on the rocks. Calmed, he explained the conclusions:

"Rely is too small using its own brand name to battle with the big boys," he said. "It's a solvent company and has a good reputation. Old Man Johnson had the right idea, but he didn't have the means to fight a good battle. Rely's future is in undercutting the private label markets. It doesn't need a slogan. Its products can be produced cheaper and sold to the big retail chains under their own name brands. The big boys want to put you out of business. The offers have risen to three million for the patent, but the potential earnings are far greater if you have the stomach to get in the game."

His glasses had slid to the point of his nose, but he was undeterred and proceeded to drop a bombshell:

"Because the company is small with extremely low overhead, I'm confident you have the ability to shave twenty percent off the wholesale price that large chains are now paying for the product and still make a profit." Morris sat back in his chair, adjusting his glasses, and waited for Jerry's reaction, smug with the knowledge that he had stunned his client.

He had. Jerry toasted the lawyer with his own scotch. Warming to the prospect of a good fight, one thought rose to the forefront of his mind:

This will be a different kind of poker game—with even higher stakes!

THE NEXT SIX MONTHS were a flurry of strategy meetings, company rallies and legal maneuvering. Cash flowed from Jerry's offshore accounts like water over Niagara Falls, but it was money well spent. Henry and the other employees were delighted. Not only were their jobs secure, but they now had a profit sharing plan. In anticipation of increased purchase orders, Jerry doubled the size of the manufacturing plant and hired an additional one hundred locals. As company president, Henry recruited a well-connected sales force to hawk product with the largest retail chains at the highest corporate levels, offering quality products at a ten percent discount.

The competition was angered but had no other choice than to match the discount. Losing all profit, they matched the discount. Rely countered by cutting an additional five percent. Lawsuits and espionage kept Simon Morris and his firm busy. Unwilling to sell at a loss, the competition folded like spiders on a hot stove. By the end of the first six months, Rely had cornered the market on all private label bladder control products. Jerry had called all bluffs, come up with four eights again, and won. David had slain Goliath!

A blizzard of orders soon overwhelmed production. Jerry re-doubled the plant size and hired another hundred locals. Income dwarfed expenses. Profits rose exponentially. Corporate clients were happy with higher profit margins. Jerry's employees were ecstatic to share a piece of the action. Morris and his partners were, too. Billable hours were up. This was capitalism at its best, and Jerry was the happiest of all. Everything he touched was turning to gold. Winning was the greatest aphrodisiac, enhanced by Miriam's sensual ministrations.

A NATION BEST SERVED HOT

Two more years went by with the business flourishing beyond his wildest dreams. Jerry was now an international financier—an entrepreneur with a bottom line rising like a tidal wave.

To Jerry's dismay, success had eroded anonymity. Costa Rican print media began publishing articles about "El Empresano Americano." When he turned down all interviews, it only fueled the intrigue. He was still a fugitive from the States, so any published picture of him could generate a request for extradition. Afraid to show his face, he stayed at home, conducting business through Adams and Morris.

Miriam cheerfully saw to his every need, but after two years, Jerry was becoming stir- crazy. In addition, he felt the distance from his business clouded his decisions. As much as he loved his villa and Costa Rica, he had to move. With instructions from his boss to hunt for local real estate, Henry found a large, twenty-acre ranch near the Juarez manufacturing plant that was for sale at a reasonable price. Jerry's money could buy protected seclusion and he would be close to the business.

Jerry knew that separating Miriam and her parents would be traumatic, so before moving, he revealed two more surprises. He had created a trust fund for her parents, giving them sufficient lifetime income so they would never again have to work. And he also purchased a lavish home for them in a pleasant San Jose suburb. Miriam was overwhelmed with gratitude, breaking into tears.

Selling his villa took Jerry less than a month. Securing Mexican visas was even easier. On Wednesday, January 2, Jerry began the year 2002 by moving his worldly possessions and devoted companion to a new life in northern Mexico. Although she would miss her parents terribly, Miriam felt her place was with the man she served, the man she loved with all her heart—

The man she would die for.

DIAPER DUTY
JUAREZ, MEXICO
2002 - 2007

WITH A HACIENDA less than ten kilometers from the warehouse, Jerry was able to study the inner workings of the business. He learned each stage of the manufacturing process with hands-on experience. Modern disposable bladder control products are simply constructed and similar throughout the industry. Consisting of three to four different layers of a micro-porous, gauze-like material—super-absorbent polymer sheets with graduated thickness—and specialized oils with perfumes to absorb odor, every diaper and pad is surrounded by and heat-crimped to an elastic shell designed to capture and contain liquids. Because of their greater absorbency, Rely's products needed only two layers of sheets, resulting in a lower manufacturing cost. In addition to strapped diapers, Rely made pads and guards that adhered to the insides of panties or briefs, and pull-ups—all-in-one undergarments.

In a lighter moment, Henry voiced a cruder description of the product line. Mimicking Tonto of "The Lone Ranger," he grunted, "We charge-um feefee for no see-um peepee."

With his limited power of attorney, Simon Morris had leased distribution centers in Newark, Atlanta, Chicago, Dallas and Los Angeles. From each center, products were shipped to all major retail customers for private labeling throughout the States. By 2007, over one hundred-thousand pieces were shipped from the factory to these centers weekly. Day and night, like worker bees, eighteen-wheelers arrived empty and left loaded with product, clearing customs and making cross-country treks to these centers. Morris rebuffed all legal challenges by the competition to clone the patented polymer and oil formula and regain market share. Only Henry and Jerry were privy to the ingredients, and Henry was a Minotaur guarding against corporate espionage.

With over a million inhabitants, Juarez was the largest Mexican city on the U.S. border. Jerry's hacienda south of town was quite different from his villa in San Jose. Sprawled over a large plateau, the home provided no scenic vistas. Jerry missed the daily rain showers. This climate was arid, hot and dusty. Instead of cheerful locals and ex-pats, these somber locals barely scratched out a living. Instead of a wide variety of fruits, vegetables and meats available locally, Jerry had to import most of his household's food from across the border. In all respects, the living experience was quite inferior in quality to Costa Rica.

As with any Mexican manufacturing company, security for Rely was paramount. Costa Rica was well-policed with a stable court system. Mexico was lacking in both. With the passing of each year, anarchy gained a stronger foothold. Turf wars between rival drug gangs made Juarez one of the most dangerous cities in the world. Murders and kidnapping were daily occurrences. Bribed into submission, local *policia* looked the other way, often assisting in the crimes. Though well south of town, security was the largest budget item for Jerry, both at his home and the warehouse. Trained guards worked for the highest bidder with no assurance of loyalty. Rely, Inc. had a small, well-paid army of round-the-clock sentinels. In addition, Jerry hired six burly American expatriates to guard Miriam and him in shifts.

Miriam never complained, but with the passage of time she grew increasingly homesick and depressed. Had she and Jerry been able to live across the border in the U.S., none of these shortcomings would have existed, but Jerry's business profile would likely attract investigation. He refused to take that chance.

Throughout his life, Jerry had been a loner, keeping thoughts and intentions private. The paths he chose were both interesting and challenging. Now his routine was a mundane exercise of watching a business run on automatic pilot. Millions would give their souls for his idyllic life—a life he had taken great risk to obtain. Great wealth, perfect health and passionate sex were at his beck and call.

He enjoyed frequent vacations with Miriam, often returning to visit Costa Rica and her parents. Jerry shared in the joy of reunion because it made her happy. His was a relationship of convenience, hers one of dependency.

Miriam was little more than a beautiful and pleasant version of his own mother, not someone with whom he could share serious thought. Yet he could not see himself living with anyone else. Like a puppy, her love and devotion were unconditional. She was a wife in everything but name. Jerry grew to appreciate Miriam more each year.

By 2007, nearly thirty-eight, Jerry felt an urge to make the first unselfish commitment of his life. Maybe it was his age, maybe a moment of weakness. The decision just felt right.

LIGHT BREEZES WAFTED through the open veranda; a half moon shone upon the solitary table for two. Jerry had reserved the entire restaurant. With a hint of jasmine wafting in the air, a single candle flicked dancing shadows on white stucco walls. From an adjacent room, a marimba murmured dulcet tones of subtle passion. A delicious meal barely noticed, words were few as the lovers' eyes spoke, promising an evening of pleasant release.

The surprise was unexpected, complete. "*Mi amour*, will you do me the honor?" he asked on bended knee, producing a two-carat diamond ring. Overcome, Miriam wept with joy and melted into his arms, shaking. Her most ardent wish had come true! Champagne in exquisite fluted crystal magically appeared. They drank deeply, toasting their future and making wedding plans. Five minutes stretched into ten. Slowly tiring, their heads nodded, eyes closed….

From the shadows on a secluded corner of the veranda, a tall, dark man waited patiently. Shortly before, the restaurant owner and his staff—all but one frightened marimba player—had fled in mortal fear of a man they recognized from newspaper photos. Using silenced pistols, the dark man and his cohort had dispatched both guards who were sitting by the entrance. Throwing on a waiter's vest while his leader poured white powder into a bottle, the assistant placed the magnum quietly beside the lovers who were deep in wordless conversation.

From the shadows, two sunken black eyes watched…and waited….

LIVING HELL
LATE JANUARY – EARLY JULY, 2007

HER PARENTS had owned a mortuary. Tracy Henderson knew she was strapped to an autopsy table. She lay naked on a ventilated platform with a drainage sink and faucets at her feet. Like a chrome swan, an overhanging halogen light loomed, revealing every detail of her shivering body.

Tracy knew death would not come easily.

El Gato inspected his captive. A menacing low chuckle revealed his tobacco-stained teeth. From a set of surgical tools resting on a small table to the left, he chose a pointed scalpel. Flashing it in front of her eyes, he looked for signs of fear.

She met his leer with defiance. Tracy was a fighter resigned to her fate, trained to withstand torture and mental abuse without breaking.

Felix Carón scowled. Visual teasing had failed to achieve the desired effect. By now all his former victims would be sniveling, crying for mercy. This one was different. She was mocking him, daring him to kill.

Tearing off a strip of duct tape, he slapped it over her eyes.

Now we'll see if she begs.

With wordless efficiency, he began with little nips to the arms and upper torso, each cut eliciting rigid tension and a short intake of breath. Trickles of blood ran from the wounds. She shivered with no verbal response.

"You take my leetle poke well, greengo puta," he growled with admiration. "Less see whachu do weeth big cut, eh?"

Taking a pointed piece of ice from a bucket below the table, he started at her neck and traced a straight line through both breasts to the pubic mound, leaving a trail of frigid cold. Tracy broke her silence with a scream of agony. Spurts of urine flowed from her crotch through the platform holes.

As El Gato ripped off the tape, her eyelids stretched to the limit before popping back in place.

"Ice feel like knife, no?" Revealing the faux weapon, he was laughing.

Signaling across the room, a huge man entered her field of vision. He unbuckled her hands as Carón released her feet. "Thees is Bolivar. You weel get to know heem well." As El Gato spoke, both men carried her squirming body to the cave wall. With arms shackled well over her head and feet to the floor, she was spread-eagled, waiting for the inevitable.

"Bolivar come back in five meenits." Carón was lowering his pants. "He get nex'," the drug lord chuckled, ramming his way home.

"Fuck wi' me, puta," he spat. "I fuck wi' you more."

THAT WAS THE BEGINNING. To her dismay, Tracy lived through the night and countless similar nights to come. Days blended together with agonizing slowness. Dressed only in a pull-over parka to ward off the cold, she shivered constantly until exhaustion led to merciful sleep. Bolivar would bring one daily meal, usually soup and bread. Keeping her hands and feet in cuffs, he would release her from the wall to consume the food and void waste in an open porta potty. Returning her to the wall, Bolivar delighted in bathing her shackled body with soap and cold water from a hose, his huge hands groping at will. Once he was aroused, Bolivar would usually follow each bath with rape or sodomy. Compared to Carón, whose assaults were accompanied by beatings and cuts, Bolivar was gentle and dressed her wounds with care.

They communicated in Spanish. At first, only he talked. Later, they shared conversation. Bolivar had known his boss since childhood, both coming from the same squalid barrio. They had scrapped for food as children, killed for advantage as teens. Carón earned his reputation by ruthless terror and cunning alliances. His status grew in proportion to body count. Bolivar bragged of his loyalty and vicious brutality. If bone-crushing strength and size weren't enough to thwart a challenge, he had no problem dealing death with knives and firearms. Together, they built an empire of drug-related enterprises. El Gato was lord and master of Juarez, fearing no man or circumstance, including clandestine raids from "greengo" drug agents.

A NATION BEST SERVED HOT

Bolivar gave Tracy pills to deaden the pain, but nothing could have prepared her for an extended stay in this dark, cold prison. At first hopeful of rescue, eventually time, torture and the reality of abandonment wore her down. Often she asked the giant, "Why am I still alive?" She never received an answer. Each day added another layer of pain and despair. Tracy Henderson wished with all her being for a death that never came.

There were others. She watched as men were brought down to suffer agonizing deaths. El Gato took delight in their screams while he tortured each before vivisection. Covered in blood, he relished waving body parts in front of her face.

Tracy retched in silence, thinking, *This man is the Devil.*

―――

TRACY ANNE HENDERSON was born in Miami Beach, Florida on August 15, 1976. As a rug rat, she was precocious, driving her parents to distraction, questioning everything and demanding attention. Both parents, Ed and Anne, provided the basics—food, shelter, security and occasional gestures of love. But they were at best inattentive, putting their own interests ahead of hers.

Tracy's father was an architect, married to his business more than his family. Anne was a free spirit who disappeared most days to walk alone in the Ocala Forest, preferring to commune with four-legged animals over two-legged humans. Tracy's younger brother Eddie was a bother, as most younger brothers are. Fragrant Mrs. Benson, the snuff-dipping nanny, was cheerful and doting, but a poor substitute for proper parenting.

"Aunt" Lena, her mother's best friend, came into Tracy's life at age four. Like a jolt of pure oxygen to a suffocating patient, she brought magic and wonder to a young girl who absorbed every offering like a sponge. Part owner of a costume business, she brought to life characters from children's classics like *Peter Pan* and *Robin Hood*, arriving with outfits to whisk mother and both children off on fanciful day hikes to Neverland or Sherwood Forest. When Tracy was a pre-teen, Aunt Lena took her on business trips to New York, London and other major cities. Bold and brash, she taught Tracy lessons in self-confidence, persistence and strategic planning. Nothing was too large, no problem too great and no one too powerful for Lena Mills. She was Master of the Universe, a larger-than-life mentor to an eager ingénue.

Teenage rebellion hit the Henderson family like a freight train. Lack of supervision and absence of boundaries led to revolt. Tracy and her brother Eddie began to run with the wrong crowd, defiantly challenging authority. Poor grades, body piercings, spiked hair and foul language were met with weak parental resistance. "They're just going through a phase," Anne and Ed agreed.

At age fifteen, Tracy's careless attitude nearly cost her life. A sleepover at a school friend's house turned into a nightmare when the sexual predator father and his two sons held her hostage, repeatedly raping and sodomizing her throughout the night, capturing every assault on film in graphic detail. Oblivious to the danger and neglecting to check about parental supervision, Anne had assumed her daughter was in safe hands. Ed was in Miami Beach, five hours away.

Tracy might have been killed if it hadn't been for Aunt Lena's chance visit to Anne's house the next morning. Sensing trouble, Lena insisted on picking up her niece from this "friend's" house.

What happened next was the stuff of legend. After encountering resistance at the doorway, Lena burst into the house to find Tracy—nude, battered and bloody, lying next to the father. Her hands were tied to a bedpost. Lena rescued her niece while incapacitating the entire houseful of sexual perverts. Grabbing the father's wallet and gun, she drove Tracy to a nearby police station and reported the incident. Pervert and his two sons were arrested, tried and incarcerated, the father receiving a life sentence. Film and equipment was confiscated and destroyed after the trials.

Thoroughly traumatized, Tracy was treated and released into parental custody. Both Anne and her daughter were forever grateful to Lena, more than willing to follow any advice coming from this amazing woman.

"Never let them see you cry." It was Lena's favorite phrase, since she herself had survived incest as a child and the seedier side of life as an adult. Strength through adversity was the lesson and the student had learned it well.

Through Tracy's four years of high school, Lena shared her past in vivid detail, describing her career as an exotic dancer, even demonstrating one of her routines—the last act of the opera *Lulu* by composer Alban Berg. Accompanied by the pre-recorded atonal orchestral score and adorned in a white virginal gown, Lena strapped herself to a male mannequin dressed in top hat and tails—Jack the Ripper in disguise. Succumbing to the advances of the handsome mannequin who removed each article

A NATION BEST SERVED HOT

of her clothing with a flourish, the music enhanced the mood of increasing intensity. Finally nude and most vulnerable, the mannequin's knife plunged twice. Lulu's death throes climaxed in orchestral dissonance. As the assailant gently laid her on the floor, the music faded to thunderous silence.

This highly successful, iconic performance had been a staple of Latin night-life for decades, often copied but rarely matched by Lena's performance as "Electra" in an Orlando gentlemen's club.

"I'm not doing this to encourage you toward my lifestyle, Trace," Lena explained. "But you need to know the power sexual suggestion holds over men and how to use it to your advantage. I'm a little rusty, but you get the idea. This was always my favorite act and the audiences gave me standing ovations."

Despite loathing the subject of sex, Tracy was fascinated and practiced the routine as well as her aunt's cosmetic techniques whenever she had privacy. A master at disguise and make-up, Lena often stated, "You never know when you might need to be someone else."

Slightly confused by the logic, Tracy took the lessons to heart. *If Aunt Lena can do these things, so can I,* swore the impetuous teen.

Off to college at eighteen, Tracy graduated in five years with honors and a Master's degree in criminology. Over-achieving throughout military training, for the last few years Tracy Henderson had been a top field agent for the Drug Enforcement Agency. Four weeks into her current assignment, she had been captured again, this time by someone more dangerous than a careless sexual pervert. This time she had been captured by a sadistic lunatic.

LIKE A RIVER erodes bedrock, time was stripping away layers of Tracy's humanity. Months of rape, impalement, whippings, tasings and knife assaults, along with disease and subterranean decay had transformed a vibrant, strong fighter into a weak, semi-lucid apparition. Bolivar began neglecting her needs, save the one daily meal. Reduced to skin, bones and blood, by day she remained shackled to the cave wall like a grotesque sculpture. At night she slept on her back atop a wooden platform with no pillow or mattress, hands and feet cuffed firmly to the surface.

Carón's visits were becoming infrequent but no less painful. While sparing her broken bones, he carved at will until there were no unaffected areas. Following each session, Bolivar dressed her wounds, keeping them sterile. Somehow her body always healed. Carón seemed determined to prolong the agony, taking pleasure in seeing her spirit wither toward eventual demise. Like a marriage gone stale, after three months when she was no longer attractive, El Gato lost interest. Sickening toward a slow death, at least she was spared further sexual abuse.

Her mind had become immune to Carón's brutality. What was once gut-wrenching became mundane, as if she were watching a horror flick rerun. Screams of other men blended with her moans of agony in an underworld symphony of pain. Days, weeks, months—Tracy had no concept of time, neither knowing nor caring how long she had been captive.

The fifth month brought a two-day interlude with the company of another female, a beautiful Spanish girl who was shackled beside her, unconscious. Upon waking, the girl was hysterical, prompting Bolivar to inject something in her arm. Through the fog of sedation, Tracy learned her name—Miriam. She kept mumbling about someone named Jerry—something about a restaurant, an engagement ring and falling asleep.

Tracy had nothing to offer but sympathy. Her own ravaged body revealed what was in store for the woman, whose teeth chattered with the cold temperature and dire anticipation.

On the second day, Felix Carón returned in a terrible mood. Snarling like a bobcat, he savagely raped the helpless woman, gripping and ripping in a bloody rampage. With one hand holding a fistful of long, black hair, the other sawed a serrated knife through neck bone and gristle, decapitating the now lifeless body. Covered in a fountain of blood, Carón waved the hideous, dripping apparition in front of Tracy's face before throwing it aside.

Like an anaconda preparing to swallow its prey, El Gato opened his mouth wide to cover Tracy's lips, exhaling nicotine-tainted brimstone, daring her to bite back. Forced to inhale, she choked on the breath of Hades, her wracked body recoiling in spasms of submission. Satisfied with his display of dominance, he withdrew, sliding blood-caked lips across her face to caress an ear. The knife rose to meet her eyes, poised to plunge. Instead, its tip brushed both eyebrows in a teasing, sanguinary dance. Flicking his snake-like tongue, the Devil licked her lobe twice before hissing, "You' mine! You' nex' to die."

With few remaining tufts of hair on her head, eyes that refused to focus, a face and body little more than skeleton and skin, Tracy shut down—

A NATION BEST SERVED HOT

willing herself to die. Her last thoughts were of Anne, Aunt Lena and her relationship to both. *Who was my real mother?* Tracy asked herself. How ironic that a stranger should share a deeper bond than her own flesh and blood. Tracy's mind drifted to the Van Gogh painting "Starry Starry Night" on Anne's wall and the last phrase of Don McLean's song:

> *Now I think I know what you tried to say to me,*
> *How you suffered for your sanity,*
> *How you tried to set them free,*
> *They would not listen, they're not listening still,*
> *Perhaps they never will....*

That was the end of remembering.

"SOMETIMES I WISH I WAS CHRISTA"
ORLANDO, FLORIDA
MAY, 2007

"YOU DID WHAT? Are you out of your friggin' mind?"

Ruggedly cut with a trim body cultivated by consistent exercise and careful diet, six-foot-eight Claude Masters was pacing back and forth, looming over his boss and friend of thirty-eight years, Lena Mills.

If time had been kind to Masters, it had been downright charitable to Lena. Midway into her fifty-sixth year, the former exotic dancer and businesswoman glowed with the confidence of self-made success. Equally vigilant with diet and exercise, she still trained and sparred with Claude, now sixty-eight, in martial arts three times a week. The product was a striking specimen of feminine firepower who looked not a day over forty.

Lena sat cross-legged on her living room sofa, countering Claude's arm-waving rant with a smug grin. She was a blond frog perched on her lily pad with a mouthful of juicy fly. Long, tapered legs disappeared into a skimpy housecoat which left little to the imagination. Any other man would have taken her dress and demeanor as a sexual tease, but Masters was happily married to Chareen, more than enough woman to keep her stud corralled for thirty-one years.

Claude's ebony contrasted Lena's ivory—two chiseled works of art. Like an older brother with his little sister, there were no secrets, nor was there any untoward lust between them. The years had only strengthened boundless trust and friendship.

"I've seen you do some over-the-top shit, but this is insanity," Masters continued his rant. "You've got it all, girl—health, looks and intelligence. You're the co-owner of one of the world's largest costume companies.

A NATION BEST SERVED HOT

You've got enough money to live comfortably for the rest of your life. All you seem to lack is common sense. Tell me you're just yanking my chain."

He's just getting warmed up, Lena thought to herself. *My, how this man can lather!*

"I said 'Yes'," she interrupted Claude's tirade with a matter-of-fact bullet to his brain. "We even set a date—September twenty-ninth."

Masters had the look of a buffalo hit with a .50-caliber Maynard. As the truth settled in, he was close to hyperventilation.

"Jesus Christ, you're really going to marry the Governor?"

"Can't you be happy for me, you lovable old geezer?" she teased, standing up to meet him. "I'm going to be the First Lady of Florida. You may kiss this." She held up her left hand. A huge diamond rested upon her ring finger. *At least two carats,* Masters guessed.

"And you can kiss my ass!" he retorted, startling her. "You can't love the bastard, the same man you taunted with a sex tape for the last God-knows-how-many years—the same son of a bitch who tried to have Anne killed."

"Win Stedman never tried to kill Anne." Lena was rapidly losing patience. "It was his father who put out the hit and you know it." She stabbed Claude in the chest with her index finger, backing him with rising ire. At five-foot ten, she was almost a foot shorter, but now seemed to tower over him.

"I don't know what love is, but whatever it is, I damn sure haven't had enough in my life. I think I've felt it with Anne and you, but that's friendship love, different than what you have with Chareen. You know my history. Maybe I'm incapable of giving myself freely to someone else. But Stedman wants me to be his wife. He says he's through catting around and knows I will keep him on a short leash. He's sixty-one, for God's sake."

Masters had backed into a wall. Logic had no effect on this woman. She was a creature of impulse. Once she made up her mind, there was no stopping her. But this behavior was out of character, even for Lena Mills. Simple curiosity made him ask the final question: "Why do you want to put yourself through all this? If it's a fling you want, go for it in private. You've spent your whole adult life avoiding public scrutiny. You know this engagement is going to be red meat to the press."

Lena sat back down, calmly gathering herself. This was Anne's fault. In the note she left, her dying words had been, "Maybe you could love him, too, if you tried."

Claude had made a good point. Seeing the pensive look in her eyes, he sat next to her, remaining silent. After a minute, Lena looked him square in the eye and took his large right hand in hers.

"You're right, of course. That's what I hate about you. You're always right. Remember Christa McAuliffe?"

"Of course. The Challenger disaster some twenty years ago," he replied. *Where is this woman going now?* he wondered.

"She had it all, too—brave, successful teacher, great family. The world fell in love with her even before she got on that shuttle. I always wonder what those astronauts feel as they take off. Words can't describe it. Even if it all ends in disaster, they have that one moment of ecstasy, that moment of awe—of being."

Lena's eyes were glowing. "Sometimes I wish I was Christa. I know I'll never be an astronaut, but that feeling is the only void in my life. Something is driving me—something I can't explain to you or anyone else. Call it restlessness. There's enough time left in my life for one grand adventure, and I'm going for it, damn the consequences."

Claude remembered a young girl with a history of abuse no one should have to endure—a young girl brave enough to enter a strip club and bare herself to a world of strangers; a young girl bold enough to captivate and conquer that world. Defying the odds to achieve wealth on her own terms, she had left the limelight at the peak of success to launch a completely different career. Blonde, brash and beautiful Electra had brought him along for the ride, and what a ride it had been!

"You're one crazy broad," he mumbled, hugging her in his massive arms.

"Does this mean you'll give me away at the wedding?" she asked, hugging him back.

Like Kenny Rogers' song "The Gambler," Claude Masters knew "when to hold 'em" and more importantly, "when to fold 'em."

He rose from the sofa and looked down at her with a rueful grin.

"Let the games begin!"

NOTHING HAD COME easily to Lena Mills. The only child of an itinerant pharmacist and acquiescent mother, she was repeatedly molested and raped by her alcoholic father until she had grown enough to resist. Born

A NATION BEST SERVED HOT

Merleen Oosterman, by the age of sixteen an awkward young blonde had matured into a striking beauty, ogled by boys and resented by girls.

Laying waste to her high school rivals, eighteen year-old Merleen was ready to escape the provincial confines of Muskegon, Michigan. With steely determination and careful planning she traveled cross-country to attend a central Florida college. Changing her name to Lena Mills, it wasn't long before she changed her career path as well. Stunning physical assets and lack of modesty bought her a well-paying job as a stripper in a gentlemen's club. Using creative skills and clever marketing, Lena—stage name "Electra"—soon became the toast of Orlando night life. Accepting fortune while rejecting fame, she learned the art of disguise to avoid the local and national paparazzi that hounded her incessantly.

Living frugally and investing wisely, in five years she had amassed enough wealth to retire comfortably. Electra's reputation increased in proportion to her Garbo-like media reticence. Relying on her wits, Lena faced every day in solitude. Assigned a bodyguard by the club owner, she slowly grew to admire and eventually trust the gentle giant, Claude Masters. Over the years and well past retirement from her career as an entertainer, Lena shared with Claude mutual respect and admiration that grew into life-long friendship.

A chance, surreal encounter during a walk in the Ocala National Forest led to her one other friendship. An opposite of Lena in every way, Anne Henderson possessed the ability to communicate with dead people and live animals. Through most unlikely circumstance, they shared one thing in common: both had bedded a rising star in Florida politics, Winthrop—"Win-at-all-costs"—Stedman III.

Through many years, Lena and Anne grew close while Win Stedman bore the scars of their creative revenge. Undeterred in his quest for sex and power, he had risen politically to become Governor of Florida, all the while harboring a secret fascination for Electra. Eventually learning her real name, he found Lena Mills to be the only woman who ever dared torment him. After thirty years of elected office, he was now ready to retire and determined to try for her hand.

Seeing her again for the first time in decades at the funeral of his old college flame, Anne Akterhoff Henderson, who had died of brain cancer, Stedman had been struck by Lena's appearance. Sitting pensively by the grave, she was every bit as beautiful as he remembered. Unlike others, age had only improved an already stunning woman. What used to be raw sexual magnetism had matured into classical elegance. With a shyness he never before experienced, Governor Win Stedman approached.

"WE'RE GOING to miss her."

He had come from behind and startled Lena. She rose to her feet and turned, at first not recognizing him.

When she did, she gasped, "Well I'll be damned."

"I'm sure that goes for both of us, Ms. Mills," said the governor, taking her hand in his.

"She was the best, Win," Lena answered, using his informal name for the first time, "the best friend a girl could have."

"I know. She was mine too." After a pause, he sighed, "Annie Akterhoff." Looking down at her grave, he added, "I was a fool to let her get away." Tears welled in his eyes.

"It was good of you to come." Lena was sincere. "I was with her these past few weeks—her personal hospice. We talked about everything, including you. She said she loved you back then. I think she would want you to know that," Lena stated, looking briefly at his eyes.

"I was a selfish bastard—still am. I didn't deserve her."

"No, you didn't," Lena answered with a slight tone of bitterness. "As long as we're in the same confession booth, neither did I."

They both looked down at the tombstone for a minute, saying nothing. Lena broke the silence. "But life goes on, doesn't it?" She started walking away.

"Ms. Mills...Lena." *He's nervous*, she noticed. "I wonder if I could impose upon you to take a ride with me. There...there's something I'd like to discuss with you."

"Like what?" Lena asked.

"Like...us." Stedman was blushing.

"Us? There is no us, Governor," Lena answered, slightly blushing herself.

"That's what I hope...I—we could change," Win stammered.

Lena was flabbergasted. This was the last thing on her mind. She was intrigued. *Is the Governor of Florida asking me on a date? In the middle of a cemetery?* Her mind was swirling with the irony. She stared at him for a good ten seconds, looking for insincerity, seeing none.

A NATION BEST SERVED HOT

"I warn you, sir," Lena said, taking his arm. "You're playing with fire. I'll eat you alive, Win Stedman." She glanced again at his face. He was starting to sweat.

"I can't think of a better way to go," he replied, slowly guiding the saucy wench toward his limo. "You ever see the movie *Casablanca*?"

"Who hasn't?" she replied.

"I'm paraphrasing the last line: 'Lena, I think this could be the start of a beautiful friendship....'"

"I'm paraphrasing myself: 'In your dreams'," Lena shot back.

"You've been in my dreams for years, Ms. Mills. You make my blood boil."

"Oh, Studley, you Wild Thing!" Lena mocked in a fake swoon, bringing her arm to her forehead.

Willie Moncrief was the governor's chauffeur—had been since Stedman took office. As his boss and a strange woman approached the limo, they were laughing. Opening the rear door, Willie shook his head in amazement. *Damn! The Gov done picked up a broad in a graveyard. Now I seen everything.*

THEY HAD RIDDEN around Central Florida for two hours in his limo, followed by two state troopers on motorcycles. Oblivious to gawkers, the two former adversaries talked not about the past, but the future. Rather, Stedman did most of the talking while Lena listened. At first skeptical, in time she was sure. He was opening his heart.

Like an old warrior weary of battle, he was ready to cash it all in at the end of his term of office in 2010. Every cause he had championed, every campaign promise made, was failing. Taxes were rising in concert with wildly-escalating real estate prices; his attempts at property insurance reform were being blocked by a Republican legislature, and burgeoning state coffers were being siphoned by costly social reforms. The worst was yet to come, he was sure. Real estate was bound to implode with sub-prime mortgages being offered to anyone with a pulse, never mind the buyer's ability to make payments. The stock market was skyrocketing toward a bubble and the prospect of another devastating hurricane season like 2004 and 2005 loomed each fall.

In the past, he would have bluffed and spun with silver-tongued oratory, blaming everyone but himself for the problems. "Not anymore," he swore.

"Gonna call 'em as I see 'em. I'm riding this galloping horse toward a cliff. Why am I the only one who seems to notice the danger?"

"You're scaring me, Governor," Lena broke in. "Why are you telling me this?"

"Because I'm tired of being alone, Ms. Mills," Stedman sighed. "Please call me Win, if you don't mind."

"I will if you call me Lena. Ms. Mills sounds like English royalty, and you know I'm anything but that," she chided.

Laughing now, he took her hand. "Let me explain something to you, Lena. Except for my father, Annie, and a few women I've jilted, no one has ever talked back to me—no one. I've never been comfortable talking honestly from my gut. I'm surrounded by toadies and 'yes' men. Do you know how frustrating that is?"

"I've often wondered how you do it, Win—keeping up the phony façade. I chalked it up to your ambition, lumping you with all other political hacks greedy for power. Since we're being honest, let me tell you my feelings. Politicians disgust me. Maybe a few get into it for the right reasons, but money and power corrupt like rust on iron. Comes with the territory, I guess. Sooner or later, it's all about re-election, greed and money—climbing the political ladder 'til you fall off."

She looked him square in the eye. "Always be honest with me," she challenged.

"That's why I like you." He glanced at the limo floor, ashamed. "I need you to slap me around—verbally, that is."

"So what do you have in mind, Win Stedman?" Lena was getting right to the point. "I'm anything but a Catholic priest. Why am I taking this ride with you?"

Stedman looked up, suddenly with a steady gaze.

"Okay. Here goes. That day at the apartment long ago—the sex was incredible. To say you made a lasting impression is an understatement. Since then I've followed your business and personal career. Aside from your roughing me up, which I deserved by the way, my admiration has grown over the years. You're a fascinating, self-made, take-no-prisoners kind of woman, Lena Mills.

"I don't expect you to like me. Can't say I like myself. You have no reason to accept my offer, every reason to turn me down, but I'll make it anyway.

A NATION BEST SERVED HOT

"I want to know you better. No sex unless you give the green light. No pretense, just honesty. I need companionship with someone I trust. Don't ask me why, but I feel I can trust you. Does this make any sense?"

Lena studied his eyes. "Eyes are the windows to the soul," had been one of Anne's favorite sayings. Stedman's eyes held the gaze of truth—the look of respect.

She remembered Anne at the end, saying, "I really loved that rascal… for all his faults." What seemed at the time ridiculous was now staring her in the face. *Anne Henderson, you witch!* A small, ironic grimace creased Lena's lips.

"It's not fair. You're catching me at a vulnerable time, Win," Lena sighed after a moment. "My best friend is dead and her daughter—someone I consider my own—is missing and presumed dead. Maybe I need someone to talk to as well."

Stedman looked shocked.

"Well, where do we go from here, Mr. Florida Governor?" Lena asked.

"Forward, my dear," he replied solemnly. "Always forward. Please… tell me everything."

ENGAGED AND ENRAGED
MAY, 2007

TWO MONTHS OF COURTSHIP, two months of high profile social engagements, two months of speculation. Tallahassee was abuzz with gossip. Other than his failed marriage, two months with one woman was a record for the "Luv Guv."

The press went wild with speculation until an older reporter for the Orlando Sun Times remembered her name and dug up some old microfilm. Pictures of a beautiful woman at ages 25 and 41 confirmed his suspicion.

Stories had run nationally for two days about Lena Mills—a former exotic dancer named Electra, who had single-handedly rescued her niece from a nest of child molesters. "BUSTY BABE BASHES PORN RING"; "KARATE QUEEN KICKS CRAP OUT OF CRIMINALS"; "AGING ELECTRA PULVERIZES PERVES"; and "DIAMOND DIVA DANCER DECKS DEVIANT DESPERADOS" were some of the sensational headlines. Hyperventilating over his good luck, the reporter burst into his editor's office with the scoop of his life.

The news hit Tallahassee like a Cat 5 hurricane. The Governor was dating a stripper! Never mind she was now in her late fifties. This was sensational! National media converged on the capitol like a swarm of locusts. Interviewing anyone remotely connected to the executive staff, reporters gobbled every morsel of gossip and regurgitated trash regardless of truth.

Lena had girded herself for public disclosure. Win had warned her of the onslaught, but nothing could prepare her for the magnitude of these vicious assaults. Newspapers screamed headlines that barely passed

A NATION BEST SERVED HOT

censorship: "SIZE MATTERS—STRIPPER HOOKS BIG ONE!"; "HAS GOVERNOR HUMP AND DUMP MET HIS MATCH?"; and "WRINKLED OR NOT, HERE THEY COME!"

"My God, the audacity!" shouted Stedman, slamming his Tallahassee paper on the dining room table. The Executive Mansion was in an uproar. All types of media laid siege to the governor's residence, straining for any glimpse of him or his consort.

Lena was in Orlando when the tsunami hit. Her cell phone had an unlisted direct line to Stedman's. "Win, what should I do?" she laughed. "They're everywhere. I can't leave my apartment."

"You think this is funny?" he replied, livid. "I'm sending in the state police for your protection. Any asshole who touches you will answer to me!"

"Love it when you're angry," she said in a sexy croon. "See you later this week, handsome." Terminating the call, she reflected: *I'll give him that. He's still drop dead handsome!*

Lena felt twenty-five again. As Electra, she had dodged the paparazzi for years, reveling in the game of hide-and-seek. The media hadn't scared her then and wouldn't now. The costume business was running itself and Claude was handling the construction of Harper Mills, a retirement home for indigent entertainers—her philanthropic endeavor. Financially set and bored, Lena was free to take on all comers.

In her wildest imagination, however, she never could have conceived something this outrageous. She was dating a raging bull and was in for the ride of her life. In spite of her ruining his first marriage, in spite of her threats to ruin his career with a certain sex tape she still had locked in her bank vault, in spite of her degrading taunts, Win Stedman was in love with her. Certainly no fool—a fool could not have risen to his political stature—this man was either delusional or masochistic. *Maybe both*, she surmised.

Although Lena felt incapable of reciprocal love, she had grown fond of this man over the last two months. Their talks had been honest and sincere. Stedman's life was chock full of narcissistic baggage he was now eager to jettison. Inside, he was a little boy who had been given too many toys. Years of unfulfilled promises to his constituents weighed heavily on his mind—promises that got him elected while piling layers of guilt upon his soul. But she was willing to bet, under the baggage lived a good man.

In turn, Lena confessed her transgressions, most born of necessity. Faced with a world of cruelty, out of self-defense she had reacted in kind, creating havoc along the way. To her, sometimes two wrongs did make a right, and she judiciously applied her brand of retribution to all who dared cross her. "In a dog-eat-dog world, it's much better to be a wolf," she confessed, looking boldly in her suitor's eyes. "Hang the consequences."

"Don't get me wrong, Win," she added. "I'm certainly not proud of the things I've done, but I won't apologize for them either. Faced with the choice of being the bug or the windshield, I've always chosen the latter."

Stedman stared in awe at this woman. Years ago as a congressman, he had traveled to England on a diplomatic mission. While there, he had met Margaret Thatcher, the retired "Iron Lady" Prime Minister. A firm handshake matched her confident gaze. Lena Mills was another Iron Lady. The word formidable came to mind. Underestimate her at one's own peril.

Governor Win Stedman had more than met his match. Instead of recoiling, he fell deeply in love. After two months, asking for her hand came as naturally to him as quenching thirst. He was more than willing to marry on her terms, if only she would have him.

"I've got three years left to undo some of the damage I've caused, Lena," he stated that night. "I need your conscience to guide me. Will you help me finish my term?"

"Governor, you flatter me," she replied. "I won't promise to love you. That may come in time. But if you're sincere, and I think you are, I would be honored to be your wife."

As he rose to embrace her, she whispered in his ear, "Just remember, you sexy son of a bitch. You cross me and I'll eat you alive."

Shocked, Stedman pushed her away.

Lena Mills was laughing.

ONE YEAR AGO, Win Stedman had been elected Governor of Florida with a firm majority of votes and a mandate for his vague agenda. A political Pied Piper, he was equally adept at teleprompter oratory and off-the-cuff banter. His was style over substance. When the Guv spoke, media lemmings jumped.

Until now, Stedman's philandering had been one of his political strengths. He was a new kind of Kennedy. With a different babe at his side every week, few seemed to care about his left-of-center leanings. Women craved his rakish lust. Men admired his roguish pluck.

Like water dousing a fire, his rumored engagement to a former stripper changed everything. Win's attempts at governing were stymied by the press and a public clamoring for salacious details. In matters of state, the more he talked, the more his legislature balked. Politically neutered, frustration grew by the day. He was damaged goods, a duck lamed by his own hand. Jilted, his constituency took it as a personal affront. How dare their Guv fall in love?

To Stedman, the next two months were a nightmare. Torn by his feelings for Lena versus his diminishing popularity, he turned inward, shunning the press in all but the most important state business. Conversely, Lena seemed buoyed by the attention. Decades of running a successful business and dealing with the public had turned a twenty-something recluse into a confident media combatant. Instead of running from the press, she relished the prospect of sparring with reporters. She vowed to be patient, deferring to her fiancé while waiting her turn for the limelight.

Her turn came almost immediately with the announcement. Stedman's press secretary, Dennis Akers, had issued a terse, two sentence announcement to the thundering media herd. He was under strict orders to answer no questions. It was like waving fresh kill in front of starving hyenas. The press demanded details. Suffering death threats, the poor soul fled for his life. There was no getting around it. The public demanded a gubernatorial command performance.

At ten o'clock on a brilliant late-May Saturday morning, with his beautiful fiancée at his side, the Governor entered the Capitol Courtyard and approached a large dais from which a gigantic phalanx of microphones rose like coiled snakes. The grounds were jammed to capacity with local, state and national media. Television cameras hummed and hundreds of cameras clicked in metallic orgasms, drowned by shouts from the unruly crowd. The beleaguered press secretary hid in his office, popping tranquilizers.

Reaching the podium, Win Stedman raised his hands, gesturing for silence. A full minute elapsed before the raucous conversation diminished, allowing him to speak. "Ladies and gentlemen, thank you all for coming," he began in a low conversational tone. "I'm not sure if you came here to see me or the pretty lady to my right."

The press resumed its clamoring. Again holding up hands for silence, he continued. "Ms. Lena Mills has graciously consented to be my wife. We are to be married in Orlando on September twenty-ninth...."

A reporter in front rudely interrupted, shouting, "Let's hear from the lady, Governor."

Rising in volume, chants of "Electra...Electra...Electra..." immediately commenced. For the first time in his life, Stedman felt the sting of playing second fiddle to another. He looked over at Lena who smiled back at him, giving a positive nod of her head. With a magnanimous gesture, he waved her forward. *God help her*, he prayed silently, stepping aside.

Other than teasing a nightclub audience with one-liners, Lena Mills had never spoken before a large crowd. As Electra, her body had done all the talking. But she felt serenely calm standing next to the podium. Nearly six feet in high heels, a silver-sequined gown accented every curve of her hourglass figure. Flowing blonde tresses still framed the face of a goddess as her eyes stared out at the sea of hostile humanity and clicking cameras. Smiling with dazzling white teeth at the cacophony of questions, she said nothing for a full minute, absorbing power like a charging battery. *So this is what it's all about*, she marveled.

Lena waited well after the last shouted word before sliding left to the bank of microphones. She had prepared her first comment, calculated to shock. After that, she would punt.

"Bet I know what you're all thinking," she began, hesitating for effect. She cupped both hands to her mouth and shouted like a foghorn: "BIMBO!"

The crowd erupted with laughter. Stedman winced, looking like he'd been broadsided. *My God! She's giving them red meat.* Like unwanted flotsam, she had tossed aside all pretense of decorum.

Waiting again for calm, she continued, "Just wanted to get that out of the way. Bet the first question you have is why—why would a randy old goat like the Guv..." gesturing toward her shocked fiancé, "want to settle down with one aging exotic dancer..." she emphasized "aging" while pointing to herself, "when he has a whole world of young babes at his disposal? Am I right?"

Another round of laughter. More shutter clicks. A few shouts of, "You go, girl!" This Electra was a trip!

Stedman's jaw had dropped open like a hooked bass. *Oh shit*, he thought, *there goes what's left of my reputation! May as well go with the flow.* He clamped his mouth shut, smiled and ruefully shook his head.

A NATION BEST SERVED HOT

"You're asking, is she that good in bed?" Lena stepped aside. In full view, she placed her hands in back of her head and thrust her hips in one sharp booty-bump.

The crowd roared with another two minutes of laughter and out-of-control shouting. Capitol police surrounded the courtyard. Until now, they were enjoying the show. The woman's bump and grind had changed their demeanor. Alert to possible trouble, each scanned the audience with practiced eyes.

Signaling for calm, Lena resumed her place behind the microphones. "I guess he has to be the judge of that," she purred, giving Stedman a seductive glance.

"You da broad!" shouted a young male reporter in front. More laughter.

Enough audience baiting, thought Lena. She held up her hands, trying for a more serious tone.

"You will no doubt raise the issue of my past indiscretions. Some I'll admit to and some you will make up. I can live with that. For whatever reasons, this wonderful man—this good governor of yours—wants me to be his wife."

Taking Win's hand, she brought him forward. The crowd had become inexplicably quiet. Like a maestro conducting her orchestra, Lena paused for effect before continuing, "And I am proud to accept his hand in marriage. I may not be the wallflower wife you expect, but I pledge to be loyal to this man and, for the next three years, to my duties as First Lady of our great state."

To Governor Win Stedman's astonishment, polite applause replaced the previous rowdy behavior. *She's won them over*, he beamed, giving her a big hug. Nothing more needed to be said. Raising their arms in a victory salute, the Governor and his consort departed like conquering royalty toward the historic Capitol Building amid loud cheers and applause.

Greeted warmly in the Rotunda by his executive staff, including one sedated press secretary, Win turned to his wife-to-be, showering her with praise. "You are one amazing woman, Lena Mills," he crowed.

"She certainly is one bodacious broad," said a large black man who approached the entourage from the corridor. Lena ran to his massive embrace.

"Win, this is my very good friend, Claude Masters. Claude, meet my future husband, Governor Win Stedman."

Shaking hands, Claude replied, "I've seen you before, sir. All of you. You just haven't met me."

Stedman was nonplussed. "Let's get a cup of coffee and I'll explain," Lena offered.

"Sounds like I need something stronger than coffee," replied the bewildered governor.

SOUL-STICE
THURSDAY, JUNE 21, 2007

LENA MILLS PUNCHED some numbers into a hand-held Garmin. Along with instructions and a letter, Lena had found the GPS when she opened a package left to her from Anne Henderson, her best friend, dead from cancer at the age of sixty-one. As instructed, Lena had waited until this day to bring the package to the Ocala National Forest. It was a hot June afternoon, but the overcast clouds made the forest temperature quite tolerable. At first disguised to avoid the press, Lena had driven alone to the forest and changed. Now dressed in jeans, tennis shoes, a loose-fitting white blouse and backpack, she followed a well-worn trail deep into the woods, head down looking at the Garmin's positioning screen. With latitude and longitude coordinates down to the second, she was close to the spot where she had seen Anne that first time so many years ago.

There it was, just off the beaten path—a small pile of stones, just as Anne had described. Taking off the backpack and removing a small folded shovel, she began digging next to the stones. The job took no more than ten minutes. Chopping through stubborn roots was the hardest part, but the hole was narrow and the shovel sharp. Three feet of dirt would be a chore for most women of her age, but Lena suffered only minor sweating. Her rigorous work-out schedule kept her in great shape. At least Studley thought so. She had to stop calling him that. It wasn't good form to give the governor of Florida an inferiority complex, but she certainly relished the role as "humbler-in-chief."

They had reached an "agreement"—that's what he named it. She called it "pre-marital détente." In return for his pledge to be through with political office at the expiration of his term, she promised to be civil and politically correct in public—as much as possible for a former exotic dancer.

She made it clear that if he ever strayed, well…she used the name "Bobbitt" to maximum effect, causing temporary shrinkage of a certain body part. He swore fidelity and meant it. From past experience, he knew she was an expert in retribution. Fear alone was enough to deter any future dalliances. Besides, he was getting too old for puckish promiscuity. Yep, Lena Mills was more than enough woman for Governor Win Stedman.

After months of badgering, Ed Henderson, Anne's husband, finally received word of his daughter. Tracy had been missing in action somewhere in Mexico since January. Though nothing was official yet, due to the mission she was on at the time of her disappearance, she was presumed dead. That was all the DEA would offer, except a long-overdue apology and condolences from the El Paso Resident Agent in Charge.

Lena was devastated but glad Anne never knew. It would have been one burden too hard for the dying woman to bear. Stubborn Tracy—she was Lena's favorite. So much wasted talent, so much wasted potential, so much wasted love forever lost. *God, life can be so cruel!* Lena had cursed. But now was now and there was a task at hand.

Digging until reaching what she thought was a three-foot depth, Lena sat on the ground to catch her breath. She picked up the instruction sheet. Each completed item had a check mark. Removing the urn from her backpack—this one had the real ashes, not wood ashes like the one buried in the cemetery back in March, she carefully dropped it down the hole. The last instruction said: "After putting urn in hole, open envelope and read letter." Lena reached inside the backpack and pulled out the envelope. Not surprisingly it was dated June 21, 2007—*today*, she noted.

Dear Lena,

I am writing this on the first week home from the hospital, while I'm still able to do so.

First, I want to thank you for following my instructions. You may wonder why I asked you to wait until June 21st to do this. Today is the Summer Solstice. I was born, married and am about to buried on a Summer Solstice.

The reason will become evident. It's not easy talking to you when I'm in a gazillion little burnt pieces, but I'll do my best. Please excuse the death humor.

A NATION BEST SERVED HOT

Second, I want to tell you a short story. When I was thirteen, Festus, Florida wasn't anything like it is now. It was still rather primitive. On one of my solitary walks about town, I was passing a dark alley. A pack of large dogs jumped out, circling me and growling. They meant to attack. If I ran or showed fear, they would jump me—probably kill me, since there was no one around to help.

Instead I stood still, stared at what I thought was the pack leader and thought, I'm not afraid to love you. I looked at each dog in turn and focused my mind. They all backed off whimpering and slithered away. It was the first time I felt the power.

I am telling you this because in so many ways you are a much stronger person than I was. You had to be to overcome what your father did to you as a child.

With business, planning, initiative, money and dealing with children, your mind has always been leap years ahead of mine. You would have drop-kicked those dogs to a pulp, then ground the meat and sold it to McDonald's (more death humor), wouldn't you? Admit it, you're one tough broad.

And looks? You're Venus and I was the bag lady. Within you is the power to change lives. Do not think you're on the downside of life. Your destiny is yet to be written.

My message to you has to do with your one weakness. Lena, don't be afraid to love. All the powers you have pale in comparison to the power of love. Don't you see? The more you give, the more you receive.

Third, please tell Ed he was a wonderful husband and lover. I am proud of both my children. Please tell them that. They need to know. Don't give up on Tracy. She'll need you more than ever someday."

"My God, the irony!" cried Lena out loud, dropping the letter, wringing her hands in frustration.

She picked it up from the ground. The letter continued:

And tell my grandchildren they were pains in the ass, but I loved them. They can burn the paddle and curse me for all I care. Life will be what they make it. Make sure Shots gets a good home. He's a good companion.

Next, please be patient and wait here until you hear me calling. Look up. I'll not be saying "goodbye." Rather "so long" until we meet again.

Last, when you're done reading this, please throw it in the hole with my urn and cover me with dirt and the pile of stones I left here. I've got to catch up on my sleep. (Enough with the death humor!)

Lena Mills, you are more than a friend or sister to me. You are my soul mate. Did you know death never separates soul mates?

You've got a lot of living to do. Follow your instincts. Give 'em hell, girl!

I'll be waiting,

Anne

The last sentence was a postscript:

P.S. Next time you're playing hide the weenie with Studley, get out a ruler. I still say it was seven inches.

Lena's jaw dropped open. *How could she have known?*

~~~

THROUGH THE HAZE of tears, Lena filled the hole and piled the stones in a small pyramid. She couldn't bring herself to toss the letter. It was her most precious link to Anne.

She sat on the ground and waited.

The forest had talked to Anne, yet Lena heard only trees rustling in the light breeze, crickets and small birds chirping, a few feral calls. She waited patiently, looking upward, knowing what she sought, wondering: would it come?

The woods were hypnotic with sounds of solemn silence.

She rested. Eyelids drooped. Her head nodded.

An hour went by. Another ten minutes.

At first faint, then growing stronger, she heard it chirping through the forest.

A lone eagle, soaring with the thermals, circled high above a few minutes before landing on the apex of a barren tree. Lena stood, eyes riveted on majesty. It looked down upon her with eyes that met hers in unspoken acknowledgement.

In a wordless trance, Lena's mind spoke: *I know who you are. I am not afraid to love!*

And then....

A NATION BEST SERVED HOT

She remembered the letter: *The reason will become evident.* A beam of sunlight found entrance through the clouds and bathed her face like a missive from Heaven. Lena fell to her knees.

"Kree."

With a sharp call, the eagle lifted, circling twice overhead before darting away.

Eyes flooded with tears, arms lifted in prayer, heart overflowing…Lena whispered, "Thank you."

THE CAVE
SOUTH OF CUIDAD JUAREZ, MEXICO
SATURDAY, JUNE 30, 2007

FIRST HE FELT the cold. Slowly coming out of a drug-induced coma, Jerry Calvin began to notice his environment. He was lying on his back. It was also dark. Many years ago, he had explored New Mexico's Carlsbad Caverns with his father. The guide had turned off the lights. Jerry remembered this kind of darkness.

Like cotton candy, fuzzy images stuck in the recesses of his mind. He was riding in a van, lying next to Miriam, stopping at a rock entrance across from an old drive-in movie theater. He knew this place. He'd taken Miriam here to see a Spanish film months ago. Carried from the van by two large men, he had passed through a tunnel around corners. A needle prick on his arm and all went black again.

Then he felt the fear. A slight draft was coming from somewhere to his right.

I'm naked, he realized. His arms and legs were tightly secured. Only his head was able to move.

He began to tremble. "H-hello?" Louder: "Anybody, a-anybody there?"

An echo? Was there an echo? Silence, except a soft dripping sound, about once a second—slow plopping like drops from a thawing icicle. *Cave*, he thought. *Surely I'm in a cave.*

To his left he detected a low moaning. Was it a female voice?

"Hello? Hey! Help me! Anyone. Why am I here?" Spurred by the sound, Jerry yelled and squirmed, trying to free any part. He was securely bound to his rock-hard...no—it was a metal platform.

His echoes receded. The moaning had stopped.

A NATION BEST SERVED HOT

"Miriam, is that you?" he asked, remembering flickering candles, the marimba, the engagement ring.

Silence. Only the distant plop, plop of liquid. A minute went by, then another.

Plop…plop…plop….

Lines from a poem entered his brain. *Dylan Thomas, wasn't it? "Do not go gentle into that good night. Rage, rage against the dying of the light."* Panic rose to match the cold that permeated every inch of his being, followed by uncontrollable shaking—teeth-rattling shivers. His head bounced off the platform. Screaming was the only thing that felt good—the only thing he could control.

"I know someone's there. Help! Somebody! Pleeeease!" Overlapping echoes added layers of mania. In full-throated, head thrashing mode, Jerry would not go gently or quietly.

Deep breaths between screams…again…again…again…again…again, until his throat gave out. Fear and anger ebbed into tears and exhaustion. Head pounding with pain, Jerry was reduced to a begging whisper: "Pleeeease."

Plop…plop…plop….

Cold.

Resignation.

His last thoughts: *How did I get here? Where is Miriam?*

Jerry slept.

"HAAAY, GRINGO." A whisper, next to his ear, followed by the stench of stale cigar breath.

Jerry snapped out of his frigid coma. "Wha? Who's there?" His mouth felt full of sand. Turning quickly to the voice, he croaked, "Pleeease, help me."

"A leetle cold, eh, greengo?" It was a full, deep voice, followed by the sound of steps walking away.

"Who are you? Why am I here?" Jerry implored.

"You owe me lot of money, greengo."

Click.

From total darkness to blinding light, the change hit Jerry like a cattle prod.

It all came back to him now—the restaurant, the proposal, champagne.... His eyes slowly adjusting, he recognized the man. *The poker game—the sunken eyes.* "Where's Miriam?" Stronger, he repeated, "Who *are* you?"

Jerry surveyed the surroundings. As he had suspected, it was a cave. *More like a dungeon,* he thought. Hand shackles and whips dangled on rock walls. Attached to one set of shackles was a woman. *It's not Miriam,* he realized. She was covered in a loose-fitting shift. Dark-haired and young, her head, arms and legs were covered in dried blood. Horrified at the sight, Jerry turned back to his captor. To his left, between his metal platform and another, a set of surgical tools sat on a small table with wheels. Both his platform and the other had faucets, overhanging lights and what looked like drainage sinks at one end. *Autopsy tables*, he thought. The drips of water came from one of those.

"Questions? You got lot questions, eh greengo?"

"Who is the girl? Where is Miriam? What have you done with her?" Jerry's head felt like it would explode.

"Pretty leetle puta, your lady frien'. Maybe I have some fun with her like thees one, eh? She Americano DEA. Try fuck wid me; I fuck wid her." Gesturing toward the shackled woman, the man was chuckling.

"What's going on here? What the hell did I ever do to you? Who are you, you sick bastard?" Jerry was screaming with the little voice he had left.

The man approached with a raised open palm.

Wham! Stars exploded in Jerry's head as it jerked to the left.

The voice was next to his ear again, hissing, "Lissen me, you punk. You owe me money and you' gonna give to me. You' gonna give me money and you gonna do everythin' I say or I cut you' pretty puta in leetle pieces and send 'em to Mamá in box. You want that, eh greengo?" Stale cigar breath and spittle sprayed Jerry's face.

Jerry had never been this frightened. "You want money? I got money. Just let us go, and I'll give you what you want," he begged.

His captor was having fun. Jerry's head had gone nuclear. He thrashed as the man tore off a piece of duct tape and forced it over his eyes, blinding him.

"Theess what it feels like to be cut, greengo." A searing pain ripped down Jerry's left side from neck to waist. "Eess what I do to you' puta. You no like, eh?"

A NATION BEST SERVED HOT

"Pleeeease." Whimpering now, Jerry felt his blood spilling from the laceration. His bladder released and he pissed in spurts.

The man was laughing. "Look like you need one you' diaper, eh?"

His tormentor let a few seconds pass before adding, "No worry now, greengo. Just some ice thees time. No cut. You gonna do what I say?"

Jerry couldn't talk. He nodded his head, weeping.

The voice hissed in his ear again. "You remember poker game two yearss ago, eh greengo? You remember fucking me out of meelion dollarss? You remember now, you leetle rat bassta punk?" More stinking spit landed on Jerry's face.

There was no arguing with this madman, no use telling him he had won the game honestly. Miriam's life was at stake.

"What do you want me to do?" he moaned, defeated.

"Thass better, greengo." The man's breath smelled like a loaded ash tray. I know we come to some kinda, how you say, *accommodación*. I tell you what you do for me. You do it, maybe you get you' leetle puta back. But I leave you with reminder so you don't fuck with me again, eh? I have dees leetle toy. He wan' play with you. Maybe he play with you' puta, too." Laughing now. "You feel thees and do what I say, eh, greengo?" Fifty thousand volts jolted Jerry's groin, fanning throughout his body, which locked in wooden agony. "You sure, eh?" the man added, zapping the taser once more.

Jerry's mouth opened in a silent scream as his shackled body danced on the table.

Passing into unconsciousness, he was never more sure of anything in his life.

⁓⌒⁓

THOUGH VIOLENT, the taser was not designed to maim, only incapacitate. Jerry awoke to the acrid odor of smelling salts, aching from head to toe. Every muscle in his body had been shocked to the limit, as if he had risen from ocean depths with the bends. He was clothed and sitting upright, bound with rope to a chair in a large, ornately decorated room. His blindfold had been removed. Across a great desk sat his captor smoking a cigarillo, puffing perfect circles in the air. Jerry instantly recalled the sunken, black eyes and mustache.

"Welcome back, greengo. I trust you like my hacienda better than cave," he laughed.

"You wan' some water?" As Jerry nodded his throbbing head, a huge man with bald head, thick mustache and scowling face appeared with a glass. Jerry drank deeply as the ogre held it to his lips.

"Bolivar, thees is Senór Calvin." Addressing Jerry, the man continued, "Bolivar has bad temper, bad as mine, greengo, but he do wha' I say. He wan' play wi' you but I say no, it taser turn. He were, how you say, disappoint,' but I say maybe nex' time, eh Bolivar?" The hulk grunted and left the room.

"Less get down to beezness, eh, greengo?"

The pain in Jerry's head was subsiding, but the rest of his body was numb. "Where's Miriam?" he asked.

"Ahhh, you' puta. Is safe…for now, greengo. Now to beezness."

"I want to see her."

"You wan'—YOU WAN'?" His captor exploded, standing abruptly, slamming his chair against the wall. "You get not'ing 'til you do what I say—not'ing, and if you don', she die. You get that, greengo—YOU GET THAT? First I get piece of you' puta, then Bolivar and taser get piece, then I cut her up in loss of leetle piece. Now you ready do beezness?"

"Okay, okay." Jerry could do nothing but appease this hair-triggered madman. He remembered his captor's insane ranting that night years ago and the physical force of his wrath in the cave. Wanting nothing more of it, he added, "Tell me what you need."

Anger slowly receding, his captor sat. "Before we begin, let me tell you. I am Felix Carón, known in thees *provincia* as 'El Gato'."

El Gato, The Cat—chief drug lord of Chihuahua province. *So this was the man,* Jerry realized—*Player Five.* Everyone knew of El Gato, his army and his ruthless reputation.

"Do not go *policia*," Carón continued. "Dey my friends, and if I find out, you' puta weel die. Do not try escape. You' puta weel die. You in my land, greengo. *¿Comprendé?*"

"Yes, I understand."

"Now I wan' my meelion dollar, plus eentres'. I theenk two meelion ees fair after all thees year, eh greengo? You get me two meelion cash, transfer to account I geev you. Now. Here. Today."

Jerry hoped this El Gato knew nothing of his Costa Rican and Cayman accounts. Two million was a small price for freedom. Thankful for offshore secrecy, he replied, "I will, but I must call my bank in San Jose to transfer the money." Carón untied him, aiming a pistol at his head. Jerry made the call, using memorized passwords for his account along with El Gato's transit and account number. In five minutes the transfer was complete.

Verifying the exchange, Carón smiled. "Now, greengo, I know you have thees nice beezness. I been thinking how you weel help with mine. You gonna get my cocaine across border, 'cause we gonna put in some of you' diaper."

Aghast, Jerry's mouth dropped open as El Gato roared with laughter. "Are you serious?"

Jamming his pistol into Jerry's throat, Carón's eyes bulged as he morphed again into rabid mode, hissing, "Do not ques'ion me, greengo. El Gato alway seriouss. You weel do thees for me or you' puta die. You fuck up, you' puta weel die first, then I come af'er you, and leel taser weel have much fun before you die. *¿Comprendé?"*

Jerry could not imagine being caught between a larger rock and harder place.

STUFFING SNUFF
SOUTH OF JUAREZ, MEXICO
SUNDAY, JULY 1, 2007

ARRIVING HOME, Jerry closed his compromised Costa Rican account, transferring the balance to the Caymans. Downing two Valium pills, he slept for twelve straight hours. That evening at eleven p.m., he arrived at the security entrance of his manufacturing plant accompanied by a young, stylish man in a tailored suit carrying a large valise. The plant was on the "graveyard shift" with a skeleton crew of workers. Jerry introduced his guest as Senór Nogales, government quality control inspector who was making a surprise visit. Surprised to see the company's owner on a weekend at such a late hour, the guard stepped aside, calling ahead to alert the night manager.

Jerry commandeered a flat cart, piled on eight shipping boxes full of pull-up diapers, secured a portable heat crimping tool, two box cutters, shipping tape and wheeled everything into his private office, where Senór Nogales waited. Closing the blinds and locking the door, they went to work. The process was simple. Nogales carefully lifted from his valise ten large plastic zip-lock baggies, each containing one kilogram—kilo—of cocaine. Jerry opened the boxes, extracting product packages. Carefully opening the packages and cutting slits at the top of each padded pull-up, Jerry held the diapers open while Nogales measured five-gram portions and, using a metal insertion tool, slipped the cocaine into each pull-up. Jerry then re-crimped the opened flaps, folding each pull-up to its original shape and piled them back into the packages, which he carefully reinserted into the boxes, sealing those with tape. With twenty-four pull-ups to a package, ten packages to a box, the added weight was about two and a half

A NATION BEST SERVED HOT

pounds per box, a barely noticeable difference. Forklifts would transfer all the boxes to shipping crates.

The greatest risk would be transporting the shipment through U.S. customs with 9/11 heightened security and drug-sniffing dogs on the prowl. But El Paso customs agents were used to daily shipments from Rely trucks. After looking at the manifests, they rarely inspected these eighteen-wheelers.

Few words were spoken during the time needed to stuff approximately nineteen hundred diapers with cocaine. It took about eight hours to complete the process, during which a new shift commenced. When Jerry and Nogales emerged from the office and piled the doctored boxes upon the assembly line for sorting and routing, the day manager had been alerted of the government inspection. Giving the manager a thumbs-up, both men piled the boxes on the conveyer. Jerry checked the manifest and made sure to place the eight boxes with the shipment headed for the Dallas distribution center, where newly-hired "workers" would be waiting to divert the product into nefarious hands. All seemed to go smoothly. He and Nogales made a show of shaking hands. A very tired and worried Jerry Calvin was free to return home and wait.

When Henry Adams arrived at the plant about an hour later, he was told of the inspection. He wondered why Jerry hadn't called him to handle this one. *Maybe he was just giving me a break,* he thought.

Adams checked the assembly line where a clueless assistant notified him the shipment to Dallas had a two-crate surplus. Henry diverted them to Atlanta which showed a two crate shortage. *Jerry would be asleep by now,* he reasoned. *No use waking him.* This was Henry's job, and he took pride in the details.

Nogales reported the successful evening to his boss. If only the shipment made it through customs, El Gato's ten kilos of cocaine would be sold to his buyers who were eager to place it with dealers on the street. More importantly, it would make a handsome profit. Sitting back in his easy chair, Felix Carón smiled and puffed noxious ringlets into the air.

STONEWALLING
DRUG ENFORCEMENT AGENCY FIELD DIVISION EL PASO, TEXAS, LATE JUNE, 2007

KEITH WESTEN, R.A.C. (Resident Agent in Charge of the DEA, El Paso Field Division) had two problems. The first had been nagging him for five months, ever since one of his teams had disappeared carrying out a clandestine mission in Juarez. Along with four Mexican nationals, four of his own best agents had gone missing on a raid against Felix Carón, "El Gato," a ruthless drug lord.

Protocol had dictated the team would be controlled by the local Mexican police contingent. Incidents of corruption had fallen sharply with the new Calderon administration, but corruption still existed. Whatever the reason, protocol had resulted in mission failure.

Juarez was a virtual war zone with mutilated bodies appearing frequently on city streets. Without news from local Mexican authorities, Westen assumed the worst. The raid had been compromised with all hands lost. Two joint search and rescue missions were deployed in the warehouse area where last communications had been received. Both yielded the same result. No news was bad news. Carón continued to operate his nefarious distribution business with impunity.

The loss was personal, the anger acute. Westen's repeated requests for unilateral action had been summarily rejected by superiors at the Department of Justice. The Bush Administration refused to consider anything that might damage the Mexican and U.S. relationship. These search and destroy missions were, after all, clandestine. Officially they never happened. Successful outcomes were accepted by both countries with a wink and nod. Failure was unacknowledged. No bodies had been returned.

A NATION BEST SERVED HOT

Admiring their skill and determination, Westen had grown fond of each agent, especially Tracy Henderson. Graduating first in her training class, she was a regular "G.I. Jane"—the finest recruit he had ever seen, outperforming her male peers in all skill sets. Destined for quick promotion, she was the agency's future.

Westen's other problem was procedural: what to tell the concerned families of each missing operative. Predictably, his superiors had circled the wagons. Since the mission was classified, he was authorized to say nothing. With hands tied and mouth muzzled, he was taking all the heat.

Now, after five months, Westen had received permission to notify each family only with: "Mission failure. All presumed dead." No when, where and how. If it were his loved one, this news would be worse than nothing.

His calls were brief and to the point, offering condolences and whom to contact for survivor benefits. They were the hardest calls he ever made. Family ire was directed at him, for he was the agency's voice.

The call to Ed Henderson, Tracy's father, was the worst. Westen learned the man's wife had just died—and now this. Henderson greeted the news with a sigh and stony silence before severing the call.

That evening, a thoroughly drained Keith Westen went home to his wife of twenty years. With tears of frustration, he polished off a fifth of scotch before passing out in her arms cursing, "Fucking bureaucrats!"

CAT-ASTROPHE
CUIDAD JUAREZ
MONDAY, JULY 2, 2007

"WHAT?" JERRY SCREAMED over the phone to a startled Henry Adams. "No, no, you didn't. Tell me you didn't divert the crates. Please tell me," he wailed. "Jesus Christ, what do I do now? God, he'll kill her!"

Henry had never heard his boss scream before, let alone rant. Jerry was always in control. Not knowing what to say, Adams waited.

"When did they go out?" Jerry demanded, collecting himself.

"Boss, what's the matter? They went out yesterday. There was an overage in the Dallas shipment and I diverted them to Atlanta, like I said. They're already there. I checked last night.

"What did I do wrong?" Henry was agitated. "What's this about 'He'll kill her'? Who's 'her'? Talk to me."

"Gotta get outta here. Gotta go," mumbled Jerry. "Henry, it's not your fault. I'm sorry I yelled. Just hold the fort for me, okay? I'll be in touch." With that, he hung up, leaving his manager all the more confused.

Never before had Jerry felt helpless. He'd give anything to rescue Miriam, but he knew it would now be impossible. She would die and he'd be next. His mind flashed back to his father, killed by angry hands bent on revenge. He was now facing the same fate.

Think! He challenged himself, hitting his forehead with the palm of a hand.

Costa Rica was out of the question, as was staying in Mexico. His only option was fleeing to the States, something he vowed never to do. At most he had one day before Carón would learn of the diverted crates. Jerry gathered the necessary personal belongings, including the contents of his

A NATION BEST SERVED HOT

home safe. Dismissing the remaining guards, at three a.m. he drove from his hacienda for the last time.

───⁂───

JERRY TOOK a circuitous route to the border, stopping for long intervals to see whether he was followed. Arriving at the border and using his Mexican passport, he filled out the necessary paperwork for a one-week business visa. Rely was a *maquiladora*—a company which manufactured product in Mexico but was domiciled in the United States. Headquartered in El Paso, Rely's big rigs were familiar to U.S. Customs agents. As company owner "on a business trip," Jerry's entry was quickly approved.

Crossing the border to his homeland, he looked at the big clock under the "WELCOME TO THE UNITED STATES OF AMERICA" sign. It read 4:58 a.m.

In spite of the tension gripping his mind, Jerry Calvin felt a wave of melancholy entering his homeland for the first time in eleven years. With two identities and three passports, he was still a man without a country.

El Gato must know of the screw-up by now, he thought. *There will be a price on my head.* From his early years, Jerry knew El Paso like the back of his hand. He felt safer from harm here.

More than anything, Jerry needed advice. From a pay phone, he made an early call to Simon Morris, setting a ten a.m. appointment at a local El Paso Denny's. There was no reason to plan anything beyond that meeting. His imagination ran wild. Over a couple of cups of coffee at a diner, he watched with worry for signs he was being tailed.

First, I have to get rid of the car, he mused. It was eight a.m. when he entered the office of a local storage company. Using a fictitious local address, Jerry rented a small unit to store his belongings. He checked his watch. With over an hour to kill, he abandoned his Lexus a couple of blocks away from a used car lot, where nine thousand in Benjamin Franklins bought a late model used VW Rabbit in record time. Producing his expired American passport, he was again Jerry Calhoun. The lot manager had successfully bid four thousand for the car at auction. A five thousand dollar profit bought cooperation with no questions asked.

Just enough time remained for a baseball cap and fake moustache at a nearby Walmart before entering the Denny's at exactly 10:08 a.m. Morris was sitting alone at a back room table. He showed no signs of recognition when his client approached. *Good,* thought Jerry. *I'm somewhat invisible.* He was wrong.

"You look like the villain in an old silent movie," Morris growled as Jerry sat across from him in the booth. "Ditch the 'stache. All it does is draw attention. My God, man! What the hell happened down there?"

"My whole world has collapsed," Jerry replied with tears welling in his eyes. It took fifteen minutes to bring his lawyer up to date.

"I'm lost, Simon," he concluded, emotionally spent. "Haven't a clue what to do."

Morris had been sizing up his client in silence. This was a different man than he had known. Haughty confidence had disintegrated into frightened panic. Skipping over empathy, the attorney cut to the chase.

"You say you know where this cave is," he asked, "the one where you saw a female federal agent being tortured?"

"I know exactly where it is," Jerry answered.

"Then forget about everything else for the time being," Simon stated. "You've got a bargaining chip. What you did over a decade ago here in the States will be forgiven if the DEA can get this agent back alive, believe me.

"I know everybody in this town," Morris continued. "The local head of the DEA is named Westen—Keith Westen. Good man. I've tossed a few tequilas with him. He'd bargain with the Devil to get one of his agents back. Let me handle this."

As Morris whipped out his cell phone, Jerry felt the first pangs of relief in days. *Nothing like a man who knows how to take control,* he thought, watching his attorney jump into action.

"Westen, this is Morris. Simon Morris. Remember me?" After a couple of seconds, he resumed, "Yeah, you too. Hey, by any chance would you be missing any female agents in Mexico?"

Holding the phone away from his ear, Simon first winced at the response, then winked at his client with a thumb up.

TUESDAY, JULY 3, 2007

A SMALL HEADLINE in the *Dallas Morning News* international section read: "JUAREZ, MEXICO: DIAPER CENTER TRASHED, SIX HELD IN CUSTODY." Under the headline, the article continued: "Early this morning Mexican police were called to Rely, Inc., an adult disposable diaper manufacturer. Six men were arrested for slashing boxes and destroying the contents. No reason was given for the coordinated attack. Employees on the scene voiced their support for the company. One employee not involved in the disorder, Oscar Skiles, stated, 'Rely is a good employer. Everyone likes it here. No one knows who these men are and how they got past security. They don't work here. We cannot understand why this happened.' None of the six arrested would talk to this reporter."

SAN JOSE, COSTA RICA
Two Days Later...

SENÓRA CARMEN DE LA ROSA answered the knock at her door. A delivery truck was pulling away as she looked down to see a large box with Miriam's Mexican return address. She smiled. *What a thoughtful daughter and son-in-law we have,* Carmen thought. The family pet, a miniature poodle named Mango, circled the package, sniffing and whimpering. Bringing the box into the house, the *senóra* noticed it was rather heavy, seemed to slosh and had a slightly unpleasant odor. Calling to her husband, she put it on the floor, found a knife and cut through the packing tape, opening the top. Shrieking before fainting, the *senóra* fell backwards into the corner hutch, which collapsed onto her unconscious body. Mango went berserk, barking furiously and jumping with excitement three times his height.

Alarmed at the sudden commotion, Jesus de la Rosa rounded the corner to see his wife covered by the hutch and broken heirlooms. Shocked by the scene before him, he was even more horrified to see the contents of the opened box. Inside a thick transparent plastic bag was an eyeless severed female head with protruding swollen tongue framed by two severed hands—all floating in blood. Before passing out himself, he heaved his recently eaten lunch, most of which splattered the dog.

Mango had priorities. Distracted from the box and his two unconscious owners by a luscious meal of regurgitated refried beans and bile, he ate himself sick.

That same day...

THE *DALLAS MORNING NEWS* ran another small headline in the international section: "DIAPER COMPANY OWNER HIT AGAIN." The story read: "A mysterious fire has leveled a large hacienda south of Juarez, Mexico. Owned by Jerry Calvin, the sole stockholder of Rely, Inc., a nearby disposable diaper manufacturing plant that was recently vandalized, the home was vacant at the time. The whereabouts of Calvin and his wife, Miriam, is unknown. Local authorities have expressed concern, but will only state that the matter is 'under investigation'."

The next day...

ANOTHER *DALLAS MORNING NEWS* headline, this time on the front page: "DIAPER DEBACLE" was followed by the story: "Two explosions destroyed the Rely, Inc. manufacturing plant near Juarez, Mexico at 3 p.m. yesterday during peak operation, killing thirty-two locals and the operations manager, Henry Adams. Ten employees have survived with severe injuries. This latest atrocity follows two recent damaging events involving the company and the nearby home of its owner, Jerry Calvin, whereabouts unknown. Local authorities express outrage and will only say that all three incidents are 'under investigation'."

Meanwhile, the tainted crates of diapers had arrived in Atlanta where they were separated and transferred to two sixteen-wheelers destined for private labeling—one with Albertsons and the other with Winn Dixie branding. The finished products were then shipped from both corporate centers for distribution to retail stores....

In Palm Beach County, Florida.

RESCUE
CUIDAD JUAREZ
TWO A.M., SUNDAY, JULY 8, 2007

THE WANING CRESCENT MOON cast a shadow from a blank movie theater screen over the cave entrance. One guard, Hernando, slept against the rock wall with a rifle resting across his lap. His loud snoring echoed through the entrance. Pedro, the other guard, was on his feet leaning against the wall, his rifle within easy reach. Deep-throated belches followed each swig of *cerveza*, often followed by a burst of flatulence from his diet of refried beans and rice. It was another boring night guarding El Gato's chamber of death.

Sometimes they got to watch. Carón and his men would bring captives into the lair for torture. So deep into the cave was the chamber, only muffled echoes from the loudest screams could be heard at the entrance as Carón and his huge assistant, Bolivar, worked over the victims. Everyone knew about El Gato's sadistic temper, yet Pedro was amazed at the creative ways his boss could inflict pain before dispatching the poor bastards.

Bolivar lived in the cave and left only to shop for supplies. He seemed to enjoy the torture less than Carón. His job was to follow orders and clean up after each rampage. Seldom communicating, Bolivar went about his business efficiently—a manservant to his crazed boss.

Then there was *la mujer,* the woman. Wrapped in a simple shift, she was always shackled to the cave wall, hanging limp and semi-conscious the few times Pedro caught a glimpse. Carón let her live. She was his play toy. Month after month, she wasted away. *The boss must really hate this woman,* Pedro surmised, feeling sorry for her. *Merciful death must be too good for this one.*

Pedro wished he were somewhere else. A wife and two young children depended on his meager wage. With little education and less motivation, he shuffled through a miserable life wishing he were anywhere but this God-forsaken town with his shitty, dead-end job. Once you were in the employ of El Gato, there was only one way you left—toes up.

Pedro checked his watch. It was time for Hernando's shift. Holding the *cerveza* in one hand and rifle in the other, he was about to kick his partner awake when he noticed a pinpoint of red light on his chest. A split second later the light traveled to his right eye, blinding him. The last sound he heard was a metallic puff just before his head exploded. A second puff followed the first. Mercifully, Hernando never woke to his fate.

Six black-clad wraiths with infra-red headgear seemed to float from the shadows to check their kills. After dragging the corpses well into the cave, two of the assassins waited outside as guards. The other four melted into the cave. Each wore padded footwear designed for silent running. Following a maze of shafts toward a dull light, after approximately fifty yards they crouched, two at each side. The leader signaled a halt and crept forward to peek around the corner into a large, lighted chamber.

The team could barely hear a cell phone ring outside the cave for fifteen seconds before it ceased.

Inside the chamber, a large hulk snored on a narrow cot. His feet were too long for the bed and hung over like two hairy clubs. The night light revealed sparse furniture—a small dining table with two chairs, a refrigerator, two storage lockers and a two-element portable range. A sink was piled with unwashed dishes and, off to the side was a doorless porta potty. Rudimentary PVC pipe led to and from the sink and a stand-alone shower. *All the comforts of home*, the leader thought.

At the other end of the chamber, a second entrance led to another dark chamber. Were there additional guards? Signaling his team to wait, the leader silently crept past the sleeping giant and craned his neck around the corner. An odor of Pine-Sol mingled with urine and excrement, permeating the largest room in the cave. Two metal platforms with overhead lights, faucets, sinks and restraining straps stood in the middle, each flanked by a side table with medical instruments.

There were no additional guards. *Looks like a crude operating room. A torture chamber,* the leader guessed. He glanced at the surrounding cave walls. Spaced at ten-foot intervals were hand and leg straps. Almost unnoticed, a wooden platform at the far corner was occupied. A limp figure dressed in a floor-length shift was shackled by the hands and feet with leather straps. From his distance, the leader could see no sign of breathing.

Looking around, he saw no other entrances or exits. *Must be the end of the cave,* he thought. Turning back to his team, he made a throat slashing gesture, pointing to the sleeping giant. As a cell phone rang next to the bed, one member secured each arm and held fast while the third made quick work of his task. The giant thrashed and gurgled blood for two minutes before finally settling to rest. Like the other phone, this one had rung for fifteen seconds and stopped.

The leader approached the limp captive. Long, matted dark hair draped over its head. *Still no sign of breathing.* He prayed it was her and she was alive.

Cupping a hand, the leader jammed it over the mouth, stifling any possible outcry as he tilted the head upward. There was no startled resistance as Tracy's eyes stared into space.

"God, we're too late", the leader moaned as the other team members approached. One felt her jugular for a pulse, waiting until he was sure.

"She's alive," he whispered, adding, "barely."

Cutting through her shackles, the leader hoisted Tracy over his shoulder. *No more than sixty pounds,* he guessed.

The leader knew Tracy well. He'd been on missions with her, tossed tequilas with her, swapped jokes with her. She'd whipped his ass in training.

While the remaining team planted c-4 explosive charges with cell phone-controlled detonators throughout the cave, he retraced the shafts to the entrance. With tears in his eyes he glanced up at the waning crescent moon. His voice held respect as he whispered to the night, "We've got you, champ. You're goin' home."

Melting into the darkness, the team was over the border and well on the way to the nearest hospital before the leader made the call....

FELIX CARÓN sat back in his easy chair, savoring a Gurka Grand Reserve, a Honduran cigar infused with Louis XIII cognac. At seven hundred dollars each, the cigar was touted as the world's most expensive smoke. Carón saved his fragrant stash for special occasions, heretofore celebrations of victory. Not this evening.

Perfect rings of smoke rose from his lips, floating like heavenly missives, gradually dissipating as they approached the twenty foot vaulted ceiling. He seemed lost in concentration, staring at the rings as if they contained answers to questions yet to be asked.

His spacious hacienda was in the middle of a five acre spread a half-mile from the cave. Circled by two barbed wire fences, he was safe from all threats. Ten Doberman pinchers and thirty guards patrolled the perimeter. Constant graft bought off the military and local *policia*. The best defense was a good offense, and he was always on the offensive against rival drug lords. His cunning and unexpected moves kept the competition at bay.

Felix had to admire that rat bastard Calvin. Many years had passed since anyone had the stones to cross El Gato. The mark of a leader was to never compromise principles. He always followed through on threats. His initial rage had somewhat dissipated since he had taken revenge on Calvin's woman, raping and cutting her to pieces before mailing her head to the parents. But a score still had to be settled.

He had sent a team to Rely's manufacturing plant to search for the shipment. Finding nothing, his men had been arrested. It was two days later. The crates had never arrived in Dallas. As he sat thinking, Carón had sent a team to torch the gringo's hacienda. Another team had been dispatched to find Calvin who had fled across the border. His car had been located in El Paso, no doubt abandoned for another vehicle. He would be found and killed. No one ever escaped the wrath of El Gato.

Today would also be the last day of the DEA woman's life. She had become useless baggage—no longer attractive, merely skin and bones. Surely she had been given up for dead by her superiors. He admired her resilience. She was tougher than any man, taking everything he gave her with stoic resistance. After nearly six months, Carón felt a certain kinship with this woman, as one gladiator to another. Was it respect…or affection? No Matter. Tomorrow would bring a necessary ending. The rings of smoke were his tribute to his DEA whore.

An underling peeked around a corner at his boss, quickly retreating. Not only had the cave guards failed to check in, but repeated cell phone calls to Pedro and Bolivar had gone unanswered. The boss needed to know, but the underling had seen the penalty for interrupting El Gato during his contemplations. His tirades were legendary.

As Carón sat back, deep in concentration, a low rumbling shook the hacienda, rattling some glass in a nearby hutch. El Gato shot out of his

A NATION BEST SERVED HOT

chair, instantly alert. Distant sirens followed the sound as guards entered the room, guns drawn, ready to protect the boss from harm.

The underling saw his opening and rattled off his report. Steam seemed to radiate from El Gato's ears. The cave! It was less than two kilometers away. The rumbling had come from that direction. Enraged, with a primal scream he opened a desk drawer, pulled out a .45 and blew away the messenger, scattering blood, bones and guts across the room. The remaining guards ran for their lives.

Once again El Gato had gone over the edge.

FORREST TO FOREST
MONDAY, JULY 9, 2007

FORREST EDWARDS was traveling north on I-25 in his spanking new Jeep Wrangler Unlimited Rubicon. It was not the most comfortable highway vehicle, but where the former Jerry Calvin was headed, comfort was secondary to off-road ability. With Keith Westen, Simon Morris had brokered Jerry's immunity from prosecution in exchange for directions and a complete description of the cave and its surroundings. In addition, Westen had negotiated Jerry's affordable income tax settlement with the IRS. His citizenship was now free and clear, but for security reasons, he now held a third identity.

Jerry had just passed Cheyenne, Wyoming when his satellite phone rang. Morris was on the line. "They got her. She's alive!" he shouted.

"Miriam?" Jerry replied. "She's alive?"

"No, I'm sorry," Simon apologized. "No word of her, but the woman in the cave was rescued—Westen's missing agent. He's grateful and wants you to know you saved her life."

Racked with guilt, Jerry's last bubble of hope had burst. Miriam was dead. He was sure. El Gato would have killed her by now. Surely she had been tortured. The Cat enjoyed playing with his prey.

"Tell Westen I'm glad, Simon," he sighed. "Just passed Cheyenne. Should be across the border by morning. I'll keep in touch. Got you on speed dial."

Jerry punched out, tears again forming in his eyes. He had been crying for three days while hiding out at Simon's home, ever since reading about the fire-bombing at Rely. Trusted Henry and thirty-one of his employees were dead plus several more injured—all victims of El Gato's revenge. Jerry's plan to sell the business, including the formula, and distribute the proceeds to his employees, was interrupted by the terrible news.

After mulling over options with Morris and Westen, the choice was unanimous. All agreed Carón would concentrate his search for Jerry in the States. Simon owned a getaway cabin in the wilds of Saskatchewan, Canada. Located three miles from the nearest town, Moose Jaw, which lay west of Regina—the provincial Capitol, it was an ideal place to hide. In three days, Westen had delivered a new vehicle, satellite phone, a forged American passport and driver's license under the name Forrest Edwards. Simon had given Jerry the cabin key.

With the chance to rescue one of his own, Keith Westen hadn't hesitated to deal with Simon. Risking an international incident, his career and pension, not to mention the wrath of clueless superiors, he secretly picked a crack team that executed a flawless mission. Consequences be damned—at least the DEA agent was now in safe hands.

Once again, Jerry was on his own. Except for money in his off-shore accounts, nothing of his former life remained. Every mile north he drove was a mile farther from Felix Carón's grasp. Only one thing kept his mind from lapsing into insanity—a famous quote by Friedrich Nietzsche. Like a tape loop, it ran over and over through his mind: *"What doesn't kill us makes us stronger."*

With an aching jaw from clenched teeth, white knuckled hands gripping the steering wheel, and summoning more hatred than he knew possible, Jerry remembered the cold cave, El Gato's colder threats, and the poker game which started it all. "You've won the first hand, Carón, he spat out loud. "Deal the cards. The game isn't over.

I'm all in...."

CABIN PRESSURE
WEST PALM BEACH, FLORIDA
SUNDAY, JULY 15, 2007

MADELYN PEABODY was late. Her 12:45 p.m. Delta Express flight from West Palm Beach to Orlando was due to leave in ten minutes. She cleared heightened security with her one carry-on, running to the gate all the way down the concourse. Madelyn's new rich husband, her fourth, had treated her to a delicious lunch at one of the airport restaurants. *Whoever said airport food was lousy has never eaten at PBI*, she thought. Her turkey salad with asparagus had been so outstanding she had lost track of time.

Running full speed at age fifty-nine was foolish. She had to pee, but there was no time. "Holding it" was becoming more of a problem lately, and she had purchased protective panties on her last trip to Albertsons. She was wearing one now, just in case. Diminutive, determined and in reasonably good shape, a sprinting senior citizen drew more than a few stares from those in less of a hurry. She thought of that sports jock, OJ—wasn't he the guy who beat the murder rap?—running and jumping hurdles in the car rental commercial. Running was bad enough, jumping hurdles out of the question for this lady going to see her first newborn grandchild from a previous marriage.

Flushed and out of breath, she arrived at gate B-6 just as they were about to close the door. Luckily she had secured her boarding pass earlier when they arrived at the ticket counter. She hurried down the stairs to the tarmac, ran once again to the cigar-shaped Canadair Bombardier, climbed the stairs and was ushered quickly to her seat. Stowing her small carry-on in the overhead, she asked the flight attendant if she could use the rear restroom, but was told she'd have to wait until the plane was airborne. Out of breath and in agony, Madelyn buckled in the aisle seat for departure. Her bladder felt like an over-inflated soccer ball. She forced a smile toward the young, good looking man in the seat next to hers, trying to think of anything but her pain.

To distract herself, Madelyn began leafing through the complimentary airline magazine until she saw the feature article about waterfalls in South America. With a groan, she returned the magazine to the pocket in front of her and tried to concentrate on the steward's seat belt, life vest and exit demonstration. She was the only passenger paying attention.

The airplane was a small mid-range carrier, holding fifty passengers, four seats across each row. It was full as usual. The trip to Orlando took only twenty minutes, compared to three hours driving time, and the price was reduced for added incentive. Flying was making a comeback after the 9/11 scare. Airlines were talking bankruptcy and the competition for passengers was keener than ever.

With agonizing slowness, the plane powered up and entered the taxiway. Madelyn noticed that storm clouds seemed to be all around and the runways were wet. After all, this was the Florida rainy season. Storms occurred with predictable regularity most afternoons about this time.

The captain announced, "Flight crew, ready for departure." Both cabin attendants buckled in, the engines roared and they were off. When the airplane reached V-1, the point of take-off, Madelyn realized this was going to be anything but a smooth flight. Heavy storm winds buffeted the plane from the beginning and the ascent was steeper than usual. Oh well, she could stand any E-ticket ride for twenty minutes. But what to do about her urge to purge?

"Ladies and gentlemen, this is the captain," the voice boomed over the intercom. "Due to inclement conditions, this may be a rather bumpy ride to Orlando. I want to assure you we're used to this. I'll try to make this trip as smooth as possible, but we will be keeping the seat belt sign on for the duration. Please do not move about the cabin for any reason."

Pilots are instructed to go around thunderstorms when at all possible. Cumulonimbus storm clouds can be a serious problem, causing random and sudden changes in air pressure. Many times, in an attempt to land, pilots have underestimated their intensity and ditched airplanes short of runways due to wind shear. A pilot at high altitude running into this condition simply rides it out. He treats it like an undertow in the ocean: no use fighting—go with the flow. When the wind shear subsides, the plane simply returns to the proper altitude and continues.

There was no circumventing this storm, however. It was socked in for hundreds of square miles, and the clouds roiled upward, downward and sideways to more than fifty thousand feet.

The duration! Madelyn thought. *No, no, this won't do.* By now she thought she would explode any minute, and drastic measures were necessary. Unbuckling her belt, she stood up and tried to make her unsteady way to the back of the plane and the head. She saw the buckled-in steward gesturing her to go back, but nature couldn't be ignored another minute. With three rows to go, it happened.

A particularly nasty shear hit the airplane from above like an anvil, forcing a thousand foot drop. Madelyn lost her grip on the seat tops and momentarily became weightless, floating toward the ceiling of the fuselage. More significantly, she lost the grip on her sphincter, releasing the contents of her bladder. While other passengers howled, Madelyn screamed in shock as she landed face first onto the lap of a smartly dressed young businessman.

Extricating herself from the shocked young man's lap and stumbling through an apology, Madelyn felt something uncomfortably warm growing between her legs and around her waist. Then she and everyone else within the back quarter of the airplane began to notice an acrid odor—the combination of paper mill, skunk cabbage and sheep excrement—wafting throughout the cabin like mustard gas. To her horror, she saw her dress ballooning outward.

"She's got a bomb!" screamed a woman across the aisle, pointing at Madelyn's waist while reaching for an airsickness bag. One of the attendants, whose name badge bore the coincidental name of Ralph, had struggled back and arrived on the scene but stopped short and bent over, gagging at the stench. The businessman and two other nearby men unbuckled and rushed to tackle Madelyn who was now lying on her back in the aisle. She met them head on with a jet stream of bile.

Like yawning, vomiting is contagious. All around the rear of the airplane, both men and women alternated between screaming and hurling. Airsickness bags were of little use with excretions of this magnitude. Like the California surf, panic and sickness roiled toward the front of the plane. Passengers who released their seat belts careened off the ceiling and back to the floor like weightless rag dolls, stumbling over each other, retching in their seats and the aisle.

A NATION BEST SERVED HOT

"Ladies and gentlemen, please return to your seats immediately. Now!" yelled the captain over the intercom, releasing the overhead oxygen masks. Forgetting to turn off his microphone, everyone heard him add, "God damn it!" and a gurgling sound. Apparently the foul odor had made its way throughout the small plane's ventilation system into the cockpit. The pilot had heaved into his own oxygen mask.

The airplane made a series of sharp turns and descended toward an emergency landing, adding to the mayhem. Madelyn remained crushed under the weight of two male passengers, both of whom had reciprocated vomitus upon her face. Her last thought before mercifully losing consciousness was, *This can't be happening!*

By the time the airplane returned to PBI, two fire engines, four EMT units and a dozen police cars escorted it to a seldom-used runway. The news media had gathered behind the crime scene tape on the tarmac. Like vultures, they waited for a sensational story once the quarantine on the airplane was lifted. Rumors of a terrorist act circulated as Action News helicopters jockeyed for the best aerial shots. All area television stations were glued to the story with live feeds to the major networks.

Madleyn, her waist bulging like a circus clown, was first to disembark. Escorted by Hazmat-suited guards to a waiting paddy wagon, she cried crocodile tears through layers of stinky facial oatmeal. The other passengers were forced to wait in filth another two agonizing hours before being released. Most swore televised revenge for their indignity and frightful inconvenience. First cell phone calls went to salivating lawyers, many of whom had already joined their vulture brethren on the tarmac.

Homeland Security agents grilled poor Madelyn for two days before determining she was anything but a terrorist. Her diaper, which had ballooned to a diameter of three feet was sent to Homeland Security for examination. The airline considered filing suit against the woman, but once she was found to be a victim, opted to recoup from the diaper manufacturer, a company called Rely, Inc. out of El Paso, Texas. The American Bar Association recommends a carpet bombing approach to pain and suffering lawsuits. Attorneys representing the passengers sued Madelyn, the diaper company, the airline, the airport, the Federal government, the pilot, the pilot's family, the pilot's relatives and, to cover all bases, the pilot's basset hound.

NEVER FORGET
WEST DELRAY BEACH, FLORIDA
MONDAY, JULY 16, 2007

SEYMOUR FLAKOWITZ was a child of the Holocaust. Born in 1932, the only child of Hans and Frieda, by the age of six the signs of trouble were everywhere in Germany. His hometown of Hamburg was no exception. After Krystallnacht in November, 1938—a nationwide Nazi campaign to round up Jews and confiscate weapons—Hans bought Seymour a one-way passage to England where he was to live with a distant cousin. Little Sy barely escaped the fate of his parents, grandparents and other relatives. A frumpy woman in her forties whose husband had fled for younger pastures, the English cousin was already saddled with three screaming brats. Good intentions were not enough and, using some of her inheritance, she shipped Sy to a distant cousin in America. When the American cousin turned out to be a con artist who stole the child's traveling money, Sy landed in a Jersey orphanage.

The people who ran the orphanage beat him every time he complained, which was pretty much always. No one would adopt him because he constantly whined. The school system rewarded his lack of effort with failing grades but passed him up the ladder to get rid of him. To spite the system, he stubbornly retained his low Deutsch accent, refusing to Americanize his tongue.

Sy was a butt of practical jokes. He maxed out at one hundred twenty pounds and five feet in height. Unable to defend himself against bigger bullies, he was constantly taunted.

As an adult, his New York number-crunching civil service career lasted forty years, rewarding Sy with regular cost of living raises for his lethargy

A NATION BEST SERVED HOT

and incompetence. At sixty-five, he was given a pension and an appropriate retirement gift—a faux gold watch which refused to work. His name was misspelled on the back.

Sy complained that the government took too much of his retirement. Each monthly payment was supposed to appear in his checking account on the first Tuesday, but never showed until the second.

He religiously played the state lottery, which fueled dreams of a permanent South Seas getaway, but instead fleeced his wallet for hundreds of dollars each year. Sy kept this secret from his wife of thirty-five years. If Sadie ever found out, he'd be in for a sound thrashing.

Sadie was his parasitic wife, a rotund bully who relished every excuse to thrash her smaller husband. Physical violence was not an option for him. It certainly was for her as well as her piece of shit dog. Sy gagged at the name. Poopsie was a miniature rat terrier that nipped at him every time he wasn't looking and was too quick for his foot when he retaliated.

His neighbors in Centennial Village, a cheap condo retirement community in west Delray Beach, Florida, were old and cranky just like Sy. Visiting grandchildren were threatened with summary execution if they dared act their age.

Sy and Sadie had no children, let alone grandchildren. They never slept together since their honeymoon, a two-day extravaganza in a cheap motel near Coney Island. After Sadie rode Sy's skanky frame for three minutes of whoopty-don't, she proclaimed him inadequate and pronounced her retirement from future lascivious behavior. If he didn't like it, he could pound sand, she stated. Sy had to look up the word "lascivious" in the dictionary. Thus ended conjugal bliss.

Next door neighbors were constantly beating on their side of the common wall when Sadie harangued him in her nails-on-a-chalkboard voice, which was again pretty much always. His neighbors hated him because he hated them. Everyone hated everyone.

Sy and Sadie lived in a culture of miserable elderly whose goal was to make someone else's day worse than their own. Most came from New York City's east side, where the Golden Rule was replaced by the Iron Pyrite Rule: "Screw unto others before they screw unto yous."

Sy craved sympathy but was lucky to receive a daily dose of apathy. The last time he could remember smiling was when he slipped tiny chicken bone shards into Poopsie's Alpo, causing a near fatal hack attack. The dog lived. Both he and Sadie were dismayed for entirely opposite reasons.

Anxious, Sy luckily avoided suspicion and was determined to try again. He'd have to be careful. Sy knew if Sadie caught him, Centennial Village would have its first rolling pin homicide.

Today started as every other, with Sadie nagging her do-nothing husband. "Seemowa, why don't you make yourself useful and go to the stowa? I'm sick o' lookin' atcha. Winn-Dixie got a special. Go get us some dollar chickens, as many as you can, and I'll freeze 'em. You don't make enough money for anything else. Why I married ya, I'll never know. You're good for nuttin'. Now get outta hea'."

Sy grabbed any excuse to get away. In silence he picked up his purple Minnesota Vikings golf hat that he'd bought for a quarter at the flea market. Dressed in his drab yellow sport shirt and candy striped shorts, his bony legs peeked out like two popsicle sticks stuffed in worn green tennis shoes. It was Sy's "pistachio" outfit. Many older men in South Florida dressed like him. It was their way of saying, "I'm retired and don't give a shit."

Sy could have walked to the grocery store. It was only a half block away. But no one in South Florida walked when they could drive. Driving was a God-given right. It was the only time Sy felt empowered. Climbing into his '95 Ford Taurus, he had to adjust the seat all the way forward. Sadie always drove when the two of them went anywhere together. He would leave the seat forward just to piss her off the next time she drove. *Anything to exact a small measure of revenge*, he vowed.

Driving to the Winn-Dixie, he steeled himself for another round of parking roulette. Always full, the lot was typically too small for traffic the strip mall generated. Sy was up to the challenge as he plunged into the fray. His Taurus bore the scars of many battles. One more fender bender wouldn't matter. He relished the chance to vent his pent-up frustration.

Reserved for the disabled, handicapped spots were nearest to the store and therefore highly prized. It seemed everyone his age had handicap cards hanging from their rearview mirrors—the prescriptions for which were purchased with bribes from their doctors. No one but suckers balked at grabbing these spots when available. Just last week he'd seen two spry old men with handicap cards vacate their cars and duke it out like kangaroos over possession of one of these cherished spots.

Sy had beginners luck this day, securing a spot next to the handicapped zone on the third go-around. An old woman walking her grocery cart was the only obstacle. He honked his horn and barely missed the crone in haste to grab the spot. The unilateral row lasted a minute. Shrill threats

A NATION BEST SERVED HOT

and shaken fists greeted Sy as he exited his car. He simply ignored her and strolled into his favorite deli restaurant next to the Winn-Dixie. The infuriated woman waited until he was out of sight and looked around for possible snitches before ramming her shopping cart into the side of Seymour's Taurus, leaving a large dent. Satisfied, she left the cart in the middle of a rare open space, flipped a bird at the irate driver who wanted it, then got in her own car and drove off to fight another day.

The Bagels and Such sports bar was Sy's favorite hangout whenever he was free from Sadie's wrath. He wasn't a sports fan and detested bagels. It was the Such that drew him to this eatery. Sadie's meals could best be described as heart attacks on a plate. Jammed with fat, cholesterol, salt and sugar, everything she prepared was calculated to shorten his lifespan. Store-bought pastries, cheese soups, eggs fried in lard, macaroni and cheese, chipped beef on toast—nicknamed "SOS," pancakes loaded with syrup and various flavored ice creams were some of her offerings. Threatening her diminutive husband with bodily harm, Sadie forced him to eat everything she served, hoping he would die of caloric overload.

Sy choked it all down, often leaving the apartment to stick a finger down his throat and heave Sadie sludge underneath the neighbor's hedge. No one could figure out why Mrs. Steinberg's hedge was so lush. It was the envy of the neighborhood.

To Sadie's dismay, Sy gained no weight and had the blood pressure, pulse and cholesterol readings of a long-distance runner. Sadie, however had ballooned like a dirigible and was doubtless destined to pre-decease him, if she continued the gluttonous diet.

Sy had one physical impairment which was common at age seventy-five. He suffered from occasional incontinence and wore the cheap, store brand protective pull-ups that Sadie bought for him at Winn-Dixie. She teased him about it, making pee-wee jokes that turned his stomach. He was wearing one today from a batch purchased yesterday.

Sy enjoyed salads—the "Such" he never got at home. Taco salads, oriental salads, even plain tossed salads, were all he ever ordered. His favorite, white asparagus with tossed greens, carrot slices, chopped tomatoes and scallions, black olives with the house vinegarette, was on the menu today. He ordered it, and for thirty brief minutes, Sy sighed in contentment, forgetting his sundry woes.

Leaving the exact amount of money for the meal on his table, Sy hurried out of the sports bar, as usual stiffing the waitress. Only suckers left tips.

He felt too good to cut short his outing, so a stop at the nearby Dollar General store was in order. Sadie would be angry at him for this extra dalliance. She wanted to know his whereabouts every minute. Whenever possible he would dally just to piss her off and assert his independence. A short period of emancipation was better than none at all.

Sy wandered the Dollar General aisles for a good half hour, not intending to buy, secure in the knowledge that he could afford anything in the store. Energized, he was now ready for grocery store war.

The Winn-Dixie on West Atlantic Avenue was a study in anthropological hostility. Most of the personnel were black. Of those, Haitians were the majority. Most of the customers were white and Jewish. It was a volatile combination. Like fire and ice, hatred was endemic. The store managers were trained in anger management but swallowed Excedrin by the handful, trying their best to deflect tension. It was a losing proposition. The store was high on the frequency list of 911 disturbance calls.

Sy grabbed a cart off the line and marched to the meat department at the back of the store. A big sign loomed over the section: "CHICKENS $1.00 EACH – LIMIT 2 PER CUSTOMER." No matter the plucked poultry were the size of Cornish game hens. This was a good deal and they were going fast. Sy, oblivious to hostile stares, piled fifteen of the bagged, bleeding chickens into his cart and started wheeling toward the checkout lines. He was a man on a mission.

"Mista, it say two to a customa," chirped a stock boy who was re-supplying the chicken section.

"Hey buddy, can't you read?" came another voice behind him.

Sy ignored both and hurried to the front of the store, dripping a trail of blood. Nothing would deter him from his appointed task. This was his day and he was empowered. He got in the 10-items-or-less lane, populated by eight customers and one young female cashier. A large black man in front of him wore a beard, a gold necklace and flashed two gold front teeth. His large head of braided hair was covered by a do-rag and his chest was covered by a cut-off tee shirt with the motto "HATE ROCKS" on the front. His cart held hot dogs, potato chips and a twelve pack of beer. When the rest of the line moved up, he was eyeing the check-out girl and failed to move quickly enough for Sy, who nudged the back of the man's foot with his cart.

All grocery carts have a lower rack for large items like bags of dog food, cat litter, and cartons of beer. The front of this lower rack is a curved

A NATION BEST SERVED HOT

metal bar that protrudes at exactly the same height as an adult Achilles tendon. Seymour's nudge registered somewhere between annoyance and pain, and the man turned on Sy with Black Panther wrath.

"Ow! You do dat again, ol' man, and I shove dis cart up yo' ass." Then he saw the chickens. "Wha' da fu'? Yo' in da wrong line an' yo' got too many dem birds an'way. Get outa here, sucka."

"I vant my sheekins," replied Seymour, crossing his arms over his chest in defiance, standing firm.

The commotion drew stares and rumblings from customers. The female cashier shook her head. Trouble was brewing. She eyed her assistant manager who loomed above the fray in his elevated observation booth.

"Mista, da sign say two to a customa. Please take da res' back," the cashier said as the manager rose from his chair.

"Yeah, ya heard her, fool." The black had right on his side and was starting to enjoy this.

"No! I vant my sheekins," shouted Sy, stomping his foot for emphasis.

Customers on both adjoining aisles were watching with interest. Some were in favor of the much smaller man.

"Leave him alone, you bully," said one.

"Let him have his damned chickens," muttered another impatient man two customers ahead in line.

Drip...drip...drip. Chicken blood formed a small pool under Sy's cart.

The assistant manager arrived and, using his best diplomacy, issued what he thought was a brilliant solution. "Sir, you may have your chickens if you go through the regular line eight times," he proclaimed, pleased with his logic.

Applause and cries of "Yeah!" from some customers broke out spontaneously.

Sy was high on adrenaline. He would not buckle under the pressure. "No, no, no! I vant my sheekins!" he screamed, pushing his cart forward, this time with gusto...into one very pissed black man's stomach.

Big mistake.

HATE ROCKS pushed back with twice the force, ramming the cart into Sy's gut. A distinct "Woof" from the small warrior could be heard three aisles down. Losing his balance, Sy careened into carts and customers behind him. A matronly woman at the end of the line had just picked up a designer birthday cake. The large box was balanced precariously on top of her cart. A domino effect of cascading bodies caused the box, cart and woman to careen into a giant pyramid of stewed tomato cans. With an extended crash, the cake and seventy-two-cans avalanched upon her head, flattening the poor woman. A few bystanders rushed to help, dragging the moaning, frosting-covered victim from the pile of cans.

The horrified manager ran to her aid. He miscalculated his approach and slid on the gooey cake frosting into an adjacent pyramid of muskmelons. Customers in other lines cheered and applauded heartily. Shopping for groceries with free entertainment—priceless!

The indignant customers in the 10-items-or-less line spewed epithets. The angry black cursed loudest, looming with clenched fists over prone Sy, who stared back up at his adversary in shock.

"Fu' yo' mama! Fu' yo' papa! Fu' yo' gramma! Fu' yo', yo' li'l shi' fo' brain assho'!" he screamed, spraying Sy's face with his spit.

Two elderly ladies in the next aisle watched the ruckus in amazement. Babs elbowed her friend, Sheila. "What's he saying?" she asked in a loud voice over the mayhem.

"I think it's called Ebonics, dear," Sheila replied with a mixture of fascination and fear.

By now chicken juice had formed a robust river of sanguine salmonella, working its way through customers' feet. All were hopscotching to avoid the flow.

Everyone was yelling. Some cursed in anger. Others howled with laughter. A hundred polarized voices picked sides. The assistant manager was new to his position. In panic, he ran for the telephone, dialing 911 and yelling, "Emergency! Riot! Winn-Dixie, West Atlantic. Hurry!"

A riot in a grocery store is an invitation to a world-class food fight. Pent-up hostilities rose to the fore. Customers emptied their carts, flinging everything accumulated from the vegetable aisle to the deli at nearby targets. Tomatoes, carrots, lettuce, cauliflower, peaches, strawberries, onions and acorn squash merged with sausage, sliced beef, liverwurst, Swiss cheese and olive loaf in a hailstorm of edible weapons. Fist fights and hair pulling broke out. Customers fell to the floor, some rolling in the chicken blood, others slipping on gastronomic debris. Over the fray, a siren could be heard approaching.

Sy was now ringed by the angry mob. He had never been so frightened in his life, even when Sadie was on the rag. The black was shaking him, one of many who were shouting and threatening violence. He closed his eyes and scrunched his neck, wishing he were a turtle. In fear for his life, Sy lost control of his bladder.

A NATION BEST SERVED HOT

As with Madelyn Peabody the day before, Sy's midriff expanded like an automatic life preserver. A massive stench permeated the crowd, gagging everyone and causing a chain reaction of vomit throughout the store.

"He's got a bomb!" shrieked a woman covered in fruit juice and bile. She was pointing at Sy's expanding midriff.

What followed made the previous acrimony pale in comparison. Like Pamplona's "Running of the Bulls," the entire store full of screaming and shoving humanity raced for the two entrances. Left to fend for themselves, the weak and infirm were trampled in the mad rush for fresh air.

Sergeant Don Budd and his partner, Corporal Jack Anders had just arrived, responding to the 911 call. The sea of humanity disgorging from the grocery store looked like suicidal lemmings about to jump a cliff. Many were covered in slime. All were choking and gasping. Anders exclaimed, "Holy shit, would you look at that!"

Budd grabbed his mike and shouted, "All units, we have a possible 10-55 or 10-81 in progress at the Winn-Dixie, West Atlantic, Delray— police codes for explosion and terrorist incident.

"Proceed stat!"

Abandoning protocol, he added, "Damn it! We need back-up!"

Sy had temporarily fainted. Waking to the stench of skunk, landfill and vomit, he immediately regurgitated his lunch upward in a viscous mass covering his face and neck like multi-colored oatmeal. His pants had split open, revealing a mass of plastic goo surrounding his groin. Looking like he'd consumed a year's supply of Sadie's cuisine in one sitting, so inflated was his waist he could neither stand nor sit.

He was alone. The store was vacant. For five minutes, he thrashed about like an overturned tortoise, listening to the commotion outside. Crying for assistance, he received none. Sy was helpless in his fragrant fate. His mind wandered to a place and time long passed. *This is what my relatives must have felt at Auschwitz,* he mused.

Four tall beings dressed in Hazmat suits busted into the store. Sy looked up at aliens looking down at him. Just before fainting for the second time, the thought occurred to him:

I am in Hell.

JAWS AND PAWS
BOCA RATON, FLORIDA
The Same Day....

*"Pride goeth before destruction,
And an haughty spirit before a fall."*

King James Bible
Proverbs 16:18

SURROUNDED BY his underlings on the front steps of the Boca Raton, Florida police station, Chief Buster Grimes was in his element. A sunny day, television coverage, something to crow about—it didn't get any better than this. A sturdy, six-foot three oak, his ruddy complexion sported a handsome age line for every one of his sixty-two years. Forty years in law enforcement. Forty years of climbing the ladder. Forty years of bureaucratic ass kissing. Three years to retirement. It was all ceremony now. He'd earned his day in the sun, and damned if he wasn't going to enjoy every moment!

Boca was awash in tax receipts, and one of the Chief's perks was a spanking new Dodge 3500. It was his toy—one of the spoils of rank. Three hundred thirty horses under a candy-apple red hood, the huge V-8—"Yep, this thang's got a Hemi"—with over 10,000 pounds of gross vehicle weight, could tow a good-sized house. But he hadn't bought it to tow. He'd bought it to show. His man machine was parked in full view of the crowd off to the building's side.

The truck was a statement, just like the six stars he wore on his uniform. If five stars were good enough for generals like Eisenhower and MacArthur, he had to have six. Forty-eight in all, with sets perched on both lapels, both epaulets, both sleeves and two sets on his cap. The combined reflected glare dazzled the crowd of reporters and onlookers, blinding the first row with beams of magnificence. He was a walking, talking constellation.

Never mind that the staff ridiculed him behind his back, nicknaming him "Bluster" Grimes. Never mind that, during the past forty years he'd only fired his service revolver on one occasion, spraying three errant shots at a fleeing rat snake daring to cross his path. It took twenty years to live down the incident some jerk coined "Bluster's Last Stand." Never mind all that. They were peasants, all beneath contempt. He was The Chief—a legend in his own mind.

"Citizens of Palm Beach County," his voice boomed over the unnecessary microphone. "Today I am proud to present your award-winning Canine Drug Enforcement Team." Grimes waved his arm toward the bottom of the stairway where two panting German shepherds and their handlers stood at attention. "They have just come back from state, capturing first place in municipal competition." The chief dazzled his pearly whites, enhancing his constellation.

"This is Bruno…with his partner, Corporal Tom Rogers." Light applause broke out as one of the dogs and its owner moved forward two steps. "And Max…with his partner, Sergeant Dusty Smith." More applause as they joined the other team. TV cameras were rolling. With ninety-four degree, sun-drenched heat, the two officers were baking in their dark uniforms. Both were silently praying, *Get on with it!*

"Years of training with dog and master have resulted in these fine specimens…"—Rogers and Smith winced at the term—"able to ferret out illegal and dangerous substances by their extraordinary olfactory acuity…"—Grimes had practiced the last two words which were guaranteed to impress the peasants and press alike—"which is hundreds of times keener than humans. We have prepared a demonstration which will showcase their skill." Like a peacock fanning its feathers for all to admire, Grimes slowly descended the stairway.

"To my left you will see forty suitcases lined in a row." He gestured with a flourish at the forty props. Reaching the bottom step, both dogs stopped panting and looked back at Grimes, ears up with rapt attention. Buster glowed with pleasure. *Even the dogs know I'm The Chief.*

"One of these forty suitcases has a small bag of cocaine inside. Each officer uses a series of German commands and hand signals. Upon command, both dogs will sniff each suitcase and find the illicit substance."

A hand from the audience went up. "Yes? A question," Grimes pointed. The deputies groaned.

"Why German commands, and are the dogs ever wrong when they do their searches?" asked a busty blonde television reporter. *She looks familiar*, Grimes thought. *Melony Major, a reporter with Action Four News*, he remembered. *What a looker!*

"Good questions, ma'am," replied the Sheriff. The reporter noted the condescension in his voice. *Ma'am,* she cringed. *What a pompous jerk!*

"These Shepherds are born and trained in Germany before being shipped over here as adults. Therefore, the handlers use the German commands they have learned. It's easier than re-training them. And as to them ever being wrong...." Grimes looked at the officers, who forced a smile and shook their heads in unison. A few cameras clicked. *Kodak moment,* thought the Chief.

"Gentlemen, are you ready for the demonstration?" The sheriff's voice boomed with pride.

Are we ever! thought the two overheated officers.

"Geh!" said Rogers, releasing Bruno.

"Auf!" said Smith, releasing Max.

"Oof," cried the Chief as both dogs flattened him. Like two lightning bolts, they had immediately turned to jump on Grimes, knocking him backwards on the department steps. TV cameras rolled as the audience members caught their breaths. Instead of running to the suitcases, a snarling Bruno latched onto the Chief's crotch and whipped it from side to side with clamped jaws. Max gripped and ripped at the chief's left arm, no doubt growling in German.

Grimes screamed, helpless under the onslaught of the two eighty-pound thrashers. "AAAAH! Get 'em off me! AAAAH, shit! Help me! Get 'em off me!"

The cameraman rushed forward, capturing every gory detail. Onlookers gasped, jockeying for a better look. Rogers and Smith couldn't believe their eyes. Less than five seconds elapsed before both officers issued stop commands and the dogs released their prey. Grimes looked like a disheveled rag doll, his constellation now merely a collection of fallen stars. His sleeve was ripped and blood flowed from the wound. His pants were torn at the crotch and blood was mixed with torn plastic—some kind of adult diaper, it seemed. Through the tear a small quantity of white powder was exposed.

Chief Buster Grimes had fainted.

Bruno retreated from his limp prey with a snout covered in the white substance. He began sneezing and jerking spasmodically. Other officers rushed onto the scene. One resourceful deputy covered the Chief's ravaged crotch with his hat. Too late. The entire incident had been captured by the television camera.

A NATION BEST SERVED HOT

Rogers and Smith leashed the dogs and whisked them off to waiting K-9 patrol cars. Bruno was still sneezing, eyes rolled back in his head, straining at his leash. The crowd had grown larger and louder. The department staff had heard the ruckus and emptied the building.

By the time the paramedics arrived and rushed the Chief to the nearby Boca Community Hospital, Melony Major was reporting on camera: "We're live at the Boca Raton Police Station. Just a few minutes ago, during a drug-sniffing demonstration Chief Buster Grimes was viciously attacked by two award-winning dogs...."

The next morning....

"I WANT SOME ANSWERS! I want some asses! God damn it, I want some nuts in a vice!" Chief Grimes was screaming at his cowering captain, Manny Arizzo, who stood by the hospital room door, ready to bolt with the first flying object. Grimes looked like an ugly newborn after a botched delivery. Red-faced and livid, he was swaddled in two wads of gauze: one that covered everything from belly button to knees, and the other wrapped around his left arm. A total of forty-seven stitches were necessary to repair the dog bites on his lower belly, genitals, and arm. A catheter snaked from the mass of crotch gauze, its long tube attached to a bedpan.

Buster was pissed. His reputation was trashed. He was the laughing stock of the county, even the country, thanks to the goddamn media. Now everyone knew he was incontinent and had to wear goddamn diapers. Worse, his own staff had arrested him for possession of cocaine. Even with the door closed, he could hear a steady stream of laughter outside his room.

To top off the indignity, the small television hanging from the room ceiling was filled with the large head of Dick Ramchez, anchor of Channel Four Action News, chuckling to his co-anchor, Susan Mitchell, about the incident. "Chief Buster Grimes. Incredible! Caught with cocaine in his diaper. This is one for Letterman's 'Stupid Human Tricks'."

Grimes picked up a vase filled with sympathy flowers. Heaving it at the television, he missed and hit the wall, showering his wife Millicent, a waifish prune, with glass shards, water, tulips and baby's breath. The tearful woman fled the room—dismayed, drenched, and deflowered.

"And this...!" Grimes threw the local newspaper at the lieutenant. It separated, harmlessly hitting the floor. The front page headline of the *Palm*

Beach Sentinel shouted: "DOGS TAKE A BITE OUT OF GRIMES." The sub-headline read: "K-9 SCRATCH AND SNIFF."

"Everybody thinks this is fucking funny!" Buster blasted his bullhorn voice.

"This just in," shouted Ramchez on the television. "We have just learned of a shocking disturbance at the Senior Samaritan Nursing Home on Forty-Fifth Street. Apparently a number of residents have been injured in a confrontation with staff. Melony Major is on the scene. Melony…?"

Distracted from his tirade, Grimes looked up at the TV. It was that bimbo reporter again. *Wonder if that's her real name,* he thought. *Sure has some knockers!*

"Right, Dick. I'm in the lobby of the Senior Samaritan, where emergency technicians have arrived and are tending to three residents. According to the staff, early this morning the three elderly gentlemen used a key to enter the storeroom and remove packages of pull-up diapers. The men were discovered by an orderly, sitting in the storeroom with scissors, cutting up the diapers which apparently contained the same white substance—presumably cocaine—that has been found in other diapers recently, like in the Grimes incident. Since the residents were threatening the staff, brandishing the scissors, police were called to the scene. Two of the patients have reportedly suffered symptoms of cardiac arrest and the other has been removed with an undetermined illness."

The camera broke in with a live picture of the three being wheeled on stretchers toward waiting ambulances. All were covered with sheets, except for their faces and hair which were dusted in white powder. Two were unconscious. The other had an ecstatic look on his face, his tongue stretching like a snail for more nearby facial powder.

"I can't get near the store room because it is heavily guarded by police, but I can tell you it looks like it has snowed in there," continued Melony.

"Shocking, just shocking!" broke in Ramchez.

"Yes, Dick. One of the residents is standing by. Maybe she can tell us more in detail. Ma'am, your name is…?"

"Bertie Begeman." The white-haired woman was dressed in a plaid robe with bunny slippers. She carried a cane and was using it to ward off people who got too close. Obviously enjoying the limelight, she exclaimed, "My, what excitement! Haven't had this much since m' dog Peaches bit the mailman in the ass."

"Can you tell us what you saw in there?" Melony asked, stifling a giggle.

A NATION BEST SERVED HOT

"Bunch o' damned fools is what they are. Think they're teenagers messin' with drugs. Snortin' diapers—never heard of such a thing. Shame on 'em." Bertie pounded her cane on the sidewalk for emphasis.

Melony wasn't finished. Flashing her gorgeous eyes, prodigious chest and microphone toward the old lady, she continued. "How did they get in the storeroom, do you know?"

"One of 'em—Watkins, I think—was watchin' the news and heard about it, this cocaine showin' up in diapers. He checked his own out and sure enough found some. Him and his cronies stole a key and made their move early this mornin'. Guess sneakin' in our rooms for slowies isn't enough excitement for 'em—they had to go an' get stoned. The damned fools."

"Slowies?" asked Melony.

"Yep, at our age, sweetcakes, we don't do quickies," Bertie cackled. Melony had walked into that one. The camera caught her blushing.

"Well, thank you, Bertie," she quickly recovered. "Back to you, Dick."

"You sure got a nice set o' lungs, dearie!" Bertie shouted off camera, before the cut-away.

Dick Ramchez was coughing—or was it laughing—when the camera returned to him. Regaining his composure, he ended with, "That's it for now. We'll keep you in touch with any further incidents as they occur. Now back to our regular scheduled programming...."

"What the hell is happening?" screamed Chief Grimes. "Get me the FBI! Get me the CIA! Get me the White House! I want answers. Now!" He threw a pitcher of water at Manny Arizzo, again missing his target by two feet. The captain left the room to grab a quick smoke outside the hospital, figuring silence was the better part of valor.

A minute later another assistant cautiously opened the door and peeked in. "Uh, sir?"

"What!?" shouted Grimes.

"Uh, crews from MSNBC and FOX are outside waiting to interview you, sir."

The partially-filled bedpan flew toward the door, followed by the long tube and ejected catheter, its balloon exploding through what was left of the captain's pride and joy. Grimes grabbed his bleeding crotch and shrieked.

Two nurses ran into the room at the roar of a wounded mountain lion. Both looked at the patient and shook their heads. Grimes was gushing blood like the man giving birth in the movie *Alien*.

Rushing toward the screaming apparition, one nurse shouted to the other, "We don't get paid enough for this shit."

CRUDE INTERLUDE
THE CAPITOL, TALLAHASSEE, FLORIDA
TUESDAY, JULY 17, 2007

"SAY WHAT?"

Governor Winthrop Rockledge Stedman III looked up from his paperwork, glaring at his Commissioner of Law Enforcement, Max Hayworth. Was he nuts?

"I know this is bizarre, but there are too many incidents coming out of one county." Hayworth was trying to keep a straight face, his portly belly shaking like Santa's "bowlful of jelly."

"Diapers? You say there's cocaine in diapers?" Stedman was incredulous. This distraction was welcome after the last two hours of reviewing mundane budgetary items, scattered on his desk like grade school book reports.

"Yep, the whole county's on high alert." The commissioner couldn't resist the double-entendre. He was clearly enjoying his moment. "There was a riot in a grocery store and a nursing home—people cutting up adult diapers to see if there's coke inside. Swear to God!" Hayworth's voice was rising in concert with Stedman's eyebrows. "Something about a plane having to land 'cause one of the passenger's diapers exploded. Everyone thought there was bomb aboard."

The commissioner saved his best for last. "And then there's Chief Grimes of Boca. 'Bout had his nuts chewed off by drug-sniffing dogs during a demonstration. Seems the ol' blowhard's incontinent..." Hayworth's face was turning cranberry red. He barely ended the sentence before collapsing in a large chair, holding his sides and guffawing, "and the dogs—har! har!—went for –har! har! har!—his pecker."

Until now Stedman had controlled his mirth. He knew Chief Grimes. Hayworth was right. The man was a peacock. The experience must have been the ultimate indignity for the conceited narcissist. The picture of him fighting dogs off his crotch was too much. Both men doubled over for two minutes, tears running down their faces. Neither had enjoyed a good laugh like this for at least a year.

"And just…just what am I supposed to do about this?" asked Stedman, catching his breath.

"That…depends…." Hayworth couldn't resist. Like two teenagers sharing a dirty joke, they resumed howling.

Stedman's intercom buzzed. It was his assistant, Maud Smith. "Is everything okay in there, sir?" she asked, no doubt hearing the ruckus from the next room.

"Yes, everything's okay, Maud. Tell you about it later," he signed off. Even stuffy Maud would get a kick out of this!

"Grimes wants you to declare a State of Emergency. His exact words were: 'Dadgumit, Hayworth, it's snowing down here!'"

"Sounds like a job for Wonder Woman." Stedman punched the phone again, still chuckling. "Maud, please find Lena and get her in here if you can. Tell her it's a State emergency."

"Har, har!" continued Hayworth, still pink around the edges.

Before Maud could answer, the governor clicked off. "That ought to put some tang in her snuff," he chuckled, double-checking to make sure the intercom light was off.

Hayworth rose to leave, still convulsed with giggles. "Let me know if you need me," he said, waddling toward the door. "Love to hear what Lena thinks."

"Oh, this is right up her alley, Max," replied the governor. "I couldn't keep a straight face in front of a camera. She'll milk this like a bitch two tits shy of a hungry litter."

"Ooo, now that's a vision!" laughed Hayworth. "Har, har, har!"

Shaking his head, he opened the door. The Gov sure had a way with words. Walking down the hall, he was full of himself. Nothing like a good laugh with the state's Chief Executive to start the day. Lena was coming toward him, deep in thought. "Ma'am," he slightly bowed, still grinning. "You're about to have a very interesting discussion with your fiancé."

Lena stopped, jerked out of her reverie. A puzzled look on her face followed the large man as he trundled out of sight. Clearing her head, she opened the door to the Executive Suite, greeting an equally puzzled Maud Smith.

METAMORPHOSIS
OLIN E. TEAGUE HOSPITAL
TEMPLE TEXAS
JULY 17, 2007

THE FIRST THING she recalled was bright light. Her eyes would not focus; everything was so bright. Then there was the pain—overwhelming pain everywhere on her body. "Tracy." A male voice. *My name,* she thought.

She turned her head toward the voice. Her head exploded and again she blacked out.

Later....

"Can you hear me?" It was the same voice, this time coming from her opposite side. *Hide and seek,* she thought, memory taking her back to childhood romps in the forest with her mom and Aunt Lena. *Come out, come out wherever you are....*

The pain hit again. *God, it hurts—everything hurts!*

"Tracy, it's me, Keith Westen." She knew that name. "Take your time, Trace. You're safe now," the voice continued.

Slowly she took stock of her environment. *I'm in a bed. I'm looking through a mask and my body is covered in something soft. There are tubes in my nose. Forced air,* she realized. Tracy tried to talk but only a gurgle escaped her parched lips.

She coughed, and once again her world exploded into merciful oblivion.

Two days later....

LIKE ROSES WELCOMING the day, Tracy's eyes slowly opened to sunlight streaming through the hospital room window—sunlight she hadn't seen in what seemed like forever. A flower garden with a meandering walkway seemed an arm's length away. *How can anything be so beautiful?* she mused.

"You're back." A voice—female this time—came from the opposite side. Remembering the pain from moving her head, Tracy remained still. Her tongue ejected pent-up phlegm onto a drool cloth as she cleared her voice to speak for the first time in months. A tube with clear liquid ran from a suspended bag to a shunt in her left hand. She was a mummy with gauze covering most of her head and body.

"W-where am I?" she croaked.

"You're in a hospital, hon," the voice replied. A forty-something black woman with close-cropped hair came into view. She wore a starched, white uniform. Her badge read "JENKINS."

"You're safe now, in a hospital. We're going to get you patched up in no time," she continued. "Baby, they won't tell me what happened, but it looks like you came up a loser in the cat fight from Hell."

Tracy began to remember: the cold, the shackles, the cuts, the beatings and rape. The devil's scent remained locked in her brain. A shiver ran the whole length of her body.

Pain!

"What day is it? What year?" she asked.

"Lemme see. It's a Thursday...." The nurse hesitated, checking her watch. "July 19th, 2007. You've been out cold for ten days after they brought your sorry ass here, Miss Jane Doe. They won't tell me your name—say it's classified. You must be one important lady. Lemme get the doc." Nurse Jenkins left before her patient could ask any more questions.

July! Tracy remembered everything now: the mission, the explosions, the dog, the abduction. *It was January then,* she recalled. *The cave… torture…murders…vivisection….* Her stomach cramped.

Six months! Six months of my life—gone, she marveled. Questions flooded her brain as the doctor and a familiar man came into view. The doctor was a tall, gangly man who resembled Dick VanDyke. His badge read "DR. CASTELEN."

"Glad to see you've finally come to." He had the deep voice of a news anchor. "You're on the mend, Miss, and we'll have you up and exercising soon. Need to get your legs back. They've…your whole body has atrophied from non-use I'm afraid. You up to talking with this man?" Castelen pointed to the other. "He's anxious to talk with you."

A NATION BEST SERVED HOT

"Yeah," Tracy responded, recognizing her boss.

Keith Westen waited until the room door was shut before speaking. Taking her right hand, he sat by the bedside and bowed his head. "God, Trace, for months we thought you were dead," he choked back a sob.

"I gave up," was all she could think to say.

"You're safe now, Trace. Still gonna take a while to heal. No one should go through what you did." Westen talked fast from guilt. "All I can say is I'm sorry, Trace. We thought your whole team was killed when you went for Carón. There was a leak and the bastard knew. Damn, what he did to you!"

"I wanted to die. I prayed to die." Tracy's voice was flat—without emotion.

"It's over now, Trace. No one knows you're alive, even your family. We'll have to keep it that way for awhile. Carón's tentacles are everywhere. We blew up the cave. I hope he thinks you were in it. If he knows you're alive, he'll come for you again. You have to remain dead. No one here knows your name. You understand?"

"My mom and dad? she asked. "They have to be told I'm alive."

"No, your dad, your brother, no one can know." Westen hesitated. "Tracy, I've got some more bad news. It's about your mother...."

THE FOLLOWING WEEKS were all about therapy and healing. Patching her body was easy compared to treating her mind. Her mother was dead. Tracy tried to cry but felt only emptiness. Losing a mother is a life-changing event for anyone, but Tracy had disconnected from Anne long ago. Her mother was a good person. She knew that. But since early childhood, their relationship had been two opposing magnetic fields.

Tracy went about the business of healing like she had approached basic training—with an iron mindset. She welcomed the pain. Pain meant she was alive—she was healing. With single-minded purpose, she drove herself toward daily goals, then surpassed them.

Upon arrival, Tracy's face had been a mangled mess. In addition to cuts and bruises, sadistic beatings had left her with a fractured nose and three cracked front teeth. After a month of dental work and plastic surgery re-shaping soft tissue to match her slightly off-center nose, her entire face was swathed in bandages. Except for generous eye, nose and mouth holes, she was a mummy from the neck upward. The wrappings had been removed from the rest of her body.

None of this hindered her training. Finally free from restraining tubes and able to consume solid food, Tracy began drawing small audiences as she moved from basic exercises through progressive judo kata techniques. Soon she was sparring with willing partners in the hospital gymnasium. Polite, rarely speaking, she garnered respect for her martial arts ability, leaving everyone speculating about this amazing, head-covered stranger.

By mid-August, Tracy was growing restive. Except for a few remaining bandages on her face, her body was healed and fit. "When do I get out of here, Doc?" she asked Castelen, who had come into the room with the same mindset, but with a twist.

The doctor had news for this still nameless woman. "We've done all we can for your body, Miss. Today is August 14th. Agent Westen has pulled a few strings. You're being transferred to the VA Hospital in Waco. Physically you're in prime condition. You've obviously been through a lot, though, and before you're fully released, you need psychiatric evaluation."

Tracy's eyes narrowed. "Who made that decision?" she asked coldly.

"Let's just say it was a joint decision between me and your Mr. Westen," was the equally cold reply. "He's DEA. I know that much, so I assume you are, too. How he got you into the VA as a civilian, I don't know. They have the best psychiatrists."

"And what if I object," asked Tracy, still fuming.

"I'm afraid the evaluation is out of your hands, Miss. If they find you're as fit mentally as you are physically, you'll be released, of course."

Tracy took stock of her situation. Like it or not, logically any objection to the quarantine would be used against her. Her mental state was yet to be determined, so she simply reacted to everyone with silence and a bitter stare.

REPARATION AND PREPARATION
PALM BEACH COUNTY, FLORIDA
TUESDAY, JULY 31, 2007

LENA'S TRIP to Palm Beach County was memorable, but not because she contributed a solution to the diaper problem. It had been two weeks since the last incident and the riddle had been solved. The tainted diapers were traced back to a shipment that originated from a company called Rely, Inc. out of El Paso, Texas. Its manufacturing plant in Juarez had been fire bombed in an obvious drug deal gone bad. The shipment was probably a one-time creative attempt to smuggle cocaine into the States. The company's owner had disappeared and the business was closed permanently.

Accompanied by Claude Masters, her huge bodyguard, the Gov's fiancée was a publicity coup for the county, embellished by Lena's visit with Boca Raton Police Chief Buster Grimes, whose ego had suffered the same fate as his manhood—emasculation. Still hospitalized and entirely deflated, he beamed as she gave him a big photo-op kiss and whispered something in his ear. As she left the room, the Chief's eyes were bulging on a face that resembled a deflated balloon.

"What did you say that got him so upset?" asked Claude as they exited the hospital.

"I asked him how his puppies were doing," she answered with a straight face.

The press circled like vultures, firing questions from all directions. "Ms. Mills—Lena. What are your comments about the cocaine incidents? What does the Governor think? Fill us in on the wedding plans."

"One question at a time, please," she begged with raised palms. "The Governor and I are very happy with the wedding plans which are proceeding smoothly. Win is sorry his schedule prevented him from coming with me. He's quite concerned about the problems you've had down here. You sure you want my opinion?"

A chorus of replies roared, "Yeah!"

The next day's *Post Sentinel* headline screamed: "GOV'S LOVE RIPS PALM BEACH." The sub-headlines quoted Lena: "COUNTY ONCE AGAIN LAUGHING STOCK OF NATION. FIRST IT WAS HANGING CHADS. NOW IT'S PUFF THE MAGIC DIAPERS."

Aside from a certain police chief, everyone seemed amused.

───※───

DURING THE SHORT FLIGHT back to Tallahassee, Lena wrestled with an idea. Matching pieces of a puzzle, a picture formed in her mind. The diaper incidents each shared common traits. Developed and controlled, these traits could yield a useful product. After meeting with Win about the Grimes encounter, she related the idea, her theory and possible application. Listening carefully, Stedman studied his fiancée, marveling at the woman's creative logic.

He picked up the phone. "Maud, get me Washington—the Secretary of Defense."

NUTS
VA MEDICAL CENTER, WACO, TEXAS
TUESDAY, AUGUST 14, 2007

DR. VICTOR HERNENDEZ, Chairman of Psychiatry, looked down at the patient who glared back defiantly. "What have we here?" he asked in a low, sultry voice. The tall, handsome Mex-Tex sported slick black hair, a thin upper-lip moustache and lightly pockmarked face. His deep-set eyes perused the bedside chart.

He sensed trouble. Taking his weekly floor check, Hernandez noticed the sign on this patient's door. "RESTRICTED ACCESS. CHECK IN AT NURSE STATION," it said. The doctor snorted as he entered the room. No one was going to restrict the department head on his own turf. The bedside chart only added to the mystery. Over the heading "NAME OF PATIENT" was stamped in red: "CLASSIFIED – NEED TO KNOW."

The patient was a woman. He was sure of that. The hair had been cut short—almost a buzz cut, and the face was partially covered in bandages. But those eyes. He searched his mind for the right word: *malevolent—eyes that could kill,* he thought.

"Who are you?"

The woman continued her wordless stare, throwing visual daggers.

He felt a tinge of danger, shivering once. This was the psych unit and she was not strapped in. Hernandez looked nervously back at the chart.

Patricia Schultz was the attending physician. There were no case notes, just a transfer chart. "Admitted - Olin Teague, Temple, 7/9/07. Transferred 8/14/07," it read. *That's today*, he realized. *I need to chastise Schultz for this secrecy.*

The Teague chart continued: "Symptoms at admission: dehydration, general emaciation including asthenia, marasmus, Addison's Disease, CLI—critical limb ischemia...."

"Rickets, for God's sake!" he exclaimed, looking up. Her stare continued unabated. He stared back. *Does she ever blink?* he wondered, looking down again.

"Contusions, systemic lesions, severe vaginal lacerations, internal and external, lesser lacerations to head, face and body, P.T.S.D.—post traumatic stress disorder."

This girl has been starved, tortured and raped, probably for a long period of time, Hernandez concluded. Nearly all patients in this ward were war casualties. This was no veteran of Iraq or Afghanistan.

Got to get to the bottom of this, he vowed. Replacing the chart and ignoring caution, he took two steps toward her.

In one swift move, the patient threw her cover aside and attacked.

The last thing Dr. Victor Hernandez remembered was falling backwards to the floor.

TRACY HENDERSON sat shackled to a chair—the only piece of furniture in a stark, off-white room. She looked up at a glass partition, behind which sat two men and a woman, each dressed in a white uniform and facing a table with small microphones.

"Why did you attack Dr. Hernandez?" the woman asked.

"Who are you?" Tracy countered, still groggy from an injection of Ativan. A nearby clock told her she had been unconscious for three hours.

"I'm Dr. Schultz and these gentlemen are orderlies, Ms. Henderson. Yes, we know your name and why you are here. When Mr. Westen learned of your incident, he released your history to us, in strict confidence, of course. We're here to help you, but we need to know why you attacked Dr. Hernandez."

Tracy assessed her situation. Poised to deliver a lethal neck twist, it had taken four orderlies to drag her off the man. Given the circumstance she decided it was time for candor.

"I thought he was my captor, El Gato, Felix Carón," Tracy answered. "Looked and sounded like him."

"Then why did you spare his life?" asked Dr. Schultz. We know you're a trained killer, Ms. Henderson."

A NATION BEST SERVED HOT

"His scent. I knew he was not Carón by his scent," Tracy explained. "Please give this Dr. Hernandez my apologies. I'm not crazy, ma'am, but I've been through…so much.…" Tracy's shoulders slumped and shivered. A sob escaped her lips as she recalled Carón's acrid breath caressing her face, neck and ears—her last memory of the cave.

Schultz studied the patient. She had thoroughly researched Henderson's classified chart. This woman was dangerous. It was the doctor's job to determine the patient's sanity and threat level to society. And then there was Hernandez. Frightened within an inch of his life, he was demanding the patient be permanently shackled and medicated.

On the plus side, no incidents had occurred during her stay at Teague Hospital. She had been a fully compliant patient—no restraint necessary—dedicated to healing and regaining physical strength. Keith Westen's account was the key. After six months of captivity, sexual abuse, mental and physical torture, any retained sanity was a miracle. How much was the question. Dr. Schultz made a calculated decision.

Signaling her orderlies to observe from their seats, she rose from the chair and entered Tracy's room. Holding her breath, she released the shackles. "Tracy, I'm in your hands now," she murmured softly. "Are you going to hurt me?"

Tracy looked up at the short, vulnerable woman with sandy pageboy locks. *Probably in her fifties,* she guessed. Schultz was visibly nervous, trying to smile with reassurance, but failing miserably. Trying to put herself in the doctor's shoes, Tracy had to admire her bravery dealing with an unknown threat.

"Nice to meet you, Doc." The patient smiled through tears, offering her hand, trying to lighten the mood. "Sorry it's under these circumstances."

In the adjoining room, two orderlies looked at each other in amazement as doctor and patient hugged like two long lost relatives.

THE BEST MADE PLANS
TALLAHASSEE, FLORIDA - THE CAPITOL
AUGUST, 2007

THREE MONTHS had flown by since the announcement and press conference in Tallahassee—three whirlwind months of planning, invitations and media massage. Lena lobbied for a small wedding with family and close friends, but small wasn't possible. Not when the governor's staff, dozens of Florida political bigwigs, lobbyists, national media, and half of New England royalty demanded inclusion.

Conspicuously absent would be anyone remotely related to Win's family. He had long since broken ties with all his Massachusetts relatives. Winthrop Rockledge Stedman II, his overbearing father, had died ten years ago from a massive heart attack. His mother followed a year later. Other than trust money which left him comfortable but certainly not rich, Win neither expected nor did he receive any additional inheritance. Millions had been left in trust to his sisters whose spendthrift husbands proceeded to squander the money. Both sisters were now divorced, bitter and destitute.

"Life's a bitch and so are you. Deal with it," shouted Win, slamming the phone down on one who called to beg brotherly assistance. *Good riddance*, he sighed. "Forget" was in the Stedman dictionary. "Forgive" was not. Stedmans held mafia grudges. Neither sister was invited to the wedding. Even if he had sent them invitations, Win was sure both would refuse to attend.

That was just the groom's side. With reluctance, Lena gave in and opened her purse, inviting the entire staff of Chameleon—her costume company, dozens of clients—both domestic and international, as well as midgets, dwarfs and freaks she'd hired in the past. With the guest list shooting over a thousand and a budget half the gross national product of Swaziland, they had reserved the huge Cypress Ballroom of the Orlando Marriott World Center for the reception.

Thankfully, the governor's staff and a dozen contracted planners handled the details, checking daily with Lena who signed off on most of their requests. Lena felt like a passenger on a runaway train. The wedding was turning into the most outrageous political soiree in Florida history.

Meanwhile Stedman had a state to govern. Often requesting Lena's opinion, he felt free to make the right decisions for his constituents, not the most politically expedient as in the past. With her encouragement and to the amazement of his legislature, he shelved every tax increase previously proposed in favor of budget cuts, most of which axed unnecessary or duplicative government services and lazy employees. To the dismay of land developers and their well-paid lobbyists, he vetoed three huge planned communities in central and south Florida in favor of water and wildlife preservation, citing a "change of heart." Florida citizens who previously had railed against the governor and all his pro-business contributors now cheered his decisions. Conservative Win Stedman had flip-flopped into an environmentally liberal head of state.

Like sand clogging a carburetor, lawsuits jammed the state court system. Without their former political leverage, the developers were left wringing their hands as dollars flew from their coffers. Empty threats were met with Stedman stonewalling. He was going out with a clear conscience, a luxury previously unaffordable. Lena found herself admiring this man who had suddenly grown a moral backbone.

In truth, she was his backbone, and he let her know it. "This is all your fault, woman," he teased, whispering in Lena's ear before beginning his scheduled August news conference. He had asked her to stand at his side during the briefing.

After the usual summation of immediate plans, Stedman took questions. The first came from Cal Edwards, anchor of FNN—Florida News Network: "Governor, recently you have changed your position on a number of bills before the Legislature. Everyone is wondering why?"

"You're looking at her." Beaming with pride, he gestured toward Lena, who returned his gaze with a smile. Cameras clicked, capturing the visual exchange. "I believe most of Ms. Mills' views reflect those of the majority in this state. I've been elected to represent those views, and until my term of office expires in 2010, I will continue to act accordingly. Lena is not just a pretty face. She is blessed with common sense, a rare commodity in today's society. There are no ambitious political bones in her body."

The second came from a beautiful but brash blonde in the second row. "Melony Major, WPBH, Channel Four in West Palm Beach," she announced. "Sir, are we to assume you've personally checked all her bones?" Spontaneous guffaws came from many in the room.

Lena sized up the reporter thinking, *She reminds me of me at her age. This girl has stones!*

Before Stedman could answer, Lena approached the microphone. Sticking her head next to his, she shot back: "I've checked his, too." She followed with a wink to the young reporter. The comment nearly caused a riot, as reporters from around the country stood and roared with laughter.

The remaining questions and answers were lighthearted, but paled in comparison. The following day, one newspaper headline summed up the event: "NO BONES ABOUT IT – GOV IN LOVE."

The press demanded more of the governor's cheeky fiancée, and with Win's permission, Lena happily obliged. Shuttling between Tallahassee and Orlando, she scheduled speaking engagements at various Kiwanis, Rotary and women's club luncheons, each attended by a phalanx of local reporters and television video cams. She was a natural at off-the-cuff banter, generating lively verbal exchange to complement her good looks. Everyone agreed this was no dumb blonde, but rather an astute debater well versed with current issues.

A foolish few who brought up her past felt the acerbic sting of rebuttal. Determined to denigrate the charming upstart, one self-righteous chubby matron fired a broadside, asking, "What makes a former prostitute like you an authority on political matters?"

The audience gasped at the woman's insult. Unfazed, Lena was ready with a one-two punch—first the charm, then the knock-out. Her lips were smiling while her eyes narrowed to venomous slits.

"Good question," she replied. "First, I'm just like most of you. I speak my mind and don't presume to be an authority on any subject." She glared at the offending woman before continuing, "Second, the word 'prostitute' should be used with care, madam. If you mean to imply that I sold my body visually for profit, I readily confess to the charge. If, however, you accuse me of selling my body for sex, you had better be able to back up your charge with proof or prepare for an expensive defamation lawsuit. I

A NATION BEST SERVED HOT

was blessed with a marketable product and nourished that product with exercise and a careful diet, unlike some..." Lena paused for effect, "who gorge themselves on Kentucky Fried Chicken and Hostess Ding-Dongs."

Thoroughly chastised, the portly accuser waddled from the room in disgrace accompanied by hisses and hostile glares from the audience.

"I ask each of you," Lena continued, scanning the remaining audience, "what is worse: prostituting one's looks for money or prostituting one's soul for power, like most of your elected representatives in state and national office?"

The crowd answered with a standing ovation.

OL' DAN DOWN THE ROAD
MOOSE JAW, SASKATCHEWAN
SEPTEMBER 21, 2007

IT WAS HIS FIRST hockey game—ever. His neighbor had told him it was one of life's imperatives to see one, so here he was, sitting second row from the ice next to the old curmudgeon, surrounded by screaming Moose Javians behind a giant glass barrier at the "Crushed Can," nickname for the oddly-shaped Moose Jaw Civic Center.

It had been two and a half months since Forrest Edwards, aka Jerry Calvin, moved into the small log cabin east of town. With nothing but wildlife for neighbors a half mile in any direction, Jerry had plenty of time to think and mourn for the people he left behind to die. Driving his Wrangler three times a week to Moose Jaw for supplies and martial arts lessons provided his only human contact, save for the grizzled old man who appeared on his doorstep a week after he moved in.

"Name's Ol' Dan Down the Road," the man announced after an iron-gripped handshake. "This here's Barf, m' cur," he added, pointing to a sorrowful bloodhound at his side. The dog looked like a tandem eighteen-wheeler, its front disjointed from the back. *Must weigh well over a hundred pounds*, thought Jerry.

The old man was wiry. *Not an ounce of fat on him. Could be anywhere from fifty to eighty,* Jerry thought. The man's face was deeply lined and pockmarked. He looked to be missing a few teeth. Those remaining were a jaundiced yellow. Tousled black hair clung like dead weeds to his chin and head. Suspenders over a plaid flannel shirt held up baggy work pants. Bulky brown boots completed the old man's provincial garb. "I be your neighbor. Thought I'd give ya a howdy-do."

A NATION BEST SERVED HOT

"Forrest Edwards," Jerry replied. "What's your real name, if I may ask?"

"That's it, Sonny—I be Ol' Dan Down the Road." He pointed toward an abandoned lumber trail meandering off to the right. Jerry had seen the cabin on one of his get acquainted walks two months ago. As far as he could tell, Ol' Dan was his only neighbor. "Done away with the rest o' the name," Ol' Dan continued. "Onliest ones interested in names be the Revenuers. Hate Revenuers—shoot at 'em on sight," he spat. "Hit one or two." He paused, giving Jerry a sly look. "You don't want to know what I did to 'em after that...."

Jerry shivered, taken aback by the stranger's provocative comment. *Was he serious?*

Ol' Dan took the one-sided conversation as an invitation. He walked into the cabin uninvited followed by the hound which plopped on the floor by the fireplace. Both acted like they owned the place.

"You on the run, eh?" asked the old man, eyeing his new neighbor warily.

"What makes you think that?" replied Jerry, unsure what to make of this brash intruder.

"Young stud, handsome, full o' vinegar, no doubt. No woman 'bout. Don't make sense less'n you're runnin' from somethin'."

Jerry was reluctant to answer the question, so he changed the subject. "Would you like something—beer, coffee, tea?" he asked.

"Got any whiskey?" was the bold reply. "Only drink whiskey and water—fire and ice keeps me in balance, eh." He chuckled at his levity.

Jerry reached for a glass and an unopened fifth of Jack Daniels he'd brought from the States. Retrieving a Molson's for himself, he set both drinks on the cabin's only table. Ol' Dan downed a big gulp of whiskey. Jerry was beginning to like the codger.

The liquor loosened the old man's tongue even more. "Come from South Florida, I did. Traded beach-front land down there back in the '50s. Made a damn killin'. That were over twenty years ago. Left the state to git far away from four theavin' wives. Took every dime. Swore off women. Pussy ain't worth all the aggravation. Bet you agree, eh?"

"Can't say I do or don't, sir. Haven't had your experience," Jerry replied with a dead pan smirk, sure he had many times the old man's notches in his belt.

"Got me a mule and this 'ere cur," the old man continued, pointing to his hound. "More'n enough company for an ol' geezer like me."

Can't hold his liquor, Jerry guessed. *He's already starting to slur.*

"Ever been to a hockey game?" Ol' Dan changed the subject, perking up.

"No, I haven't, sir," answered Jerry, wondering why he brought it up.

"Quit callin' me sir, dammit," spat the old man. "'Sir' is for ass kissin', an' I sure 'nuff don't want you kissin' mine. You ain't no faggot, now are ya, eh?"

"No, no, but what do you want me to call you, just Dan?"

"Call me Ol' Dan. Earned ever' one of my seventy-five years, and I be proud of it. Back to hockey, y'say y' never been to a game? That means you never experienced real life, Sonny. Hockey is life, don'tcha see?" Ol' Dan was on a roll. "Ain'tcha never heard the phrase: 'Went to the fights and a hockey game broke out', eh?"

Jerry laughed, shaking his head "No."

"Jesus, Mary and Joseph, this boy's from Pluto!" Ol' Dan exclaimed to his dog, downing the rest of his drink in one huge gulp, sliding his glass toward Jerry for a refill.

Two more refills and Jerry poured the old codger into his Jeep and slowly drove the half mile down an old pot-holed lumber road to his run-down cabin. Like John Wayne on a bender, Barf followed, six-inch jowls sashaying in sync with his lopsided gait. Met by a braying mule at the outside entrance, Jerry gingerly carried Ol' Dan through the door and placed him on a rickety bed.

As Jerry left the cabin, the old man was half snoring, the other half slurring, "Goddam revenuers n' scuzzy bitches." The hound and mule gave him a good sniff before letting him pass and return to his Jeep.

One day I gotta see one of those hockey games, he swore.

"KILL THE SON OF A BITCH!"

Jerry looked up two rows from his seat to see someone's red-faced grandmother shaking her fist and screaming above the roar of similar hysterical fans. It was the third period and the Moose Jaw Warriors had just scored the tying goal on their hated rivals, the Swift Current Broncos. The fight started with both teams in a scrum at the Bronco net. Two opposing players dressed like Ninja Turtles broke out of the crowd to fling their gloves on the ice—the hockey equivalent of flipping each other the bird—

A NATION BEST SERVED HOT

and flail at each other. The object was to grab hold of the enemy's jersey with one hand and beat the snot out of him with the other—a circular Kabuki dance of arms and fists enhanced by the audience's thundering cheers and jeers. The skirmish was accompanied by flying objects hurled from the stands: raw squid, dead squirrels, wool caps, half-eaten wieners and beer cups.

Fights were the main attraction. Jerry had seen NHL games on television. Occasional fights broke out but were quickly subdued by the refs. Those games were important, with large sums of money at stake. The minors, like the Western Hockey League of Canada, were filled with players either on the way up to or just coming down from the bigs. The former were eager to catch the eyes of major league scouts with their stellar play. The latter were embittered has-beens determined to wreak havoc on the former. The refs let the show go on for a minute or two before attempting to break up the fight. The fans were getting their money's worth.

Rarely televised, these matches had to be seen in person to be believed. Raw aggression accompanied by blood on the ice—it didn't get any better than this!

Moose Jaw defenseman Jock Sutter was getting the best of Bronco Brady Leavold, beating the poor slob mercilessly. Granny Two Rows Up shouted, "Kick him in the nuts, eh!" Ol' Dan Down the Road grinned and threw his empty beer cup at the glass wall, shouting in Jerry's ear, "Our guys always win the fights but lose the game, eh." His eyes were bloodshot and his mouth sprayed Molson-tainted foam.

"I thought you said you only drink whiskey," Jerry shouted in Ol' Dan's ear.

"I lied. He, he, he," he giggled like a mischievous pixie.

In any other venue, Granny and Ol' Dan would be declared rabid and shot, Jerry was convinced.

"What I tell ya, eh?" crowed Dan, lifting his arms to the gods of hockey, as the refs led both miscreants to their respective penalty boxes amid a deafening chorus of boos. "Dees 'ere's a real sport—da best!" His face beamed like a Christmas bulb as the final seconds of the period counted down and the horn sounded. The game was going into overtime and the fans rushed up the bleacher stairs toward the concession stand, no doubt to reload their Molson passion.

Ol' Dan was in his element teaching this young pup the nuances of the game. "These fights are nuthin'. Shoulda seen Ol' Moose Lallo in his prime. Best damn defenseman ever. Wide as he were tall, dat one, eh. Called him 'de enforcer'. He pick out a big stud, skate 'tween his legs and high stick him in the nuts. Most penalty minutes in the history of the league, dat one. Weren't no cup or jock strap could stand the blow he give, nossir. Nex' thing you know, the stud be singin' sopranny in a Sunday choir." Jerry winced at Ol' Dan's hysterical cackle, wondering whether some contagious disease lurked in his spittle.

The overtime game ended on a breakaway goal by one of the Swift Current forwards. Just like that it was over. Jerry had to admit there was never a dull moment as he propped Ol' Dan toward the Jeep. The crowd, though disappointed, had exhausted itself and staggered out of the Civic Center quietly as if exiting a church function, everyone dreading the next day's hangover.

Fifteen tow trucks lay in wait. The fender benders on game night provided a month's worth of usual revenue. Police stood by to mediate arguments, but they had learned years ago to ignore the inebriation after each game. It was logistically impossible to issue DWIs to the entire population of Moose Jaw.

Jerry counted twenty-two accidents on the way out of town, and judiciously gave wide berth to any vehicle in sight. Ol' Dan, buckled and bloated, snored like a road grader all the way home this moonlit night in central Saskatchewan. Passing by deer grazing the roadside, a skittering fox on a solitary hunt and raccoon eyes staring from the bush, Jerry remembered a passage from Genesis he'd heard as a child: "All God's creatures, great and small...."

I wonder if God has ever been to a hockey game, he chuckled.

CASH FOR STUNKERS
MOOSE JAW, SASKATCHEWAN
OCTOBER, 2007

AT THE AGE of thirty-eight, Jerry was a late-comer to the disciplines of jujitsu and karate. With no television, radio or Internet connections, except for a weekly call to Simon Morris, he effectively shut off the outside world. Diving into both arts with single-minded purpose, he progressed through kata techniques in his cabin up to eight hours a day. Jerry's senseis were amazed at his progress through the respective skill degrees. In less than three months, he had achieved an orange belt in both sports.

The desire for revenge was his motivating force, Felix Carón the focus of his determination. With money safely hidden in offshore banks, his fiancée murdered by the crazed drug lord, a decimated career in business and a shattered ego, Jerry's life was one-dimensional. Live or die, money be damned, he set about maximizing his chances with careful planning.

Eat, sleep, train and plan. Day after day he continued his routine with few distractions. Ol' Dan Down the Road, his trainers and a few merchants still knew him as Forrest Edwards. Summer gave way quickly to autumn in southern Saskatchewan. Fall was also short, as Arctic fronts blew through with increased frequency toward the dead season. Jerry kept to his routine, altered only by preparation for a winter he never before had experienced. The challenge and hardship would be penance for his accumulated life sins.

Thanksgiving came and went. Jerry ignored the holiday but couldn't ignore the blast of cold that bit to the bone. He added chopping wood for a long winter's rest to his daily regimen. Power would be unreliable for months to come. He stocked extra provisions, should he be snowed in. Trips to town would be fewer and only during lulls between storms.

The Moose Jaw Public Library, a modern Federal style building on Athabasca Street, was Jerry's favorite stop. Books were his singular entertainment. He checked out ten to twenty at a time—non-fiction books on martial arts, warfare strategies and anything related to Central American drug cartels. Taking advantage of the library's anonymity, he scoured the Internet for news of Felix Carón. Every mention reinforced the drug lord's image as a despot running rampant with impunity. Butchered victims appeared with increasing frequency in Juarez alleyways and side streets. Like his four-footed namesake, El Gato was marking his territory.

Jerry held no illusions. He was an irritating mouse The Cat would never stop trying to kill. He was the one who got away. The odds of success against Carón's well-financed army were slim, but an eventual showdown was a matter of when, not if.

Lawsuits against Rely from South Florida were piling up, reported Simon Morris during one of their phone conversations. The tainted diapers had surfaced in Palm Beach County. Bizarre stories of apparent product malfunctions—explosions, disgusting odors, drug-snorting seniors and riots were all over the local media. "They're all true," Simon swore. "Somehow the combination of Johnson's formula, the cocaine and urine occasionally combine to produce a volatile reaction."

"What do you mean by 'occasionally'?" asked Jerry, skeptical and surprised.

"The feds have been doing research," Simon replied. "The supervising scientist called yesterday to say there must be a missing ingredient, because there are no adverse reactions with the basic combination. Since urine is the only variable, he thinks they've found the key but won't discuss it with me, declaring the matter 'classified'."

"What the hell could be so important to make them classify the results?" Jerry asked, neither expecting nor receiving an answer.

Morris continued, "People are pissed—pardon the pun. This is where it gets really crazy. Today I got a call from Senator Brian Dobbs, chairman of the Armed Services Committee. The feds want to buy Johnson's patent and are offering you ten million dollars. Ten million!" he shouted.

"Simon, I checked the calendar," Jerry laughed. "It's not April Fool's Day. Either you're smoking something, or…."

"Shut up and listen, dammit!" Morris was screaming. Jerry sat down in shock. Simon was always calm under fire. He never shouted. "Look, I know you think this is preposterous. I do, too. But this is no joke. The feds must think they can make some kind of weapon with the combination of ingredients.

Years ago when you hired me, I legally separated the patented diaper formula from the company, placing ownership under a new dummy corporation in the Cayman Islands—in effect protecting it from mainland creditors. Since the plant bombing, the rest of American-domiciled Rely has no remaining asset value. I don't know the details, but the feds are willing to pay you for the formula. Once you sell it, the government simply 'classifies' the project, sheltering the formula from creditors."

"Can't the creditors come after me once I have the money?" Jerry asked.

Morris concluded, "The government isn't dealing with you personally. The payment goes to the dummy corporation in the Caymans. Nearly all your money is in offshore accounts, Jerry. With my power of attorney, your name stays out of the limelight and your assets remain free from attachment. Don't you see?"

Jerry's mind was spinning. He was already worth a few million. If Simon were right, he was about to be very rich. As he sat in silence holding the phone to his ear, one thought overrode all others: *all that money could buy a small army.*

"You still there?" asked Morris after fifteen seconds of silence.

"Yes, Simon," Jerry replied, coming out of his reverie. "You continue to amaze me. Please follow up thoroughly and get back to me. My anonymity is paramount. If a deal can be arranged, the price is okay with me, but my name has to be kept under wraps, understand? You have my power of attorney. I repeat: whatever you do, my name stays out of it."

"Got it. Over and out," answered Morris, hanging up the phone.

Jerry sat back, deep in thought. Here he was, in the middle of nowhere, while forces beyond his control were at work manipulating his future. Had Providence dropped another big one in his lap? He smiled at the irony. *Exploding diapers, for God's sake!* he mused. *If life gives you lemons, don't make lemonade....*

Make stink bombs.

THE WEDDING
ORLANDO MARRIOTT WORLD CENTER RESORT
SATURDAY, SEPTEMBER 29, 2007

THE MONTH OF SEPTEMBER flew by like a hurricane. Indeed, everyone connected to the wedding was glued to tropical forecasts, praying for good weather on the wedding day. Karen, a small tropical storm east of the Bahamas, was losing strength. Other than the normal afternoon shower pattern, all signs looked good for the event.

Win had stopped attending the Catholic Church many years ago following the divorce from his first wife. Lena had no formal church affiliation. They both decided on a civil wedding. Zelda Zoe Zinsser, Lena's business partner—nicknamed Trip, short for "Triple Z"—was a notary, authorized legally to certify the marriage. Asked to perform the ceremony, she was flattered and eagerly accepted. As secret and Spartan as the reception was public and ostentatious, the marriage would take place in the resort's King Suite immediately prior to the gala affair.

The day arrived amid a frenzy of activity. Anne's widower, Ed Henderson, his son Eddie and wife Donna arrived with their children. Eddie had taken his mother's dog, Shots the vizsla, to live with his raucous family in Virginia. High strung like Eddie's children, the dog had adapted to his new and frenzied environment.

All rooms at the World Resort and nearby motels were booked with media types and invited guests, each vying for a glimpse of the bride and groom. Lena and Win had reserved the suite, which doubled as Preparation Headquarters before the wedding and their bedroom following the reception. Feeling cramped, Lena walked about the grounds with her cell phone, barking last minute orders to her coordinators. To thwart the ever-present media, she was in disguise. Everyone thought Lumpy Lena was one of the wedding coordinators going about her business.

At six p.m., she retired to the suite. Attended by Trip and two other Chameleon employees, she morphed from lumpy to luscious, emerging after two hours in an off-white, strapless wedding gown. Designed by Vera Wang, the A-line skirt was made of light organza silk fabric, showcasing intricate beading and appliqué. A grosgrain ribbon fell over her chapel train, accenting her hourglass figure. She rejected a matching train, veil and sprinkled pearl beading in her uplifted hair, considering all three cumbersome and gaudy. Simple yet sleek, Lena Mills was regal as any European monarch about to review her subjects.

She was joined by her fiancé, who looked elegant in a classic black tuxedo. Claude Masters and his wife, Chareen, were to be Lena's witnesses. Both were dressed to the nines and beamed their approval.

Win was long since estranged from his former wife and children, all of whom considered him a lower life form somewhere between pond scum and plankton. Marrying the bitch who caused their 1975 divorce was the final straw for Marcia Stedman. In profanity-laced diatribes, she vented to any and all who would listen. Few did. After years of this behavior, the media considered her poison—a jilted, crude harpy bent on destroying the career of a popular politician. Claims of a sex tape had long since fallen on deaf ears. After years of searching, no evidence had surfaced, and Marcia's rants were dismissed out-of-hand.

Instead of family, Win's witness was Maud Smith, his long-time assistant. Nearing seventy, she knew every secret, mannerism and intention of her boss, keeping all in strict confidence. Uttering nary a word of criticism, she had been through thick and thin, extinguishing every firestorm with professional aplomb.

The past few months she had studied this Lena Mills with a practiced eye and found her honest and strong. *The Guv met his match with this one,* she mused, pleased to see him finally settling down. Dressed in a simple, gray floor-length gown befitting her age and demeanor, she joined Claude and Chareen, standing behind the two lovers.

With daughter Becky at one side, Trip began the formal ceremony, "Dearly beloved, we are gathered here...."

In five minutes it was over: Prince kissed Princess. Documents were signed, followed by hugs all around.

"Win, are you okay?" Lena whispered in his ear after the vows. He looked tired.

"Haven't slept in two days," he replied with a drawn smile. "I'm fine, Mrs. Stedman. How could I be any different? I'm married to the most beautiful woman in the world," he crowed with pride, taking her arm. "Let's knock 'em dead."

It was 8:30 p.m.—show time.

"LADIES AND GENTLEMEN, it's official." Press Secretary Henry Akers announced, his voice quelling the conversational drone filling the nearly two and a half-acre Cypress Ballroom. Placed strategically around the perimeter, one hundred off-duty state troopers and local police had been hired to assure a peaceful event. One hundred twenty-five round banquet tables, each decked with name cards, white linens, crystal glassware, ornate china and elaborate flower arrangements, were positioned in a semi-circular pattern facing the twenty-yard wedding party table. In the middle stood a podium garnished with red, white and blue bunting, the front of which displayed white gardenias surrounding a large state seal.

The fabulous Florida fiesta was a Mardi Gras sans confetti and parade. Over the past two hours, enough adult beverages to float a medium-sized barge had already been consumed by the inebriated throng. Members of the media mingled with sequin gowns and elegant tuxedos, fawning over any and all celebrities in search of an interview. So large was the sparkling venue, two bands were entertaining their own audiences on platforms above segregated dance floors at opposite ends of the building.

When the Press Secretary tapped his microphone for attention, all music and conversation had ceased. A thousand heads turned in unison toward the speaker.

Akers continued, "It is my great pleasure and distinct honor to introduce to you Governor and Mrs. Winthrop Rockledge Stedman III."

Behind the podium, two massive doors opened. To everyone's surprise, the University of Michigan fight song "Hail to the Victors" boomed over the P.A. system. Several Florida Cabinet members and their wives emerged, followed by ten midgets and a bevy of aging freaks. Throughout the room, jaws dropped and cameras clicked when Lobster Man, who sported claw-like hands; Liverlips, the two-headed woman; Stork Woman, Bearded Lady and the Conjoined Twins scrambled from the opening as if disgorged from some underworld lair, to take places at the head table.

A NATION BEST SERVED HOT

Unnoticed, Claude and Chareen Masters were next, followed by Trip Zinsser, her daughter Becky and Maud Smith.

Just as the cymbal-crashing, brass-blaring fight song ended, an unseen drum roll sounded, followed by a brass fanfare, presenting the beaming bride and groom. Standing, the audience greeted the stunning couple with a three-minute ovation. Like two rock stars, the Guv and his First Lady ascended the raised dais and acknowledged the huge crowd, waving and pointing to favored friends. Stedman approached the microphone and gestured for silence, mouthing "Thank you" a few times to a chorus of cheers as the applause faded.

Lena stood at his side, marveling at the spectacle before her. *This is way over the top*, she told herself, *but we asked for it.*

Stedman took stock. Maybe it was his fatigue, possibly the admiration pouring from the largest crowd of friends and acquaintances ever assembled in one place. Without a prepared speech, he was suddenly overcome with emotion.

He waited for near total silence before beginning: "In my sixty-one years, I've never been as happy as I am right now in this place, in this moment. I am humbled by your warmth."

Interrupted by applause, Lena could see he was weeping. *This isn't like Win*, she told herself. Concerned, she approached and took his hand, squeezing it firmly. As the applause died, the tears only increased. Turning toward Lena, Win's eyes were begging for assistance. She gave him a big hug and a long kiss, setting off a new round of cheers.

Lena switched places with the Governor, who now stood at her side at the podium, dabbing his eyes with a handkerchief. As the applause again calmed, she spoke: "You'll have to forgive my husband. He needs a stiff…" She paused two seconds, looking at Win with a sly leer, "drink."

Laughter cascaded throughout the building for another minute, finally calming enough to continue. "This is the first time I've seen His Majesty speechless." Another round of guffaws.

She looked around at the spectacle before her. "Isn't this something? It's like a gigantic cruise ship. I'm told that it's almost two and a half acres, 105,000 square feet—the largest pillar-free indoor ballroom in the country.

"Perhaps you were shocked by the Michigan fight song as we came in the room," Lena continued. "Believe me, that was Win's idea. He went to school there." Feeling the urge, she whispered conspiratorially into the mike, "I'm a Gator, myself." Hoots and a few catcalls from Seminole fans were overwhelmed by most of the audience cheering and doing the two-armed Gator Chomp.

"Some of you may wonder about members of my wedding party," she continued, gesturing toward the freaks and midgets. "I want you to know they are all long-time friends of mine. They may look a little different, but I assure you each is a wonderful human being. Please come up and introduce yourselves. They won't bite, I promise." With perfect timing, she paused before adding, "Well...Lobsterman there may pinch the ladies." Lena giggled as she left the podium, stood behind and wrapped her arms around the crustaceous character. He blushed red as if being dunked in boiling water.

Stedman had regained his composure. Returning to the mike, he proclaimed, "My wife, the stand-up comedian." More cheers. "Everyone, please eat, drink and be merry. Enjoy the evening," he concluded.

Both bands started in unison as the crowd dispersed to find their assigned seating. Win joined his bride who was going down the line, hugging everyone at the wedding party table. "Thanks for rescuing me, darling," he whispered. "Don't know what got into me."

"You sure you're all right, Win?" Lena noticed beads of sweat lining his forehead.

"I'm okay, really," he answered, starting to greet well-wishers.

Three hours of press interviews, fifty toasts and a thousand greetings later, Win was exhausted. Bride and Groom had little time to nibble on food which did nothing to sober their champagne buzz. After the ceremonial cutting of ten large cakes, countless dances with well-wishers, a thousand poses for pictures and smooches on demand, the bride was still radiant. Her husband looked like an old warhorse with lipstick battle scars.

Maud Smith looked concerned. Approaching Lena and touching her arm, she whispered, "Get him out of here, honey. The man's had it."

Lena looked Maud in the eye and replied, "I agree. When was his last physical?"

"Ha!" Smith scoffed. "He hates doctors and blew off the last two physicals. Said he was too busy, the stubborn jackass."

Lena was shocked. "I'll try, Maud. Thanks." She approached the Governor, who was deep in conversation with a cabinet member. Both were shouting to be heard over the nearest band, which was blasting "Get Down Tonight" by KC and the Sunshine Band. Surrounded by dancing couples, she thought, *He doesn't want to leave, but I know how to get his*

A NATION BEST SERVED HOT

attention. With one hand lightly touching an elbow and the other discretely massaging a chunk of buttock, she whispered in Win's ear, "Green light, honey. I've had enough. Let's blow this place and do some gettin' down of our own. I've got a surprise for you." She emphasized the last with a gluteus grab.

Stedman had been patiently waiting for her "green light." For seven months Lena had teased him mercilessly with foreplay, but insisted they wait until marriage for consummation. He wasn't about to let exhaustion interfere with the moment.

Apologizing to those around them, the newlyweds made their way to the door, waving to the crowd. The press secretary quickly ascended to the podium and boomed over the massive din, "Ladies and gentlemen, as they depart, let's give it up for the Guv and his Luv."

Another round of heartfelt applause followed the regal pair out of the Crystal Ballroom. Outside, climbing in the back seat of a chauffeured golf cart for the short drive to their suite, Win and Lena were lip-locked, ignoring the leading cart with three guards assigned for their safety. Coming up for air, Lena murmured in his ear, "Is this becoming of a governor, sir?"

"My 'becoming' hasn't started yet, wench," he whispered back with a wicked grin. Lena giggled, lightly massaging his bulge.

Facing him, she continued with her best Little Red Riding Hood imitation: "My, what big…eyes…you have."

"You better stop or I won't make it to the room," Win cautioned. Until then he hadn't noticed the driver, Willie Moncrief, his personal chauffeur, who was trying in vain to stifle laughter. "Hey, Willie, this thing got an overdrive?" Stedman asked.

"No suh, but apparently you do." All three busted out laughing. The guards in the leading cart turned to look back at the ruckus. The driver missed a turn and barely avoided a manicured hedge, causing more laughter all around.

Somehow making it safely to their room, after hanging the "Do Not Disturb" sign on the knob, the couple closed and safety-locked the door. After a couple of minutes passionately kissing, Lena backed Win into the bedroom, motioning him to sit.

"You'll have to wait another few minutes while I change out of this gown, darling," she said. "When I come back, I have a surprise for you."

Stedman was running on fumes. It was sleep he needed most, but wanted least. While she retired to the bedroom bath, he used the second bathroom to remove his clothes and shower. After dimming the lights, he was waiting naked under the covers in bed as Lena's door opened. Blonde hair flowing to her neckline, she was Venus wrapped in a terrycloth robe. Eyes glued to her lovely torso, his one-track mind had vacated the cranium and migrated south, evidenced by an undercover tent just below his waist.

"What's this surprise you mentioned?" Win croaked.

Lena opened her purse and removed a compact disk. "I had this burned from the original '75 film. I destroyed the original. This is the only copy left, I promise, darling." Lena popped it into the CD player attached to the room TV. "Thought you'd like to see us thirty-two years ago, lover." The ten seconds it took for the CD to start were enough for her to strip off the robe and climb into bed next to Stedman.

Win watched in amazement as Lena stroked his Minuteman missile. "My God, did we really do all this? Jesus, if I tried that position now, I'd get a hernia." He laughed at the sexual gymnastics on the screen before them.

"You up to the task, Governor?" teased Lena, throwing back the covers, revealing all. She had a small six-inch ruler in one hand.

"What's that for?" he asked.

"Scientific research, darling," she said, lightly grabbing his boy toy and measuring it. "Ha, I was right!"

"What the...?"

Tossing the ruler aside, she climbed on top of his body. "Prepare to be vanquished, sir. Let's rock and roll!"

She rolled onto his rock and rode him like a rodeo queen. Cries of ecstasy came from both as they smashed and mashed in sweet, sweaty, insatiable sex for the next hour. "Come on baby. You up for more?" she urged her lover after each launch, stroking his missile to life after a few minutes of recharge. Win was hyperventilating, his face and body bathed in sweat. Lena knew something was wrong, but animal lust trumped common sense.

The third and final moon shot was Win's last—literally. With an anguished feral cry he fell back on the bed, limp and motionless. Lena rolled off, horrified. "Win? Win, darling." First a gentle nudge, then a hard shake. No response.

Lena looked down at her husband in horror. With vacant eyes, Winthrop Rockledge Stedman III, Governor of Florida, was smiling—deader than a beached carp.

She glanced at a nearby clock. It read 2:15 a.m. She had been First Lady of Florida for less than six hours.

THE PRODIGY RETURNS
DEA FIELD DIVISION, EL PASO, TEXAS
TUESDAY, NOVEMBER 13, 2007

A CALL FROM DR. SCHULTZ had warned him of her arrival. It had been four months since agent Keith Westen had seen Tracy Henderson. The face and body had been swathed in bandages. He remembered her before all this: the eager-to-please, chip-on-her-shoulder combative young star. Mysterious and edgy rather than outwardly beautiful, she was more like a brunette Ellen Barkin: slightly off-centered nose; flat, sultry lips; eyes that had witnessed less good than bad and ugly. Her body matched the face: a filly lean and mean from all the training, yet sexy in a stand-offish way. When she walked through his door for the first time, Westen remembered thinking: *easier to tame a bobcat.*

What walked through his door this time was a classic beauty. No more off-center face, rather movie star symmetry. No more filly with attitude, this time mare with flare—still lean but with fully-developed, pollen-to-bees attraction. All six of the office staff looked up from their computers. At first curious, they were stupefied when the stranger addressed them by name. "Hey Al...Sonja...Beau," she waved. "How ya' doing? Good to be back." Six jaws dropped as she breezed by them toward Westen's door.

"Well, I'll be damned! Is it really you, Trace?" Westen rose from his chair to embrace her.

"Any wise-cracks about Barbie Doll looks and I'll deck you," was the smiling reply as she reciprocated. *The bobcat's still there,* Westen marveled.

Eight mouths began talking at once as everyone joined in welcoming back their living legend. Five minutes of questions, hugs, back slaps and high fives later, the staff retreated to their posts, still shaking their heads at Tracy's metamorphosis.

"Please close the door, Trace," motioned Westen, sitting behind his desk. It was time for frank talk.

"God, you look…well, different," Keith caught himself, seeing the look of defiance on her face. He could tell the change in appearance wasn't entirely to her liking.

"I've heard from your doctor. She says you're completely healed physically. Mentally, well, it's her opinion with what you've gone through, that there's no telling how long it will take you to return to normal, if ever."

Tracy's demeanor had turned serious. "I know. She and I had long talks. Dr. Schultz says I won't be healed inside until I let it go. Guess she told you I'm on psych medication, something called Zoloft. She doesn't understand. What that animal did to me…it haunts me at night. I wake up in a full sweat. I'll never let it go until he's dead."

Westen studied his young agent. "No one can understand what you've been through. The mission was compromised. We sent teams to look for you and your men and found nothing. For six months we thought you were dead. You must have known that. Damned Mexicans," he spat. "I'm so sorry, Trace."

A fine line stood between frankness and condescension. He knew she would rebel against the latter.

"I want to go back, Keith—finish the job." Her jaw was set in stone.

"I'm afraid that's impossible." Westen shook his head. "Doctor's orders. Besides, things have changed diplomatically in the last year. Bush has gone politically correct: let the Mexicans handle their own drug problems—a new hands-off approach. Your team died for nothing, Trace. God knows I hate it, but there's nothing I can do about it.

"Go home to your family. It's been months since we rescued you, and from what we can tell, Carón thinks you died in the cave. Your father and brother need to know you're alive. I've arranged for unlimited disability benefits until you and your doctor decide it's time for you to come back to the agency."

Tracy was shaking her head, the anger building. "And then do what? Would you put me on a desk job, take me off the field?"

"I'm giving it to you straight, Trace. We can't have an agent take it personally. You know that from training."

Six months of torture at the hands of a madman. The only way she can *take it* is *personally*, he thought.

A NATION BEST SERVED HOT

Tracy stood up, fire shooting from her eyes. Deep down she knew it couldn't be any other way. Still, this cut to the quick. Leaning toward him, hands firmly planted on the desk top, her eyes bored into his soul. With a voice like fingers on a chalkboard, she rasped, "I want one thing."

"Anything, Trace, anything I can legally do, I will. The agency, the whole damned country owes you a debt of gratitude it will never be able to repay."

"I will go home in time, but first I want to thank the man who saved me, who saw me in that cave and told you where to find me. I want his name and where he can be found."

Keith Westen sighed in relief. "You must meet a lawyer named Simon Morris," he returned, picking up his phone. "He'll give you directions to the person you want. His name is Jerry Calvin."

The hard part was over. *She knows,* he thought, *she'll never see action again.*

He was wrong.

HEAD OVER HEELS
MOOSE JAW, SASKATCHEWAN
SATURDAY, NOVEMBER 17, 2007

TRACY ARRIVED on a bitterly cold and windy day. Snow clouds were forming, a prelude to the season's first blizzard. Moose Javians generally kept to themselves. In a town the size of Moose Jaw, the arrival of any stranger elicited a trickle of gossip. Dressed in a warm, hooded parka, gloves and stylish black boots, this stranger opened a flood.

The definition of beauty varies geographically. In Miami, SoCal or Rio, places awash with gorgeous, often scantily-clad women, exotic beauty is common. In a small southern Canadian town with a harsh climate, high caloric diets and questionable hygiene, feminine appearance ranked somewhere between "strong like moose" and "built like brick shithouse." Generations of hard labor and multi-national immigration resulted in hearty stock. Local beauty was defined by a bevy of harlots who hung out at the Sugar Shack, the town's only brothel. Like the women, male clients came in all shapes with one common adjective—hefty.

When the sleek and redesigned Tracy emerged from her Toyota Land Cruiser, passers-by stared. When she entered the general store and removed her parka, the world ceased rotating. She was still getting used to her classy chassis. Lustful glances from a group of slobbering males was convincing: here was the place to experiment with her new sexual magnetism.

"Name's Kitty Daniels," Tracy announced to the slack-jawed owner. "Short for Kitten," she added with raised eyebrows and a wink. Ted Campbell was standing a few feet away. He elbowed his buddy Mike Jones, who had just awakened from his daily nap and responded with a startled

"Humph." Both gulped, eyes glued to the heavenly vision before them. The stranger turned her thousand watt smile toward the weak-kneed pair and asked, "Does anyone know a man named Forrest Edwards? I'm told he lives around here somewhere outside of town." Tracy oozed sensuality. Old Ted and Mike oozed infatuated pheromones.

"Yes'm, but he's here in town today," offered Mike.

"Over at the judo place, flippin' people," echoed Old Ted, doffing his plaid hunting cap. He couldn't resist a follow-up. "You his wife?"

"No, no, nothing like that," she returned with a dazzling smile. "Just a...friend he hasn't seen in a while."

"Two blocks down on the left," pointed Sam, the store owner, rather gruffly. His two buddies were making damned fools of themselves, slobbering over the young woman. "Sign says Judo and Karate. Y'can't miss it."

"Thank you, boys," purred the woman named Kitty. "Can't wait to see him flippin' people," she laughed. All three men ogled with bobbing Adam's apples as she slithered back into the parka, bundled her jet black hair into the hood and waved, exiting the store. All three would later agree that watching the young lady dress beat the annual Moose roping contest, hands down.

"Bye-bye, gentlemen," she cooed. "Sure got a nice town here."

Tracy slid back into her Land Cruiser and backed out of the parking spot. Looking in her rear-view mirror, she could see the three men had followed her out of the store and were staring. *Get a life, guys*, she chuckled. She drove the two blocks and parked in front of the converted strip mall. The storefront sign said: "Judo – Karate, Lessons for the Young and Young At Heart." *Nice touch*, she thought, climbing again out of her vehicle to enter the dojo.

The inside was just what she expected. Typical of most martial arts training facilities, a small entrance led to a large staging area, bare of furniture except a few chairs off to the side, with most of the floor covered in padded mats with guidelines. A number of grade school children, two teens and three adults, were standing at attention while the sensei and another teen demonstrated the uki-goshi hip throw. As Tracy removed her parka, all eyes left the demonstration to focus on the newcomer.

"May I help you?" asked the sensei, a slim, forty-something Asian who was irritated by the interruption.

"I'm sorry to intrude," Tracy said. "May I be allowed to observe your class? I promise to be quiet as a mouse."

"This is closed session, Miss—students only," he objected.

"I do apologize, sensei. I'm a student from out of town, passing through." She turned to leave.

Curiosity got the better of the sensei. "What level, if you please?"

"Nidan, sensei," was her reply, followed by the customary bow with hands in the prayer position. Nidan—the Japanese term for second degree black belt. Tracy glanced at his waist. His belt was brown with stripes.

The sensei rushed forward. "We would be honored by your presence, Miss...."

"Daniels, sensei, Kitty Daniels. The honor is mine."

"We would be pleased to have you join us. I was just demonstrating some basic moves...."

"Yes, the uki-goshi was flawless, sensei," she replied. *Never hurts to slather on the praise, even though he was rather mechanical*, she thought. "I would be doubly honored to join in. Please allow me to get my bag and change." Another bow and she left. The class took a break, murmuring about the stranger.

Five minutes later, Tracy emerged from the changing room, dressed in a white gi. All eyes were glued while she seemed to glide through a series of warm-up exercises: rotations, twists, bends and stretches. Observing the beautiful stranger, the sensei made comments on her technique, utilizing a precious teaching moment. Completing her routine without breaking a sweat, she bowed again, this time to the class, glancing at the single adult male who seemed no more interested than the others. He was wearing an orange belt. *Must be Forrest Edwards—Jerry Calvin*, she surmised.

The sensei clapped his hands and the class again lined up at attention. "I was about to demonstrate two new submissions, Ms. Daniels—the twister and crucifix," he continued. "I am sure you are familiar with these, no?"

He's testing me, Tracy said to herself. She nodded her head yes.

"Perhaps the class would like to see a nidan demonstrate these." The sensei bowed again. Was he daring her?

Time to introduce myself to the man who saved my life, Tracy thought, bowing back with a smile. "I will need a volunteer, perhaps the handsome man over there?" She pointed to Jerry, who walked toward her. "Your name, sir?"

"Forrest Edwards," he replied, bowing formally.

"Thank you, Mr. Edwards. Let's begin." She assumed her positions and guided him through both exercises, commenting as she executed each phase. It had been two weeks since her last judo workout. The exercise felt good. Her nervous partner flowed through the moves with a minimum of resistance. *Smells good—an Aqua Velva man like my father*, she noticed.

The room full of eager eyes followed the supine ballet. The sensei looked for flaws. This woman was good, very good. He bowed low at the completion. "Excellent, sensei," he gushed, paying her the ultimate compliment. She had become the teacher, he the student. He clapped again. "That will be all for today, class. Let us give our new sensei a warm thank you."

Applause and smiles broke out from all as the class departed to the dressing rooms. A few, including her partner, remained to shake her hand. "Mr. Edwards," Tracy smiled, taking him aside, "you were an able assistant." He blushed lightly and murmured thanks. *I like him*, she thought.

Waiting a few more seconds for the remaining students to depart, she captured his eyes with hers and asked, "Perhaps I could buy you a cup of coffee. I've come a very long way to meet you...Jerry." She leaned in to whisper the last word.

The name hit him like an electric shock. Tracy sensed his alarm and continued, "Simon told me where to find you." Relief replaced shock. She could tell by his eyes, gentle eyes that had seen the same horrors, sensed the same fear. She took his hand and followed with, "I owe you my life."

Jerry gathered his wits. *The cave! Was she the one?*

"I'll buy the coffee," he said.

THEY BARELY MADE IT to the cabin before the blizzard hit with the force of a tsunami. Snowdrifts piled against the cabin's west side, soon obscuring both vehicles from view. The phone and electric lines went down. Heat from the fireplace made the cabin within a cozy oasis from the harsh assault. Stranded by nature, initial awkwardness soon gave way to familiarity. It was as though they had known each other forever.

Interrupted by brief periods for eating, bathing in the secluded corner shower and resting on training mats before the fire, Jerry and Tracy talked for three days—for each, three days of catharsis. The memory of one brief encounter in the most heinous environment had forged a unique bond. Like long-lost twins leaving nothing untold, both shared secrets neither had ever before dared reveal to another.

She told him about a mother who paid more attention to animals than to her children, a father who paid no attention at all, a brother lost in his own world, and tough-as-nails Aunt Lena, who loved her most and taught her to survive.

Aunt Lena was her mother's best friend. Newspapers Tracy read during rehabilitation chronicled a Florida soap opera that strained credibility. Lena married? That was amazing on its own. But to marry the Governor of Florida who died of heart failure on their wedding night? Nothing about the woman had ever shocked her, but this story was over-the-top! Then Lena had vanished. It was so unlike her to run from anything. "Curiosity is killing me, Jerry. I'd give anything to blow my cover and go find her. I owe her my life. But I have to wait."

Tracy told him of a little girl who sprinkled pixie dust in the forest, thinking the world was good and full of magic, only to be raped and tortured as a teen. She told him of an iron will to succeed in a world of evil, training to be better than the rest, a sense of accomplishment with the DEA, and six months of hopelessness, abandonment, cold and pain at the hands of a madman in the cave. She told him of rehabilitation into an uncertain future with retribution her single-minded goal.

Humbled and attracted to the woman before him, Jerry opened up, relating a past filled with financial fortune and hedonism until his luck ran out. He told her of Miriam, his fiancée—the woman he was to marry, whose life was brutally cut short by the same demented drug lord. "We have one thing in common, Tracy," he explained. "Both of us live for the same goal. I know Felix Carón. I've studied him across a poker table and under the threat of torture. One thing is certain. Neither he nor I will give up until one of us is dead."

Without so much as a hug, by the third day Jerry had fallen in love. It was more difficult for Tracy. She had long since barred the door to trust and happiness. The concept of love was, to her, foreign as fire to ice. They had reached a crossroad. She asked herself, *Will he understand?*

Taking his hands in hers, Tracy looked into his eyes. "I know what you want—what you need. I owe you my life, Jerry, and if you insist on having sex, I will submit. But understand, with all I have been through, at least for now I am incapable of loving anyone in return. I am damaged goods, physically and mentally."

Tears were streaming down her face as she ended with two heartbreaking revelations: "I'll…never be able to have children. Carón made sure of

A NATION BEST SERVED HOT

that." She hesitated before ending with a sob. "I'm thirty-one goddamn years old and have never been kissed."

Filling that void in her life was the easy part. Throughout the following hour, fully clothed and locked in each other's arms, Jerry was in agony trying to convince himself abstinence was the better part of chivalry.

THE BLIZZARD LASTED two days. It was followed by two weeks of melt-off. A dazzling, warm Indian summer brought a final respite before months of closed-in winter. They took advantage, exploring the surrounding forest and nearby lakes. Tracy felt young again, reborn. Memories of the only time she ever felt happiness flooded her mind. She hungered to keep this feeling alive, knowing Life had another plan.

One morning, after their customary brisk walk, Ol' Dan Down the Road showed up with his hound. Jerry opened the door and the old curmudgeon marched in with a customary, "Howdy-do." Barf, exhibiting even less class, ignored Jerry and marched up to a startled Tracy, scenting her crotch.

Jerry made the introductions. Tracy laughed and began petting the rude beast. "Think he likes ya." Ol' Dan warned, "Watch out, ma'am. He ain't seen nuthin' female in years. No tellin' what he might do." Tracy bent down to receive Barf's slobbering kiss. Jerry recoiled in disgust.

"I love dogs," she said, playfully grasping the hound's droopy ears.

Ol' Dan remarked, "See ya got a life, after all, Sonny. She's a looker, too!"

He's tactless as his dog, Jerry thought.

"Got any whiskey left?" the old man followed, hoping for a handout.

"Chrissake, Dan. It's nine in the morning." Jerry complained. Tracy was laughing.

"Oh, all right, I can wait. Say, don't remember the last time I had company over for vittles. Been cookin' up some mean stew over t' cabin. How 'bout you and the lady here come by 'bout five tonight?" Ol' Dan was on a roll, visibly excited. "Ya get a show with supper, too!" he added.

Before Jerry could politely decline, Tracy chimed in, "We'd love to, Mr....?"

"No mister, ma'am." The old man was beaming. "Like I told lover boy here..." He elbowed Jerry in the side, "name's Ol' Dan Down the Road, or just Ol' Dan—no last name, y' see."

"C'mon, dog. We got some cleanin' up to do. They be a lady comin' to dinner."

Jerry was mute as Ol' Dan and Barf, who was reluctant to leave his new girlfriend, exited the cabin.

"Wow!" exclaimed Tracy. "Some character, that one. Any more like him around here?"

"No, thank God," Jerry answered, shaking his head. "Just don't get him started about hockey."

IT WAS DARK when Jerry and Tracy arrived at Ol' Dan's cabin. Saskatchewan sunsets arrived early this time of year. The old man was sitting in a rocking chair on his deck as Barf loped to meet the guests. Again ignoring Jerry, Barf gave Tracy a few slobbering dog licks and trotted back to the cabin.

"Yer just in time for the show," the old man greeted the couple.

"What show?" asked Jerry, growing anxious as Ol' Dan reached for his rifle.

"C'mon up here and take a seat," he gestured toward two deck chairs next to his. "Now, lookie up there in the trees." He pointed toward the nearby forest.

Tracy's jaw dropped open. Jerry gulped as both looked up to see moving colored lights dancing throughout the upper branches. "Like Christmas, ain't it?" Ol' Dan chuckled.

"What the...?" Jerry gasped. "What are those lights?"

"You'll see," was the old man's answer as he took aim.

BAM!

The rifle exploded, startling Tracy, even though she anticipated the sound. One of the lights floated to the ground.

"Barf, fetch!" barked Ol' Dan, as the dog trundled to do his master's bidding. He promptly returned with a dead squirrel in his mouth, dropping it at his master's feet. The squirrel's tail was florescent orange in color. Ol' Dan was cackling, seeing both youngsters with mouths open in amazement.

"Imagine this in Florida. People'd pay to see a show like this," he bragged. "I'd call it 'Glow World.' Put it right next to Disney."

"But how...?" Jerry asked.

A NATION BEST SERVED HOT

"Set some traps, see?" Ol' Dan explained. "Catch 'em little buggers and spray the tails different colors of glow paint, then let 'em go." After a pause he continued, "Get hungry, shoot a few. Skin 'em first, of course," he added.

"That's disgusting!" Tracy blurted out, unable to contain herself.

Ol' Dan's expression matched that of his bloodhound—hang-dog hurt. "Gee, ma'am, I'm sorry." He looked crushed and, head bowed, turned to enter his cabin. "Guess you won't be wantin' supper, then…squirrel stew."

NIGHTS AND EARLY MORNINGS were spent training—she the sensei and he the student. The cabin's main room was cleared of furniture, the floor covered in padded mats. Jerry was eager to please, but Tracy knew his inexperience would only hinder a close combat situation, especially in a life or death battle.

She was brutally honest. "You must understand. I've trained for years to kill with my body and weapons. Not to brag, but I'm damned good at it. You will only get in the way when the time comes."

"I have to try, Tracy," he replied. "It's the only thing I live for, just like you."

So they trained each night, slept side-by-side and by day walked hand-in-hand, savoring this time together.

On Monday, December 3rd, the cabin phone rang. A call from Simon Morris marked the end of pleasant reverie. "You're a very rich man, Jerry," he gloated. "The government deal for Rely went through. After my commission and expenses, I just deposited a little under nine million in your off-shore accounts. Your net worth is slightly under fourteen million, guy. What do you think about that?"

Jerry had prepared for this news. "I think I owe you, my friend," he sighed. "But now I need you even more. Tracy Henderson is still here. I have a plan, but I need to pass it by her." Before Simon could comment, Jerry ended with, "Call you back in a day or two. Hang tight."

Tracy had listened to the conversation with a questioning look on her face. Within a few hours, she learned of his wealth and details of his plan, marveling at both.

The next four days were filled with phone calls as they made contacts, modified strategy and packed to leave. Reality is often a road scarred with bumps, laying waste to well-financed intentions. Together they charted a collision course with destiny, unaware fate would leave a pothole in the middle of the road.

"THE CAT" LOOSES A HOUND
CUIDAD JUAREZ
FRIDAY, NOVEMBER 23, 2007

FELIX CARÓN paced back and forth across the spacious veranda above the manicured courtyard of his fortress. He looked to the ominous sky. Storm clouds were approaching from the west.

His hacienda was patrolled by thirty well-trained assassins, six Dobermans and sixteen closed circuit cameras mounted strategically upon two rows of electrically-charged chain link fence—all topped with razor wire. Two sets of entrance gates were each camera-monitored and manned by armed guards ready to blow away anything or anyone who approached uninvited.

El Gato was a man marked for death by his adversaries and a few straight shooters in government who had refused his bribes. He had countered all threats by assembling a hand-picked army of former Mexican soldiers trained in offensive and defensive combat, stationing them inside his impenetrable fortress. Only an overwhelming assault could breach the perimeter. Carón used his vast wealth to buy off the *Federales* and dominate the competition.

Security was not on the mind of El Gato this day. His mood matched the approaching storm. Four months had passed since that piss ant gringo diverted his shipment of cocaine and disappeared. From hysterical media coverage of strange related incidents, he knew the cocaine had terminated in Palm Beach County, Florida. Police and federal investigators had descended like flies on shit.

Four months had also passed since he'd lost his only friend, Bolivar, in the nearby cave explosion. "*¡Pendejo!* Loose ends!" he cursed. Carón hated loose ends. He controlled his territory with iron-fisted autonomy. Any breach of security drove him mad. With vast resources, Felix Carón was an octopus whose tentacles reached in all directions. He had paid a small fortune searching the states for all Jerome, Gerald and Jerry Calvins. Over three hundred matches had come up negative. Obviously, the irritating gringo had changed identity and was hiding somewhere. But where? The only contact with his diaper company was a lawyer in El Paso named Simon Morris who had been followed since late July. Targeted bribes had yielded phone records of his law firm. Each attorney in the firm used his own set of segregated land lines. During those weeks, Morris and his assistant had made same-number calls to many clients as well as personal contacts. It had been an exhaustive study matching each number with a name or business. Again all proved negative.

That left cellular calls. With encrypted digital technology, no chance existed of tracing the numbers from Simon's cell, except through his Verizon account. Again, after expensive bribery which yielded the past four months of records, all repeatedly-called numbers were negative… except one weekly call to a land line in Moose Jaw, Saskatchewan.

It was this news that had the drug kingpin pacing his balcony, anger rising like a rash on the back of his neck. *Did I find you, fucking gringo? I will squash you like a bug!* Felix Carón seethed with vitriol reserved for his most hated enemies.

Summoning his aide, he slammed a piece of paper into the man's hand and barked, "*Jorge, envíelo el albinos a esta dirección.* Send the albino to this address. *Cerciórese de que su pasaporte sea activo.* Make sure his passport is active. *Haga que él mate a quienesquiera que vivan allí luego tomar una foto de las caras.* Have him kill whoever lives there and photograph the face." Enrique Ramos, "The Albino," was the most skilled assassin on the payroll.

"*Y Jorge,*" Carón growled, "*Tráigame una puta—un poco más vieja esta vez.* Bring me a prostitute—a little older this time. *Las jóvenes tiemblan y gritan.* The young ones, they tremble and cry. *A mí me gusta una puta sazonada con una cierta lucha.* I like a whore seasoned with some fight. *Mi azote se necesita el entrenamiento.* My whip needs a workout."

Felix Carón pushed aside his anger for growing lust, his lips curled in a lurid sneer.

Jorge Cruz was El Gato's personal assistant. Like Bolivar, he was from Carón's barrio and had catered to the older thug from an early age. Now

A NATION BEST SERVED HOT

in his mid-thirties, unlike Bolivar and his bachelor boss, Cruz was married with two young children. A devout Catholic, Jorge wished for any other life free from servitude, but his local knowledge, fear for his family and a generous income had bought many years of obedience and feigned loyalty.

He bowed and backed away, grateful for the change in El Gato's attitude. A call to the usual pimp would yield the perfect mouse for The Cat's appetite. As he had many times before, Jorge felt remorse for another unwary woman who would fail to leave the compound alive.

A RECIPE FOR STARDOM
EL PASO TO NEW YORK
1988 – 2007

MARY LOU MOOTHART, JR. was born in El Paso, Texas on September 20, 1988, of an unknown father and mother who died giving birth. She was raised by her cranky maternal grandmother with the same surname. Shortly after Mary Lou's birth, a busybody stickler for proper etiquette chastised the new grandmother. Looking down her nose over half glasses, the woman huffed, "The title 'Junior' is reserved for male children only."

Big mistake.

"Screw you and the horse you rode in on," spat Gramma Mary Lou. "I'm stuck with the goddamn brat." Pulling meat from a pork roast, she shooed the woman out of her restaurant with greasy hands, adding, "I get to remind the little shit who raised her."

Gramma's fourth husband had been a weak-minded drunk. Before running him off with a pitchfork, she gave him a choice: sign over his modest inheritance or become a two-legged pin cushion. Using the coerced settlement to buy space in a local El Paso strip mall, she furnished it with restaurant supplies and opened Mary Lou's Sweet and Sour Spaghetti Shop. The only menu item was a recipe by the same name handed down from her deceased mother. That recipe, tossed salad and the best French bread she could find, kept the place full with waiting lines from day one. Word got around. People swore the recipe was so addictive it must contain something illegal. The same people became regulars, returning in droves for another hit of Mary Lou's spaghetti. Sly Gramma Moothart closely guarded the secret ingredient, padlocking the refrigerator. In the dead of night, she would cook a fresh batch of sauce for the following day's consumption.

A NATION BEST SERVED HOT

The mystery substance was so exotic no one could replicate her recipe.*
*She flatly refused all bribes to release the secret, even to her employees. It seemed the more she raised the price, the more people came to quench their habit.

The two Mary Lous made a feisty pair: a trash talking senior citizen and a caterwauling baby. "Kid's got lungs," proud Gramma proclaimed. "Go ahead, girl. You tell 'em!"

Doting on little "Junior" became a passion she never felt with her own three children. Fearful of their mother's wrath, her two boys from previous failed marriages were now adults and never called. Gramma described them in five words: "Stale seed begets worthless crops."

Like honey to bees, her only daughter attracted drones. Mother's birth control advice went unheeded and daughter was pollinated by a slick-talking car salesman during a one-night stand. The daughter died giving birth to Mary Lou's obstreperous namesake. From a very early age, little Junior badgered her grandma for parental knowledge. "Your mom and dad weren't worth knowing, precious," Gramma always replied. "Let the dead be buried. Someday when you're ready, I'll give you the facts."

Junior's first memory was the smell of Gramma's recipe. Seemed the only thing that would quiet the screaming child was the pungent odor. As a baby, she slept peacefully through each day in the restaurant's back room. At age five, she started waiting tables after kindergarten class. Her feisty bantering and occasional dropped plates provided entertainment with the meal. Customers, sated and magnanimous, left the little towhead big tips in exchange for wide smiles and eager-to-please service.

Soon there were two restaurants, then three, plus two take-out shops, forcing Gramma to make sauce in a locked kitchen, days as well as nights. Producing enough to satisfy five outlets was now a full-time job, and she wasn't getting any younger. At the age of twelve, little Junior wasn't little any more. She was an easy learner with the stamina of a racehorse, earning straight "A"s in school. Long, coltish legs were offset by an angelic face framed by graceful blonde tresses. Her chest seemed to expand by the day.

In addition to school, the pre-teen now monitored operation of all five stores. Too young to drive, she was shuttled everywhere by a lanky Mex-Tex bodyguard, Jesse Lopez, whose family emigrated across the Rio Grande from the barrios of Juarez. Jesse came from honest, hard-working

---

*   See recipe at the back of book.

people Gramma hired to oversee her home and help with the business. She trusted him with her precious granddaughter, but not before having a candid talk with the young man in her kitchen. Pointing to her collection of very sharp knives, old Mary Lou let it be known her granddaughter's virtue was sacrosanct and Jesse was one flirtation removed from castration.

Jesse was suitably terrified. Polite and attentive to Junior's needs, at age twenty he couldn't help noticing the blossoming young filly in his charge. Strong cautions from his family, along with Gramma Mary Lou's graphic admonition, kept lascivious thoughts deeply recessed in his mind. Instead, he dedicated himself to her safety and shared his street-wise knowledge during daily trips on El Paso byways.

Junior soaked up knowledge like a sponge, asking frank questions to someone more her own age. Boys and sex entered her mind casually as school subjects, and she used Jesse as a sounding board, torturing the young man who returned frank answers while squirming in his seat to hide an erection. One day, casually commenting on her prodigious assets, he used crude Spanish slang she would later modify into a professional name—"*mayor melones,* major breasts." Mary Lou looked down and, using both hands to cradle her *melones*, replied, "I wonder how big they'll be when I'm twenty."

Stifling a groan, Jesse nearly drove off the road.

KISMET CALLED shortly after her fifteenth birthday. A local television station, KTEX, ran a series on area restaurants. One of the obvious choices was the wildly-successful Mary Lou's Spaghetti chain. Gramma was camera-shy and foisted the interview onto her granddaughter, now a raving beauty. Naturally poised and refreshingly candid, the interview was a smash hit. Calls to the station came in by the dozen. Everyone wanted more of this photogenic natural.

The station director phoned Junior for a screen test as a walk-on weather girl. The day came and Jesse could see she was nervous. He delivered her to the station primed with two Dos Equis *cervezas*. After a brief logistical run-through with the back screening process, the slightly smashed ingénue winged it. Introduced as Junior Moothart, she looked straight into the camera and smiled, ignoring protocol. "This is El Paso, Texas, y'all," she announced, pointing to western Canada on the map. "Give me a break. It hardly ever rains, but if by some remote chance it does tomorrow and you're under it, the chances of precipitation are one-hundred percent." She giggled and waved, signing off with a brazen bootie bump and a giggle, "I'm Melony Major, and remember, when a flock of buzzards fly overhead, don't look up."

The station director choked on his Pepsi, bubbles painfully shooting up his sinuses. After cutting to commercial, the cameraman and various assistants broke out in applause, ushering their new star off the set. Jesse was waiting in the wings, cringing with worry. What was this about buzzards... and "Melony Major?"

"Crissake, Jun. Where did you come up with that?" he scolded, giving her three chocolate mints on the way to the car. Any hint of beer on her breath, Gramma would filet his skanky ass.

"I hate my name," the tipsy teen replied with marinated inhibition. "Mary Louuu Mooothart." She drew out the vowels with stretched hand gestures. "Sounds like an owl or a moose." A sly wink and two hands cradling her twin assets answered his question. "*Mayor melones*, remember?" she teased in a low, sexy voice.

Jesse muttered Spanish expletives all the way home.

⁓⌣⌣⌣⌒

LIKE A SAILBOAT tacking to a changing wind, Junior devoted all her energy to course correction. Finishing high school was her top priority, classes in broadcast journalism at a local community college, second. Sporadic appearances on KTEX rounded out her schedule. That left no time for the restaurant business.

Gramma accepted the inevitable. With her only successor rocketing toward a different career, in late 2003 she sold the business and her precious recipe to a salivating entrepreneur, retiring with a hefty buy-out pension and stock portfolio. Exhausted by the pace of running the seven-day-a-week business, the shock of retirement was like hitting a wall. With no hobbies or goals, after three years of gluttonous luxury, she piled on fifty pounds of artery-clogging corpulence. Mary Lou Moothart died of cardiac arrest at home during a west Texas sandstorm in early June, 2006. The next day, after ringing her doorbell five times, a neighbor peeked through the kitchen window to see Gramma lying face down in a plate of her favorite spaghetti.

"A fitting end for the saucy bitch," one of her two sons remarked after learning both had been cut out of their mother's estate. Costly legal attempts to invade the will were rebuffed. Her considerable assets were locked tighter than a tick in a bank-managed irrevocable trust. Granddaughter Mary Lou was the sole beneficiary. The trust would provide her income with one third of the corpus distributed at five year intervals, starting at age thirty.

Now eighteen and an adult with a driver's license, the youngster mourned the only parent she'd ever known. Jesse was twenty-six and no longer threatened by Gramma's knives. He was in love and fought off other young studs on the scent.

Junior was well aware of her allure and enjoyed the attention, but she remained laser-focused on her career. More valuable than tangible assets, Gramma had trained her young charge in self-reliance and determination. She graduated high school with honors, petitioned the state for a name change and, with a glowing referral from the KTEX manager, accepted an entrance level job as an apprentice reporter at WPBH in West Palm Beach, Florida.

The scheduled day of departure came with agonizing slowness for Junior, all too soon for Jesse. Her late model Mercedes packed to the grille, she took the lovesick friend aside to give him a first and last kiss. "I'll never forget you and hope you understand," she murmured, breaking away from his ardent embrace. "You're a good man, Jesse Lopez... my big brother." The three words cut him more deeply than Gramma's sharpest knife, but they needed to be said. "Now go find someone more worthy."

With that, emancipated Melony Major sped off to face the future, leaving El Paso, Texas and her past in her rearview mirror.

SHE WAS A NATURAL. After a brief training period as an apprentice, Melony went solo on assignment around the state. Live on-scene interviews with the cocaine diaper incidents and her press conference question with the governor and his fiancée earned effusive praise. She was quick on her feet and eye candy to the local Palm Beach viewers. Calls came in demanding to see more of the vivacious reporter. WPBH news ratings went up as her assignments increased.

A NATION BEST SERVED HOT

Offers from the major networks were inevitable. CBS, NBC and FOX courted her with juicy contracts. She polled different agents who came calling, most of whom recommended the youngest and most aggressive of the three networks. FOX NEWS was only eight years old but had assumed prominence in cable and satellite ratings.

Melony Major had never been to New York. The city was overwhelming to a newcomer, but she was even more awestruck with the network studio. A 24/7 beehive of activity, the "Fair and Balanced" news crew was a study in creative efficiency. Media mogul Rupert Murdoch sought the brightest and best, and most of the news crew was young and eager. He was known to hire based equally on looks, poise and intelligence. Melony's interview with FOX president Roger Ailes was pleasant and to the point. He expected excellence from day one. Success was pass/fail from the get-go.

Armed with a signed contract, a thick corporate get-acquainted portfolio, a generous expense account and an open-ended round trip airline ticket back to Florida, Melony was given her marching orders. She was assigned a seemingly impossible task. Three of her FOX predecessors had failed to locate Lena Mills Stedman and get an exclusive interview. They weren't alone. No one had seen the late Florida governor's wife in over two weeks. Elusive as Garbo with equal mystique, she was every reporter's dream assignment. But where had she gone?

"Use your intuition. Be creative. Ask questions. She has to be somewhere. You're up against the best jackals in the business. Can you handle it?" asked Ailes, looking for a crack in Melony's armor.

The brashness of youth showed through her answer: "Watch me." Ailes liked her pluck. "Go get her then," he ordered with a smile.

Just like that the interview was over.

Heady stuff for a veteran, let alone a rookie.

Melony Major left on assignment, determined to make the spirit of Gramma Moothart proud.

INTERLUDE
OCALA NATIONAL FOREST
OCTOBER, 2007

ANNE HENDERSON'S INTERMENT in June had been a brief, emotional, one-day trip to the forest. With this extended stay, Lena noticed how much the forest had suffered from human pollution over the past thirty years. Lena saw it every day on her walks: garbage strewn on previously pristine pathways, inconsiderate hikers scaring off wildlife with raucous chatter, abandoned campfires destroying acres of virgin foliage before being extinguished. In the distance, a never ending buzz of all-terrain vehicles drowned out what used to be soothing forest solitude.

Yet Lena relished this hiatus—the not caring about time, the lack of schedules and appointments, no harsh demands of fame. Surrounded by nature, she was her own person again.

It was another brilliant late October day in the forest. The temperature was pleasant, somewhere in the seventies. Sitting in Anne's favorite $4.99 Walmart folding chair, one of two retained from her friend's estate, Lena stared at the small pile of stones beside the pathway. She came here each day to talk with her friend. How ironic it seemed: Anne claimed as a child to converse with the dead. The table had turned. Now she was underground—at least her ashes were.

"How I wish you could talk to me," Lena Mills-Stedman whispered each time to the stones before her, willing her mind to listen for a reply she knew wouldn't come.

On this day, the sound of approaching voices interrupted her reverie. A young backpacking couple rounded the corner and stopped to stare at the woman in a chair. "Hello," the young man offered. "Are you okay?"

A NATION BEST SERVED HOT

"Couldn't be better," Lena returned with a smile that mirrored the dazzling day. "Just enjoying the forest, like you two."

The youngsters walked past slowly, still staring back at her, eventually disappearing. Lena was all too familiar with their "I've seen this person somewhere" look.

The pain from losing Win and the wedding night aftermath still lingered one month later. Her life had fallen off a cliff. The over-the-top wedding with good will, smiles, speeches, champagne, the furious love-making, the ecstasy on Win's face—all things she wanted to forget, but couldn't. She had lost control of her life. The baffled doctors, harsh police, demanding lawyers, relentless press, never-ending flashbulbs, accusations—everyone wanted a piece of her when she had no more to give.

What drove them all crazy was her lack of tears. A widow should cry, they all said. How could she be so stoic? Unable to answer, she felt only numbness.

Three coroners had come to the same conclusion: death was from an acute myocardial infarction—a massive heart attack. The state and national press had a field day skirting around the obvious question on everyone's mind. One alliterative headline summed it up: "DID LENA LOVE GOV TO GRAVE?"

Only Christ's Second Coming could have trumped the titanic tabloid titillation. Was Lena another Mata Hari, a Jill the Ripper, or just an oversexed victim of circumstance? Secretly envious of her charms, women feigned shock toward the "brazen bitch." Men gathered at water coolers to swap one-liners.

"Got what he deserved, sure 'nuff," one opined. The Governor's exploits with women were legendary.

"Son of a bitch died the way he lived—screwing another constituent," a jealous political foe remarked. "I should be so lucky!"

"Some broad! 'Nuff to make the South rise again," a third exclaimed amid a chorus of chuckles.

Hounded day and night, Lena's only option was to disguise herself and flee. Millions who relished every tidbit of tabloid trash were left to wonder and speculate. Only her best friend, Claude Masters, knew of her plan to disappear to the place where they had fled together over thirty years ago. Exonerated from blame, two weeks after "that day," she vanished. Lumpy Lena had tuned up her old camper and disappeared into the Ocala National Forest.

We would have had a hell of a ride, she thought. Win Stedman had changed over the past year. He was near the end of his political career. *Maybe it was stress or his age.*

Maybe it was me, Lena concluded. Then she discarded the thought. *I would have been good for him,* she was sure. With his political clout and her backing, they could have made a difference. All the possibilities had evaporated with the heart attack.

I was just beginning to love you, she mourned.

For the first time since she left Michigan as a teen, she was alone. Anne was gone. Tracy had disappeared. Claude was wrapped in his own life, watching his family grow and overseeing the retirement home. She hadn't seen him since the day after the wedding.

Day after day, Lena hiked to sit at the shrine of rocks. Day after day, she conversed with herself, losing track of time. Today was no different. It was so peaceful here, even with the mechanical bees buzzing in the distance. Anne was right. This place was Home.

Sitting in the chair, Lena closed her eyes and slowly drifted off. She was floating, letting the thermals take her to and fro, eyes fixed on a dozing woman far below....

A freshened zephyr woke her. Or was it someone else approaching? How long had she been out? From a thicket across the path a lone doe was staring at her. She could almost reach it but stayed still, fearing the deer would skitter off. Lena's mind flashed to Anne thirty years ago, her arms outstretched upward through a beam of light....

Who are you? she thought, staring at the delicate doe, taking care not to move a muscle.

Yesssss. More whisper than voice, the reply echoed in the canyon of her brain—a dream-thought dissipating. Surprised yet calm, Lena continued staring at the doe, daring to hope this moment was real.

"Anne?" Lena concentrated with every ounce of being as she whispered the name. Flinching at her lip movement, the deer was on edge, ready to bolt at first threat.

Yesssss. This time a little stronger. *Don't be afraid,* the thought continued.

The doe turned to leave.

"Don't go!" Lena reached out as the deer scampered off. "Damn! I've lost you," she wailed, standing, beating her sides in frustration.

I'm down here, girlfriend, came the thought—a thunderbolt that nearly knocked Lena off her feet. *Down here, right where you planted me.*

A NATION BEST SERVED HOT

She looked at the pile of stones. Was it suddenly an oracle? *This must be a dream,* she thought. Lena slapped her face—hard. The pain was sharp. "Ow!" she cried out.

Hurts, doesn't it? How I wish I could hurt again, the voice replied.

"B-but the doe…." Lena stammered.

…a deer, a female deer. Ray, a drop of golden sun, was "The Sound of Music's" sing-song reply. *I never could carry a tune.*

Lena was mesmerized. No more whispering or thought-speak. She cried out, "This is really happening! Tell me this is for real. Tell me I'm really talking with you, Anne."

I'm proud of you, sis. You're a slow learner, but you've finally crossed over. Anne's voice had leveled off to conversational telepathy. *Takes a little getting used to it, but once you're comfortable, it's like riding a bike or having sex. In your case, less dangerous.*

There was no doubt. The voice was Anne's. Lena shook her head, still in shock, babbling, "I'm talking w-with…a freakin' pile of rocks!"

Hey, give me some credit, okay? They're just stones. Remember me telling you I used to talk to "grounders?" Well, I'm one of them now, so show some respect.

God, I'm dying to give you a hug! Lena bent over to touch the rounded apex.

Careful with the "God" and "dying" stuff, woman! You're not ready for all that yet, and beside, hugging's not all it's cracked up to be. I can't eat baby back ribs. You can't hug me. I call that even, okay?

Lena decided to play along whether this was real or a dream. "How'd you get so cynical?" she asked, still feeling awkward, looking around. She was alone. "You were always so serious."

Got that from you, Sugar. Can't do all the neat things with you yet. Baby steps. But we can still mess with the masses, if you get my drift.

"No, I don't get your 'drift'," Lena shot back, irritated. "Why can I talk with you now when I couldn't all the times I came here before? And what do you mean, 'mess with the masses'?"

One thing at a time, Lena, AnneVoice countered. *Sit down. Take a load off.* Lena obeyed, planting herself once again in the Walmart chair.

Connecting is an acquired skill. Takes total commitment and concentration. Your mind took a while to train. Why do you think you kept coming back here every day? Think about it. You knew deep inside I was here for you. The note I left you hinted at it, but I hadn't passed yet when I wrote it, so I wasn't sure. As for the masses, stick with me, Honey. You're about to embark on the wildest trip imaginable.

"What the hell does that mean?" Lena asked, not sure she wanted to play this game. This AnneVoice was not at all like the reserved, living friend she remembered.

I repeat: careful with the Heaven and Hell stuff, kiddo. I could tell you things, but all that is way beyond your corporeal pay grade. Yes, you have doubts. Of course you do.

Let me explain. By connecting with me, you've already got a head start. Do you know how the Internet is called the "Information Superhighway?"

"Go on", Lena replied with growing curiosity.

Well, you've just tapped into the Future-mation Superhighway, girlfriend, and I'm one of your spirit guides. Very few Earthbounders have the ability. You've just won the lotto.

"Okay, now you've done it. I'm totally confused." Lena shook her head like a dog shedding water, hoping to clear her mind of supernatural cobwebs. "Why me?"

Ah, that's the question, isn't it? Like a breath of wintergreen, AnneVoice mind-sighed. *I'll try to put this in your terms because you'd have to be here to understand the rules in what you call Heaven.*

The Masters oversee everything that goes on in your dimension. Each Master has lived many previous human lives. Think the "Founding Fathers of America" as an example and you'll get the idea. After eons of experiments failed to form the "More Perfect Union," these few extraordinary men got together, took what concepts seemed to work, discarded what didn't, and came up with the Constitution, the foundation of laws for the United States of America. This grand experiment wasn't perfect and needs tweaking now and then with amendments, but the Constitution has lasted as mankind's Beacon of Hope for over two hundred years. Are you beginning to understand?

"You still haven't answered my question: why me?"

Patience, woman. Patience is the backbone of knowledge.

"Y'all must be smoking some great weed, wherever you are," laughed Lena, trying to inject some levity into the ethereal conversation.

Anne's spirit deflected the humor and continued. *Please, there is nothing humorous in what I'm trying to communicate. You must concentrate. What you're about to hear next you will not at first believe. I repeat: have patience. Only time and experience will convince you.*

"Why do I need to know if I will not believe?" Lena interrupted, feeling like a dog chasing its tail.

Anne's mind-thought abruptly changed timbre. A deeper, masculine one had replaced hers, commanding: *You have the power to lead, and lead you must! Use this power wisely....*

"Wait a minute! Who are you? Where is....?"

SILENCE!

The thundering command hit Lena's brain like a bolt of lightning. She fell backwards onto the ground. Stunned with mind voltage, her last thought before losing consciousness was, *What have I done to deserve this?*

SHE WOKE WITH a pounding headache. Daylight had waned to cooler dusk. The forest was quiet save for rustling leaves. Recreational vehicles had ceased their distant whining. She shivered. *Damn,* she thought, *what a nightmare!*

Lena picked herself up and sat in the Walmart chair. Had she really communicated with Anne? "You still there?" she spoke again to the pile of rocks, hoping her memories were not just a dream.

No response. The spell—whatever it was—had disappeared.

She tried again. "What am I supposed to do, Anne? I'm still full of life. I've got the energy of a twenty-year-old...well, maybe thirty," she reconsidered.

"More like forty," boomed a deep voice behind her. Lena bolted out of her seat, startled for a third time. Reality had returned in the form of Claude Masters. She squealed with delight and rushed into his huge arms. Dropping a small handbag, he lifted her in a great bear hug, chuckling.

"I'm slipping. You never used to be able to sneak up on me, you big lug."

"So this is where you buried her." Claude looked down at the pile. "I never thought she was in the graveyard."

"It was our secret, and I hold you to it. You must never disclose this location to anyone. I mean it, Claude!" Lena replied forcefully, releasing herself from his embrace. The bizarre encounter with Anne's ghost was still fresh in her mind. "I can't say any more. You'll think I'm batty."

"Okay, okay," he answered, palms outstretched in agreement. "Woman, you passed batty thirty years ago and cruised into demented," Claude laughed, buying himself a sharp jab in the arm.

He abruptly changed subjects. "Had enough of your little vacation yet, enough of the four-legged world? The two-legged one awaits your return."

"Return to what, more slanderous accusations? More ridicule?" Lena spat. "If I wanted more abuse, I'd sign up for Masochists Anonymous. I'm a freak, Claude. Now I know how Misty Mathers felt screwing up her face for profit. People didn't come for her act. They came to laugh at her, to feel superior."

"Guess you haven't been paying attention to the news lately, right?" he asked, knowing the answer.

Lena shook her head while Claude pulled newpaps out of the handbag. "Read the headlines," he said. "This is just a sampling from the past two weeks."

"LENA, ALIVE OR DEAD?"; "MYSTERY WOMAN DISAPPEARS – GONE FOR TWO WEEKS"; "GOV'S LUV IN CLEAR, WON'T APPEAR"; "LENATICS WITHOUT LEADER"; "FANS THRONG STADIUM IN CANDLELIGHT VIGIL."

"Lenatics?" she gasped, looking up. "What is all this?"

"You're an icon," laughed Claude. "Apparently many people were taken with your appearances over the past year. You've got a huge fan club clamoring for your return, and I guarantee it's not because they want to laugh at you."

Lena returned the papers, folded the chair and started back to her camper with Claude. She was puzzled. "I don't understand. I was just campaigning with my future husband, going through the motions."

Claude shook his head. "It's hard for me to understand it, too. You just seem to have a way of attracting people to your side of an issue—a bold, frank, cool-under-fire way of cutting through crap and getting to the point. People say you were better than Stedman, and he was a master in logic and winning arguments."

That word "master" again. Lena remembered Anne's use of the term.

The big man continued. "Couple that with your looks and the disappearing act and you're now a cult figure."

"What if I don't want to be this icon, Claude?" she asked, looking up at his face.

"Sister, I know you too well," he smiled, meeting her glance. "Stop bullshitting me. This is what you've been waiting for all your life."

A NATION BEST SERVED HOT

Mighty words echoed through her mind: *You have the power to lead, and lead you must!* Looking back at the small pile of stones, she put her free arm through his. With a hesitant smile, she answered, "If we thought the ride before was wild…."

Arm in arm, they walked back to the camper. Rounding the last corner, they were startled by a beautiful young blonde who sat in Lena's second Walmart chair. "Who are you?" barked Claude, fully alert, eyes scanning the perimeter for additional strangers. He'd taken great pains to disguise his trip to the forest and was upset anyone had followed.

"I'm alone," replied the woman, standing. "I trailed you here, Mr. Masters. I've been following you for two weeks."

She looks familiar, thought Lena.

Holding out her hand, the woman introduced herself. "Melony Major, FOX News. A pleasure to meet you again, Mrs. Stedman."

Claude rushed forward to eject the brash youngster, who was suddenly terrified.

"Hold up, Claude," Lena raised her left hand, remembering. Instead of shaking the woman's hand, she pointed. "News conference. Something about checking bones." Claude's mouth dropped open.

"Your memory is as good as your rhetoric, Mrs. Stedman." Melony had again gathered her wits, turning a light shade of red.

"She reminds me of myself at her age," Lena remembered thinking. A flash of inspiration wormed its way into the recesses of her mind. In the first of many times to come, she heard herself speak involuntary words conjured from a spirit. Instructed to accept this stranger without reservation, she gestured toward Melony, "Call me Lena, young lady. Sit. This may be your lucky day."

DEATH COMES KNOCKING
MOOSE JAW
DECEMBER 3, 2007

THE ASSIGNMENT was simple: execute a gringo living in a log cabin miles away from civilization. The photo depicted a typical smiling WASP. The description included the words "businessman untrained in self-defense or use of weapons." After the kill, the assassin was to take pictures of the gringo's corpse, torch the cabin and return home.

The venue was the problem. Enrique Ramos had never been north of Denver. He hated cold, and December in Saskatchewan had cold written all over it. He'd already banked a quarter million US, the largest retainer of his life. Pony up the evidence to El Gato and the other half was his. Bottom line: a hot half million took the edge off a cold assignment.

Five foot even, bald and wrinkled with an oversized head and pale Dresden skin, the forty year-old Mexican national was born with a rare form of albinism. Instead of a pinkish hue, Enrique's retinas lacked pigment. Catching his eye, one could see into his brain. More alien than human, children stared in awe. Adults shied away. Looking at him made everyone nervous.

From the beginning, he was different. A product of drunken lust between two vagrants, Enrique survived by begging for handouts, picking pockets of unwary marks and pilfering garbage in the barrios of Mexico City. He was one of thousands—orphans roaming the streets risking death each day for a slice of tomorrow. Known only as "*el albinos*, the albino," as a teen he grew tired of being nameless. Finding the name Enrique Ramos in someone's pilfered wallet, the name seemed to fit, so he adopted it as his own.

A NATION BEST SERVED HOT

Oddly, it was his strangeness that scored greater handouts, earning him sustenance while others starved. Like Jack Dawkins, the Artful Dodger in Dickens' *Oliver Twist*, Enrique lived on wits, deception, acting ability and luck. People felt sorry for such an ugly, sub-human so they doled out to him more than his share. To their dismay, generous donors discovered their handouts far exceeded voluntary offerings, losing wallets and other valuables to his nimble fingers.

Ramos had one other trait necessary for success: a cold, sadistic mean streak. Killing began at an early age. He loved squeezing the life out of small animals, hearing the pitiful cries of desperation, seeing their little eyes pop before death and dismemberment. He soon graduated to small children who were helpless under his spell. Body parts strewn in alleyways were gruesome calling cards.

Loved by none, feared by all, Enrique earned his reputation based on deeds as well as superstition. He was *el loco látigo del barrio*, the crazed scourge of the barrio. To know this two-legged nightmare was to die. While other survivors formed gangs and fought over territory, Enrique foraged solo and was left alone. His visage struck fear into the most heinous minds.

At sixteen, Enrique Ramos turned a sadistic passion into a business for hire. Contract killing felt no different. He was now paid for something that came naturally. It was his ticket from squalor to luxury. A perfectionist, he never failed a mission and covered his tracks with meticulous detail. Smaller than most, Ramos never felt the need to learn self-defense. Hand-to-hand combat was unnecessary in his line of work. Killing with pistols and long range rifles, victims were merely targets—coupons to the next payday. Now in his fourth decade, Ramos had executed dozens of hits.

He packed only a small carry-on. Dressed in a casual suit, he took an early morning United flight from El Paso to Regina with one stop in Denver. Canadian Customs took note of the odd-looking stranger before welcoming the Latin businessman to Saskatchewan. His contact was waiting with a hooded winter parka, gloves, boots, a small digital camera and a loaded 9mm Sig Sauer P 226 X-Five pistol. With few words spoken, Enrique took possession of a rented late model sedan with snow tires and a map to the target's cabin.

Four-foot drifts and a minus five degree Celsius temperature greeted Enrique as he exited the airport. He had never driven in the white stuff, so he carefully guided the car through freshly-plowed city streets onto the slick highway. Traffic was light, but time was a factor with less than three hours of daylight left. The few slips and over-corrected slides brought no danger to his mission, only Latin curses. The damned cold seemed to permeate his very being, even with the heated car and hooded parka. *Cute and harmless,* he thought, seeing the reflection in the rear view mirror. *Damned if I don't look like that phone-home movie midget.* The sooner he could finish the job, the sooner he could return to the airport, ditch the car and leave this forsaken ice box for the warmth of Mexico and the remaining half of his pay.

The sixty-nine kilometers to Moose Jaw took two hours and the short side trip to the cabin another half hour. The contact had scouted the route. Enrique left the car by the road and walked a short distance through snow drifts to avoid notice. This was the hard part. Enrique shivered through seventy yards of torture before sighting the cabin. There were two vehicles. He expected only one. In addition to the target, one or more additional people were likely inside.

A second or third person meant uncertainty. Ramos hated uncertainty. On a warmer day, he would have waited and gathered information, making sure of the odds. Waiting was not an option at dusk and minus five Celsius. Pulling out his pistol, he softly climbed three steps to the deck and entrance door.

TRACY HAD JUST WALKED out of the bedroom. Packed and ready to leave, she was carrying a large suitcase in one hand and travel bag in the other. Jerry was tidying up the cabin, not wanting to leave a mess for the next occupant. Simon had arranged everything. They were to drive south and in three days meet the team of thirty hired mercenaries at a designated warehouse in the outskirts of El Paso. Former CIA, Marines, Rangers and trusted civilian commandos, all battle tested killers, would be given individual duties in a clandestine, surgical night strike.

The weather was clear. Usually talkative, both Tracy and Jerry were lost in thought as they prepared for an evening departure. Neither doubted the finality of their mission. Both knew it was their lives against Carón's. Death was certain for at least one person. Tracy had decided to resign from the DEA. It was important she carry out the mission as an individual, not as a government employee. Her pre-dated termination letter sat on the dining room table to be mailed on the way south.

A NATION BEST SERVED HOT

The planned attack was in direct violation of laws and agreements between the two countries. Anything less than total surprise and perfectly executed success would result in an embarrassing international incident. The odds against success were enormous under the best conditions. Something always seemed to go wrong when so many operatives were involved. Beside the generous advances, the only leverage against leaks and subsequent mission failure was a large bonus promised to each mercenary for his silence and a successful completion.

A loud knock interrupted their reverie. "Has to be Ol' Dan," Jerry said. He glanced at Tracy, admonishing her, "Now be nice." Reaching for the latch to open the door, he added, "You were pretty rude to him last night and...."

A strange, hooded apparition stood at the entrance. Jerry recalled seeing something like it in a popular children's movie. Before he could speak, the creature's right hand rose with a pistol. "What the...?"

Tracy had come up behind a second too late. Reacting with instinct, her lifting toe-kick altered the pistol only slightly as it fired. The bullet tore the flesh from Jerry's left underarm, knocking him backwards. Her second hinging kick landed squarely on the assassin's midriff. With a woof, he fell backwards down the three stairs onto the frozen walkway.

Stunned, Enrique Ramos realized too late he still held the pistol. Following the short creature down the steps, Tracy stomped hard onto his wrist, forcing the gun from his grip. Like an anaconda seizing its prey, she fell on him, entwining her legs, arms and body, lashing his limbs in a two person pretzel. She cracked his neck viciously to the left. Enrique's last sensation before blacking out was extreme pain. Every joint in his body had been stretched to the limit.

Her opponent subdued, Tracy retrieved the pistol and frisked the man's clothes for additional weapons. Finding none, she rushed inside to Jerry, who was sprawled in shock on the cabin floor and bleeding. Grabbing a towel from the bathroom, she whipped it into a tourniquet, wrapping it tightly around the arm to staunch the flow. Absent spurting blood, her training told her no artery was hit. *Just a painful flesh wound,* she thought. "Hold this tight," she admonished Jerry. "You gonna faint on me?"

"No, no," he mumbled, barely coherent. "What the hell just happened?"

"Bastard tried to kill us," she replied, leaving him to grab her tote bag and scrounge for handcuffs. "It was a hit, Jerry. You're very lucky. Six more inches to the left and you'd be dead."

Finding the cuffs, she returned outside, flopped the comatose victim on his face and secured the wrists behind him. She dragged the body inside, letting the small man fall in a lump, and closed the door.

"First aid kit is in the closet," Jerry pointed with a stronger voice. "Bet anything this is Carón's work," he followed with a nod toward the hooded captive.

Five minutes later, with the wound bathed in antiseptic and tightly taped in gauze, Jerry sat in a chair as Tracy pulled back the assassin's hood, revealing a bald gnomish head.

"Bastard looks like E.T., doesn't he?" exclaimed Jerry.

"What are we going to do with him?" asked Tracy, finding a pulse in the man's neck. Rummaging through his pockets, she removed a small digital camera and a set of car keys. "Rental car; has to be close by. Bet he was going to shoot you and take pictures to prove the hit. Don't know how long he'll be out."

An ominous thought crossed Jerry's mind. "What if he wasn't alone?"

"Back in a few." Tracy grabbed the Sig Sauer, checked the load and gave it to Jerry. "If he comes to, either bash him with this or shoot him. Don't care which." Taking the stranger's keys, she pulled on her parka and boots and grabbed her pistol. Cautiously opening the door, she surveyed the area in a crouch before leaving to search, following the man's snow prints.

She returned in about fifteen minutes. The assassin was still out cold. Jerry was sitting in the same chair. "Nothing. He's solo," she said, pointing to the assassin. "Car's parked at the driveway entrance. It's a rental from Regina. I checked the glove compartment. Found these."

Tracy dropped a number of items on the table. Beside a local road map was the rental agreement, an airplane boarding pass for a return trip to El Paso the next day, and a Mexican passport, all in the name of Enrique Ramos. "Definitely a hit," she said. "Felix Carón is written all over this guy."

"What should we do with the little creep?" Jerry asked, leafing through the documents. "Don't want the law involved. We've got a schedule to keep."

Tracy sat beside him at the table and traded ideas. After a few minutes discussing scenarios like killing and burying the body, she offered, "What about Ol' Dan Down the Road?"

A NATION BEST SERVED HOT

ENRIQUE RAMOS woke slowly to a cold dog nose sniffing and prodding his face. His first sensation was pain. Every muscle and joint was on fire. He lay on a wood floor completely naked except for boots. His wrists and ankles were shackled with taught rope. Like a roll of thunder, the dog commenced a low growl before backing off to reveal a disheveled man staring from a nearby chair.

"Finally awake, eh?" the man chuckled. "Damned if you don't look like a giant grub worm."

"*¿Quién...donde?* Who...where?" Ramos stammered with a mouth dry as parchment. It all started to come back: the door opening, his gun firing, some banshee woman kicking and wrestling him to the ground.

The old man rose and, with a savage yank, grabbed the tied wrists, dragging him closer to the fireplace which crackled with flame.

Enrique screamed through excruciating pain. Wrenched upward from the back, his arms felt on the verge of separation. "Fuckin' beaner," spat the old man. "Try to kill my friend, eh? Now I kill you. Been a while. Squirrel 'n deer get old. A bit puny, y'be, but you'll taste mighty good roasted on a spit with seasoning." He chuckled and left to retrieve something from the table.

Ramos could not believe his ears. He'd never felt such intense pain, but the old man's words were more ominous. He stammered incoherently in Spanish as the man returned with three cans and began spray-painting his nude body, starting with the buttocks. "Gonna have some fun first, ain't we, Barf?" the old man laughed. The dog opened its large mouth and began panting, rivulets of saliva falling from its giant, slack-jawed tongue. Its eyes were glued to the victim who was rapidly becoming a bald-bodied candy cane.

¡Santa Madre de Dios, estoy en el infierno! Mother of God, I am in Hell! cringed the helpless Mexican, as the old man finished his multicolored art and yanked Ramos to his feet. Throwing open the cabin door, the frigid Canadian night air pricked at Enrique like a thousand needles. Ol' Dan's boot shoved him through the door into a snowdrift.

"Y'got a five minute start, spic," shouted the crazed geezer. "Then me 'n ol' Barf, we be comin' fer ya."

Enrique Ramos began to run—a fluorescent apparition staggering into the frozen darkness. Shocked with cold, he made it only a few dozen yards before falling again, knowing the Devil had come for his due. *How ironic,* he thought as a blanket of numbness slowly replaced the needles of pain, *to die in a frigid inferno.* Looking up, his last conscious vision was of colored lights dancing through the trees, as if tiny ghosts of Yule had come to usher him home.

JERRY CALVIN and Tracy Henderson never heard the two shots echoing through the forest. They were halfway to Regina. Arriving at the deserted airport, Jerry had parked the rental car, depositing keys and agreement in the external kiosk. He wore leather gloves to avoid leaving fingerprints in the vehicle. No one saw him climb in Tracy's SUV and return to the cabin. Stowing their belongings in both vehicles, they departed Moose Jaw. Jerry would never forget the cold Canadian wilderness, where life and death were reduced to rudimentary terms. Ol' Dan Down the Road and his lopsided cur belonged. He did not.

Heading south, both Jerry and Tracy were lost in thought. Ahead lay a deadly battle with a vicious drug lord and his Mexican army. Hell would be paid.

Only the price remained uncertain.

JABBERWOCKY
AMERICA AT LARGE
DECEMBER, 2007

THE VOICES wouldn't leave her alone. Like uninvited relatives, they came to visit Lena's subconscious every night, interrupting badly needed sleep. They were masculine voices, insistent, demanding attention, filling her mind with unwanted instructions and facts.

Where was Anne? She could answer Anne. Not these mental harbingers who were cramming her brain with information.

SILENCE! She was almost getting used to the abuse. It was how she imagined Marine Corps basic training: hurry up and learn; shut up and listen; ***MOVE YOUR MENTAL ASS!***

Every morning she would wake up exhausted, as if she had run a marathon, only to face another day of appearances. After an extensive interview and short trial period, Lena liked what she saw in Melony Major and hired the fiery young woman as her personal publicist and appearance coordinator, doubling her FOX salary. In the last two months since Lena emerged from forest seclusion, Melony had booked her seventeen times for Florida and national appearances. Miami, Orlando, Chicago, New York, L.A., back to New York. Glitzy parties, book offers, radio and television interviews. Everyone wanted to know: "What really happened on your wedding night?" and "Why did you disappear soon after your husband's death?"

Her answers to FOX's Greta Van Susteren were typical. "Win was stubborn. He skipped his last two physical exams. Said he didn't have the time and thought he was in excellent health," she explained. "According to the autopsy, he was a heart attack waiting to happen. The duties of governor plus the stress of the wedding caught up to him. The dear man died in my arms.

"As for my disappearance, I just wanted to be alone for a while," Lena continued with tears in her eyes. Pausing for effect, she concluded, "Anyone who has lost a beloved spouse should be able to understand and respect my privacy to mourn a man I had grown to admire and cherish. The State of Florida lost a good leader. I lost a husband."

Reaching for wads of Kleenex, viewers across the nation had fallen in love with Lena Mills. Even the stoic Van Susteren seemed to shed a tear.

Radio and television talk shows vied for Lena; paparazzi stalked her; fans—"Lenatics"—followed her; newspapers filled columns with sensational tidbits of her life, mostly fabricated.

Depending on perspective, Lena was either blessed or cursed with good looks. She accepted most of the notoriety and posed for pictures with grace, but she drew the line with *Playboy*'s six figure offer for a photo spread. It was not because she lacked confidence in her fifty-seven-year-young physique. Rather, Melony got wind of the proposed insipid byline: "DID THESE THIGHS OF THUNDER PUT LOVE GUV SIX FEET UNDER?" and leaked it to the press.

Sensing an opportunity to humor her saucy reputation, Lena endured three days of badgering, waiting for the perfect venue to retaliate—a scheduled interview with Oprah Winfrey, undisputed queen of daytime television talk shows. After the usual fawning banter, Oprah boldly breached the subject of *Playboy*'s offer. "Don't you think it rather amazing that you've been asked to do a nude pictorial at your age? If you don't mind me asking, aren't you in your late fifties?"

Feigning indignity and trying her best to keep a straight face, Lena answered by taking a completely different tack. "I'm fifty-seven and damned proud of my figure, Oprah," she huffed. "Thunder thighs, indeed." Looking straight into the camera, she continued, "Hugh Hefner, you're eighty-one, an octo-trog. You should crawl back under a rock." She added a challenge: "Meet with me face to face. Man up and take your Hef-a-lumps, you girlie geezer. I'll box your ears and wash your mouth out with Geritol!"

Eyes big as saucers, Oprah's jaw dropped. The talk show queen fell backwards on the stage sofa, holding her sides in laughter. The studio audience members rose to their feet in unison and exploded, chanting "LENA! LENA! LENA...!"

Next day the press went ballistic. Newspapers across the country vied for the cleverest headline: "LENA LOBS ONE AT HEFNER"; "LENA

A NATION BEST SERVED HOT

SAYS, 'PUT 'EM UP, GIRLIE GEEZER!'"; "LENA RIPS HEF A NEW ONE"; "MAE WEST LIVES! – HEFNER LENA-TIZED"; and "THIGHS OF THUNDER TEAR HEF ASUNDER."

The following week, on an appearance with Katie Couric, the CBS Evening News anchor, Lena experienced her first live mystical intervention. She had begun the interview with light-hearted bantering, admitting the *Playboy* dust up was "blown out of proportion" by the press.

"I have nothing against Hugh Hefner," she stated. "As a matter of fact, he called me a few days ago and we had a good laugh over it."

Suddenly turning serious, Lena surprised her host as well as herself. In a deeper, insistent voice, she leaned toward her host and abruptly changed subjects. "Katie, last June my husband warned everyone who would listen there is a dark financial period is coming to our country, indeed the world. Win was sure we're due for another big recession." Turning toward the camera, she continued. "Stock values have grown to all time highs and the real estate market is out of control. The fools in Congress have relaxed the rules for obtaining mortgages, encouraging home sales to people who can't afford the payments."

Lena felt like a passenger on a runaway train. *What am I doing? Why am I saying these things?* She realized too late it was one of the Voices speaking through her.

"I believe we're just now seeing the beginning of this downturn, and our country—indeed the world—is in for the worst recession since the Great Depression."

Katie Couric looked across the table in amazement. Her guest had a far-away, trance-like look. "You're scaring me, Lena, and I'm sure you're scaring everyone watching you," she said, wondering what these proclamations would do to her ratings. Sensing a gotcha moment, the news anchor seized the opportunity to take down this celebrity upstart. "What makes you so certain of what you are saying? After all, you're not an economist?"

Still in a trance, Lena ignored the loaded questions and continued. "I advise everyone to get out of the stock and real estate markets immediately and put your money into cash. Mark my words: this time next year the American stock market will have lost half its value, big banks will be on the verge of failure, credit will dry up and most businesses will all but come to a halt...."

Out of the corner of her eye, Katie Couric could see her producer giving her a throat slashing sign. She interrupted the crazed woman before her with an outstretched arm. "I'm sorry, Lena. We're coming into a hard break." Looking into the camera with a nervous smile, Katie ended with, "We'll be right back."

The camera's red light blinked off. Couric was livid. "Just what the hell do you think you're doing?" she spit. "I've had enough of you. This interview is over. Get out!"

Too stunned to answer, Lena rose from her chair and walked out of the studio in a daze. *What just happened? I'm out of control.* She was trembling.

Melony Major met her backstage. Draping a comforting arm around Lena, she ushered her to the ground floor and their waiting limo, thinking: *The poor woman is exhausted. She's having a nervous breakdown.*

"Cancel all my appearances. Get me out of New York. Take me home." Leaning into Melony, Lena was shaking as she sighed, "I've lost my mind."

OPERATION "CAT SCRATCH FEVER"
EL PASO/CUIDAD JUAREZ
DECEMBER 6 - 9, 2007

LETTERS AND NUMBERS were used. Names got in the way. Simon Morris had coordinated everything through a retired Special Forces one-star. Loyalty and secrecy were paramount to success. Jerry had authorized Simon full access to the Rely payoff, but money was secondary to the thirty steel-hardened mercenaries arriving singly and in groups at the empty El Paso warehouse. Trained sharpshooters, all were retired from active service. Most had fought in teams from Desert Storm and Shield operations. No stronger bond exists than the loyalty of battle-tested platoon mates—"Bands of Brothers." Backslaps, grins and mock profanity echoed through the building as the warriors converged, reunited after years of absence.

Logistics were complete. A month long campaign of costly espionage and detailed satellite downloads had yielded schematics of the compound, its alarm system, patrol schedules and other operational routines. El Gato's personal contacts and habits had been crunched for maximum vulnerability. The compound was designed to thwart the most probable threat—an all-out frontal assault. Since the cave implosion, the drug lord rarely left his main house. It would be most difficult to strike at him holed in his den—difficult, but not impossible.

Tracy, Jerry, Simon and the one-star planned strategy while the soldiers were assigned motels and told to await further instructions. The general lobbied for a coordinated, bastion-storming night attack. "These men are trained for this," he argued.

"Too messy. Maximum casualties," vetoed Tracy, not at all intimidated by the one-star. "We have to assume this kind of attack will trigger additional reinforcements and the local police. The worst case would be a prolonged battle. We have to strike quickly, quietly with precision. El Gato is the target, not half the population of Juarez."

All agreed an element was missing to a successful assault. They needed the assistance of someone inside—someone who had gained the war lord's trust. From discreet payoffs to multiple sources, one name surfaced as the clear choice.

WELL PAST MIDNIGHT, an exhausted Jorge Cruz pulled into his driveway, anticipating a few hours of respite before another round of brow beating by his boss. His ulcer was acting up again, and before exiting the car he swallowed another antacid. El Gato's violent temper kept him on edge. The vision of a bullet entering his predecessor's head constantly haunted him. "Don't shoot the messenger" meant nothing to Felix Carón. Working for the crazed tyrant meant every day could be Jorge's last. Paid well for his service but hopelessly indentured to the Devil incarnate, no amount of money was worth the stress he endured.

Margarita and the children were his whole life—his only reason to exist. Home was Jorge's only refuge. Opening the door, the last things he expected to see were a pistol pointed at his head and his family huddled in a corner guarded by two burly gringos. Suddenly the painful ulcer was the least of his worries.

THE PLAN WAS SIMPLE, its execution complex. Tracy was adamant. The motel room was small, but her words seemed to echo off the walls. "I have to do this, Jerry. The risk is irrelevant."

"You'll be alone. Even if Cruz cooperates, at least two other guards are in the hacienda at all times," he argued.

"You have to understand," she replied. "I know this man. He will want to be alone with me. He doesn't like an audience when he rapes. I can handle him while the other guards are distracted by the assault outside."

"What if he recognizes you?"

"He won't. Not only have I gone through extensive facial restoration, but I have learned to disguise myself. Aunt Lena taught me well. Carón will be focused on his lust until all hell breaks loose. Cruz will cooperate.

A NATION BEST SERVED HOT

We have his family. Once he gets me in, I will do the rest."

Jerry objected, "I don't like it, especially the part about me staying out of the action."

"You're still injured and would only be in the way. Face it, Jerry. The rest of us are professionals. You supplied the money and you'll coordinate the extraction."

"What did the general say about your plan?"

Tracy shrugged. "He thinks I'm nuts too, but it's my ass. He's concerned with the mission, not me."

Jerry looked deeply into her eyes and saw the futility of further argument. Jaw set in granite, the love of his life stared back. The look on her face frightened him. Tracy Henderson was a force impossible to deter.

It was Sunday, the day of reckoning. Death would come knocking on the Devil's door this moonless December night.

EXECUTION
NEAR CUIDAD JUAREZ
SUNDAY, DECEMBER 9, 2007

"Before you embark on a journey of revenge, dig two graves."
Confucius (BC551-BC479)

FELIX CARÓN sat back in his spacious lounge chair with a cigarillo in one hand and snifter of expensive brandy in the other. He exhaled a sigh of contentment. A bit of culture would top off a day filled with the rewards of recent commerce. Five million US in hundred dollar bills sat in his safe, proceeds from three successful shipments to brokers in the States. The money more than made up for the irritation he felt toward Ramos, who had not checked in since last Monday. His rental car had been returned to the Regina airport, but Ramos had missed his flight home. Six days and no phone call from the albino. *He's either dead or skipped out with his retainer,* Carón had fumed. A simple job: knock off the damned gringo, was all he expected. *I'm surrounded by incompetents.*

The recently completed theater was about to be christened with a gringo actress performing his favorite operetta, known locally as "Lulu's Dance of Death." According to Cruz, the actress was strikingly beautiful. She'd better be. He had nearly choked when his aide told him what he'd paid for the command performance.

El Gato had seen the act many times in nightclubs around Mexico. The memory of Jack the Ripper plunging his knife into a luscious virgin aroused his libido. *I will get my money's worth,* he sneered. *Tonight I will be El Ripper!*

Stage lights dimmed as a recording of Alban Berg's twelve tone dissonance commenced. A beautiful, dark haired dancer entered from the side. Dressed in a white gown and glove while strapped to a handsome mannequin dressed in top hat and tails, she flowed across the small stage, whirling effortlessly to the music.

A NATION BEST SERVED HOT

Cruz was right, nodded Carón to himself, his groin beginning to stir. *This one is a beauty.*

First at a distance, with every turn she inched closer, her eyes focused on the one man audience. *She has fire, passion!* thought Carón, staring back. *Those eyes.... Where have I seen those eyes?*

From months of close contact, Tracy knew El Gato's expressions. *Does he recognize me?* she wondered. *I can't wait any longer.*

In a gesture too quick to notice, one of her free fingers pushed a tiny button concealed in the glove's heel. The real show was about to begin.

Carón put aside his cigarillo and brandy, stood and took a step toward Tracy. "You!" he snarled, bending over to reach for a knife strapped to his right boot.

With a single motion, Tracy ripped away the Velcroed mannequin, leaving her in a sleek white spandex leotard. A raucous alarm rang out. Shouts came from the adjoining room as she leaped at the drug lord with a vicious leg kick to his head, sending him flying backwards over the lounge chair. Twelve tone recorded cacophony blended with alarm blasts as Tracy pounced on his torso with a thump. Felix Carón howled as she ripped arm and hand tendons while stripping the knife from his right hand with a vicious side armbar. Scrambling to a mounted headlock, she grasped the knife in her free white-gloved hand, bringing it to eye level. Tracy's lips nestled next to his left ear as she hissed, "Not so brave without your fat sidekick, are you?"

¡No, no debieses estar viva!" No, no, you're dead!" he cried.

"Saluda me al Diablo." Give the Devil my regards." Tracy rasped as she sliced deeply across his throat from ear to ear.

El Gato's scream lapsed into a bubbling gurgle as blood gushed in spurts from the lethal wound.

With months of repressed rage, lightning eyes and a feral cry, Tracy Henderson went to work....

OUTSIDE, ALL HELL had broken loose. Thirty riflemen, dressed in black hooded assault gear, had surrounded the compound some thirty yards from the perimeter. Through a series of taps and whispered commands on their shoulder-mounted radios, each had positioned with ideal vantage to specified human and canine targets. Adjusting NightForce scopes and tripods on their special order NSWC "Crane" SEAL Recon Rifles, they focused on their prey and waited patiently for Tracy's signal. Equipped with KAC Quick Detach sound suppressors, at the signal all thirty rifles spit in close unison. Heads exploded, bodies wrenched backward and dogs yelped, most writhing in brief dance before collapsing lifeless to the ground. Someone inside the long security building set off an alarm as the remaining guards raced outside with two men from the hacienda. Within seconds, all met the same deadly fate.

Jerry and the general watched the action from one of the extraction vehicles. "Like a state fair shooting gallery," Jerry remarked, in awe of the carnage.

The general remained silent, focused on the big picture. The initial volley was over in fifteen seconds. "Phase two, phase two," he barked into his radio. Like shadowed wraiths, all thirty mercenaries stormed through gates to finish off the wounded, steadily working their way toward the hacienda, alert for additional guards. Seeing none, a steady stream of "Clear"s sounded. Jerry and the general raced to the compound.

JORGE CRUZ had braced for the worst, convinced he was living his last moments on Earth. He had followed instructions to perfection, first convincing the boss to hire the dancer—*"Ella es una belleza, una buena cogida.* She is a beauty, a good lay,"—then arranging her passage into the compound. Ushering the dancer through the back entrance, he had never seen such a cold, determined stare. It was as if the woman were in a trance. Before leaving her in a small dressing room to prepare, he was shaking as he implored, *Señorita, mi vida no vale nada.* My life is nothing. *¡Téngase misericordia a mi familia por favor!* Please have mercy on my family."

For an instant the brunette beauty broke from her trance. Wordlessly, she reached out to gently grasp his hand. Was she crying or smiling?

The door closed and Jorge gathered himself for the inevitable, seeking to inform the boss the beautiful senorita awaited the pleasure of his audience.

Fifteen minutes had elapsed. Jorge and two guards waited outside the closed theater door as the music commenced. Unfamiliar orchestral dissonance wafted from the adjacent room. The guards jammed ears to the door with voyeuristic anticipation, betting each other how long before the

A NATION BEST SERVED HOT

woman's screams would rise above the strange music. One had wagered three minutes, the other four.

Both were wrong. Slightly less than two minutes had elapsed when the alarm blasted, knocking them back in shock. Anticipating the raucous sound, Jorge sprang to action. Drawing his pistol, he shoved both guards toward the front door, shouting, *"Fuera. ¡Apúrase! Comprobaré encendido a El Gato.* Outside. Hurry! I will check on El Gato."

Guns drawn, the guards flung open the ornate front door. Taking only two steps outside before each head exploded in a shower of bone and bloody brain matter, both torsos jerked a ten second Saint Vitas' Dance as spasms of blood shot from headless arteries over the Grecian marble foyer.

Jorge Cruz surveyed the carnage in shock. Inside the theater, El Gato's brief scream interrupted the orchestral score as it rose to an apex of intensity. Sliding against the wall to a sitting position, Cruz flung aside his pistol and prayed to his beloved Christ for undeserved mercy.

Over the next three minutes, muffled rifle shots grew louder as the mercenaries approached. The first team member arrived at the open front door, stepping gingerly over the two headless corpses. Waving his rifle from side to side, he spotted a suppliant Jorge sitting against the wall, quivering with tears streaming down his face and hands raised in surrender. A voice shouted from behind, "Stop! He's a good one."

Jerry Calvin approached and kneeled before the sniveling man, pulling him to his feet. "This one lives. Let him go to his family." Jerry's mind was on Tracy inside the theater as he shoved the trembling man toward the front door.

Cruz stumbled outside in a fog of cautious euphoria. *Could it be? Am I to be spared to join my beloved Margarita and the children?* Looking to the star-lit sky, he never saw the general approach from behind—never felt the shot that blew his head away.

"No witnesses," mumbled the one-star, disgusted with civilian sentiment. The general glanced toward Jerry with disgust and defiance.

Witnessing the execution, his anger rising, Jerry vowed the arrogant general would pay. But now he had a more immediate concern.

※

AS HE ENTERED the theater, Jerry would be haunted for the rest of his life by the scene before him. The music had run its course. Tracy was a scantily-clad apparition covered in blood. As he approached to take her in his arms, he pulled up short.

Her lips formed a hideous snarl—half smile, half grimace. Tracy's eyes seemed to be staring through him to another dimension. Kneeling over the naked corpse of Felix Carón, she was a lioness on a fresh kill. With eyes and mouth wide open from his final scream, the drug lord's body had been stabbed from head to toe like a birthday piñata. In her right hand Tracy held a large, blood-soaked knife. Only when he saw the gaping hole at Carón's crotch did he recognize the bloody objects she held in her left.

"Holy Mother of God!" exclaimed the general from behind. Not since 'Nam had he seen such subhuman butchery.

"Leave us." Jerry pointed to the door, fighting back the bile in his throat.

"Ten minutes and we're out of here," barked the one-star, resentful of the order. Hoots of surprise could be heard from a nearby room. The general went off to supervise the looting of El Gato's safe.

Stripping off Tracy's leotard and guiding her to a back room lavatory, Jerry was shaking as he turned on the shower so he could gently scrub blood from her hair down to her toes. Tracy stood in a wordless trance, neither assisting nor resisting, as he dried and dressed her with the clothes she had worn to the compound. Gathering everything including the orchestral CD, he exited with her through the back door to a waiting SUV.

ALL RIFLES, remaining ammunition, bloody leotard and the lethal knife were buried in a deep grave a good distance away from the compound. After an hour of site preparation leaving a staged killing field, the team crammed into ten ordinary cars and SUVs, melting into the moonless night. Entering the U.S. sporadically over a half hour period, all vehicles and passengers made it through Customs without extensive searches.

Mission accomplished. No casualties. Mexican authorities would assume the massacre to be a territorial turf war between rival gangs. After a series of skirmishes and assassinations, the lucrative void would be filled. A thriving drug trade with its graft and carnage would resume with minor interruption. Only the names would change. Felix Carón, El Gato, would be remembered as one of a long list of ruthless drug lords who died as they lived—violently.

In the back seat of his SUV, driven by a nameless soldier, Jerry cradled and rocked the only person he would ever worship, murmuring through his own tears, "It's over; it's over." The border guard looked through the window and assumed Tracy was sleeping. Only Jerry could feel the soundless, wracking shudders of a warrior who had prevailed to give her enemy more than his due—someone who had followed her victim into Purgatory.

Safely back in the States, Jerry phoned a very relieved Simon Morris with two cryptic requests. "Meet me at the warehouse with a doctor and a strong sedative, no questions asked. Also, arrange for a waiting helicopter to fly both Tracy and me to the Waco VA Hospital within the next hour."

At the warehouse, Jerry handed her off to the waiting doctor, walked inside and instructed Simon to distribute the final payments to the soldiers. Morris could only stare and shake his head as a five million dollar bonus caused a roar to rise from the troops. "You men have earned every dollar. I don't want the blood money," he stated with handshakes all around.

Taking Simon aside, he instructed, "Let them divide the contents of the safe. Release the hostages and give Cruz's widow the general's share."

Morris objected, "He's not going to take this well. What if he threatens to expose the operation to the feds?"

"The asshole still gets his fee for services rendered," explained Jerry. Gesturing toward the mercenaries, he continued, "Before you are thirty reasons he won't talk. In addition, he wouldn't dare jeopardize his own federal pension."

Morris was visibly shaken, objecting, "You mean I'm the one who has to confront the general with this news?"

"Get a grip, Simon," Jerry ordered. "Go earn your million dollar bonus. I have a more important problem."

After the short conference, Jerry carefully loaded a heavily sedated Tracy into the Bronco for the short trip to the airfield. *I hope Simon is as fast on his feet as he is with his mouth,* Jerry rationalized.

As the helicopter flew east with the pilot and two passengers to meet dawn's early light, one question lodged in Jerry's brain like a malignant tumor: *Was anything human left in Tracy Henderson?*

VA HOSPITAL
WACO, TEXAS
MONDAY, DECEMBER 17, 2007

"Where there is love there is life."
Mahatma Gandhi (1869 – 1948)

DR. PATRICIA SCHULTZ looked down upon her restrained patient. In her twenty-three years of practice, Dr. Schultz had lost count of the number of post-traumatic stress disorder patients she had treated, nearly all victims of war. With proper and consistent medication, counseling and time, most had been released with confidence into society. An unfortunate few would never recover and were permanently institutionalized, deemed too risky to chance an experiment with freedom. No amount of medication or counseling could mitigate these minds, whose hope of rational sanity was forever lost.

Then there was the third group, the recidivists who seemingly responded to treatment but retained stubborn demons. These patients eventually returned, most in worse condition than before.

She was looking at one of the latter. Not only had Tracy Henderson responded well enough to her treatment and medication to qualify for prior release, but she was actually cracking jokes. All of this was a façade, of course. Upon seeing Tracy return, Dr. Schultz had re-studied the woman's history, chastising herself. *I should have known. I should have seen the signals.*

Prior sexual abuse and the recent six months of torture had eaten at Tracy like a virile cancer that neither medications, counseling nor time could cure. Just below a surface of normalcy lurked a visceral hatred reserved for the Mexican drug lord, Felix Carón. Tracy hid it well, the doctor had to admit. She could see it clearly now. This personal mandate for revenge had simply been too strong for conventional therapy.

A NATION BEST SERVED HOT

Because she posed no outward signs of danger to others or herself, Tracy had been released. At the time, Dr. Schultz rationalized the obvious. It would be suicide for Tracy to act out her revenge alone on someone as powerful and protected as Carón. She was a survivor, a strong woman, certainly not prone to suicide.

"Tracy Henderson's release is conditional," she had written Keith Westen, the DEA supervisor. "I trust you will prohibit her from acting out any fantasy of retribution. If this means desk duty or a leave due to disability, I will underwrite your decision. For the foreseeable future, she must be prohibited from any field duty that includes the possibility of violence."

That was then.

This was now. It had been a week since the handsome young man brought Tracy back to her care. Other than cries of "No! No!" in response to attempts at rousing her from a constant stupor, Tracy remained unresponsive. Nourishment, medication and liquids had to be administered intravenously. Locked inside this defensive shell of lethargy lived a once vibrant woman. Finding the key to the lock was looking more doubtful with each passing day.

As it was with her colleagues, years of service had numbed Dr. Schultz against pity toward her patients, allowing her to concentrate on clinical solutions. Tracy Henderson's ordeals were so grievous, they touched the doctor's soul. Since early childhood, the poor woman had never enjoyed happiness or security. Sexual abuse and torture had banished a normal psyche, substituting basic survival instincts and a singular feral focus on revenge.

What had happened since Tracy's release took even that away, leaving a breathing but shattered carcass. *Life hands everyone lemons,* Dr. Schultz mused. *This poor thing never had a chance to make lemonade.*

The man who delivered Tracy to the hospital seemed devastated. He was someone who obviously cared, spending every day patiently waiting for updates. Schultz had grilled him that first day about the specific trauma Tracy last suffered. She purposely met him in Tracy's room, hoping some of the conversation would register in the comatose woman's mind.

"What I have to say is strictly between us and must never leave this room," Jerry Calvin stated. "I'm talking doctor-patient confidentiality, right? I cannot stress how important this is to her safety, and her safety is your top priority. I must have your word, Dr. Schultz."

"Of course you have it," Schultz had replied to the cryptic demand, unaware she was being prepared for an astounding revelation.

Jerry produced an El Paso newspaper. The headline screamed, "DRUG LORD MASSACRE – 'EL GATO' SLAIN." Two sub-headlines read, "RIVAL CARTELS TAKE CREDIT – VIE FOR CONTROL" and "ANARCHY IN THE STREETS OF JUAREZ."

"The assassination of Felix Carón and his gang was no cartel takeover," Jerry explained. "Neither was there any official U.S. intervention." Jerry was used to studying faces for signs of weakness. Finding none with the doctor, he continued, hardening his demeanor as he dropped the bomb: "Tracy resigned from the DEA a week before we met with a group of hired mercenaries. We took out the son of a bitch and his whole compound of thugs. Tracy personally killed Carón."

Patricia Schultz gasped, "Who are you? This better not be some kind of a sick joke. Are you telling me the truth?"

During the next half hour, Jerry described his and Tracy's histories with Carón along with the planning process and execution of the raid. Dr. Schultz listened without interruption, studying the man. He had an underlying confidence, a boldness stopping short of arrogance. Jerry Calvin knew what he wanted and how to get it. He was a gambler unafraid of risk. Tracy complemented him with her stubborn determination. The gambler had no doubt met his match.

"I've never met a braver person in my life," he summarized. "Over my objections, it was her plan to confront the bastard one-on-one. She not only killed the drug lord, she butchered him. When I came upon the bloody scene, the look on her face convinced me she had snapped. Butchering Carón drove her over the edge.

"I love this woman, Doc. Please tell me you can bring her back. I'm begging you."

The confident Jerry had disappeared. He was crying. Dr. Schultz also felt tears building, but knew she had to speak unvarnished truth. "Mr. Calvin, I fear this is going to be a long rehabilitation. At worst, she'll never respond. You are welcome to visit her any time or stay with her. Talk to her. Keep asking her to come back. Physically, she is in perfect health, but over time her body will atrophy, possibly shut down. Her will to return to a world where she's only known abuse and violence will depend on someone breaking through, convincing her that two things she's barely known—love and security—await.

"We can keep her comfortable and calm. Someone she trusts will have to do the rest. I sincerely hope you're that person."

A NATION BEST SERVED HOT

With that, she rose to hug the young man lost in grief. "May I ask—are you religious?"

"No, doc," Jerry admitted. "I don't know what I believe, especially now."

"Neither do I," she whispered. "But for times like these, I feel prayer has no address or statute of limitations."

With that, she left the room to a helpless man so used to control. Jerry pulled a chair next to the bed, held the patient's hand and whispered, "Please come back to me, Trace."

"I CAN SEE CLEARLY NOW...."
Johnny Nash - 1972
OCALA NATIONAL FOREST
SATURDAY, DECEMBER 15, 2007

HERE SHE WAS, on a brisk, sun-filled day, stuck outside an old camper in the middle of nowhere. It was the same spot she had first met Lena Mills Stedman, the most exasperating person she had ever known. Melony Major was fuming at herself for taking big money to nursemaid a borderline schizo over a promising career at FOX. How could she have been so stupid?

Sure, Lena was exciting, creative, captivating—all those things and more. She was the best spellbinding, off-the-cuff speaker Melony had ever seen—a woman with unlimited leadership potential. Call it what you will—charisma, pizzazz? Things that drew her to Lena were the same things that captured her many followers—the magnetic aura of self-confidence, mid-American values and common sense. She could debate with the best on almost any subject. Unpredictable, Lena could turn on the southern charm one minute, crack a good joke the next or lash out with biting sarcasm, leaving her foes as stammering shells of submission. Two months of building that aura with the media, and with it the rush of being close to a star on a meteoric path—all of it had been dashed in one embarrassing breakdown on national television.

They had returned to Lena's Orlando apartment, where both packed suitcases with a week's worth of attire. All of Melony's clothes were business chic, so Lena financed a complete casual overhaul for her young assistant. After catching up with Claude's business affairs and introducing Melony to the staff at Chameleon, Lena took her old camper out of storage again and they headed north to the same remote Ocala Forest campsite.

A NATION BEST SERVED HOT

Melony had canceled all Lena's appearances "until further notice." Here they were again, hiding in exile. What was it about this place that so fascinated Lena Mills?

"Someday I'll tell you, when you're ready to know," her boss replied to the question.

"You sound like my Gramma." Melony was miffed but let the subject slide.

Lena had asked politely, but Melony could see it was more of an order: "Please stay put at the campsite until I return. By the way, this came for you yesterday." Lena produced a package with an El Paso return address: Carl Blackstone, Esq., Cantor, Morris, Blackstone, et al, Attorneys at Law, P.A. It was Gramma Mary Lou's trust attorney. "I had to sign for it, so it must be important."

Since agreeing to work for Lena, Melony had notified the law office, changing her forwarding address to Lena's apartment. Setting the envelope aside, she asked her boss, "When do you think you'll be back?"

"Don't know, my dear," Lena replied. She started walking with that cheap folding chair down the wooded pathway, adding cryptically, "I have to find some answers."

Setting off down the path, Lena had a faraway look in her eyes.

Find some answers. In the woods? Was her guru a sasquatch? Oh well, Melony thought, *I'm nineteen years old; I can always get another job; the pay is great and there's always Prozac. Think I'll ride this train a little longer.*

Melony sat in the lawn chair and looked around. At least it was a peaceful day. Peace was as foreign to her as rain to a desert. Gramma Mary Lou had been loud from the minute she woke to the minute she dropped off to sleep, and even then the old woman snored like a hibernating bear. Her restaurants were always noisy, filled with hungry, boisterous customers clamoring for more of that special spaghetti, rolls, salad or drinks. Then there were the television studios where talking never stopped. Throughout Melony's life, noise had always come with the territory.

Yawning, Melony stretched her arms and legs, closed her eyes and relaxed into semi-consciousness. Like an explorer at sea, she let her mind drift with the waves of forest solemnity. Before falling asleep, she would later remember feeling: *I could get used to this....*

LENA SAT IN her Walmart chair, staring at the pile of rocks. Any doubts of cross-dimensional communication had disappeared with the Couric interview. *Where are you, Anne? Don't send those grumpy old men this time. I want to talk with you!* Her mind was a cudgel, eager to smash the damned rocks to bits. *The Voices are driving me insane. After the last interview, everyone thinks I've gone crackers. What's this about the financial markets going to hell? At least they could give me a warning when they're going to pull a stunt like that—taking over my mind and speaking for me.* She was beginning to hyperventilate. *Talk to me!*

Nothing. No response. Lena realized anger was getting her nowhere. *I must relax, she thought. But what about Anne?* She was the first to communicate, but had deferred to the Voices ever since. Lena's mind wandered: *How do the mediums do it? How do they channel other dimensions at will? If I now have the power, I must learn to control it, not have it control me.*

"It's my mind you're messing with, dammit!" she yelled out loud, quickly looking around for witnesses to her ranting. Seeing only the surrounding flora and feeling a slight breeze, she sat back and looked up through the muted canopy. *This could take a while,* she resigned herself, sighing….

A small nearby branch fell to the ground, waking her. Lena glanced at her watch: *3:17. I've been here for over two hours.*

You calmed down now? It was Anne. *Had your panties in a wad, didn't you?*

"Anne, thank God it's you!" Lena cried, standing.

Let's get something straight, sis. I'm not your Fairy Godmother, replied AnneVoice. *We were cut off last time when Claude barged in, so maybe this time we can straighten things out, okay? You've got a lot of work to do, Ms. Hotshot Celebrity. Time doesn't stop for needless hysterics.*

Okay, okay. I'm listening. Lena reverted to mind-speak.

That's better. You're learning, AnneVoice answered. *Before I resume, you must know I can only introduce you to the Masters. I cannot act on Their behalf. They may seem grumpy, intimidating, whatever, but you must realize They speak the truth. Do not doubt Them. Do not defy Them, for They will reveal the Future and your course of action.*

But…. Lena started to ask a question.

Uh, uh, uh…! You're doing it again, Lena. For once in your life, just shut up and listen!

Anne was never like this before, Lena thought.

A NATION BEST SERVED HOT

No, I wasn't. Now listen!

Okay, I'll shut up.

AnneVoice continued. *Think about this. Your reality, your world exists in four dimensions—length, width, height and depth. You have been chosen to be a conduit between your reality and the fifth dimension....*

"This is the dawning of the Age of Aquarius ...." The 1969 Fifth Dimension's hit song rang through Lena's head.

Yeah, I know... "When the Moon is in the Seventh House...." *Yada, yada, yada,* answered the AnneVoice. *I was a college hippie, remember? Let's get back to the subject, shall we?*

OK, I'm the condom.... Lena couldn't help the levity.

Conduit! Not condom, twit.

Glad to see you still have a little sense of humor, girlfriend, added Lena.

AnneVoice resumed. *Here is where it gets complicated. You have to take this on faith, Lena. Trust me like you did when I was alive, please. The fifth dimension is a combination of the Past and Future. It's the "when" dimension. Don't get freaked out when one of the Masters occasionally takes control of your mind and actions. He will do this for two good reasons: to warn of impending disasters and to influence the actions of your contemporaries.*

But....

Let me finish. Then you can ask questions, okay? AnneVoice insisted.

Lena willed herself quiet.

You're getting better at this. It will be the same for the interventions after one or two more. You will never achieve total comfort with your loss of control. But like anything else, the more you do something, the better you get at it.

Lena, once people learn you speak the Truth, you will find there is a fine line between them accepting your proclamations versus accusing you of heresy, especially the Bible thumpers. You must use your powers of persuasion to assure them of your good intentions. Some will think you're a Prophet. Others will think you're the Devil....

"Now wait just a damned minute!" Lena broke away from mind-speak and yelled out loud. "Why are you saddling me with this, this...?"

Responsibility? AnneVoice finished Lena's sentence. *Let me ask you a couple of questions. Do you love your country—are you patriotic? And are you willing to sacrifice your life, fortune and sacred honor for it, as so many have in the past?*

But I'm just a fifty-seven-year-old woman..., Lena mind-babbled.

Your age is irrelevant and you know it, Lena. Now answer the questions, AnneVoice insisted.

I've never thought about it, but yes, of course....

Think of it as being drafted. The answer to "Why me?" is simple. Remember the note I left you, when I wrote, "Within you is the power to change lives.... Your destiny is yet to be written?"

Yes, but....

At the time I felt like you do now: why am I writing this? It was a Master who penned those words through me. Remember I also wrote, "Don't be afraid to love." Confess. You weren't afraid when you married Win.

Lena, don't be afraid of your destiny—leading people to proper paths and punishing those who take advantage of others. Embrace your destiny with confidence knowing you're a Chosen One.

A beam of light shone through the canopy upon Lena's face. Her eyes welled with tears.

"Anne, please show me something, something to convince me what you're telling me is real," Lena spoke once more, this time in a whisper.

I'll do better than that. Go immediately to the Waco, Texas VA Hospital. Someone there needs you desperately. Ask for Tracy Henderson.

Please save my daughter from herself.

Lena sat back in the $4.99 Walmart chair, dumbfounded. *Tracy's alive? My God, I thought she was dead, missing in action!*

My mission is complete. AnneVoice was fading. *In your future you may feel me, but this is the last you will hear my Voice.*

Godspeed to you, Lena Mills—my forever friend.

"No, don't leave me!" Lena rose to her feet again, wringing her hands in frustration. Feeling liberated yet enslaved, she railed, "I came here to find answers. Don't you dare leave me with more questions!"

Like a cool zephyr soothing a sultry day, calming assurance enveloped Lena's mind. Looking upward through the trees, she welcomed the beam of light with outstretched arms, remembering, as if it were yesterday, a young woman beseeching Heaven so many years ago. High above the trees, soaring with the thermals, was a lone eagle.

Lena Mills choked back a sob, tears flowing freely down her face.

The eagle flew off in one fading cry.

Then, like a question unasked, it never was.

A NATION BEST SERVED HOT

REFRESHED FROM HER NAP, Melony had retrieved and opened the envelope. Inside were two letters—one from the attorney, the other from Gramma Moothart—and a certified bank check for $100,000, payable to Mary Lou Moothart, Jr., aka Melony Major. After a full minute adrenaline rush, the shock of seeing the check gave way to curiosity. She read the letter from Gramma first. It was dated three weeks before her death.

Wednesday, May 24, 2006

Dear Junior (Regardless of your stage name, you'll always be Junior to me).

When you were knee high to a stump, I promised you this letter, to be opened when you were old enough to understand. That time is now.

Of all the persons I have ever known, you are my favorite. Unlike all of my husbands, children and acquaintances who have disappointed me, you've grown into a smart, hard-working and sassy broad with a bucket load of common sense.

That's the first thing I want you to know: I'm proud to call you my own. There is no doubt in my mind you'll be successful. My only hope is that, with your success, a lot more happiness than I've had comes your way.

Second, I must tell you about your birth parents. Your mother's name was Emily Sue Rogers, product of my second husband, Henry (Hank) Rogers, a sorry son-of-a-mule I married one week and divorced the next. (No use digging into that closet!) Like her two brothers from prior marriages, Emily Sue grew up stubborn (got that from me, no doubt) and to my mind, worthless. None of my children have your drive and common sense. But Emily Sue was a beauty on the outside, attracting men like a fresh kill attracts jackals.

You are the result of a one night stand with a slick talking salesman. Your mother never told me his name. She died giving birth to you, the only selfless act of a vain, selfish woman. I know it is a terrible thing for a mother to talk this way about her child, but from the moment your mother was born, we butted heads over everything. When you were born, I accepted you as penance for my failure with my own children, but over the years I have grown to love you for who you are and what you can become.

DAVID CARL MIELKE

The only other good to come out of my life is a small fortune from the business. I have put everything into a trust for your benefit, managed conservatively by an attorney and his financial advisors. It will give you income immediately and eventually control of the principal. Invest the money wisely and it will help supplement your future. Spend it carelessly and, like my life, it will have been wasted.

I hope you have it your heart to forgive my transgressions and think kindly of this cranky old failure. Find your passion and hang on tight.

Give 'em hell, girl!

Your loving Gramma Moothart

The attorney's letter was all business. The check represented one year's interest from trust assets totaling slightly over two million dollars.

Melony was staring at the check when Lena returned. Both had tears running down their faces. Both had no idea why the other was crying. Instinctively, both knew words would ruin the moment. They hugged and quietly packed to leave.

REVELATIONS
EN ROUTE TO WACO, TEXAS
TUESDAY, DECEMBER 18th, 2007

ASIDE FROM TYPICAL Homeland Security hassles, the flights from Orlando to Waco by way of Dallas/Fort Worth went smoothly. Lena had purchased first class tickets to DFW, which stifled most autograph hounds and gave them time to compare notes. Melony told Lena about the letters and her unexpected wealth.

"For the first time, I learned the name of my mother," she gushed. "I'd love to know who my father is and whether he's still alive. But without a name, I guess I'll never know."

Lena listened with half her mind, the other half still trying to digest Anne's revelations. These unpredictable interventions would be difficult. They could strike at any time, rendering her helpless to control speech, let alone explain her behavior. It was as though she suffered Tourette syndrome. Should she warn Melony? *She already thinks I'm a little nuts*, Lena thought to herself. *This could drive her away. I need her now more than ever.* Deciding a little knowledge was better than none, she broached the subject during the flight.

"Melony, how much do you trust me—my judgment?" Lena asked.

"What do you mean?" Predictably, Melony answered the question with another. *Not a good start,* cursed Lena under her breath. *Screw this. I'll just come out with the truth, consequences be damned.*

"Remember what I said when I walked off into the forest?"

"Yeah, you had to find some answers. I wondered what kind of answers could be found in the woods?"

"Well, I found them, and believe me I don't like what I learned. You're going to have to take what I tell you on faith. Hopefully, you won't think I'm crazy, but here goes:

"My best friend died the beginning of this year. She had brain cancer."

"Yes, someone named Anne. You mentioned her to me before," Melony broke in.

"Well, I buried her ashes in the forest. That's where I went yesterday—to that spot."

"O...kay...?" Melony drew out the response, urging her to continue.

"The day I met you, until Claude found me and interrupted, I talked with her spirit. It happened again yesterday."

Looking for an adverse reaction and seeing none, Lena continued. "Here's where it gets really 'Twilight Zone'-ish. First let me give you some background...."

For the next hour, Melony sat and listened, fascinated by Lena's story from her early life: the exotic dancer years, Claude Masters, the costume business, her friendship with Anne Henderson and their mutual connection to Win Stedman. She omitted the gruesome acts of revenge. "Let sleeping dogs lie," she reasoned.

"When she knew the end was near, it was Anne's idea to be buried in the forest. The spot was holy to her. Now it is to me.

"Anne never understood her paranormal ability. She just accepted it. I was always skeptical until she died, but the day I buried her, something inside me changed—something I ignored until the interview with Katie Couric."

Lena barged ahead, "Have you ever said something and immediately wondered why you said it?"

"Yes, I guess everyone has at some point," replied Melony.

"Well, that's what happened. During the interview, I lost control of my thoughts and speech. Talk about the willies! I thought I had gone bonkers from stress and lack of sleep, but knew there had to be another reason. That's why I made the second trip to the forest.

"Anne's thoughts came to me again, this time without interruption. Without going into details, Anne told me I have been given a power to read minds, to know things—sometimes incriminating—about total strangers.

Melony had been silent long enough. "Lena, I like and respect you, even admire you...."

A NATION BEST SERVED HOT

"But you don't believe me, do you?" Lena finished her sentence. "I can't blame you. If the tables were turned, I wouldn't either. You want proof? Are you ready for this?"

"Ready for what?" asked Melony. *This has to be an elaborate joke,* she thought. *She's putting me on.* "Sure, give me your best shot, boss," she grinned.

"Okay, you've told me about your Gramma who raised you, but you never told me about Jesse Lopez, the young man who loved you."

Melony's mouth dropped open in surprise.

"You also never told me about your sex life," Lena continued, watching Melony's expression. It was time to drop the big one and hope the girl would forgive. "You're nineteen and never had sex with a man, right? By the time I was your age, I had screwed half a high school football team and worked as a stripper in a nightclub."

As if clobbered with a two-by-four, Melony Major gasped and turned white as a sheet.

LENA MILLS hit the VA Hospital like a west Texas sandstorm. Followed by her pretty young assistant, she blew into the lobby, startling the elderly greeter who had nodded off with boredom. "Where's my niece, Tracy Henderson?" Lena thundered. All eyes in the lobby jerked toward the ruckus.

"You're...you're...." babbled the flummoxed volunteer, certain she had seen that face many times.

"The name's Lena Mills Stedman. What room is Tracy Henderson in?"

"She's in a restricted access area," rumbled a deep voice from behind. Lena turned to see a tall, swarthy Latin man in an expensive suit. The badge on his left breast pocket read "DR. HERNANDEZ."

"Are you Tracy's doctor?" asked Lena.

"Dr. Victor Hernandez, Chairman of Psychiatry, madam," replied the man, holding out his hand. Hernandez had been passing by the entrance just as Lena and Melony approached the greeter.

Lena shook the hand and continued. "We've flown from Florida. I must see my niece, sir."

"Unless you're immediate family and can prove it, I'm afraid that will be impossible," the doctor replied, folding his arms and looking down his nose over half glasses, both gestures of intimidation. "The patient is high risk and cannot be disturbed. You may check in daily for an update, but unfortunately, that's all I can offer you. Now if you'll excuse me…." As he turned to leave, Lena lightly gripped his arm.

"Are you her attending physician?" she repeated, refusing to be dismissed. His aura of hostility convinced Lena she would get nowhere with this man.

"No, that would be Dr. Schultz," sighed Hernandez, glaring at her hand on his arm with growing impatience.

"Then let me speak with this doctor," insisted Lena, trying to remain pleasant, refusing to release her grip.

As Melony watched the duel of wits, the term "Mexican standoff" came to mind.

"Out of the question. Now unhand me, woman," Hernandez glared, "or I will call security to have you removed from this facility."

Melony saw a strange look come over her boss—the same look from the Couric interview. *Oh, oh,* she thought, *here comes trouble.*

Lena seemed to grow six inches on demand, reaching eye level with the doctor. "Step over here," she hissed. The grip on Hernandez had turned to steel. He winced in pain as Lena guided him a few paces aside. In a whisper, she spat, "Look, you pompous asshole. I'm used to eating guys like you for lunch and spitting out the gristle. You've got a choice. Take me to this attending physician or know that I will speak to the hospital director. There's a certain nurse you've been banging in your office for months. Does the name 'Rosie' ring a bell?"

Like a cat hacking a hairball, Hernandez wheezed, his mouth flopping open in guilt-ridden surprise. "What the…?" he stammered. "W-who *are* you?"

"You're worst nightmare if you won't let me see this Dr. Schultz immediately," Lena whispered. "Look, jerk. I'm trying hard not to make a scene. Don't blow it in front of the help."

Hernandez was in shock. His mind screamed, *How could this strange woman know about Rosie?* Shaken but realizing at least twenty pair of eyes were focused on them, he attempted to gather himself.

"Of c-course," he stammered. "Please come this way." His demeanor had changed from haughty to subservient.

Thirty feet away, Melony couldn't hear the short exchange but marveled at the effect on the doctor. Lena signaled her to follow. Wordlessly, the three walked through an automatic door and down two corridors. In a trance, Lena's face was rigid until they reached an office marked "Dr. Patricia Schultz, Psychiatry." Hernandez knocked on the door.

"Enter," spoke a muffled voice from within.

"These people are here to see you about Tracy Henderson," Hernandez announced. Turning to Lena, he begged, "You won't...."

"As long as I can see my niece, no, I won't," said Lena in an Alpha tone of voice. "Please leave us." She pointed toward the door.

As if dismissed from a fate worse than death, Hernandez hurried off, muttering Spanish invectives, certain he was in for major damage control. *Bad enough the dangerous patient almost killed me,* he grumbled. *Now this fruitcake waltzes into my turf threatening me.* A sudden thought ruined the rest of his day:

Ohmigod, are there pictures?

"Won't what? What's this all about?" Schultz asked, rising to greet the remaining pair. "Dr. Hernandez looked like he's seen a ghost. Hey, aren't you...?"

"Lena Mills Stedman, Dr. Schultz. I'm Tracy Henderson's adopted aunt," Lena interrupted, seemingly back to normal. "This is my assistant, Melony Major. Your Dr. Hernandez needs a few lessons in bedside manners."

As the three shook hands, a still shaken Melony stood in awe with newfound respect for her boss, thinking, *It's one thing to have a great fastball; quite another to know how to pitch it for strikes. I'm working for freakin' Nolan Ryan!*

This woman is famous, Patricia Schultz mused, searching her memory for Tracy's background. She had mentioned an aunt during her first round of therapy. "The only person I would trust with my life," was her comment. *Why didn't I think to contact this "aunt" upon Tracy's readmittance?* Schultz chastised herself again.

"Come with me, please." She guided them up two floors to the restricted ward. "We need to talk. I've done all I can to bring Tracy out of her coma. Maybe you can help."

As the three walked into Tracy's room, a man was asleep in a chair next to the bed, his head resting next to hers. He was holding Tracy's hand. "This is the man who brought Tracy in," whispered Schultz. "Name's Jerry Calvin. Says he loves her."

Lena looked down at the sleeping girl, thinking *This can't be Tracy.* Searching the girl's tortured mind, she realized it was.

Dr. Schultz motioned them to the hallway. "I see that look on your face, Mrs. Stedman. You don't recognize her, do you? She's had reconstructive surgery since you saw her last. This woman has endured more extended abuse—physical, mental and sexual—than anyone I've ever treated. Tracy has lapsed into what we call a catatonic stupor. Sometimes a body's reaction to an extremely traumatic event is to fall asleep—somnolence. It's an avoidance response, a refusal to confront and understand a traumatic event. The young man brought her in just like this almost a week ago. Neither he nor I have been able to bring her out of this condition.

"Does her family know she's here? Are her mother and father on their way?" the doctor asked.

"No one else knows she's here," Lena stated. Her mind was doing somersaults. The Voices were in overdrive cramming her brain with waves of information. "It's a long story. It has been about a year since anyone has heard from Tracy. We were all told she was presumed dead from some clandestine DEA raid months ago. Since then her mother has passed. She may not have heard about that."

"If she ever comes out of the coma, we must not tell her right away," Schultz remarked. "A blow like that could put her right back out."

"What about this man? What is his connection to her?" asked Melony, finally gathering the courage to interject.

"I don't have the whole story. He has told me little, other than Tracy saved his life. He'll have to fill you in. She is my only concern."

"Of course," Lena responded, looking around the corner, studying the young man.

"You're the professional, doc. I'll call her father and brother later today. Tracy and I have shared a strong bond stemming from her early childhood. She trusts me."

"Yes, she told me. You're the widow of the Florida governor, aren't you?"

Lena nodded affirmatively. "I believe I can help, Doc. She needs to know I'm here. Please give me a chance."

Over the past week, Schultz had tried all clinical and medical approaches. Receiving no response, time remained the last option. "What do you propose?" she asked.

"I need to lie beside her. Maybe hearing my voice will work."

"I must be in the room with you," the doctor countered. "There is no predicting Tracy's behavior when she wakes."

"Deal," Lena replied, watching as Schultz gently woke the young man.

"Jerry, I'm Tracy's aunt and this is Melony Major, my assistant." Lena studied the man's mind. *This one has a good heart,* she knew instantly.

Still groggy from sleep, tears welled up in Jerry's eyes. "Thank God you're here," he sighed, surprising Lena with a hug. "Tracy's told me about you. How did you find us?"

Ignoring the question, Lena drew him aside, saying, "I need you to fill me in, young man. Please tell me everything."

Over coffee in a nearby private room, Jerry spent the next hour with Lena doing just that.

TRACY BELL was two and a half years old, romping again through the Neverland forest with her favorite friends, Peter Pan and Wendy. Throwing small fistfuls of pixie dust on nearby shrubbery, she was shouting, "Poof, you're a toad," and "Poof, you're a lion."

Putting on the small costume back at the house, she had tugged at Anne's hand, asking, "Mommy, is Aunt Lena a magic lady?"

"We'll have to find out about that, won't we?" replied her mother, smiling.

Tracy looked up at Lena, dressed as Peter Pan. "Can you fly?"

"My pixie dust is rather flat," Peter had answered. "I'm walking today. Borrr-ing! Would you like to go on a picky-nick with Wendy and me?"

Would she ever! Boldly leading the threesome down well worn pathways, wide-eyed Tracy Bell was on alert for dangerous foes, especially Captain Hook and tick-tocking crocs. Coming around a corner, she spotted three deer ahead—a mother and two fawns. She turned to Wendy and Peter and put a small finger to her lips. "I see deers! Be quiet. They might hear us and run."

Wendy bent down to whisper, "Tracy Bell, you stay here with Peter, okay? Be still and don't make any noise. I'm going to try something." She rummaged through her backpack and removed some peanut butter-flavored kibbles.

Tracy Bell and Peter watched as Wendy walked slowly toward the deer with hands outstretched, calling to them in soothing tones. The doe looked up and prepared to bolt, but instead approached her. Wendy sat on the trail holding out her right hand as the mother mouthed the kibbles. With her left, she caressed the doe's flank. Each fawn followed, shyly nibbling from the cupped hand. Then in a flash they were gone.

"Mommy, Mommy," Tracy Bell cried, running toward Wendy. "You're the magic lady!"

"It's not magic, honey," laughed Anne, hoisting Tracy in her arms. Animals seem to like and trust me. That's all."

"Lady, you're one hell of a sorcerer," commented Lena as the three prepared to enjoy one of many picky-nicks to come.

Tracy was lost in early childhood, the only time in her life she felt secure, surrounded by happiness and love. Past was present. Time ceased to exist.

Strange voices were coaxing her back to a life of danger and terror. "No! No!" she moaned in protest at each tactile attempt. *Leave me alone,* cried her mind. *Let me stay. I don't belong in your world.*

Sometime later, a different, more familiar voice breached her wall of resistance—a voice belonging to someone she loved.

"Tracy, it's me," the voice gently whispered in her ear. "It's me, Aunt Lena. I'm here to take you home."

I am home, her mind argued. *It's where I belong.*

The voice continued: "You are needed here. People who love you are waiting. Be strong." Like a kitten treed by a pack of dogs, Tracy was torn between the comfort of the limb and the arms of its owner. She recalled the sing-song phrase from hide-and-seek games: *Come out, come out, wherever you are....*

Lured by the gentle prodding, Tracy's mind slowly relented.

Her lips moved, at first with no sound, then with a breathy sigh: "Aunt...Lena?"

"Yes, child, I'm right here lying beside you. I love you. Come back to me."

Eyes fluttered, adjusting to harsh fluorescence. Lena put a hand under Tracy's chin, smothering her face with kisses. "Poof, you're a Tracy Bell," she chuckled in relief.

Tracy coughed to clear away dried phlegm. "Magic...lady," she croaked. A waterfall of tears streamed down her face as she threw both arms around Lena, hugging with all her might.

"Easy now, Trace. I'm getting older. Save some of that for this young man."

A NATION BEST SERVED HOT

Standing beside the bed, a sobbing Jerry Calvin replaced Lena on the bed. "Welcome back," he cried, shaking with emotion. "You're safe now, in a hospital again. Carón is dead. It's over."

Dr. Patricia Schultz stood off to the side, shaking her head, amazed at her patient's transformation. A week of therapy had failed to achieve what this woman had with fifteen minutes of loving encouragement. There were times when all her training and experience weren't worth a flip compared to a gentle human voice.

Melony Major stood at the doorway, astonished at the bonding. A tinge of jealousy crept into her mind. *Will I ever feel this way about someone?* she asked herself.

Dr. Schultz took Melony's hand, breaking into her reverie. "Come on. I'll buy you a cup of coffee," she urged her out of the room into the hospital corridor. "You must tell me all about this remarkable woman."

Melony replied, suddenly upbeat. "We don't have enough time for the whole story, but I'll give you a synopsis." Changing course, she added, "You like spaghetti?"

"Yes, of course. Why?"

"Have I got a recipe for you!"

Dr. Patricia Schultz, healer of fractured minds, laughed like she hadn't in months.

"I CRACKED, Aunt Lena," Tracy explained, her head down in shame.

Jerry Calvin sat next to her on a couch in a vacant waiting area. Sitting opposite her for the past half hour, Lena had learned of El Gato's demonic hold on both their lives, the reasons for revenge and the successful raid upon his compound.

"I've been trained to execute without emotion—get in, kill, get out," Tracy explained.

"The plan was flawless. Everyone did their job," added Jerry.

"Alone with the bastard, killing him wasn't enough," continued Tracy. "Something in my mind snapped. I found release. I actually enjoyed mutilating his body." Holding her sides, she shivered. "I'm no better than the animal I killed."

"You know that's not true." Jerry was trying to help, encircling her in his arms. Her vacant eyes told him the condescension, though well-intended, was of little help.

Lena remembered a teenage girl and her night of abuse by the sexual predator and his two younger accomplices. Thanks to her aunt's intervention, Tracy was rescued and the men arrested. With positive reinforcement, Tracy had set aside the trauma to become a successful law enforcement officer, only to suffer six months of torture at the hands of the vicious drug lord. As it was with the teenage attack, Lena's own history, skill, and tough love—not pity and soothing words—were needed now.

"Don't think you're the Lone Ranger, kiddo," she admonished Tracy, shocking her. "You've been through the pits of hell during your short time on earth. You've been robbed of a normal life by sick, perverted men who gripped and ripped at you to the brink of death."

Jerry's mouth had dropped open. Lena looked at him square in the eyes and asked, "Young man, could you give us some time alone? What I have to tell Tracy is strictly between us. If she cares to tell you later that will be fine, but for now, I need to share a few things with her in confidence."

Jerry rose from the couch. He had read about this woman. Tracy had described her as kick-ass confident, always in control. Face to face, he felt inadequate. The term "primal force" came to mind. Squeezing Tracy's hand, he smiled and said, "I'll go find your assistant, ma'am. She went off with the doc. Come get me when you're ready." He bent to kiss Tracy and left.

Lena's eyes were on fire as she took Jerry's place on the couch. Holding both of Tracy's hands in hers, she commented, "That man's a keeper, girl. I can feel it."

Tracy could only nod. Lena continued, "Not one in a million could come back from what you've been through, honey. Yet you're made of stern stuff. I can't say that my experience rises to your level, but some things in my life have come close. You know about my early childhood, but there are other things, things involving your mother, Claude and Deppidy Don you should know about. Now is the time."

Over the next hour, Tracy learned for the first time things she could barely believe: how her grandparents died in a fiery car accident, and how two Cubano hit men chasing her mother caused the crash. She learned about a crusty old sheriff named Elmo Parker and cringed at the story of swift country justice—how, according to Anne, the Cubans were fed alive to a huge alligator named Ol' Clyde.

If she was shocked by that, the next story made her gag. Her mother Anne had discovered three forest squatters—cannibals, who kidnapped

A NATION BEST SERVED HOT

hookers from Orlando streets and brought them back to their campground where they were raped, killed, dismembered and eaten. Forest rangers refused to investigate what they considered wild fiction. While Anne stayed home, Deppidy Don, Claude and Lena planned and executed a night raid on the camp.

Catching the three cannibals by surprise, they hogtied and took them to the same gator hole, again feeding them alive to Ol' Clyde's offspring.

"I'll never forget hearing the bones crunch, just as you will never forget mutilating Carón, Tracy," Lena stated. "The guilt I felt that night stayed with me for a long while. You can either dwell on it or move on. I chose the latter, and you will, too. We're human, Trace. This 'turn the other cheek' thing is bullshit. We're all made of better angels and bitter demons. Evil exists. You can let it beat you or you can beat it down. Sometimes, in the heat of the moment, we can't help kicking it a few more times than necessary. There's an old saying: 'No use beating a dead horse'. It should be followed by: 'unless you really hate it'."

Tracy's mood changed on a dime. Laughing, she asked, "Where did you hear that one?"

"Made it up myself. Seems to fit two sinners like us, don't you think?"

Dr. Schultz had rounded the corner just in time to hear Tracy laugh. "Now that's a sound I like to hear from one of my patients. Mind letting me in on your joke?"

"We were just talking about a dead horse," giggled Tracy.

"I'll have to adjust your medication, young lady," scolded the doctor, wagging her finger in mock rebuke. "Your happy pills are too strong."

All three laughed. Tracy had to admit, it was good to be back.

Looking up at Schultz, Tracy asked, "What do you think, Doc? How long before I can get out of this place and go see my father and brother?"

Lena gasped. Tracy couldn't know about her mother. *How could I be so stupid?* she chastised herself.

"What's wrong?" asked Tracy.

Lena gathered herself, looking up at the bewildered doctor for strength. Tracy was still fragile. One more volley of bad news could ruin her niece's recovery.

Grabbing her in a bear hug, she cried, "Oh, girl, after all you've been through, it's been so long you couldn't know."

"Know what, Aunt Lena?"

Tears well again in her eyes as Lena, with cracking voice, explained,

"Honey, your mom passed last March from inoperable brain cancer."

Lena clung tight, willing her mind to concentrate on Tracy's pain, asking her niece to accept the truth. Dr. Schultz fell to her knees and looked into her patient's eyes for signs of relapse.

"I knew that. Keith Westen told me a while ago," was Tracy's solemn reply.

For the second time that day, Schultz was blown away. What she saw in her patient's eyes wasn't shock. Neither was it grief or hysteria. Tracy Henderson's eyes glowed with something that could only be described as grace.

After a pause, Tracy released Lena's embrace to look in her eyes. In a soft, reassuring voice that defied all clinical explanation, Tracy spoke to her aunt, "I understand.... Mom's not really dead, is she?"

―――

"SO TELL ME about yourself, how you met Mrs. Stedman." Jerry was sitting across the coffee shop table from Melony—*a strikingly beautiful blonde, the kind I used to like in my younger days,* he thought.

Dr. Schultz and she had exchanged only small talk earlier. Melony had taken care to avoid conversation about her boss, spending most of the fifteen minutes writing down the spaghetti recipe. "Try it. You'll like it, I promise, Doc," she bragged.

Likewise, the doctor had revealed nothing about Tracy, citing doctor-patient confidentiality. Schultz had left the table two minutes before Jerry took her seat.

"I think she prefers Ms. Mills, or just Lena, Mr. Calvin," replied Melony, thinking to herself, *If this guy was twenty years younger and wasn't in love with Tracy, well....* "As you must know, she was only married to the governor for a few hours."

"Please call me Jerry. Yes, I read about it. Pretty bizarre, but then everything about your boss is a little, shall I say, eccentric?"

"Yeah, she's a piece of work, all right," chuckled Melony. "Never a dull moment. That's why I stay. I think she's out to change the world."

"What's your background? How did you two meet?" Jerry asked again, sipping from his cup of tea. "Coffee makes me jumpy," he had explained earlier to both Dr. Schultz and now Melony.

A NATION BEST SERVED HOT

"I'm a west Texas girl, born and raised in El Paso by my Gramma. She was a pistol, like Lena," she answered with a smile. "Maybe that's why I'm attracted to the boss," Melony added.

"That's a coincidence. I'm a Texan by birth, too. Lived and worked my first jobs in El Paso when I was in my late teens." Warming to the young lady, Jerry added, "My dad was a gambler who cheated death until someone called his bluff. We were in Dallas then. After he was killed, my mom gave up living and I left home, if you could call changing motel rooms home. Heard she died shortly after him. I know it sounds cold, but I could never stand weak dependents."

"Sounds sad," commented Melony. "I never knew my dad, don't even know his name, and my mom died giving birth to me, according to Gramma Moothart. She took me in and raised me all by herself. She told me I was a product of a one-night stand, if you get my drift. West Texas is a good place to be from, don't you agree?"

"Yep, sand in your teeth and hot sauce with every meal," Jerry answered.

This guy's a charmer, thought Melony. Opening up to him came easy.

"Anyway, Gramma owned a small chain of restaurants in the area—specialized in an exotic spaghetti sauce. Drew customers by the truckload. From an early age I served tables, delivered meals, and later did most of the accounting. At age fifteen, I auditioned at the local TV station as a weather girl, changed my stage name from Moothart to Major, and eventually landed a network job in Florida. That's where I saw Lena for the first time, during a short interview at a governor's press conference. She and Stedman were engaged at the time. She told me later she remembered me for the funny question I asked, which got a lot of laughs. Something about 'checking each other's bones'," she giggled. *I'm rambling like a school girl,* she admonished herself.

"Go on. This is fascinating," Jerry prodded. *I feel twenty years younger listening to this young woman,* he thought. *I'm old enough to be her father.*

"Well, shortly after the governor died, I got an offer from FOX Network, flew to New York, and was assigned to find Lena and get an exclusive interview. Pretty tall order, since I was only nineteen and one of a hundred reporters with the same assignment. She had disappeared for more than two months right after her husband's death, making her story tabloid gold. Guess I was more persistent than everyone else. Maybe just smarter. Tailed her best friend, a man named Claude Masters, for a couple of weeks until he sneaked off to the Ocala National Forest. It was there

I found the boss. She took a liking to me and the rest is history, or in her words, a 'prelude to history.' I resigned from FOX and went to work for her as publicist, scheduler and all-around assistant.

"Now you owe me. Tell me about yourself and how you met Tracy," Melony ended, swallowing a big gulp of coffee.

She could see the hesitation in his eyes. "Come on, now, no fair! I told you all about me. It's your turn."

She's flirting with me! thought Jerry.

Melony wasn't through. Boldness overcame sense as she coyly asked, "Don't you want to know how I chose my stage name?"

"How was that?" he laughed. Flattered by this intriguing young lady's attention, he found himself attracted to the Texas Southern Belle.

"Not until you spill, sir. I repeat: it's your turn."

Lassoed by her charm, Jerry relented, but not before admonishing her. Turning serious, he gazed into her eyes. "You were a reporter. How well can you keep what I tell you in strictest confidence?"

Melony was caught off guard with the change in his tone, but answered, "If it's that serious, of course I promise to tell no one. But I warn you, Lena has a way of reading people. Tracy will probably tell her everything that's happened between you two anyway."

"Fair enough," Jerry replied, asking himself, *What does she mean by "having a way of reading people?"*

For the next half hour, Melony learned more about the raw side of life than she bargained for. Leaving out Tracy's butchery, what Jerry described sounded more like an action movie script than plausible fact. She had read about the demise of Felix Carón, reported in the news as a territorial takeover by a rival gang. Two people with thirty mercenaries wiping out an entire drug cartel seemed preposterous. The man before her was either a great actor or deadly serious.

Jerry ended his story by gripping both her hands for emphasis. The look in her eyes revealed fear. *I've told her too much,* he realized and apologized. "I'm sorry, Melony. It sounds far-fetched, but you wanted the truth."

"I'm stronger than you think, Mr. Calvin," Melony retorted. Miffed by his condescending tone, she reverted to his formal name.

"Whoa, tiger! I apologize again. You've got a backbone like Tracy." He sat up straight, sliding his chair two inches in full retreat. Melony decided to cut him slack and lighten the mood.

A NATION BEST SERVED HOT

"Okay. I'll assume you're telling me the truth. Lena will get it from Tracy anyway. Now, don't you want to know how I chose my name?"

Jerry nodded yes.

Wordlessly wiggling her shoulders, Melony allowed her low cut dress to flaunt her two perfectly proportioned assets. "These babies are called *major melones* in Spanish."

Everyone within the coffee shop and down the adjoining hospital floor jerked their heads toward a sound almost never heard in the psych ward—boisterous belly laughs.

―⌒⌒―

IT HAD BEEN a most extraordinary day. Dr. Schultz sat behind her desk. Lena asked a simple question: "When may I take Tracy home?"

The answer was anything but simple. Tracy Henderson was the most challenging patient Schultz had ever treated. Inside a normal exterior, this beautiful, charming young woman harbored a cocktail of personality disorders, the sum of which defied clinical definition. She was both a psychiatrist's dream and potential nightmare. Leaving Tracy in lockdown for study was out of the question. She was a human being, not a lab rat.

Tracy was also a trained killer. Schultz found it hard to swallow the story behind her relapse. All the media concurred: Felix Carón and his gang were eliminated in a raid by a rival cartel. The story Jerry had told was logically implausible. Yet Tracy's trauma, mental and physical, had been real.

Each year, thousands of people in the armed services were trained to kill enemies of the state with impersonal efficiency. If the story were true, Tracy's violent behavior was, in contrast, very personal and directed toward one man who was now deceased.

Schultz was a one person parole board. Her decision must come down to an educated hunch. Was Tracy capable of repressing violence, or was she a hair-triggered time bomb of lethal rage?

Lena studied the doctor, reading her mind. "I know this woman—what makes her tick, Doc. She is no threat to society.

"I know…" Lena caught herself before continuing, "I think I know what must be going through your mind: if Tracy snaps again, the blame will be yours, right?"

Schultz nodded wordlessly, eyes locked on Lena, looking for any sign of insincerity, seeing none.

Lena continued. "I'm so certain she's no threat that I'll take personal responsibility for her actions and put it in writing, if necessary."

The doctor waited a few seconds before relenting. "I must keep her here under observation and verbal therapy until the Zoloft takes hold, usually about one month. When I'm as sure as I can be that she's no danger to herself or others, I'll release Tracy into your care, Mrs. Stedman. Two conditions, however. For at least the next two years, she will need to stay on the meds and call me once a week. I expect you to keep her on a short leash and will hold you responsible to continue the therapy."

"Deal, Doc. You've made a courageous decision, one I guarantee you'll not regret."

Lena rose to shake hands and left to tell Tracy the good news.

God help me if the decision is wrong, prayed Schultz. *What a day this has been.* She locked her office, walked down the hallway and punched the down button. As the elevator approached her floor, she could hear Dr. Hernandez berating someone at the top of his voice.

The door opened to reveal red-faced Hernandez towering over a terrified, weeping nurse—Rosie Gonzales. Upon seeing Schultz, Hernandez snapped back his raised right fist, followed by the rest of his body. "I'll... take the next ride," offered Patricia, stepping back.

The door closed. *Whew! What was that about?* she wondered. Deciding to hoof the few floors down to the garage, she couldn't wait to get home where six squawking cockatoos, two bouncing Jack Russell terriers, one irrationally sane husband and a normal life of pleasant mayhem awaited her return.

During her descent to the garage and the short walk to her late model, candy apple red Porsche Boxter, two competing thoughts captured her mind:

There must be a full moon, and *I need a stiff drink!*

WINGING IT
EN ROUTE TO ORLANDO, FLORIDA
WEDNESDAY, DECEMBER 19, 2007

"SO TELL ME what fascinates you about Tracy, Mr. Calvin." Sitting next to Jerry in first class, Lena took a swallow of complimentary J&B scotch on the rocks. Before leaving Waco, she had called Tracy's father and brother with the good news, telling both surprised men the abbreviated story and Tracy's pending release date.

At Lena's insistence, Melony sat separately in coach on the return flight home to Orlando. Since Anne's forest revelation less than a month ago, Lena had discovered some minds were harder to read than others. Jerry's was the most difficult she had yet encountered. He was trying to forget a past filled with remorse—that much was evident, but the details were somehow hidden from her telepathic probing.

Melony had related what she had learned during Jerry's coffee shop conversation. It all meshed with Tracy's story, but other than the brief history of his childhood and parents, he hadn't filled in the years before seeing Tracy shackled in Carón's torture cave. With Jerry, Lena would have to take the direct route by asking questions.

Jerry looked Tracy's aunt in the eye, remembering what Melony had said about her boss: *She has a way of knowing people....*

"Famous, formidable, wealthy, fiercely loyal" were some terms Tracy had used to describe Lena. "Kick-ass confident" was another. A self-made stripper in her younger years, now nearing sixty she was still a looker. "Trifle with her at your own risk," Tracy had warned him. "Deception is out of the question. Honesty isn't just the best policy, it's the only policy."

"I'm not bragging, just telling the truth," Jerry began reciting his past, sipping a complimentary Bloody Mary. "I've known many women in my life. I was even engaged to be married. Her name was Miriam. She was a gentle soul. Worked for me when I lived in Costa Rica, and I moved her with me to Mexico."

Jerry's mood turned dark. Hands balled into fists, he continued, "Felix Carón murdered her and butchered the body. I learned much later he mailed the bloody head to her parents." His head was bowed and he was shaking with anger.

Lena gripped his arm. "God, you poor man," she consoled him. "No wonder you hated him. He took away part of your life, just like he did to Tracy."

"That's one reason why I love Tracy, ma'am," Jerry continued. "We have that in common, as well as our revenge against the bastard. But there's more...."

"I'm a gambler. Got that from my father...."

"Tracy has told me that about you—your nomadic childhood and your father's death," interrupted Lena. "Someday I'll tell you about my childhood. It wasn't a bed of roses, either. Sounds like we both used the experience positively. The old saying, 'What doesn't destroy you makes you stronger' applies, don't you think?"

"Amen to that, ma'am," Jerry answered.

"Please...call me Lena from now on, okay?"

"I'd be honored," Jerry replied, smiling.

"Oh, now you're toying with me and making me feel old. Cut the crap, Mr. Calvin, or I'll take you over my knee right here on the plane!" Lena laughed.

Any ice that remained between them thawed instantly. Jerry chuckled and raised his hands in submission before continuing. "Anyway, Tracy is simply the most fascinating person I've ever known. She came to Saskatchewan to thank me for arranging her DEA rescue from Carón. We spent the time planning the raid and getting to know each other."

Jerry felt free to clear the air: "We never had sex, if you're wondering. I respected her and what's she's been through too much, and I'm willing to give her all the time she needs...."

Like a flower opening to the sun, Jerry's mind blossomed. Lena could now read his pain. The man was truly in love. "I haven't asked her yet, but someday when she's ready, I'll ask her to marry me."

He added, "Carón's torture made it impossible for her to conceive. Did she tell you this?"

A NATION BEST SERVED HOT

It was Lena's turn to ball her fists. "That sick bastard! I wish he were still alive so I could kill him again," she blurted out, almost knocking her glass off the tray. "No wonder Tracy butchered the son of a bitch."

The outburst reinforced Jerry's opinion. *Tracy was right,* he mused. *This is one tough broad!*

He continued, "In case our raid failed, Tracy resigned from the DEA a week before the execution. Luckily the assault went down better than I expected and an international incident was avoided. I guess you could say we're both unemployed now, although I'm independently wealthy."

"How did you make your money?" asked Lena. "If you're going to be Tracy's husband someday, I've got to be nosy, you understand."

"First, my real name is Calhoun. I was a salesman, and a damned good one, in El Paso," he stated. "Cars, then life insurance. I made a killing on insurance commissions but found the products were crap and blew up on the customers after a year or two. I'm ashamed to say I ran from the country to avoid prosecution. Changed my name to Calvin and ended up in Costa Rica with my money in offshore accounts. I was bored and turned to low stakes poker, losing more than I won. Along came a big stake, winner-take-all game. Gambling is like catnip. I couldn't resist. All the players were anonymous, but I later learned one was Felix Carón. Long story short, I won everything with a lucky draw on the last hand—walked away with millions, one million of which was the drug lord's money. There was no way I could have cheated, but he thought I had, so he vowed revenge. In addition, from another player I not only won his ante but also his company. It was called Rely, Inc. and manufactured adult diapers.

"I moved to Mexico near Juarez to be near the plant. Carón found out, kidnapped my fiancée and forced me to smuggle cocaine in a big shipment of these diapers. It was destined for Dallas but ended up in Florida by mistake...."

"Whoa, stop right there!" Lena interrupted.

Jerry held a confused look as she explained, "Those diapers ended up in Palm Beach County under different labeling and caused all kinds of mayhem."

Lena shook her head, laughing. "I'll be damned. Mystery solved. Rely—Calvin, of course! You're the guy no one could find. Your company went belly up and you disappeared."

"Yep," he answered. "That's when I went to Saskatchewan—to get away from Carón and all the lawsuits. Left everything with my lawyer,

Simon Morris, with a power of attorney. He folded Rely under Chapter Seven. When I won the company, he separated ownership of the diaper formula, putting it with another corporation in the Cayman Islands, sheltering it from creditors. Morris is an amazing man. Very smart," Jerry concluded.

"Did you ever find out why the formula explodes when mixed with cocaine?" Lena asked, still marveling at the coincidence.

"I have no clue," Jerry replied, wondering how this woman knew so much.

"I had the governor send some of the diapers off to the FBI for analysis," Lena explained. Turns out there was a missing ingredient, a liquid trigger that caused the diapers to explode. The byproduct is an incredibly vile stench, described by some as a combination of sheep excrement, the scent of paper mill and Korean kimchi."

"What's kimchi?"

"Nasty smelling skunk cabbage," she replied. Jerry's stomach lurched at the thought.

"And what was the trigger?"

"There's a chemical term, but in lay terminology it's called asparagus piss," Lena replied with a straight face. "The reaction only happened when people who ate asparagus later peed in their diapers."

The look on Jerry's face made her laugh.

"My idea was to research it as a weapon, kind of like a smoke bomb, to flush out cave- dwelling Taliban and Al-Qaeda," Lena added, still chuckling at Jerry's expression.

"Now it all makes sense." He shook his head in wonder. Morris sold the secret formula for ten million to the government, no questions asked. The money financed the raid on Carón."

It was Lena's turn to be surprised. Shaking her head and taking a deep swallow of scotch, she let out a long sigh, declaring, "What goes around sure as hell comes around."

Fill-in-the-blanks small talk made up the rest of the flight. She probed the young man, listening intently to his answers, searching his brain. *He's thirty-eight years old. Tracy's thirty-one. Confident without being cocky. Knows what he wants but has the patience to wait. Tracy will need much of that,* she thought.

She liked this young man, but something about him nagged at her mind. There was a loose end, a missing piece to the puzzle that was Jerry Calvin.

Like Felix Carón, Lena hated loose ends.

A NATION BEST SERVED HOT

~~~

THE HOMECOMING was a flurry of activity. After a cab ride to Lena's apartment, the three talked until two a.m. The next day, Lena and Melony took Jerry to visit with Claude and his wife Chareen. Lena's Harper Mills Retirement Home was still in the planning stage. Claude had agreed to a few changes with the architectural rendering. Overall, she was pleased with the progress. Then they drove to see Lena's partners, Trip and her daughter Becky, at the costume business, Chameleon. At age sixty-seven, Trip hadn't changed. She was the same no-nonsense manager. Like her grandmother who founded the business, forty-seven year-old Becky was a natural at bargaining with show business impresarios. Consequently the costume shop was making more money than ever. Lena expected nothing less.

Along the way, Melony asked to stop at her bank branch to deposit the huge trust check. At lunch, Lena asked her to read Gramma Moothart's letter. Hearing the woman's testament, a thought formed in the corner of Lena's mind. Too far-fetched to mention, she kept it to herself.

Still in demand, Lena gave Melony the go-ahead for more press interviews. Within three hours, fifteen had been booked over the next three weeks. With her provocative statements and biting humor, once again Lena Mills was on the tip of everyone's tongue.

During this time, Jerry flew back to Waco, not only to see Tracy but also to meet with Simon. Tracy continued in good spirits with the goal of a quick release from the hospital. She was Jerry's top priority. According to the attorney, Jerry remained in legal limbo. Lawyers representing Palm Beach governments and individuals were still after his personal assets, all of which remained in Cayman accounts with Morris in control. Starting a new U.S. business venture was out of the question. Jerry resolved to wait for Tracy's release before entertaining any career possibilities.

Tracy's emancipation day came at last, on January 15th. After winning an internal battle with Dr. Hernandez and a long video conference with Lena Mills, Dr. Patricia Schultz signed Tracy's paperwork and released her from the hospital into Jerry's arms. "Know this, young lady," she cautioned with a stern voice. "I'm taking a great risk for you. This is conditional. One more relapse and you'll likely never be free again."

"You're not my doctor anymore. You are my friend," Tracy smiled with confidence. "I promise to be a good girl and can't thank you enough for your trust in me. I'm determined to earn that trust."

"Go with my blessing, Schultz smiled. "No one deserves this chance more than you."

Was that a tear in the doctor's eye, Tracy wondered?

After hugs all around, Tracy walked out of the hospital lobby for the last time. Jerry was waiting for her in his rental car, and after a long kiss, they drove to the airport, giddy as school-children on a field trip to Orlando. During the trip east, certain only of their love for each other, both remained locked in thought. Jerry was determined to marry but was uncertain of the timing. Tracy thought she was ready but uncertain he would ask. Holding hands would have to do for now.

A surprise waited at Lena's apartment. Tracy's father Ed Henderson and Eddie, Jr. had flown from Miami and North Carolina. Shouts of delight echoed down the condominium hallway as the door opened. Lena's neighbors, accustomed to peace and quiet, rushed out of their apartments at the ruckus to witness the joyful reunion.

"Jesus, Mary and Joseph," exclaimed Eddie upon seeing his new and improved sister for the first time. "Who plunked you with the 'magic twanger'? You're gorgeous, Trace! If you weren't my sis,...."

"Hold it, hot pants!" grunted father Ed, as Tracy blushed fire engine red. "My turn with the babe," he chuckled, grasping Tracy in a bear hug. Holding his daughter, his mood changed on a dime, remembering all he'd been told she suffered. "What have they done to my girl?" he cried.

"You should see the other guy," Tracy replied, hugging back. "On second thought,...."

Melony watched in joyful awe. With no family of her own, she had only seen this type of behavior on TV. "What am I, chopped liver?" she interjected, pointing to her prodigious chest. Four jaws dropped in unison. Her boldness shocked everyone.

Lena nearly slipped and fell on the floor, holding her sides as introductions were made between hearty guffaws. Down the hall someone shouted, "Hey, pipe down! I didn't know this was 'Animal House'."

The six comedians piled into the apartment and were still laughing ten minutes later.

IT'S A SMALL WORLD
ORLANDO, FLORIDA
The same day…

AN HOUR HAD PASSED since Lena and Melony had left the apartment to run errands. Four hours earlier, Tracy's father had left for Miami and brother Eddie had a plane to catch. For the first time since Moose Jaw, Tracy and Jerry were alone in a quiet atmosphere. Disappearing into the bathroom for ten minutes, Tracy called to Jerry in a tentative voice, "I have a surprise for you."

"What's that?" Jerry asked.

Tracy emerged wearing only a bath towel. Walking slowly to toward him, she whipped it off. "Me," she said.

Surprised, both Jerry and his toy soldier stood at attention. Folding herself into his arms and rubbing herself against the horizontal hardness straining against his shorts, she stared into his eyes and purred, "I'm ready now. It seems you are, too." She framed his face with her hands. "I only ask that you to be gentle with my damaged goods."

Jerry croaked, "Damaged goods, hell. I'd take your damaged chassis over anyone else's showroom model every time. I love you, Trace."

Later, during the height of passion, Tracy purred, "I never thought I could feel this way. Show me how to love you back." Whispering in his ear, she added, "Sensei."

Making gentle, languorous love, Jerry would always remember this as the happiest two hours of his life.

WHEN LENA AND MELONY arrived back at the apartment, they were met by two lovers wearing only skimpy underwear and shit-eating grins. "Hope it's OK." Tracy giggled, hugging her surprised aunt. "At least we changed the sheets." Jerry and Melony wore shocked expressions. Lena thought, *Who has the redder face?* It was a close call. Both resembled peeled beets.

After a good five seconds, Lena broke the ice. Turning to her niece, she smugly replied, "I do believe your therapist is blushing, my dear."

Jerry rebounded with: "Clinically speaking, I made a breakthrough."

All four collapsed, again holding their sides.

Once levity and clothing regained a semblance of normalcy, Lena's tone grew serious, as though she were about to lecture an audience. "All right youngsters. This old woman has a proposition for all of you. Except for Claude, you two ladies know my weird personality better than anyone else. I've lived my whole adult life either hiding from or courting the media. First it was my looks that fascinated. Now it's my eccentricity and my brief marriage to a governor. The press, television and radio people still hound me for interviews.

"I've been successful as an exotic dancer, then as a businesswoman, and lately in the political arena with Win Stedman. But you know all of that. For reasons I don't understand, the rest of my life has been ordained to exploit the public pulpit toward a goal. That goal is to shake up the political establishment, to weed out the primary players responsible for rampant theft and corruption in Washington."

"Aunt Lena, all my life I've believed in you. Now you're making no sense," broke in Tracy. "You sound like the intro to the old Superman reruns: '...and who, disguised as Lena Mills, fights a never ending battle for truth, justice and the American way'," she paraphrased in a deep announcer voice, causing all to chuckle nervously.

"Give her a chance, Trace," argued Melony. "I've seen her in action and believe me, what I've seen has made my hair stand on end."

Lena continued, "With the exception of Claude, who's convinced I'm nuts but accepts me anyway, if I said these words to anyone else other than you two and Jerry, I wouldn't be given a chance to explain. I'd be dismissed and shunned as an egocentric fool. I ask all of you for three favors: to accept what I do with an open mind, to keep what I say to you secret from everyone outside this room, and finally to consider joining me in what promises to be a wild adventure.

A NATION BEST SERVED HOT

"I have no idea what the future has in store. But I can promise you each a steady paycheck—money is no object, that I will not knowingly break the law in anything I do or say, honest and loyal friendship for as long as you care to put up with me, and the knowledge that you are doing something to help your country."

Melony was first. "I already told you, Lena, I'm in, for better or worse."

Tracy looked at Jerry, who asked the obvious question, "What do you want us to do for you?"

"Melony will do what she has been doing—lining up interviews and arranging my schedule. She'll be kind of a press secretary. Tracy, you'll be in charge of security. There will be times, I'm sure, when I rub powerful people wrong, and I'll need you by my side at all times and to assess the prospects for danger. You are used to firearms and tactical weapons, and if the situation warrants, you can hire and direct additional security."

Still not convinced, Tracy interrupted with a hint of sarcasm, "Sounds like it's right up my alley. From the DEA to your Secret Service."

In too deep to stop now, Lena bulled ahead. "Jerry, from what you have told me, you're not afraid to gamble if the odds are right. I need someone like you to advise me how to keep one step ahead of my adversaries. You'll be my idea man in charge of overall strategy."

She turned to address all three. "I'm going after powerful people—people who, when threatened, may retaliate with more than just words. I know it sounds vague and incredible, but I have the power to know things that can destroy their careers. I'm determined to bring these things to light. It's a given they won't go down without a fight."

"What do you think?" asked Lena. Had she gambled her credibility and lost?

The room was silent. All three were being asked to follow her blindly down a "yellow brick road"—this woman with a mercurial mind, unproven power and some preordained vendetta against unnamed enemies.

Jerry looked at Tracy. *She's not far off with the Superman analogy,* he thought. He decided to lob a fast ball. It was a perfectly thrown strike.

"Sounds like fun," he replied flippantly, hoping to lighten the mood, "as long as we don't have to drink Kool-Aid."

No one laughed.

Lena couldn't blame him for his persistent doubt. Proof was necessary, and the kind of proof she had ran the risk of losing the loyalty and respect of all three before her. She knew there would be times when her power was a curse rather than a blessing. This was one of those times. Lena threw the dice, hoping with all her might they wouldn't come up craps.

She stared at Jerry like a cobra and struck: "Does the name Emily Sue Rogers mean anything to you?"

Two feet away, Melony gasped. White as a roll of Charmin, she fell to the back of the sofa in shock.

Challenged by Lena's hypnotic stare, Jerry stayed silent. At first puzzled by the abrupt change of subject, seeing Melony's reaction caused his mind to dig deep into the past. Emily Sue Rogers? During his early years he had carelessly slept with dozens of women. Back then, selling cars and insurance were down the list of priorities compared to his insatiable urge for sexual conquest. If it were difficult to remember the number, it was impossible to remember all their names. But something about a woman with three names snagged his memory like a gaffed fish.

"I...I...." he stammered. His legs turning to rubber as the pieces began to fall in place, he sat in a lump next to Melony.

She's nineteen. His mind was sorting through the facts: *By coincidence both of us lived in El Paso. I would have been eighteen when she was conceived.* He remembered the conversation in the hospital coffee shop and his reaction: *She's flirting with me.* He remembered thinking, *I'm old enough to be her father.*

Tracy looked on, fascinated. There was a resemblance. The jaw lines, blond hair, slightly upturned noses, especially the eyes. Both had blue eyes. Turning her attention to Lena, she stared daggers. What was she doing? Why was she doing it?

Lena cursed the Voices in her head, *God damn you!* She had dropped a bomb. No apology could cure the devastation she had wrought. Damage control was the only option.

Everyone was too shocked to speak. She had the floor. "It came to me on the flight back from Texas, talking with you, Jerry. It was more than a hunch. I can't expect any of you to believe what seems preposterous—that I can read minds, interpret the past, discover the truth. Billions of people are on earth. The prospect of two souls related by birth accidentally finding each other defies coincidence. Please," she begged, "if you both agree, check it out with a paternity test."

She added with certainty, "But you'll find I'm right."

Lena bowed her head contritely. Speaking softly, she concluded, "I ask you for forgiveness. It was necessary to prove my point. I wouldn't blame either of you for leaving and never seeing me again."

Overwhelmed, Melony broke out crying with tears streaming down her face. Tracy sat next to Jerry, throwing her arms around her bewildered lover who sat stiffly as if goosed by a cattle prod. *What a day!* she thought. *Poor guy—straight from making love, he's zapped by the greatest shock of his life.*

It was a scene from an Edgar Allen Poe story. Funereal gravity blanketed the room. Lena's grandfather clock was the only sound: *tic-toc, tic-toc....*

Seconds turned to minutes...*tic-toc, tic-toc....*

Tracy broke the pregnant pall. Releasing Jerry from her embrace, she stood and asked, "Isn't anyone going to say something?"

Her mind a maze of conflicting emotions, Melony turned to Jerry and touched his arm. "If you're my father, does it mean I get to kiss you?"

Lena and Tracy grinned like Cheshire cats.

Jerry was a pat of butter on a warm pan, melting into his daughter's waiting arms.

SQUASH
WASHINGTON, D.C., NBC STUDIOS
MEET THE PRESS
8: 50 A.M. - A SUNDAY MORNING
LATE FEBRUARY, 2009

"WHY AM I HERE with this bimbo?" demanded Dermott Flagg, Democratic Chairman of the House Ways and Means Committee. Host Gregory Davis was frantic, having been notified two hours before air time that Republican Congressman Hugh O'Connor's assistant called, saying his boss would be a no-show—"gall stones" the stated reason.

"Get Lena Mills!" the show's director had ordered. She was in town and available, according to the press which followed her every move. Melony Major answered Lena's phone, yelled to her boss and confirmed the interview. Postponing a lesser appointment, Lena dressed quickly. Accompanied by Tracy, she took a cab from her nearby high rise condo to NBC Studios, arriving fresh and ready for battle with five minutes to spare.

The show's producer was licking his chops. *Meet the Press* was still the highest rated Sunday talk show, but was losing ground to the other network copycats. Instead of the regular one-on-one format, followed by a panel discussion, the producer ordered a full hour of four-on-two questioning, the four being Davis and a panel of three regular journalists. Seating loose-lipped Lena next to the congressman might be just what the doctor ordered. *Like tweaking a volcano with a nuclear warhead,* the producer anticipated.

Well aware of her reputation, Dermott Flagg wanted nothing to do with Lena Mills. If it had been any other venue, he would have bolted for the door. But no one walked out on the longest-running show in television history.

A NATION BEST SERVED HOT

Feeling setup only increased his ever-present anger. Dermott—"He's a Grand Old Flagg"—looked angry even when he was happy, which was rare. Pudgy jowls accented a mound of Brillo black hair, bushy eyebrows and a face lined with battle scars resembling rocky crevasses along the coast of his ancestral Ireland. All these features made for a hideous countenance that terrified small children and made elderly women void in their Depends.

Kissing babies was not on his campaign agenda. In fact, Flagg had never campaigned, coming from a "safe" Connecticut congressional district with nearly seventy percent registered Democrat constituents. A scrapper since early childhood in the Hartford suburbs, he took pride in two things: never running from a fight and crudely running his mouth—any subject, anytime, anywhere. Thus the nickname penned by his adversaries: "Dirtbag Dermott."

Yes, he had a long history of sex with younger male partners. But this character flaw was not only ignored by supporters, it was considered fashionable in modern progressive society.

The year 2008 had been eventful for Lena Mills and her loyal entourage. Tracy and Jerry had married in June with a small, family-only ceremony. Already winning her way into Jerry's heart, daughter Melony had talked him into confirming Lena's "hunch" with a home paternity test. It was positive, of course. By then all three had accepted Lena's extraordinary gift, remaining somewhat spooked by the prospect of her reading their minds.

For her part, Lena vowed never again to use her power to intimidate friends or adopted family. If she learned anything untoward or tawdry, she kept it to herself.

Turning down offers to run for local, state and national political office, Lena opted for what she did best—TV and radio talk show interviews. The more months that went by, the more her fame and credibility was enhanced by reruns of the old Katie Couric interview. She was one of only a few who had predicted doom for the American economy, and by now the worst recession since the Great Depression held a vice-grip on the lives of most Americans. This fame gained her access to the powerful. She took full advantage of personal meetings to read minds, find skeletons, secure proof of legal and moral wrongdoings, then issue private ultimatums to those with nefarious and greedy intentions at taxpayer expense.

Most of the targeted politicians went quietly, resigning "to spend more time with my family." The few who fought her lived to regret their choice. After public flogging by a press eager for tawdry tidbits, the end result was always the same. Lena never asked for credit and most of the time received none. Behind the scenes, however, the mere mention of her name was known to cause the deodorant of the most audacious politico to fail.

As the year wore on, Americans were too concerned about their 401(k)s, the dramatic decrease in home values and loss of jobs to notice the large number of congressional resignations from both parties. The country longed for a "Change We Can Believe In", and in November, 2008, voted an avalanche of Democrats, including America's first black president, to replace discredited Republicans in both houses of Congress.

Professional politicians like Flagg, who was in his fifteenth two-year term of office, were an arrogant bunch. They were also the biggest abusers of the public trust. Until this day, Dermott had successfully dodged the "Angel of Death," as Lena Mills was known to the Washington elite. Like a patient spider, she went about her business stinging profligates less senior in congressional stature.

Today, firmly entangled in her web, was a senior committee chairman whose day of reckoning had arrived. She carried the lethal dose in her purse.

Ignoring Flagg's initial volley, Lena calmly sat next to him, leaning as far away from the tempestuous troll as possible. The theme music played, host Gregory Davis made the perfunctory panelist introductions, and commenced with, "Today we are pleased to have as our guests Dermott Flagg, Chairman of the House Ways and Means Committee; and Lena Mills, self-styled congressional critic and, some would say, prognosticator of American financial and political trends."

For different reasons, both Lena and Flagg winced at Davis' description.

The moderator continued, "I'll begin the questioning with you, Ms. Mills. Ladies first." As he said the last two words he glanced at Flagg who grimaced, sensing a dig at his sexual orientation. "Where do you see the American economy going, and why?"

"Gregory," Lena replied, looking at the camera, "short term, and by that I mean the next six months to a year, the markets will continue to decline, then rise in value once they hit bottom about March. But as long as the administration continues to degrade the dollar with all their spending programs, for the long term, commodities will be where you want to put a good percentage of your assets. Sometime in the not-so-distant future, we're due for a tsunami of inflation."

Flagg ground his teeth, impatiently waiting his turn. *Tsunami?* he groused to himself. *I'll show the bitch a tsunami.*

Lena continued in a pleasant conversational tone, as if giving a weather forecast. "If the current administration stays its course, I see the dollar sinking so low against other major world currencies, countries like China which are propping us up with loans will stop putting good money after bad. What happens then is anybody's guess, but all scenarios spell disaster for the American economy."

She then thrust a personal jab at the smug curmudgeon on her left. "Thanks to destructive policies of the past and current president and members of Congress like *this* man..."—she pointed an accusing finger at Flagg who was turning a bright shade of red, "our country is in real trouble."

Dermott Flagg's Irish was up, primed for a frontal assault. Davis turned to him, asking, "How do you respond, Congressman?"

Huffing like a blowfish, he launched, "I'd like to know why you invited this…this *harlot* on your program." Mucous missiles spewed from his mouth toward the host, who deftly dodged the offending globs.

At the word "harlot," Deidre Kendell Godwin, one of panelists, rose out of her seat, something never before seen in over sixty years of the program. "Now just a minute!" she lashed at the offending gnome. "How dare you use that language, you sexist pig?" The other two male panelists were trying to remain calm but were chuckling.

In less than two minutes, this normally staid— some would say stuffy— program had deteriorated into a pissing contest. The host knew he was in trouble. He couldn't see the show's producer who was in the control room clapping with glee.

"Now, everyone calm down," Davis shouted, standing as well. "Please, everyone stay civil." All the while he was thinking, *Why don't we tape this damn show in advance?*

Addressing the hostile congressman who was standing as well, Davis admonished, "Mr. Flagg, sit down. Ms. Mills is a respected political analyst who just happened to predict this recession correctly over a year ago. People want to hear her opinions, as they do yours. With all due respect, sir, that's why she's on this program."

Flagg wasn't through. He was just getting started. Reluctantly sitting, he continued, "She holds no office, and the only credential she has is being a trophy wife to a governor for less than six hours. She's a former stripper, for God sake!" he retorted, again standing and waving a hand dismissively at her. "Nothing this woman says is legitimate."

With a smug expression, he sat back again and crossed his arms, satisfied he'd made his point.

Gregory Davis looked at Lena with a combination of pity and fear. The woman was sitting with a tranquil look on her face. There was no way to tell what would come out of her mouth next. "Ms. Mills, what do you have to say to these accusations?" he asked, praying for an ending to this nightmare.

Lena studied her opponent. Reading his mind, she thought, *This naughty lamb is ready for slaughter. Best get it over with.* Like a fighter assured of a first round knockout, she reached into her purse and pulled out a small pile of photographs. Putting them face down on the table in front of her, she stared her fat foe in the face. After a pregnant pause, with a low venomous hiss, she struck.

"I thought you'd be like this, you nasty puss. I brought you a present. It was given to me by one of your jealous former boy toys. Don't worry, I made lots of copies."

Like an attorney assured of victory, Lena rose, picked up the pictures and slid one across the round table to Davis and each of the panelists, saving the last for her adversary. Seeing the evidence, every jaw in the room dropped open in shock. Every jaw but one, belonging to Dermott Flagg, whose eyes bulged like a gigged frog. Sounding like a half-dozen vacuums simultaneously sucking air from the room, a chorus of gasps gripped the studio.

Upon seeing the picture, Davis' face paled. He turned toward the unseen producer, whose smug countenance had morphed from the thrill of victory to the agony of defeat. With a throat slashing gesture and a mind full of doubt, Davis croaked to the camera, "We'll be back."

Cocksure Congressman Flagg held in his quivering hand the only thing that could harm him, the one thing that could lay waste to his lengthy career: a photograph his turncoat lover had promised to destroy that night of drunken, unbridled debauchery ten years ago at a sleazy bar in Tijuana.

For however accepted it was to play Irish organ jigs with younger men in the privacy of one's home, it was quite another matter to be pictured wide-eyed in flagrante delicto…

Ramming his five-inch fugue into the backside of a donkey.

A NATION BEST SERVED HOT

IN OVER SIXTY YEARS of weekly programs, only one edition of *Meet the Press* finished with a rerun.

HEADLINE IN THE WASHINGTON CHRONICLE
TUESDAY, FEBRUARY 24, 2009:

"CONGRESSMAN DERMOTT FLAGG,
CHAIRMAN OF THE HOUSE WAYS AND MEANS
COMMITTEE, RESIGNS"

SUB-HEADLINE:
"GIVES UP SEAT AS CHAIRMAN AND MEMBER OF CONGRESS
'EFFECTIVE IMMEDIATELY – TO SPEND MORE TIME WITH
MY FAMILY'."

AFTER EXTENSIVE RESEARCH, no one in America or Ireland was able to locate any living relatives of former Congressman Dermott Aloysius Flagg.

"...AND THE HORSE YOU RODE IN ON!"
THE ED SULLIVAN THEATER NEW YORK CITY CBS STUDIO 50 A WEDNESDAY, MID-JULY, 2009, 5:00 P.M.

IT WAS ALMOST UNANIMOUS. Tracy and Melony urged Lena not to do it. Even Claude Masters put in his two cents: "Look what he said about Sarah Palin's daughter. He's a ruthless, sarcastic bastard. He'll say anything for a laugh, even when it's not funny at all. And the TV audience is always on his side."

Melony added, "No matter what you say, he'll twist it to make you look foolish."

"I can handle myself," Lena objected. "Don't you have any faith in me by now?"

They were backstage at the Ed Sullivan Theater, minutes before taping of this evening's *David Letterman Show*. Lena sat in the middle of the three pacing worry-warts, patiently absorbing their concern with a calm confidence. Only Jerry Calvin sat off to the side, expressionless and quiet.

"You don't need this, Aunt Lena," Tracy chimed in. "Your popularity is through the roof. Aren't you doing exactly what your 'Voices' want? And so far, you've been wildly successful. Half of the worst congressmen in Washington have given up power or announced they won't run for another term. Look at what you did to Flagg. The bastard is still in hiding! You and others are playing your parts in a grass roots movement that will throw most of the rest out in 2010. Why take the chance?"

"Because she's got something up her sleeve," Jerry broke in, finally joining the debate. "She's a gambler, like me. Am I right?" He looked at Lena with raised eyebrows.

"Nothing ventured, nothing gained," Lena replied with a sly smile.

A NATION BEST SERVED HOT

As the Paul Shaffer CBS Orchestra commenced the show, Lena rose from her seat. She was wearing a sleek gray and wine-red combination that accented her attractive figure and carefully coiffed hair. Her demure serenity enhanced the confidence she felt. "How do I look, gang?"

"Like a lamb going to slaughter," Tracy worried.

"Like my best friend on a date with the guillotine," echoed Claude, ever the pessimist.

"Like my dad says," Melony added, changing her tune and giving her father a hug. "You look like someone about to draw on an inside straight."

A knock on the dressing room door interrupted, followed by a voice. "Two minutes, Ms. Mills. Please follow me to the curtain."

Jerry opened the door and, as Lena brushed by him, he whispered in her ear, "Flatten the son of a bitch."

⁓⌇⁓

THE PRODUCER had argued she would bring a great boost to his ratings. David Letterman hesitated before giving the blessing to the interview. Lena Mills was unpredictable. That was *his* gig—being unpredictable. Her reputation was legendary: "Takes no prisoners; uncanny ability to know what you're thinking; hits your weak spot; two-legged nitro"—all comments by television hosts who had weathered her searing wit. Yes, Letterman had hesitated, but only for a second. His haughty ego made the decision: *I'm the best. I'm bullet-proof, and no washed up former stripper is going to make a fool out of me.* "Book her," he had ordered. "We'll see who gets the last laugh."

⁓⌇⁓

LETTERMAN HAD COMPLETED the preliminaries—bantering with Shaffer and his band, a brief monologue with a few sarcastic political jabs, and a run-through of the evening's light-hearted "Ten Stupid Pet Tricks" list. After a brief station break, the show resumed.

"Now, the one you have been waiting for," the host announced. "I've never met this woman in person before, but I'm as intrigued as you are about our first guest. Let's welcome Lena Mills, everyone."

It was a setup. Shaffer's band was at the ready, grinding out the theme to David Rose's 1962 *The Stripper* in raunchy overdrive. Instead of a normal entrance, Lena made a reflex decision. Angling toward the host, arms on hips, she booty-bumped with the music and the drummer's rim shots. The audience applauded with cat-calls, whistling and laughter.

Letterman leaned toward her for the standard Hollywood kiss, which Lena deflected to a simple handshake—the first indication she was in charge. At the last bump ending the song, she plopped down in the chair beside the host, waving to oversexed males in the audience who continued whistling.

She waited fifteen seconds before exclaiming, "Wow! You make a girl feel right at home, Dave. Last time I had a cheer like that, the joint burned down!" Shaffer's drummer was alert and thwacked a "bada-boom" on his snare and bass drum.

Another round of cheers and cat-calls followed, as Letterman fumed inside. *Less than two minutes and she's hijacking my show!*

Projecting his patented combination smile and sneer to the crowd, he opened with, "Well, I guess we picked the wrong song, didn't we?" Letterman winked at the audience.

The joke fell flat. Everyone was still locked onto Lena, who rescued her host with a Marilyn Monroe breathy imitation, "Heaven's no, Dave. It made me tingle—all over!" As she stood again, her hands outlined her hourglass figure, driving the audience to distraction again.

Cries of "LENA, LENA, LENA…" mixed with another ear-splitting cheer, lasting another thirty seconds. Letterman was helpless. He'd never seen a reaction this intense for any guest. But laughter was the lifeblood of the show, so he decided to go with the flow.

Relative calm resumed after another thirty seconds. *I haven't even asked my first question,* the flustered host groused to himself. He was anxious to put this presumptuous prick teaser in her place. It was, after all, his reason for inviting her.

Using his serious face, he leaned toward the guest and began with, "Ms. Mills,…"

"Call me Lena, Dave," she interrupted, adding to his anger.

"Okay…Lena," he continued. "You've made quite a splash this year: predicting the stock market, the recession, your one-night stand as First Lady of Florida…."

A few hisses could be heard from the audience. Letterman was treading on dangerous turf. This was someone many in this crowd admired. *I better lighten up*, he chastised himself.

"It's rumored that you had a hand in a few Washington politicians suddenly retiring," Letterman followed, changing course.

A NATION BEST SERVED HOT

Expecting sarcasm but angered by his bald-faced insult, a suddenly serious Lena stared blankly at the host, giving him her "I-dare-you-to-say-it" look.

"Some people think you're a witch—that you can read minds." Then Letterman boldly went where no man had gone before:

"Can you read mine?" he insinuated with a sardonic wink at his audience.

Without hesitating, Lena faced the audience and pouted, "Whatever you say, David Letterman, I will **not** sleep with you!"

It was bomb of epic proportion. Letterman sat back, stunned. His audience erupted with cheers and a standing ovation. The drummer hit a rim shot and cymbal crash, not realizing he had just committed employment suicide.

Lena realized she had won the battle, but couldn't resist another parting shot across the bow. *I'm going to make short work of this asshole and leave*, she vowed. Raising both hands to calm the audience, she waited until the noise settled for her voice to be heard. Letterman, looking like a little boy caught by his mother with a dirty magazine under his bed, sat with his patented smile hiding a devastated ego, too helpless and confused to comment.

"One more thing, Dave," Lena resumed, standing and looking down on the host. "Sarah Palin sends her regards. She's in Alaska teaching her daughters how to field dress a talk show host."

A chorus of "Oooooos and Aaaaaahs" accompanied another standing ovation. Lena Mills marched off the stage like a victorious gladiator, waving to her minions. With sweat pouring from his brow, David Letterman anxiously signaled his producer for a hard break.

DISTRACTED BY THE UPROAR, no one noticed Jerry Calvin and his mini-cam recording the sequence from the dressing room monitor. That night, the CBS television audience was treated to an unexplained *David Letterman Show* mid-week rerun.

The next day, a *FOX News* nationwide audience was treated to the original sequence, which was then repeated throughout the day and aired by all the other major networks. Roger Ailes was ecstatic. Melony Major, his former employee, had given his network an exclusive coup! CBS lawyers sharpened their talons with a flurry of lawsuits but the damage was done.

David Letterman, the network's nighttime "Golden Boy", had been humiliated. A headline in the following day's *Wall Street Journal* said it all: "THE HOST IS TOAST!"

PLAYING WITH FIRE
AUGUST, 2009

"Those who live are those who fight."
Victor Hugo (1802 – 1885)

BY AUGUST, Lena was well aware her life was in danger. The Voices told her. In fact, the Voices were running her life now. Each day consisted of strategy sessions with her crew, approving or rejecting upcoming speaking engagements and following through with these engagements. She was a rock star, far more popular than ever before. The liberal-leaning media eviscerated her every appearance, every statement, every move. The more she was criticized, the more her "Lenatics" adored her. She was "Everywoman"—telling their stories, reflecting their views, fanning the flames of liberty from the status-quo of tyranny, upholding the Constitution against those who would tear it down. She was a powerful voice of the majority against the minority in power.

Death threats were inevitable. If there was any doubt before, the Letterman fiasco proved that Lena Mills was a formidable threat to the Washington elite. Former enemies became allies. Clandestine calls were made. Secret meetings were held. Whispered plans were put in play.

Surrogates were solicited—professionals who specialized in elimination. One came forward with enthusiasm claiming, "This is personal." Big money was exchanged. The bitch was dynamite and must be killed.

Lena's entourage had grown to twenty. All but her core group were part-time body guards. Tracy supervised the security detail, hiring only highly-trained personnel and placing them strategically at each speaking venue. Over initial objections, Jerry, Claude and Melony convinced Lena to start charging a nominal fee for these engagements, over and above the rental charges for each venue. She agreed, but only to the extent ticket prices offset expenses. "Everyone who wants to should be able to afford to see me in person," Lena argued. "I don't ever want it said that I'm in this for the money."

Melony hired a booking agency with a cast of accountants in charge of financial matters, which answered to her on a weekly basis.

Beginning in August, the star kicked off her "Lenatization Tour" in smaller venues like state fairs and race tracks. Volunteer country-western and pop music bands lined up to help, and soon each stop turned into an extravaganza of warm-up acts prior to her appearance. Selling out each concert in minutes, after three of these events, it became clear the largest stadiums could be filled. Melony hired a staff of experienced, out-of-work "roadies" to coordinate each concert's logistics.

In September alone, Lena appeared at Comerica Park in Detroit to an audience of 40,000; Vanderbilt Stadium in Nashville—40,000; Tiger Stadium in Baton Rouge—90,000; and the Cotton Bowl in Dallas—92,000, drawing capacity audiences at each venue. Nationally-known musical acts now vied for inclusion with her appearances—dubbed "Teed-off Parties."

"LENA FOR PRESIDENT" signs began appearing and soon numbered over a thousand at each event. Running for office was the last thing on Lena's mind and agenda. "All this is spiraling out of control," she groused to Jerry, backstage before her Cotton Bowl speech. The Charlie Daniels Band had just finished his signature song "The Devil Went Down to Georgia." Screaming fans out front were chanting "LENA…LENA…LENA…."

Amazed with each concert's success, Jerry could only laugh. "You're in Texas, boss, hitched to the biggest bucking bronco of your life. Head 'em up, move 'em out, rawhide!"

"Yahoo, Aunt Lena," Tracy shouted over the din as her idol marched on stage, following Melony's introduction. A full three minutes of shouting, chanting and screaming accompanied the musical intro, as Lena grabbed one of the musician's ten-gallon hats and square danced around the stage with the fiddle-playing Daniels. Half the massive audience rose out of their seats to join in a spontaneous close-quarter dance of merry mayhem.

When the music ended, Lena hugged the gentle giant, who marched offstage with his band members to raucous applause. It was Lena's show from now on.

Holding up her hands in a call for silence, Lena finally quieted the crowd before shouting, "HELLO, WASHINGTON!

A NATION BEST SERVED HOT

"Dallas has a message for you: DON'T MESS WITH TEXAS!"

A thunderous roar went up from the crowd. Onstage, Lena was rocked by a decibel level louder than jet engine blast. *My God!* she thought, suddenly frightened, looking over the sea of friendly faces. *How do I top this?*

As the Voices took over her mind, a blanket of familiar calmness enveloped her. After another two minutes, the exhausted crowd sat and waited in rapt attention. Lena waited another full ten seconds before speaking. Her demeanor had turned serious. Starting in a soft voice, she addressed her audience:

"Accounts receivable tax, business property tax, building permit tax, cigarette tax, corporate income tax, dog license tax, excise tax, federal income tax, federal unemployment tax, fishing license tax, food license tax, fuel permit tax, gasoline tax, gross receipts tax..."

Taking an exaggerated deep breath, Lena continued, "hunting license tax, inheritance tax, inventory tax, IRS interest tax, liquor tax, luxury tax, marriage license tax, Medicare tax, personal property tax, real estate tax, Social Security tax, sales tax, recreational vehicle tax, school tax, state income tax, state unemployment tax..."

The crowd was getting restless. Shouts of "Enough already!" and murmurs of disgust could be heard over Lena's ever-increasing volume and litany of outrageous offenses.

"You want more taxes?" she asked.

"NO!" the audience shouted back.

"Too bad. Hide your wallets," she cracked, continuing, "telephone federal excise tax, telephone federal universal service fee tax, telephone federal, state and local surcharge taxes, telephone minimum usage tax, telephone recurring and non-recurring charges tax—that's a tax on a tax, people—, telephone usage charge tax, utility tax, vehicle license registration tax, vehicle sales tax, well permit tax, workers compensation tax."

By the last two items, her voice had strained to a high level. After pausing for effect, she ended with, "Not one of these taxes existed a century ago. The United States of America was the most prosperous nation in the world. We had no national debt. Now our debt is over $10 trillion dollars—that's trillion with a 'T'! Anybody know how many zeros are in ten trillion?"

A few shouted out numbers. Most were wrong. "That's right," Lena answered, "THIRTEEN!

"What the hell happened?"

Shouts of "You go, girl", "Yeah, you tell 'em" and "Right on!" followed her question.

"I'll tell you what happened," Lena continued, her voice a battering ram of reason. "One hundred senators, 435 congressmen, one president and nine Supreme Court justices equals 545 human beings out of 300 million—who are directly, legally, morally and individually responsible for the domestic and financial problems that plague your country. That's what happened."

"BOOOO! YEAH!" answered the crowd.

"They, and they alone, are responsible. When you grasp the truth that 545 people exercise the power of the federal government, you realize what exists is what they want to exist.

"These 545 people spend most of their time and energy trying to convince us what they create is not…their…fault."

"YEAH!"

"How many moms are out there—grandmas, too?" Lena shouted. "Stand and be recognized!"

Over 50,000 flag- and banner-waving women rose as one with a minute-long, shrieking cry of defiance. Men covered their ears and cowered beside their "better halves."

"You ladies," Lena continued after a slight reduction in volume, "you're the ones who should be fightin' angry. Those 545 people in Washington are messin' with your kids' future, saddling them with debt that can't be repaid. Rise up and tell those bastards—write them, call them, let them know you're MAD AS HELL AND YOU'RE NOT GONNA TAKE IT ANYMORE!"

The men stood to join their women in a deafening roar.

After another two minutes, Lena held up her arms for silence. The audience slowly sat, as the mood changed from outrage to somber.

Lena waited until the crowd calmed before resuming in a low voice, "I want you to meet four people who have gone belly up, either with their business or personally, because of the crippling taxes I just listed. These are your neighbors, and but for the grace of God, you could be next."

Two men and two women walked on stage, nervously waiting to be introduced to the humongous crowd. During the next half hour, each citizen told heart-wrenching stories of struggle, success and eventual bankruptcy through no fault of their own, but because of confiscatory taxes and

A NATION BEST SERVED HOT

over-regulation by local, state and federal governments. The last to speak was a successful, award-winning and profitable auto dealer forced out of business because of industry bail-outs and an arbitrary decision made by Washington bureaucrats. His brother, a partner in the business, had committed suicide rather than face an impossible future.

After giving each a hug, Lena joined the audience in ushering them offstage with heart-felt applause. She returned to the microphone with a sober look and scanned the crowd. Across the vast stadium, not a single dry eye could be seen. Again starting softly, Lena continued:

"Politicians are the only people in the world who create problems and then campaign against them," she began. "Have you ever wondered—if all the politicians are against inflation, a large deficit and high taxes—why we have inflation, a large deficit and high taxes?"

A low-volume smattering of "BOOOO"s followed.

Lena's voice was rising with each damning sentence. "You and I don't write the tax code. Congress does."

"YEAH!"

"You and I don't create fiscal policy. Congress does."

"YEAH!"

Cleverly, Lena broke with the pattern. "There's a sign in the House of Representatives men's restroom that says, "If pro is the opposite of con, what is the opposite of progress?" She paused again.

"CONGRESS!" she shouted with a raised fist.

The audience roared with laughter.

"If voting could really change things, Congress would try to make it illegal. A dog barks for food. A congressman lies for votes." She was almost shouting now.

More laughter.

"Don't let these 545 people shift the blame to bureaucrats, lobbyists or regulators. Don't let them con you into believing mystical forces like "the economy," "inflation," or "politics" prevent them from doing what they took an oath to do. There are no unsolvable problems. There are only 545 power-hungry maggots out to lie like a rug, take our money and…

"RUN…OUR…LIVES!"

Another round of "BOOOO"s, this time much louder.

Most of the audience members knew what was coming, having seen Lena's previous televised rallies. All broke out with spontaneous applause, which continued through the rest of her speech.

"Let's start to take our country back next year at the ballot box.
"KICK THE ASSES OUT OF WASHINGTON!"
"YEAH!"
"SEND THOSE PACHYDERMS PACKIN'!"
"YEAH!" roared the crowd again. Standing en masse, everyone prepared for the anticipated conclusion.

As Lena took a deep breath to shout the climactic last line, coordinated with the deafening broadcast sound of a flushing commode, the image of a huge toilet appeared on the giant LED screen behind her. Cranking her arm with a downward motion, she screamed, **"FLUSH…CONGRESS!"**

"FLUSH…FLUSH…FLUSH…FLUSH…." chanted the angry crowd, cranking their arms with the same motion. As Lena waved and marched off the stage, the chanting dissolved into a five minute roar which shook the stadium stands. Over 90,000 "Lenatics" begged for an encore, but she was exhausted and took only two curtain calls before collapsing on a dressing room chair. "I'm dying of thirst. Will you get me a beer?" she asked Melony, who met her boss with a wide towel and wider smile.

Melony beamed like an angel, "God, I swear you could own the country, boss. You were fantastic! Your people out there were hanging on every word."

"Please, no backstage visitors this time. All I need is a beer and some good rest." Like a sack of flour, Lena sagged in the chair. Closing her eyes, she implored the Voices to leave her alone for one night. *What more do you want of me?* she asked….

Unaware her greatest sacrifice lay ahead.

"DON'T CRY FOR ME...."
MICHIGAN STADIUM
ANN ARBOR, MICHIGAN
MID-WEEK, LATE OCTOBER, 2009

IN A COUPLE OF WAYS, it was good to be back to her birth state of Michigan. Lena had always loved the fall season with its bitter coldness and colorful dying leaves, now symbolic of the state's unemployed who, like the leaves, were just trying to hang on in the face of bitter economic times.

Lena had never been to Ann Arbor, but through her friend's description of the university with its ivy-covered traditions, she felt a strange but certain familiarity with the campus. It was here Annie Akterhoff had met and fallen in love with Win Stedman during the tumultuous late sixties when sex, drugs and rock and roll were the order of the day.

Dressed in disguise, Lumpy Lena wandered, knowing she was taking the same paths her best friend and soul mate walked those many years ago. What used to be roads were now strictly pedestrian thoroughfares. Despite the cold, she felt a blanket of warmth, as though another shared her body during this excursion.

Now I know why you loved this place, Lena thought to herself, hoping she was speaking to Anne. *Gainesville has its charm but pales in comparison.*

The Voices entered her mind, interrupting her reverie. *There is danger here. Cancel the concert scheduled for this evening,* they insisted.

More than any other state, the people of Michigan need me, she argued. *It is my destiny that I speak the truth here, for they must know there is hope.*

Forces of evil have come to destroy you, the Voices warned.

My mission is more important than my life. Your words, not mine! she railed.

We cannot predict when, just where. We cannot predict what will happen if you go onstage, the Voices countered.

If I die, so be it! Lena's mind screamed. Her head pounded in pain.

"For this once, I'm calling the shots. It's my life and I'll damned sure do what I want with it!" Realizing she had yelled out loud and passers-by were staring, Lumpy Lena blushed and kept walking, hoping her outburst was taken as just another silly senior citizen talking to herself.

The Voices were quarreling, sending mixed messages.

Maybe I am *just an old geezer with an addled brain,* she thought, waiting patiently.

Then we can only do what we must, a single Voice returned in cryptic summation. Leaving her mind as they always came—suddenly, the Voices were gone.

"A GOOD WALK SPOILED." Lena remembered the phrase from someone's description of golf. If this were her last day, she was determined to enjoy it.

As if on cue, the delightful tingle of bells from the Burton Tower carillon sprinkled musical charm over the campus. She stopped at a pathway bench and sat, enjoying the heavenly concert, which was ignored by everyone but her. Lena's mind flashed to the Ocala Forest and the small pile of rocks. *If this is my last day on Earth, at least I have this moment of grace,* she beamed. Tears of joy were running down her cheek.

"Ma'am, are you all right?" asked a young man walking by, hand in hand with his pretty girlfriend.

"Couldn't be better," she smiled, remembering a similar incident in the forest. At long last, Lena Mills was at peace with her world.

TRACY AND JERRY compared notes. By reputation, stadium security was tight. No bottles, cans or backpacks were allowed past the gates. Hundreds of trained personnel were strategically placed at every home game and event. Besides doing their assigned jobs, all were on the lookout for any signs of trouble. Add in Lena's sixteen guardians and Tracy felt reasonably assured about Lena's safety.

But Lena Mills drew capacity crowds wherever she spoke without the advanced screening and protection of the Secret Service, which was provided only to top political candidates and elected officials. Because of their sheer size, these major venues always made Tracy nervous. "Comfortable" was a word absent from her vocabulary.

The "Big House" was the largest-capacity stadium in the country, with seating for over 107,000. The huge press box had been torn down and was in the process of renovation. Like a giant root canal, a gaping hole marred the maize and blue ambiance. The large stage at one end of the field seemed small in contrast with the massive bowl of seats surrounding the game turf. A sea of chairs had been set up on the playing field for the event. Every ticket had been sold days before, guaranteeing a record army of "Lenatics" in attendance. The cool fall air was mitigated by the sold-out crowd of warm bodies who had come to blow off the steam of hopeless oppression. Lena Mills was just the tonic needed for Michigan's financial influenza.

"I don't have a good feeling about tonight, Jerry," Tracy yelled at her husband over the blaring music of the final opening act. "Lena seems more distant than usual, as if she has the same feeling, but she won't talk about it."

"Everything and everyone is in place, Trace," replied Jerry, cuffing his hand to her ear. "You're nervous about every concert, remember? Comes with the territory. The security here is tops, I'm told."

"I'm going onstage with her and stand off to the side, if only for my peace of mind," Tracy yelled back. "I've done it before."

"If it will make you feel better, go ahead. It's your call. Nothing's going to happen, I'm sure," Jerry smiled, giving her a peck on the cheek before wandering off to a concession stand.

Gotta admire his fortitude, Tracy thought. *How he can eat at a time like this is beyond me.*

As Jerry disappeared down the corridor, Melony approached. "How's it going, Trace?" she shouted. Her sexy cowgirl outfit, complete with chaps and a holstered toy gun would have made her look foolish any other time, but the Dolly Parton look fit perfectly for the Country-Western musical theme Lena preferred to launch her onstage. As emcee, Melony was the young firecracker to Lena's mature Roman candle.

"Fine, I guess," Tracy shouted back. "How's the boss?"

"I don't know. You can ask her," Melony pointed to Lena, who had just come into view. Beautiful as ever, she was dressed conservatively but stylish, in a light blue business top with white blouse and a mid-knee-length gray pleated skirt. Surrounded by four huge, black-suited bodyguards, each sporting an ear piece and shoulder radio, she seemed small, belying her formidable demeanor.

"You look maaa-velous, madam," drawled Melony toward her boss, who answered with a wordless smile. "Ready to rock and roll?"

Normally excited with backstage jitters, tonight Lena was serene. Saying nothing again, she simply kept smiling.

Something's bothering her, Tracy thought. She knew the look well. *Aunt Lena's in a trance again.*

Onstage, the music stopped, followed by a huge roar from the crowd. Chants of "LENA...LENA...LENA..." began in anticipation of her entrance.

"That's my cue. Knock 'em dead, boss!" Melony bounded out the entrance like a football player and onto the stage amid thundering applause.

"Are you ready for some FOOTBALL?" she shouted into the mike. The crowd loved the opening line, shouting its approval. Like a cheer-leading rabble-rouser, Melony played the massive audience like a violin, stoking the flames of passion with her pre-set routine of jokes and booty-bumps coordinated with the previous band's drummer.

"And here's who you've been waiting for...." Melony paused for about five seconds before continuing, driving the crowd crazy.

"My friend and yours...." Another pause.

"The champion of common sense...."

"YEAH!" cheered the crowd.

"The voice of democracy against the status quo of hypocrisy...."

"YEAH!"

Over 110,000 fans stood on their feet. They knew the final line like they knew the Lord's Prayer.

"The sword of truth against the LYING...THIEVES...IN WASHINGTON...."

"LEEEEENAAA!" screamed Melony, quickly backing off the mike and disappearing backstage amid a roar every bit as strong as a Michigan touchdown against fierce rival, Ohio State.

Backstage, like a switched-on light, Lena snapped out of her trance, grabbed Tracy in a fierce hug and shouted in her ear, "Don't cry for me! Never doubt my love!"

Abruptly, she turned and marched forward, leaving a shocked and puzzled Tracy to follow a few feet behind.

A NATION BEST SERVED HOT

TO FANS ACROSS the giant field and up in the stands, Lena and Tracy looked like two ants marching onstage. Amid a sea of camera flashes, the band played as loud as it could, but produced music no one heard over the deafening applause.

Like a conquering hero returning from battle, Lena strode with confidence toward mid-stage, waving to some, smiling to all. Few noticed Tracy as she followed only two steps behind.

No one heard the shot that came from the dark recesses of rubble, steel and pilings that was formerly the old press box. No one saw Lena make a slight movement to her left at the same instant. Everyone saw the woman following jerk backwards.

Tracy's head exploded in a sea of blood and bone. Thousands screamed as the nearest band members threw down their instruments and tackled Lena to the floor. They were followed quickly by four bodyguards, who dragged her offstage in a phalanx of protective custody.

The security personnel could only watch as mass hysteria gripped Michigan Stadium. In a scene reminiscent of 9/11 New York streets, over 110,000 screaming people trampled each other toward the exits, leaving dozens of victims crushed dead and hundreds injured.

The Gates of Hell had opened.

The Spirit of Felix Carón had returned to claim his bride.

DAVID CARL MIELKE

*RECIPE FOR MARY LOU MOOTHART'S
SWEET AND SOUR SPAGHETTI

INGREDIENTS:

5-6 lb. boneless pork roast
4 - 12 oz. cans tomato paste
1 ½ large cans tomato juice (Sacramento brand is best)
1 tsp. spaghetti seasoning
½ tsp. each – rosemary, oregano, sweet basil
5 large sweet onions, chopped fine
¼ cup maple syrup
¼ cup light brown sugar
3 - 16 oz. cans mushrooms (drained)
Seasoning Salt and pepper

SECRET INGREDIENT: 1 cone Sap Sago cheese – grated by hand (caution: this a very hard cheese and will break most automatic food processors!)

INSTRUCTIONS:

Pre-heat oven to 500 degrees. Rub roast with seasoning salt, pepper and sage. Place in roasting pan on middle rack of oven and sear for 10 – 15 minutes. Without opening oven, turn heat down to 350 degrees and cook 30 minutes to the pound.

Remove roast and let cool until you can shred the meat into bite-sized pieces (pulled pork tastes much better than cut cubes).

SAUCE:

In a large stock pot add tomato juice, tomato paste, chopped onions, mushrooms, brown sugar, maple syrup, grated Sap Sago cheese and all spices. Let simmer while roast is cooking. Then add shredded pork and at least a half cup of drippings from the roast (drain most of the fat and keep the natural

A NATION BEST SERVED HOT

gravy, if possible). Stir well and frequently while the pot simmers at least another two hours.

SERVE OVER DRAINED SPAGHETTI.

Note: This recipe makes lots of sauce and will serve at least twelve. Left-over sauce can be frozen for further meals. Serve with heated garlic bread and salad.

Try it – you'll like it!

P.S. Most Natural and "Whole Foods" grocery stores will carry both Sacramento Tomato Juice and Sap Sago cheese, but you may have to special-order these ingredients. Everyone who consumes the result says it's worth the hassle.

ACKNOWLEDGMENTS

AS I MENTIONED in my previous novel *A DISH BEST SERVED COLD*, bits and pieces of people I have known through my life make up the characters in my stories. Though the reader may infer actual persons through context, most of the names in these works are fictional, with the exception of a few public icons such as Katie Couric, David Letterman and Charlie Daniels.

For most of my information, I relied heavily on search engines such as Google, Yahoo and AOL, as well as reference sites like Wikipedia, various almanacs, encyclopedias and dictionaries. As an example, I acknowledge journalist **Charlie Reese's** e-mail article as the source for Lena's list of taxes during one of her speeches.

However, one cannot complete a work like this in an Internet vacuum.

I wish to thank the following family members, friends and acquaintances, who not only helped me with specialized facts and procedures, but also nourished this fledgling author with constructive encouragement:

Keith and Dan Weis, sons of **Jean Weis**, in memory of whom I dedicate this novel. Keith is a high-level DEA agent, recently Resident Agent in Charge, Boise, Idaho. He is currently coordinating drug search-and-destroy missions in Afghanistan. Keith provided valuable DEA educational, procedural and tactical information. I continue to follow his Afghan exploits (occasionally featured on major news networks), admire his courage and pray for his safety during the two-year assignment in a very hostile and dangerous environment.

Dan is a Captain in the Osceola County, Florida Sheriff's Department. Like his brother, he's enjoyed a long and distinguished career in law enforcement. Dan helped me with the use of police 10-codes, typical arms used in police activity as well as communication equipment and procedures.

As with the previous novel, dear friend **Tina Carberry** helped with Spanish translations. She teaches high school Spanish in New Jersey.

Another friend, talented artist **Sally Cummings Shisler**, provided assistance with basic judo and karate terminology. She has been a student in martial arts for three years.

Jeff Rancour, former patrolman with the Lighthouse Point, Florida Police Department, provided information about canine drug teams and their reactions to hidden illegal substances.

Mary Lou Moothart, who was going to take her rich and marvelous spaghetti recipe to the grave…until I talked her into giving it to me as a wedding present. I cherish her memory and continue to enjoy her delicious legacy.

In both novels, the character **ANNE HENDERSON** is loosely based on real life friend **Anne Lippert.** Anne is an eclectic mix of dog whisperer, armadillo stalker and outspoken Conservative. She keeps me stocked with hilarious local yokel exploits and historical lore. We are perhaps each other's greatest fan.

Longtime friend **Patricia Schultz, ARNP** (Advanced Registered Nurse Practitioner), specializes in adult and child psychiatric care in Eustis, Florida. I relied heavily on her knowledge of medications and treatment procedures with **TRACY HENDERSON**. In the story, she is elevated (or is it demoted?) to the status of MD. Pat's professional dedication, sincerity and compassion are second to none.

Graphic artist extraordinaire **Ethel England**, who designs my covers and continues to amaze me with her talent.

Editor **Tyler Tichelaar**, whose perfect mix of encouragement and constructive criticism strengthened this work immeasurably.

My family: daughters **Mary Arnst** and **Laura Gardner** not only provide me with inspiration and encouragement, but also convince me there is hope for future generations; grandchildren **Allen** and **Caitlyn Arnst**, who promise to postpone reading my books until they're old enough to understand Grandpa's "dark side."

And, of course, my wife of forty years, **Cathy**, who suffers the brunt of my good-natured sarcasm and promises, out of the goodness of her heart, to keep me out of the loony bin as long as possible….

Unless she changes her mind.

DAVID CARL MIELKE

TO THE READER: If you liked *A DISH BEST SERVED COLD* and this sequel *A NATION BEST SERVED HOT*, please be on the lookout for the final book of the trilogy *FLUSHED*, available early 2011 – Lord willing and the creek don't rise.

The Author

ABOUT THE AUTHOR

DAVID CARL MIELKE lives just outside of Mount Dora, Florida at *One Mielke Way**, home of One Diabetic Grandpa, One Sweet Grandma, One Candy-assed Dog and One Sour Puss. In addition to visits from family and friends, who come for snickers and snacks and such, he whiles away the remaining years with hobbies and frequent naps. Strapping on a suicide word processor, he commits jihad on the English language, hoping to earn his seventy-two virgins—not that he would know what to do with seventy-two virgins. He is simply curious…

Of course.

* The address *One Mielke Way* is a confection of the author's mind.